but before they moved back toward the surface, each of them touched her with an electrical tendril. A moment later she was alone, floating in the stygian gloom.

In spite of the darkness and the isolation, she wasn't afraid. Although the symbionts had not communicated with her verbally, their meaning seemed crystal clear to her. *They aren't abandoning me. They want me to continue downward, but they can't—or know they mustn't?—go below this point.*

Another thought, less benign, occurred to her: *They don't know what's down here any more than I do.*

She noticed that the increasingly viscous water seemed to be fighting her, almost as though Mak'ala itself was trying to reject her presence.

She glanced at her wrist-mounted sensor display. As far as she could tell, the dark cavern into which she was descending was bottomless; she knew that at some point her suit would no longer be able to take the pressure.

Keep breathing, she thought, concentrating on taking normal, shallow breaths. Not for the first time, she wondered if Julian hadn't been right when he'd tried to tell her that she was embarking on a fool's errand. Why did he have to be right so damned often?

Just as she was about to activate her suit's wrist lights, she glimpsed a dim, orange-green glow lining a nearby cavern wall. Her tricorder identified it as a colony of bioluminescent microorganisms, evidently growing out of a side channel that appeared to be an ancient, partially collapsed lava tube. As she watched the mat of glowing microbes, the pool's currents carried some of its tentacle-like fronds away from the wall and toward the surface. *Maybe this is what they eat when they're living down here unjoined,* Ezri thought, finding it curious that she couldn't recall the Dax symbiont's experiences in the caverns with any degree of detail. *Maybe the symbionts don't share everything when they join with us.*

That thought made her more determined than ever to continue her descent. To get to the bottom of things, as it were.

WORLDS OF
STAR TREK
DEEP SPACE NINE®
VOLUME TWO

UNJOINED

MICHAEL A. MARTIN AND ANDY MANGELS

FRAGMENTS AND OMENS

J. NOAH KYM

Based upon STAR TREK®,
created by Gene Roddenberry,
and STAR TREK: DEEP SPACE NINE,
created by Rick Berman and Michael Piller

POCKET BOOKS
New York London Toronto Sydney Trill Bajor

This book is a work of fiction. Names, characters, places, and incidents are products of the author's imagination or are used fictitiously. Any resemblance to actual events or locales or persons, living or dead, is entirely coincidental.

An *Original* Publication of POCKET BOOKS

POCKET BOOKS, a division of Simon & Schuster, Inc.
1230 Avenue of the Americas, New York, NY 10020

This book is published by Pocket Books, a division of Simon & Schuster, Inc., under exclusive license from Paramount Pictures.

Planet art by Geoff Mandel
Cover design by John Vairo, Jr.

ISBN 0-7434-8352-9

First Pocket Books printing February 2005

10 9 8 7 6 5 4 3 2 1

POCKET and colophon are registered trademarks of Simon & Schuster, Inc.

Manufactured in the United States of America

For information regarding special discounts for bulk purchases, please contact Simon & Schuster Special Sales at 1-800-456-6798 or business@simonandschuster.com.

TRILL

Unjoined

Andy Mangels and
Michael A. Martin

ABOUT THE AUTHORS

Andy Mangels is the coauthor of several *Star Trek* novels, e-books, short stories, and comic books, as well as a trio of *Roswell* novels, all cowritten with Michael A. Martin. Flying solo, he is the best-selling author of many entertainment books including *Animation on DVD: The Ultimate Guide* and *Star Wars: The Essential Guide to Characters,* as well as a significant number of entries in *The Super-Hero Book.*

He has written hundreds of articles for entertainment and lifestyle magazines and newspapers in the United States, England, and Italy. He has also written licensed material based on properties from many film studios and Microsoft, and his comic book work has been published by DC Comics, Marvel Comics, and many others. He was the editor of the award-winning *Gay Comics* anthology for eight years.

Andy is a national award-winning activist in the Gay community, and has raised thousands of dollars for charities over the years. He lives in Portland, Oregon, with his long-term partner, Don Hood, their dog Bela, and their chosen son, Paul Smalley. Visit his website at www.andymangels.com

Michael A. Martin's solo short fiction has appeared in *The Magazine of Fantasy & Science Fiction.* He has also coauthored (with Andy Mangels) several *Star Trek* novels (including the forthcoming *Titan: Books One* and *Two; Star Trek: The Lost Era 2298—The Sundered; Star Trek: Deep Space 9 Mission: Gamma Book Three—Cathedral; Star Trek: The Next Generation, Section 31—Rogue); Star Trek: Starfleet Corps of Engineers* #30 and #31 ("Ishtar Rising" Books 1 and 2); stories in the *Prophecy and Change* and *Tales of the Dominion War* anthologies (as well as in the forthcoming *Tales from the Captain's Table* anthology); and three novels based on the *Roswell* television series. He lives with his wife, Jenny, and their two sons in Portland, Oregon.

ACKNOWLEDGMENTS

The authors owe a debt of gratitude to: Christopher Teague and René Echevarria, who first established the truth behind Trill symbiosis (DS9 "Equilibrium"); Robert Sabaroff and Tracy Tormé, who introduced the alien parasites that infiltrated Starfleet in 2364 (TNG "Conspiracy"); S.D. Perry and Robert Simpson, who gave us the ever-vigilant Gard ("Allegro Ouroboros in D Minor" from the *Lives of Dax* anthology); the conjoined literary entity known as L. A. Graf (Karen Rose Cercone and Julia Ecklar), who unwittingly did some geographical, pharmacological, and zoological spadework for us ("Reflections" from the *Lives of Dax* anthology); Diane Duane, whose novel *Intellivore* provided some inspiring scenery; John J. Ordover, David Mack, and Andrew Currie, who helped set up the contemporary political climate on Trill (Wildstorm's *Divided We Fall* comics miniseries); the aforementioned S. D. Perry, who embellished the histories of the symbiont and parasite species in previous volumes of this series ("Sins of the Mother" from the *Lives of Dax* anthology and the novel *Unity*); Michael Jan Friedman, for whom we nicknamed one of our Guardians; Ronald D. Moore and Joe Menosky, who introduced a certain fossil civilization (TNG's "The Chase"); Jeff Lang, who took good care of one of our favorite supporting characters during his tenure aboard the *U.S.S. Enterprise-E* (in his *Next Generation* novel *Immortal Coil*); Scott Anderson and Scott Gutierrez, both of whom furnished some much-appreciated scientific background information regarding symbiosis and parasitism; Marco Palmieri, editor extraordinaire; and Rick Berman, Michael Piller, Ira Steven Behr, and Gene Roddenberry, the giants upon whose shoulders we stand.

HISTORIAN'S NOTE

This story is set in early October 2376, approximately one week after the conclusion of the *Star Trek: Deep Space Nine* novel *Unity*.

We are not enemies, but friends. We must not be enemies. Though passion may have strained, it must not break, our bonds of affection. The mystic chords of memory, stretching from every battle-field, and patriot grave, to every living heart and hearth-stone, all over this broad land, will yet swell the chorus of the Union, when again touched, as surely they will be, by the better angels of our nature.

—ABRAHAM LINCOLN, FIRST INAUGURAL ADDRESS, MARCH 4, 1861

If you want to know who you are, it's important to know who you've been.

—JADZIA DAX ("EQUILIBRIUM")

Stardate 53777.5

Dante could not have crafted a more explicit version of hell than the one that existed in this place. As a doctor, Julian Bashir was used to trauma and suffering—he had dealt with severe episodes of both during the Dominion War—but those chaotic, bloody moments had not been entirely unexpected.

Here, however, in the bedlam of Trill's Manev Central Hospital, things seemed very different. As the overflowing triage center filled with cacophonous screams and tortured wails, Bashir and the other physicians and medics struggled against a tide of death whose source had been both surprising and invisible.

And though Bashir's medical conscience did not want to admit his own personal fears, the worst part for him was having no way to know whether Ezri had survived the initial bioelectric attacks—or even if she was in danger at all. But as Trill society continued to collapse around him, and reports kept coming in of hundreds—or maybe thousands—more casualties, he could only respond to the unfolding crisis as best he could, while striving to avoid considering the personal loss he might have to face in the very near future.

A pair of med-techs attempted to move a hover-gurney through the corridor as panicked personnel moved quickly out of its path.

"I'm a medical doctor. Can I help?" Bashir blurted out as they passed him. He had already asked this question six times during the last few minutes, and had been ignored or pushed aside each time. He imagined the lack of spots on his face made them distrust his claims of medical expertise. Why should he expect them to let their guard down sufficiently to allow a non-Trill to help them?

One of the med-techs, a young woman, called back to him, either unmindful or unconcerned about his species. "In here! Help us, please!"

Bashir followed the nurses and their patient into a vacant treatment alcove. One of the medics locked the hover-gurney into a wall unit, transforming it into a stable biobed, complete with a detailed display screen.

"Who is he?" Bashir asked. He noticed that the med-techs were treating their unconscious charge with a degree of deference that few of the triage center patients were receiving.

"Doctor Rarn just transported here from the Symbiosis Commission," the first medic said as she monitored the man's thready vital signs. "We don't know if he was injured in the attacks, or if the transporter sent him into neural shock."

Of course, Bashir thought. *Some symbionts don't tolerate transporter beams as well as Dax does.* Once again, he had to actively banish his worries about Ezri.

Bashir tapped at the keypad of the wall-mounted scanner, his eyes quickly absorbing the statistics and numbers displayed there. "His dreoline levels are spiked. It's definitely related to the transporter." He turned to the second nurse. "Three hundred cc's of drenoctazine."

His eyes wide, the male medic punched a code into a keypad mounted in the wall, and a fine mist sprayed into an attached hypospray device. "Are you sure that's not too much? Trill physiology is—"

"Yes, I'm sure," Bashir said firmly. "If he's going to live, he'll need at least this much. Possibly more."

"He was *told* not to transport," said the first medic, her eyes flicking back and forth from the scanner to Bashir. "There's so much comm traffic right now that the transporter network isn't reliable."

"The subspace bands are probably filled with emergency

chatter," Bashir said, nodding. "The government needs to shut down the public transporter grid, or else there'll be a lot more of this. Can you get them to do that?"

"I can try," the med-tech said. Then she hesitated, obviously unwilling to leave Rarn's side.

"Go!" Bashir barked. "We're doing everything we can here. More lives will be in jeopardy the longer the public transporter system stays up and running."

As the woman left, the male medic injected the patient with the hypospray. For a moment, the man convulsed, then arched his body before landing back on the biobed. Rarn's breathing quickly resumed a normal pattern, and only minor twitches in his fingers betrayed the fact that he had just had a seizure. The medic smiled grimly, pointing to the scanner. "It worked. He's back."

Bashir felt some measure of relief, though he was well aware that many more such battles lay ahead. "Good," he said, instinctively taking charge. "You need to stay with him for a little while to make sure his condition remains stable. Then I'd like you to get back out there to help with the others." Heading out of the alcove, he added, "I'm going back to triage now."

Stepping into the corridor, Bashir had to quickly sidestep another passing hover-gurney. He winced as he moved, feeling the pain in his side from the beating he had experienced a short time ago. Cautiously rounding a corner, he saw a black-garbed policewoman carrying an unconscious preteen boy in her arms. All of the bustling medical personnel appeared to be ignoring her, despite the fact that she was bleeding profusely from her forehead. Bashir saw that the boy, too, had livid facial lacerations.

"This way," Bashir half-yelled as he neared them, pointing back in the direction from which he had come.

"Thank you," the policewoman said, her voice ragged. Bashir took the boy from her arms and started to turn, then noticed that the officer was turning to go back outside, wiping the blood from her eyes as she weaved toward the door.

"I meant *both* of you," he said. "You can't go back out there in your condition."

The woman turned back to him, her clumsy swaying prompting Bashir to wonder if she had suffered internal injuries.

"You know what's happening out there?" she said. "There are

others like him all over the street. There are people lying dead everywhere. Or dying."

"You can go back out after you've been treated and stabilized," Bashir said, trying to maintain an emphatic tone. "Please."

Her shoulders fell slightly as she accepted his gentle logic. Although she was unsteady on her feet, the woman followed Bashir back into the alcove he had just left. The male medic there looked up in surprise.

"Is he stable enough to be moved?" Bashir asked.

"I think so."

"Then please move him over to one side of the gurney. This boy needs immediate help, and space seems to be at a premium."

The medic hesitated. "But he's . . ." Bashir saw something flicker across the man's features. *Doubt? Fear?* And then he did as he was told, carefully moving the Trill doctor as close to the edge of the conveyance as possible, leaving barely enough room for the unconscious boy.

Bashir set the child down, then turned to the medic, who was already recalibrating the scanner for the second patient. Bashir read the medic's name tag. "It appears you're to be my nurse for a while, Mister Jenk. So, whatever Trill medical secrets you may believe need to be kept, please leave those aside. We are in a crisis situation, and given the current overflow of patients, you're going to have to trust that I know what I'm doing."

Jenk eyed him for a few moments, his expression guarded. Then he gave Bashir a curt nod. "Understood, Doctor."

"How did this happen?" Bashir directed his question to the policewoman with a glance, then returned to viewing the multicolored monitor.

"When the bomb went off, a lot of people were injured, even those who were standing fairly far away from what we assume to be the epicenter of the flash," she said, still holding one blood-soaked sleeve up to her head. "Several of the skimmers and hovercars nearby crashed, either because of the electromagnetic pulse waves, or else because their drivers passed out. This boy was the only survivor of a three-way hovercar pileup. His mother and sister died."

Bashir quickly finished his initial trauma scans, both of the boy and the police officer, the latter of whom showed no evidence of internal injuries. The boy, however, had not been so fortunate.

"It appears that in addition to severe multiple fractures throughout this child's body, a fragment of one of his ribs has entered his spinal column." Bashir took a closer look at the biobed monitor, tapping the console so that the scanned X-ray graphics rotated for a view from the underside.

Jenk inhaled sharply. "Can you extract it safely?"

"Even if I can, it's possible he'll be paralyzed for the rest of his life," Bashir said.

The policewoman stood shakily, all color draining from her face. "I didn't . . . I didn't make it *worse,* did I?"

Bashir pointed back toward the chair. "Sit! You're making it worse on *yourself.*" He turned to the medic. "Get sterile instruments ready. We're going to try to save him."

"Are you—" Jenk didn't finish the question, as Bashir shot him a look that was meant to remind him of his earlier admonitions. The med-tech entered a sequence of numbers into the keypad on the wall, and hidden trays slid out.

"I'm going to need more people helping," the medic said quietly.

"We don't have more people available," Bashir said curtly. "It's going to be you and me. And the officer here. Do you have a dermal regenerator?"

Jenk handed Bashir the requested instrument, then began donning a surgical gown taken from a sealed package that lay on one of the wall trays.

Bashir moved over to the policewoman and crouched beside her. "This won't hurt nearly as much as it already does," he said with a grim smile. Activating the instrument, he moved it over the woman's lacerated scalp and watched as the skin quickly sealed itself. Unfortunately, he lacked the time to do more than a cursory job. *She can get the scar removed later. Right now, I'm going to need her help.*

"What's your name?" he asked.

"Rame Sagado," she said, wincing slightly as she rubbed her newly repaired scalp.

Bashir set the dermal regenerator down on one of the trays. Pointing to a nearby washbasin, he said, "Well, Officer Sagado, I need you to wash up, put on a sterile gown, and get some gloves on. You're going to help us here."

"But I need to go back to my post," she protested.

Bashir steered her toward the basin. "Not to be pessimistic, but you're in no condition to face rioters, or to drag more injured people out of the crowds. For now, let's concentrate on saving one life at a time."

Bashir once again checked the monitor, and then began to carry Dr. Rarn from the biobed. Before Jenk could react, he said, "His condition is fully stabilized. He may even be conscious within the hour. He doesn't need this bed as badly as the boy does. And we need this space to work." He gently deposited the unconscious doctor on the wide chair that Sagado had vacated, then moved to get himself gowned, gloved, and prepped for surgery.

Minutes later, the trio began operating on the young Trill. Bashir made an incision through the pouch below the boy's stomach, the place where the symbionts nested in the joined. Sagado was helping keep the pouch flap open with retractors, while Jenk administered drugs as needed, handled the surgical instruments, and watched the vitals on the monitor.

It would be easier to go in directly through the stomach, but with this much chaos going on, I can't risk an infection from a nonsterile environment, Bashir thought, focusing past the screams he heard coming from the triage room outside the alcove. He was so deep in concentration that he almost drowned out the cacophony from the rest of the hospital, not to mention the occasional phaser bursts and explosions that were still audible from the street.

But even as he worked delicately to finesse the broken bone from the boy's spinal column, Bashir's mind was awhirl with questions. "Officer Sagado, do they have any clue what happened out there? I know it was some kind of radiation-producing bomb, but I haven't seen many of the concussive injuries one would expect from a weapon of that type."

"The comm channels are still pretty scrambled," the policewoman said. "But we think that the blasts were some kind of neurogenic radiation, along with an electromagnetic pulse. Leran Manev wasn't the only city hit. There were reports from Gheryzan, New Scirapo, and Bana the last I heard, and there are fears that some of the symbiont spawning grounds have been attacked as well."

Bashir felt his blood chill. Ezri was at the Caves of Mak'ala right now. If a bomb had been detonated there, she could be dead. *And there is so much left unresolved between us.*

"Did you hear anything about Mak'ala?" he asked, his voice barely above a whisper.

"No," Sagado said simply.

"Do they know which of the radical groups is responsible for this?" Jenk asked the officer.

Sagado seemed relieved to continue discussing something other than the emergency surgery she was assisting with. "Given their choice of targets, I'd bet on one of the anti-joined groups. Probably the neo-Purists."

From what he already knew about the chaotic political situation on Trill, Bashir thought that was a safe bet indeed.

"Widen that spreader," he said to Sagado, then spared another quick glance at the monitor. He was forced to move millimeter by millimeter now; the smallest twitch of his hand could cause fatal neurological trauma.

Bashir heard feet scuffling at the entrance of the alcove, but didn't divert his attention from the delicate task at hand. He heard a harsh male voice. "We need this alcove."

"It's in use," Bashir said, his voice stern and clear. "I'm trying to save the life of this child."

The voice grew closer, became more demanding. "From the looks of the scans, this child is beyond saving. We have a very important doctor from the Symbiosis Commission that needs to undergo surgery right *now.*"

Bashir kept at his exacting work, sparing another glance at the monitor. In the glass he could see ghostly reflections of a pair of medics, a security guard, and a body on a hover-gurney. The guard was apparently the one who had been speaking.

"This child *will* survive, sir, because we will keep working until we save him," Bashir said in his most commanding voice, though he remained bent over his small patient. "And if *you* want to save your commissioner, I suggest you find another alcove before it's too late." Uncertain how the guard would react, he tried to keep his breathing steady.

Bashir knew that if the man were to try to physically remove him, his patient would almost certainly die.

2

Stardate 53757.6 (approximately one week earlier . . .)

Every time he stepped into the expansive chamber, Leonard James Akaar felt an almost primal apprehension. With the immense metal doors to either side and the rear, and the illuminated risers placed along the walls, the Federation Council assembly hall had the feel of a gladiatorial arena. Capellan tribesmen had once fought each other to the death in such places—though the combat venues had been much larger, and did not feature polished black opalite floors—and Akaar imagined that some of his countrymen probably still conducted such blood rites in Capella IV's backwater provinces.

Akaar knew that the main Federation Council chamber was built for both function and grandeur. The acoustics of the central space not only allowed speakers to be heard clearly from any section of the room, they also imparted a stentorian resonance that befitted those who assembled before that august body to represent their respective homeworlds. But even though he had been born to a line of hereditary monarchs and was now an in-fluential fleet admiral in Starfleet, Akaar was more comfortable in humbler surroundings; simple tents were far better suited to the martial tastes of a Capellan *teer,* even one in exile.

Akaar's high birth notwithstanding, the political coup that had forced him and his mother, Capella IV's Regent Eleen, to flee their homeworld during his childhood meant that he currently held no Capellan titles or lands. Because of this, he tended to look with disfavor upon councillors and dignitaries and political functionaries. They had their place—and he was in one of those places now—but he felt little kinship with them. It was an aspect of his personality that he tried to conceal from all but those closest to him.

He stood to one side as the councillors filed in to take their seats. Today's briefing was not meant to be a full quorum session of the Federation Council, but instead was comprised of the representatives of the Federation Security Council.

The Tellarite Councillor Bera chim Gleer was Akaar's least favorite of those in attendance. Like most of the Tellarites Akaar had dealt with over the years, Gleer tended toward rash emotionalism. Though the passionate warrior aspect of Akaar's personality could empathize with that trait, he still found Gleer frustrating at the best of times. On the other side of the spectrum was Councillor T'Latrek, a Vulcan who was in charge of her world's external affairs. After eighty years on the Council, she had seen many members come and go, and had witnessed the eruption and resolution of numerous wars and crises. But, true to the culture in which she'd been raised, she seemed completely unencumbered by emotion, expressing her thoughts in the rational and occasionally didactic manner of her people.

Somewhere between Gleer's fire and T'Latrek's ice was Councillor Matthew Mazibuko, representing Earth, whose diplomatic career had thrived by avoiding temperamental extremism. It was a trait, Akaar knew, that tended to be mistaken for a lack of decisiveness and conviction—a fallacy many of Mazibuko's opponents on issues brought to the floor of this chamber had learned to their great regret. As the human took his place among his peers, his vividly colored ambassadorial robes adorned in the intricate patterns of his native Africa, Akaar reflected that it was precisely this tendency to underestimate human subtlety that had enabled Earth to become such a formidable member of the Federation.

Akaar caught the gaze of Charivretha zh'Thane for a moment, but the Andorian councillor broke eye contact almost immediately, her antennae twitching in a manner that Akaar knew signified embarrassment. He'd heard she had been recalled to her homeworld and would be departing shortly after this meeting. When he had asked her earlier in the day if the rumor was true, she had deflected his question with several pointed inquiries of her own about Capellan notions of privacy. Akaar had taken the hint and withdrawn, unoffended, imagining that whatever the reason for zh'Thane's return to Andor, he would learn about it in due course—or not.

Several of the other councillors had already taken their seats, among them Huang Chaoying from Alpha Centauri, Ra'ch B'ullhy from Damiano, and Dynkorra M'Relle from Cait. But Akaar's attention was soon diverted by the arrival of the Federation president, Min Zife, who entered through the side door, flanked by several Starfleet security guards. The Federation's affable chief executive strode forward with confidence, his blue Bolian features complemented by his smartly tailored, light gray civilian suit.

"I call this session of the Federation Security Council to order," Zife said after he had taken his place behind the podium emblazoned with the Federation seal. All talk in the room dropped away sharply as the gathering turned its whole attention to the front of the chamber. "Today's meeting is to be considered sealed, unless the entire Council votes, at a later date, to reveal the proceedings herein."

Zife gestured toward Akaar, who squared his shoulders and stood straight, drawing himself to his full 2.2-meter height. He stood at attention as the president continued. "We will first hear from Fleet Admiral Akaar about the situation in question, then discuss the Council's best course of action. Admiral?"

Akaar stepped forward, bowed his head respectfully to the president, then turned to address the councillors seated along either side of the chamber. "Thank you, Mr. President. Esteemed Councillors, I trust that by now all of you have read Starfleet Command's official after-action reports on the recent crisis on Bajor, and its apparent connection to the world of Trill."

Councillor Gleer raised his porcine snout truculently. "I most certainly have, Admiral Akaar. And I am greatly displeased by the many questions they leave unanswered."

Unsurprised by Gleer's attitude, Akaar met the Tellarite's glare impassively. "I will be pleased to answer any questions that you or any of the other esteemed councillors present may wish to raise, Councillor Gleer."

Apparently unimpressed by Akaar's attempt at openness, Gleer pounded one of his hirsute fists on the table before him. "How could all of this have been kept secret for so long?" he bellowed.

Akaar found that Gleer's blunt question brought him up short. "To what are you referring specifically?" he asked after a moment's consideration.

"*All* of it! These parasites and their apparent genetic relationship to the Trill symbionts, a fact that the Trill authorities must have been concealing from us for quite a while—just as they used to hide from friend and foe alike their true nature as a joined species. Then there's the matter of the Trill government's use of assassins against other Federation heads of state. The Federation Council cannot countenance the wanton—"

Growing irritated by the Tellarite's peremptory tone, Akaar interrupted him. "I am prepared to discuss Starfleet's operational knowledge of and involvement in last month's parasite-related incidents. However, it might be indecorous of me to use this venue to speculate about the internal workings of the Trill government."

"Indeed," said Councillor T'Latrek, raising her right eyebrow in what Akaar interpreted as a display of curiosity. "Inquiries into the Trill government's knowledge about the parasites—and its apparent sanctioning of the assassination of Bajor's First Minister Shakaar—would be more appropriately directed to the councillor representing Trill."

It had not escaped Akaar's notice that Councillor Jerella Dev of Trill was conspicuously absent.

"Just why *isn't* Councillor Dev present at this meeting?" asked Ra'ch B'ullhy, the representative from Damiano. "For that matter, I would think Bajor, given the manner in which it was directly affected by Trill operatives, would demand representation at these proceedings as well. We *are* talking about an act of aggression by one Federation member world against another, are we not?"

Akaar's gaze shifted to the presidential podium, behind which Zife stood. The Bolian looked uncomfortable, apparently at a loss for words. Not for the first time, Akaar wondered how this president had gained his reputation for decisiveness, and how he had maintained it during the tumultuous years of the Dominion War.

"To their credit, and our good fortune, the Bajoran people have not been blind to the extenuating circumstances surrounding the death of their leader," Councillor zh'Thane said, cutting short the embarrassing silence from the podium. "Their own doctors have agreed that Shakaar Edon had irrevocably ceased to exist well before his parasite-dominated body was shot and killed aboard Deep Space 9. Understandably, the Bajoran government continues to demand a full investigation into Trill's handling of this crisis, about which no Bajoran or Federation officials were ever consulted. However, the Bajorans have agreed to wait for this Security Council to issue its recommendations before bringing the matter to the floor when the full Council reconvenes later this month." Zh'Thane paused before continuing. "As for the other matter, our business today very much concerns Trill, and might well be hampered by the presence of a representative from that world."

"But must we conduct this business behind the backs of the Trill people?" Councillor Huang wanted to know, her obvious distaste for subterfuge emphasized by her grim countenance.

"Why not?" said Gleer, his voice a low rumble. "The Trill have never had a problem concealing essential truths from other Federation member worlds. It seems to come naturally to them. Consider the manner in which they used stolen Starfleet property to achieve their ends on Bajor!"

Hiziki Gard's isolation suit, Akaar thought. Ordinarily utilized for benign covert cultural study of prewarp civilizations, the Starfleet "cloaking" garment had become the means by which Shakaar's killer had hoped to evade capture while he remained hidden aboard Deep Space 9. Gard said he had obtained the suit through black market channels, a claim supported by the fact that the suit's serial number tied it to the *U.S.S. Kelly,* which had been destroyed at the Battle of Rigel during the war. Ships of the Orion Syndicate were known to have ventured into the debris field in the aftermath of the battle, salvaging what they could from the wreckage before Starfleet could claim its own. It made Akaar wonder how much classified Federation technology had been recovered in the same manner by unscrupulous parties. Another postwar headache to deal with.

"In light of its government's actions," Councillor M'Relle

was saying, his usually purring tones sounding jangled and dangerous, "a reevaluation of Trill's status as a Federation member may be in order,"

"I agree," said Gleer, prompting Akaar to wonder whether the Tellarite councillor had ever before uttered that particular phrase.

Councillor Rach gently shook her horned, cerise-hued head. "That might be a bit extreme."

"I concur," said Matthew Mazibuko. "All the facts are not yet in, and it would be well for us not to rush to judgment, despite the shocking nature of recent events. Moreover, even with the Dominion War behind us, the Federation can't afford to simply cut loose long-standing member worlds. Our postwar recovery depends as much upon our continued political cohesion as it does upon mere physical reconstruction."

T'Latrek nodded at Mazibuko. "Perhaps a vote for censure would be more appropriate."

A buzz of cross conversation steadily rose among the members of the Security Council, and Akaar patiently waited for it to subside. Standing behind the podium as though using it for cover, President Zife seemed to wish he were light-years away. *Perhaps he regards the dissension surrounding Trill as a personal failure on his part,* Akaar thought.

"As deserving as the Trill government is of our criticism, we cannot afford to let that distract us from clear and present dangers," Gleer said, his nasal voice cutting through the cross talk like a rodinium-tipped mining drill. The Tellarite's stern gaze fell directly upon Akaar.

If Gleer had expected Akaar to flinch, he was disappointed. "To what are you referring, Councillor?"

Gleer snorted. "I should think my meaning is obvious. I'd like to know how we can be certain that the parasite crisis is indeed over. After all, twelve years ago—after the creatures temporarily seized control of Starfleet Command—the threat was thought to be ended. But this year they've managed to return, popping up on *Bajor* of all places. If these organisms can wreak havoc with the Federation's newest inductee, then how can we really know we're rid of them?"

The perspicacity of Gleer's words was underscored by a renewed barrage of cross talk that erupted across the chamber. Akaar waited until it had died down before replying. "You raise a very good point, Councillor Gleer. At the moment, all we have is the testimony of Captain Benjamin Sisko that the immediate threat is over . . . and the complete absence of any evidence disproving that assurance."

Gleer grunted derisively. "Far be it from me to doubt the testimony of the Emissary of the Bajoran Prophets," he scoffed.

"What my esteemed colleague means," interjected Mazibuko, shooting Gleer a sharp look before turning to Akaar, "is that the responsibilities of this Council to the people of the Federation require that we test those assurances, Admiral."

"Agreed," Akaar replied. "It should therefore please the Council to know that during the four weeks since the crisis on Bajor ended, all Starfleet databases, as well as those of local peacekeeping authorities, have been sent explicit declassified information about the parasites, including data gleaned from the encounters on both Deep Space 9 and Bajor.

"Additionally, Starfleet teams are even now reconstructing the travels of everyone known to have become infected by the parasites, in order to determine whether any residual threat yet exists."

Charivretha zh'Thane leaned forward in her chair and spoke. "Admiral Akaar has so far neglected to mention that the Trill government has asked Starfleet and this Council to withhold from the public certain salient information, namely, the genetic similarities between the parasites and the Trill symbionts."

Akaar found zh'Thane's gaze and tone grating. Was she always this condescending? Or had he gotten on her bad side when he'd asked about her recall? "Thank you, Councillor zh'Thane," he said, concealing his irritation behind a stoicism perfected by long decades of practice. "You have anticipated the next item on my agenda."

"And have we accommodated the Trill government's request?" M'Relle of Cait asked, his tail twitching absently near his right shoulder. The graceful felinoid seemed unaware of the tension between zh'Thane and Akaar.

"So far, Councillor M'Relle, neither the Federation Council nor Starfleet Command has revealed anything the Trill government has requested be kept secret," Akaar replied.

President Zife cleared his throat quietly, bringing everyone's attention back to the podium. "I have been in communication with Trill's President Maz, who has informed me that her government is undertaking a full investigation of the parasite issue, including an exploration of the apparent genetic links between the parasites and the symbionts. She respectfully requests that the Council grant the Trill Senate adequate time to conduct these proceedings before taking any precipitate action regarding Trill. President Maz has assured me on her honor that she knows nothing more than we do at the moment."

Akaar wondered briefly whether Maz was telling the truth about her personal ignorance, or was engaging in the time-honored political practice known across the quadrant as "plausible deniability."

Having evidently got his second political wind, Zife continued. "President Maz has also informed me that her people are currently experiencing considerable domestic political stress. I believe this underscores the necessity of honoring her request. It is, after all, in the interests of this Council to help Federation member worlds to maintain domestic social stability—providing they can do so without violating the Guarantees of the Federation Constitution.

"I therefore recommend that this Council allow President Maz and the Trill Senate a reasonable period of time to complete their own public inquests into the parasite affair before we make any public statements—or calls for a censure vote of any kind against Trill."

"Does the Trill government truly believe that news of the parasite-symbiont connection won't become public before it completes its own investigation?" Rach asked, her crimson face a mask of incredulity. "I find that ridiculous. If I understand the admiral's report correctly, dozens of people—perhaps even *hundreds*—already know all about this, from Starfleet to Bajor to Cardassia. It seems certain that the story will leak to the general public no matter what either the Trill authorities or this Council does."

"The odds in favor of that eventuality are high indeed," T'Latrek said. "Word of this *will* get out. It is just a matter of time."

Akaar stopped himself from nodding as the councillors conferred all around him, conversing quietly with one another in low tones.

As the members of the Council began their official vote on the matter, Akaar found that he agreed wholeheartedly with Rach and T'Latrek. Whatever domestic political problems lay ahead for the Trill people, he hoped their leaders were prepared to deal with the havoc that was sure to be unleashed, once the secret of their relationship to the parasites stood revealed.

3

Stardate 53768.2

Looks like we've reached the bottom of the world, thought Lieutenant Ezri Dax as she stepped carefully over the vast field of scattered ice and stone. She didn't think this place was quite as cold as the Tenaran ice cliffs could get during the dead of Trill's northern winter, but it was certainly chilly enough to make her grateful for her insulated field jacket and gloves.

A persistent, frigid wind numbed Dax's ears and the tip of her nose as she trudged forward, trying not to slow the away team's progress. A dull, coppery sun hung low in a duranium gray sky, barely peeking over the huge slabs of ice-slicked rock that extended to the horizon in every direction. The flattened stones, some of which appeared to be more than three meters in length, were arranged at crazy, random angles, as though the spin of some great cosmic *tongo* wheel had determined their final resting places. The slender rocky shapes cast long and sinister shadows that sometimes caused her momentarily to lose sight of the other members of the away team.

A streak of light near the horizon briefly caught her eye. At first she thought it was a meteor burning up in the atmosphere—until she saw it abruptly change its trajectory, obviously preparing to make a soft landing at one of the supply depots that dotted the lower latitudes.

Another cargo ship, she thought. The irony was inescapable; once an object of Cardassia's insatiable lust for interstellar conquest, the planet Minos Korva—situated on the edge of Federation space just four light-years from the prewar Cardassian border—now served as one of the busiest transit points for aid shipments bound for Deep Space 9, the hub for all Federation relief cargoes bound for Cardassia Prime, the Cardassian Union's war-ravaged heart.

As the evanescent streak of light vanished below the horizon, Dax turned her attention back to the frozen tableau that lay all around her. Minos Korva's south polar region reminded her of a hurricane-battered cemetery. Despite her ambivalence about the notion of death and burial—an attitude characteristic of joined Trills—she found some comfort in the permanence of the image; though grim, it helped buoy her hopes that the object of today's search not only was dead and buried, but also would forever remain that way. Like the legions of multilived Trill whose conjoined thoughts and memories eventually ended up, according to myth, enfolded safely but inertly within *Mak'relle Dur,* the Trill afterlife, deep in the bowels of the homeworld.

Dax was startled out of her reverie when she saw Dr. Vlu's arms start to pinwheel wildly, the diminutive Cardassian doctor's feet evidently having slipped on a mirror-smooth section of the frozen, rock-strewn field. Even as she moved toward the physician, Dax knew she wouldn't be able to stop her from tumbling onto one of the many steeply inclined slabs that dotted the area. Vlu shouted a pungent Cardassian curse as she started to go down, her flailing limbs casting long, spiderlike shadows across the ice as she fell toward the opening of a shadowy crevasse.

From Vlu's other side, a thickly muscled arm reached out, clutched the back collar of her field jacket, and lifted her as though she weighed nothing.

"You must be more careful, Doctor," said Taran'atar as he set Vlu on her feet beside him with a gentleness that belied his fierce countenance. The Jem'Hadar's rough, cobble-textured skin and brutish features looked as cold and hard as the frozen stones that stretched to the horizon. "These surfaces are not to be trusted."

Scowling, Vlu rubbed her throat with a gloved hand, messaging the spot where her jacket collar had constricted her neck when Taran'atar had pulled her back. "Neither is your strength. I think you dislocated a few of my neck bones."

"Are you all right?" Dax asked, reaching Vlu's side at the same time as Julian Bashir and Lieutenant Ro Laren. Dax offered an arm to steady the wobbly-looking Cardassian. She could feel Vlu's convulsive shudders right through the thickly insulated jackets they both wore.

Vlu's dark, penetrating eyes were still fixed on Taran'atar. "Please do me a favor," she said, rubbing her neck again. "Next time, just let the safety line catch me."

The Jem'Hadar's eyes narrowed as if Vlu had just spoken in an unfamiliar language. "That would have been an unwise risk to take. You might have pulled me into the crevasse along with you."

Vlu's scowl melted into a shuddering nod. "And put the rest of the team in jeopardy."

"Not to mention the mission," Ro said, her breath joining the great cloud of vapor that was accumulating over the heads of everyone on the team. Her tether, too, was hooked onto Taran'atar's belt.

"Ah. The mission," Vlu said, failing to suppress another spasmodic shiver.

The mission, Dax thought darkly, suppressing a shiver of her own—one that had little to do with the temperature. *To march right into the very place where those . . .* things *lured Shakaar Edon and hijacked his body.*

Though Dax had been in the Gamma Quadrant when her fellow Trill Hiziki Gard had assassinated Bajor's first minister in order to kill the sentient parasite that had seized control of him, she knew the story well—as did all the other members of the away team. That knowledge had apparently made the entire team extraordinarily alert.

Ro had given everyone present a thorough briefing on Shakaar's death and on her investigation into the circumstances that had led up to the parasites' initial attack on the first minister. After compiling a list of planets where Shakaar's infection might have taken place, Ro had quickly eliminated most of them. During the months prior to his becoming infected, Shakaar had toured a number of Starfleet facilities and Federation worlds, including a pair of highly secure starbases, the planets New France, Deneva, and Betazed, and then the final place that Ro hadn't been able to eliminate from her "possibles" roster: the sparsely populated Federation colony at Minos Korva.

"You don't look so good, Doctor," Bashir said as he unlimbered his medical tricorder. He seemed as oblivious to the cold as was Taran'atar. Though she recognized the feeling immediately as irrational, Dax knew a momentary surge of shivery envy.

To her left, her peripheral vision registered that Taran'atar had moved into a crouch, his attention apparently drawn to something in the ice.

"I'm fine, Doctor Bashir," Vlu said, gently pushing Julian's tricorder away. "I just wish the trail had led to that nice, warm mountain region the local officials were supposed to have been showing Shakaar during his visit. We Cardassians simply aren't suited to cold climes like this."

I guess doctors really do *make the worst patients, no matter what planet they're from,* Dax thought. She suppressed a grin as she recalled what she knew of the western mountain ranges of Minos Korva; though they were situated well within the planet's temperate zone, they wouldn't be significantly warmer than the south pole, at least not at the higher elevations.

A sharp crack interrupted her train of thought. Taran'atar started to rise and turn toward the rest of the team.

"Run!" he shouted, and took a step toward Dax.

The ice she stood on tossed her into the air. Landing on her side near a section of the icy floor that had suddenly reoriented itself vertically, she scrambled with both hands and feet to keep from sliding into the crevasse that suddenly yawned beneath Taran'atar's feet. Luckily, her boots immediately came into contact with a solid horizontal surface.

Dax felt her tether line go slack as the Jem'Hadar's massive body plunged into the shadows. *He's disengaged his safety line,* she realized with dawning horror.

The away team froze, stunned by what had just transpired and worried that another misstep might trigger additional breakages in the ice. Into the widening silence, Ro said, "I think I'm picking him up on my tricorder. He's alive."

Dax heaved a sigh of relief. "Dax to Taran'atar," she said, tapping her combadge. A burst of crackling static came in response.

"Something in the ice and rocks must be interfering with

your signal," Ro said. She scowled at her tricorder, leading Dax to conclude that it was working only marginally better than her combadge.

Then she pointed toward the east, and the rest of the group fell into step behind her. Though trapped underground, Taran'atar was evidently on the move, perhaps searching for an alternate exit to the surface.

After fifteen minutes, the party crested a low, ice-covered rise. "Here!" Ro said, gesturing with her tricorder at a tumble of rocks and ice that lay at the bottom of the other side. Dax, Ro, and Julian quickly fell to the task of clearing away icy debris from what appeared to be a narrow cavern entrance.

Several minutes later, Taran'atar's arm emerged from a rocky crevice nearby, and soon he was standing with the rest of the group. As the Jem'Hadar soldier silently reattached his safety line, Dax studied his stony, impassive features. Perhaps it was only the dim lighting, but he looked almost . . . fatigued.

"Are you sure you're all right?" Julian asked, concern striating his forehead. Dax wondered if he had noticed the same thing about Taran'atar that she had.

"My injuries are trivial, and I heal very quickly," said the Jem'Hadar, sounding annoyed, either at the situation or at himself for having fallen in the first place. "Let us resume our search for the parasite nest. You needn't waste any more time or attention on me."

"A way into the underground chamber we identified from orbit is less than fifty meters from here," Ro said, once again intent on her tricorder's display. If not for Taran'atar's accident— and the abundance of scan-reflective refractory minerals present in most of the surface rocks—the team would doubtless have reached its goal a good half hour earlier.

"Good news, Lieutenant," Julian said. Turning his attention back to Vlu, he added, "Maybe we can get you warmed up once we get belowground."

"That sounds positively lovely," Vlu said, as more uncontrollable shudders seized her. "In the meantime, would you remind me again why I agreed to come along on this little junket?"

Dax felt her own teeth beginning to chatter, perhaps in sympathy with Vlu's predicament. Smiling, she said, "Because you said you didn't want me to have to do all the griping myself."

Vlu smiled in response, apparently warmed by Dax's gentle humor. "What is that expression some of you Starfleet people are so fond of using? 'It's a dirty job, but somebody has to do it'?"

"Precisely," Dax said, returning Vlu's smile. As the group resumed moving forward, her thoughts darkened. After all, the real reason for bringing Vlu along was starkly apparent to the entire group: the away team had to include members who wouldn't be vulnerable to being biologically co-opted by the parasites; an earlier failed attempt by one of the creatures to infect Gul Akellen Macet had demonstrated that Cardassians, like Jem'Hadar, were incompatible with the parasites' physiology and thus completely resistant to their influence.

The fact that the Cardassians and the Jem'Hadar weren't first cousins to such monsters made Dax experience another stab of envy. To put that thought out of her mind, she once again considered their mission's twin goals: to find out precisely how and where Bajor's late first minister, Shakaar Edon, had been attacked by the hellish aliens who had very nearly brought destruction to the Trill homeworld; and to make certain that no more of the creatures still lurked in the deep places of Minos Korva, despite the enigmatic assurances of her oldest friend, Benjamin Sisko, who had returned after an eight-month absence from the linear continuum.

After a few more minutes of walking, Ro—who had remained at the head of the tethered procession—came to a stop. The rest of the team followed suit as Ro gestured with her tricorder toward the heavily shadowed cavern entrance that lay ahead.

"Here it is," Ro said. "Everybody ready?"

Dax's eyes darted from face to face, starting with Julian, who apparently wasn't trying to hide his trepidation over coming to this place. She glanced next at Vlu, who looked similarly discomfited, evidently as much by the cold as by whatever might await them below the icy surface of Minos Korva. Only Ro and Taran'atar appeared impassive, the former's pale Bajoran features evidently schooled to give nothing away, the latter's stony visage all but incapable of expressing anything recognizable, other than the most primal of emotions.

Ro activated an intense wrist-mounted light. Then she raised her phaser, as did Taran'atar. "Then let's go," she said.

The lights revealed a pile of icy rocks and scree that formed a crude stairway leading down into the shadows. The team moved forward, their lights pushing the darkness into full retreat. Soon the frozen crust of Minos Korva completely enclosed them, and still they walked downward, following a winding, narrow passageway. The icy rock walls were encrusted with mineral formations that revealed a panoply of subdued colors under the team's moving wrist lights; Dax noted shades ranging from dull milky opals to ugly grayish pinks. The place seemed to be a hideous parody of the Caves of Mak'ala, where the Order of the Guardians carefully tended the breeding pools of the Trill symbionts.

Moving with deliberate steps, the group pressed forward, darkness enveloping them entirely except for their wrist lights. The ice beneath their feet gave way to a moraine of gravel. The gentle slope of the progressively narrowing passageway confirmed what Dax's inner ear had already told her: they were continuing to move steadily downward. For uncountable minutes, she forced herself to concentrate on her footing as they continued making their slow descent. She almost succeeded in not thinking about what might lay ahead.

But not quite. "Anything on the tricorder?" Dax asked Ro. Her voice cast eerie multiple echoes against the cavern walls.

"I'm reading minute DNA traces on some of the rock faces," the Bajoran said, neither lowering her wrist light nor turning to look back in Dax's direction as she spoke.

"Confirmed," Vlu said, consulting her own tricorder, her earlier discomfort now apparently forgotten. "Some of them are Bajoran."

Julian's tricorder issued three sharp beeps. "More specifically, they're Shakaar's," he said.

Ro grunted an affirmation. "Shakaar was a resistance leader long before he became a politician. He wouldn't have gone down without a fight. I don't wonder that he left some of his own blood behind."

Not that fighting would have done much good against even one infected host, Dax thought grimly, recalling how the creature that had possessed Jayvin had made him both preternaturally strong and invulnerable to all but the most intense phaser settings.

The team continued forward and the passageway abruptly

widened around them. Dax noticed that Taran'atar had stopped
walking only when she nearly ran into Vlu's back. The
Jem'Hadar was slowly craning his head from left to right, scowling
as he scrutinized the broad chamber.

"Turn off your light, Lieutenant," Taran'atar said as he extin-
guished his own.

"Are you crazy?" Ro said.

Taran'atar betrayed no sign of having been offended. "Indulge me for a moment."

Through the weird shadows cast by Ro's twin lights, Dax
could see her own skepticism mirrored on the security chief's
face. Leaving her own wrist beacon dark, Dax quietly moved her
hand toward her phaser. *What if he* did *somehow fall under the
influence of a stray parasite while he was alone under the ice?*

"All right," Ro said, scowling at Taran'atar. "But this had better be good."

Dax heard a click, then saw nothing but blackness punctuated
by bright retinal afterimages of Ro's wrist light. The spots before
Dax's eyes lingered for a protracted moment before yielding to
the stygian gloom. She drew her phaser.

"All right," Ro said tartly. "What am I supposed to be seeing?"

Then Dax saw it: a wan, greenish-yellow glow that seemed to
ooze from every pore of the passage's rough-hewn walls. Meandering horizontal grooves in the passage glowed more brightly
than the surrounding stone, forming crude lines that seemed to
beckon the team forward. The chill, stale air stank of death and
corruption.

Dax wanted to run, but she forced herself to remain where
she was. Before her lay what might well have been the last sight
that met Shakaar's eyes before his parasite-infected Minos Korvan hosts led him down here to face an unimaginably horrible
fate.

And she knew that she had seen these phosphorescent
striations—and their sickly, bilious glow—before. *No, not me,*
Dax reminded herself as her eyes began to adjust more fully to
the darkness. *Those memories belonged to Audrid.*

She walked toward Ro, whose tricorder readout shone as
bright as a welding torch in the surrounding gloom. "Life
signs?"

"Nothing definite," Ro said. "But the material in these rock faces seems to be the product of some sort of biological process."

Julian was moving his tricorder along one of the chamber's faintly glowing walls. "Bioluminescence. But whatever produced it no longer appears to be active."

"I would estimate that it died on the order of five weeks ago," said Vlu, studying the glowing face of her own tricorder. "The bioluminescence we're seeing now is simply a residual effect of life processes that have ceased."

"Can you be sure of that?" Dax asked, addressing both doctors at once. "What about the refractory mineral interference we noticed earlier? Couldn't that be hiding a few live parasites?"

"I seriously doubt it," Julian said. "Those minerals appear to be most heavily concentrated in the surface layers, as geologically unlikely as that sounds."

"Then perhaps it has more to do with tactics than with geology," Taran'atar said, his rich voice reverberating in the large darkened chamber.

Dax frowned. "What do you mean?"

"The parasites may have deliberately scattered those minerals on the surface, hoping to conceal their exact whereabouts. Since that time, they may have either left or died."

"Makes sense to me," Ro said, then raised her phaser. "Still, I'm not going to take any chances."

"I agree," Vlu said. "I'd feel a good deal better if we could actually find some dead parasites here. That would tend to prove that the entire hive died when the main reproducing female was killed."

"At the very least, we have to verify that this . . . nest is empty," Julian said, nodding.

Despite the wan light, Dax could see that Ro was turning in a complete circle, her tricorder raised. "I'm all for that," Ro said. "The question is, where exactly do we look?"

Dax's eyes flitted back to the cave walls, whose glowing, veinlike markings now seemed to call to her, even as they continued to churn up some of Audrid's most painful memories.

"This way," she said. She began moving forward, following the faintly glowing lines in the stone—

—and she was once again deep inside the frozen comet where more than a century ago Audrid, her husband Jayvin Vod, and a

Starfleet team had encountered the first parasite, a creature whose genetic makeup and biological processes had scanned as so similar to those of the Trill symbionts. How excited Audrid been at the prospect of exploring that relationship, perhaps even discovering the long-debated origin of Trill symbiosis.

But that wasn't what happened.

Quicker than any predator Audrid had ever seen, the creature launched itself through the faceplate of Jayvin's environmental suit. It didn't take long for the thing to hijack the body, intellect, and soul—both humanoid and symbiont—of the man who had fathered Audrid's children.

Speaking through the enslaved Jayvin, the creature referred to itself as "the taker of gist," and called the inhabitants of Trill—its genetic cousins—"the weak ones." It said it was paving the way for the arrival of countless others of its kind, creatures whose only desire was the indiscriminate destruction of the Trill. It called the comet a "ship," sending it on a Trill-ward trajectory using directed surface outgassing—a process evidently mediated by the "veins," the creature's term for the multitude of branching lines that scored the comet's complex network of interior passages.

Ezri Dax stared in fascination at the "veins" as she continued leading the group toward whatever lay at the nest's center. Though she found the striations disturbing, she also found she was having great difficulty looking away from them. She reflected that the markings here couldn't have fulfilled the same function as those Audrid and Jayvin had found inside the comet so long ago; rather than steering the parasites toward their intended victims, perhaps the lines here served as lures for the humanoid pawns they needed in order to bring their inexplicable hatred to fruition on Trill.

If this place were still full of live creepy-crawlies, we might all be helpless or dead by now, Dax thought. *Maybe even Vlu and Taran'atar.*

The group came to a stop before a raised, rocky formation that appeared to have been thrust up from the stone floor eons ago; the natural structure stood about a meter high and vaguely resembled a cylindrical altar. A small basin had been carved into the top face of the stone; it was filled with a congealing, half-frozen mass of viscous, faintly glowing material.

Dr. Juarez, the xenobiologist from Fleet Captain Pike's Starfleet team, stood before the rocky basin where the mysterious entity lay below a gleaming sheet of cometary ice. "There's a life-form of some kind in there . . . complex arrangement, carbon-based, it should be frozen, but . . . I can't get an exact size, it seems to be shifting—"

Run! Ezri Dax shrieked from behind an impermeable veil of memory. But these were Audrid's recollections, not hers. There was nothing she could do to change what was about to happen.

"Between eight and twelve centimeters long," Juarez continued, studying his tricorder closely. "And according to this, it's at least four thousand years old."

Audrid knew from the far more precise scans that she and Jayvin had already performed that the creature was actually at least two millennia older than that—

Ro reactivated her wrist lamp, forcing the glowing striations to vanish from Dax's sight. Once again, Dax blinked rapidly as dark spots briefly danced before her dazzled eyes.

Ro bent over the fetid mass inside the basin, inspecting it.

"No!" Dax shouted.

Something shot out of the ice-covered pool, something small and dark. Simultaneously, the liquid's frozen surface splintered into innumerable flechette-like shards.

Jayvin staggered back silently, engulfed in the horrible glow, the atmosphere venting from his environmental suit's shattered helmet in a rapidly crystallizing halo—

Audrid saw Jayvin turn and snatch a phaser from the grip of one of Pike's security officers. Jayvin shoved the man down, shattering his helmet. Then he raised the weapon and fired—

Audrid Dax knew she had lost Jayvin Vod forever.

Dax suddenly realized that everyone was staring at her, their wrist lamps throwing bizarre, tentacular shadows across the chamber.

"Ezri," Julian called, his voice tinged with worry. He approached, his medical tricorder pointed toward her. "Are you all right?"

Damn. Damn. Damn!

"I'm fine, Julian. You can put that away. What's the verdict on the life signs?"

"Nothing, Lieutenant," Vlu said carefully, as though she were repeating herself. "We found the remains of several parasites in the pool, but none were still alive."

Dax felt a rush of relief at the news. Then she noticed that Julian had not yet put his tricorder away. He was continuing to scan her.

"Really, Julian, I'm fine."

He paused his scan, scowled at the tricorder display, then closed the instrument. Fixing her with a piercing stare, he said, "Is there something you'd like to tell me?"

She felt her hackles rise. Why couldn't he leave well enough alone? "You tell me, Julian. I'm sure it's nothing your tricorder can't pick up."

"This is one of those times when my instincts are telling me more than my tricorder can. You cried out as though you were having a nightmare. Or reliving a traumatic memory."

"We've already established that the parasites possess limited telepathic abilities," Vlu said. "Perhaps their decomposing nervous tissue can exert some residual influence on members of related species." The Cardassian doctor's gaze momentarily lit upon Dax's abdomen as if to underscore the close relationship that existed between the symbionts and the alien parasites. Dax frowned silently at the unspoken comparison.

"Some of the creatures may have abandoned this place in favor of a more secure nest," said Taran'atar, who appeared impatient to get the mission back on track. Dax was grateful for the interruption.

"I doubt that," Ro said. "I think it's likelier that they all died down here after they lost their telepathic link with the reproducing female."

"Why?" Vlu asked.

"Because I think they're smart enough not to leave any bodies behind for us to study. If any of them had survived, they probably would have tried a little harder to cover their tracks as they fled."

Vlu nodded as she conducted some additional scans of the cave floor. "You may be right. One would think they would have taken more care not to leave so many DNA traces lying about, come to think of it. One of their hosts could easily have eliminated those simply by using a phaser on the way out."

Dax thought this scenario made perfect sense. But she also

wondered if this was because it was exactly what she wanted to believe.

"None of this tells us why they chose such a remote base of operations as Minos Korva in the first place," Vlu said. "I don't understand why they would set up shop so close to Cardassian space. They don't appear terribly interested in us, after all. Cardassians, I mean."

Ro shook her head. "No, they don't. But they *are* interested in Trill. I think they originally intended to mount their next offensive on the Trill homeworld directly from here. But getting hold of Shakaar gave them something even better: the opportunity to infect a population of billions on a world about to enter the Federation. The damage they could have done from a position like that would have been incalculable."

"Trill appears to have dodged a bullet," Julian said. "That's something to be thankful for."

Dax nodded, her spirits buoyed by the prospect of leaving this horrible place forever. She could only hope that her homeworld could soon put the parasite horror behind it and move on.

"If there's nothing more to see here, I'd like to get back to the runabout," Dax said, taking a step backward.

She felt something hard crunch and scrape between her boots and the cold stone floor, breaking her chain of thought. Turning her wrist light back on, she cautiously dropped to one knee to take a closer look at whatever had gotten underfoot.

She stood, holding up a curved shard of pottery that measured perhaps a few centimeters across. It was clearly a manufactured object, and looked extremely old.

"Can anyone hazard a guess about this thing?" Dax said.

Julian shrugged and offered her a lopsided smile. "Perhaps the parasites enjoy making ceramics. Even monsters must need hobbies."

Dax felt a tart rejoinder springing to her lips, but it was diverted by the chirp of her combadge. Since everyone who might be communicating with her via combadge was present, it had to be an incoming signal from the runabout they had left parked at their landing site a couple of klicks to the north.

Handing Julian the ceramic fragment, she tapped her combadge and said, "Dax here. Go ahead."

"Incoming priority message from Captain Kira Nerys on

Federation Starbase Deep Space 9," the runabout's computer reported, its pleasant alto voice displaying not a trace of emotion.

"Send it through."

"Channel open."

"Dax here. Go ahead, Captain."

Though the scattering effects of the refractory minerals in the topsoil overhead created a background wash of low static, the runabout's powerful subspace transmitter had established a strong connection with Dax's combadge. A familiar voice reverberated through the tomblike chamber, muffled only slightly by the dozens of light-years that separated the station from Minos Korva. *"How's the search going, Lieutenant?"*

"It's going just the way we hoped it would," Dax said. "We found the parasites' nest and confirmed that First Minister Shakaar was lured here and probably infected here as well. The parasites themselves are all dead now, and have been for some time. We've found no trace of infection among the planet's population."

Kira paused a moment before answering. *"Good work. That goes for all of you. Well done."*

Despite the congratulatory words, something in Kira's tone warned Dax that whatever else she had to say couldn't be good.

"Ezri, Starfleet Command has just informed me that the Trill Senate is planning to conduct official inquests into the entire parasite affair."

Dax's eyebrows climbed skyward. "That's kind of surprising, Captain. I thought the last thing the Trill government would want right now is publicity about the parasites' attack on the homeworld."

"I'm sure you're right about that, Ezri. But the government no longer seems to have any choice in the matter. The word has already gotten out among the Trill populace. Your people are demanding that their leaders come clean."

"About the relationship between the symbionts and the parasites?" Dax imagined she could feel her symbiont squirming uncomfortably in her abdomen.

"That seems to be part of it. They also aren't happy about the fact that officers of the Trill Defense Ministry have participated in the assassination of a high Bajoran official. However justified."

Dax clearly heard the pain that underlay this reference to

Shakaar, who had once been Kira's lover and whose orders Kira had followed during her years as a resistance fighter.

"The parasites and the assassination have caused ripples that go way beyond Trill," Kira continued. *"Officials on other Federation planets are starting to howl about 'Trill secretiveness,' and they're making demands that something be done about it. Starfleet Command believes that the Federation Council might even be forced to take action if things don't calm down soon."*

Dax swallowed hard as she imagined the worst possible outcome: Trill's status as a Federation member being placed in jeopardy.

When she replied, her voice came out almost as a croak. "What can we do?"

"I think the question is, what can you *do?"* Kira said.

"Me? Come again?"

"You're a joined Trill and *a Starfleet officer, and you have contacts in the Trill government who could use your guidance and assistance."*

Dax considered reminding Kira that her closest contacts inside the Trill government—Hiziki Gard, an internal security operative, and Taulin Cyl, a general in the Defense Ministry—were the very ones responsible for Shakaar's assassination. As longterm "watchers" of the parasites, as well as keepers of the now-compromised secret of the parasite-symbiont genetic relationship, Gard and Cyl were arguably part of the current problem more than part of any solution. Of course, the creature that had hijacked Shakaar's body had left Gard and Cyl little choice other than killing him. But still . . .

"My . . . guidance," Dax echoed incredulously, though she knew what was probably coming next.

"Also, Admiral Ross and I agree that your testimony at the upcoming Trill public hearings could be invaluable in heading off a real crisis," Kira said. *"We need you on Trill, Ezri."*

No. The one you need is Curzon, Dax thought. *A real career diplomat, not just someone who hears the echoes of his memories.*

Aloud, she said, "All right. We're just about finished mopping up here. Once we get back to the station, I'll—"

"I want you to take the Rio Grande *directly to Trill,"* Kira

said, interrupting. *"Immediately. Tenmei is en route to Minos Korva in the* Nile *to pick up the rest of your team. You should get them back to the Federation settlement as soon as possible."*

Dax hesitated only a moment before answering; ever since she'd made the switch from a counseling career to Starfleet's command track, she had always tried her best to expect the unexpected.

"Yes, sir. I'm on my way."

After returning with the team to the surface, Dax wasted no time ordering the *Rio Grande*'s computer to begin preflight preparations and to beam everyone in the party aboard the runabout. Seated beside her in the cockpit, Julian silently stared out at the icy, twilit wasteland of Minos Korva's south pole as Dax operated the transporter controls, sending Vlu, Ro, and Taran'atar directly to the nearby Federation settlement.

She turned her seat toward him. "Your turn, Julian. It's time I got under way to Trill."

He nodded absently, then rose slowly from the copilot's chair. But instead of walking aft toward the runabout's transporter pad, he doffed his heavy field jacket and tossed it beside hers on one of the other cockpit seats.

"I'm going with you," he said simply.

Ezri shook her head gently. "I'm not sure that's such a good idea, Julian. This is Trill business, and—"

"—and Trill are notoriously reticent about letting non-Trill in on their affairs, yes, I know." Though he had interrupted her, he continued to smile ingratiatingly as he resumed his place beside her in the copilot's chair.

"I appreciate the offer, Julian," she said, looking directly into his dark eyes. "But I really think this is something I ought to handle on my own."

"And I think you're going to need my help. Or at least my moral support. You told me yourself how guilty you feel over Audrid's cover-up of the discovery of that first parasite more than a century ago. And I've seen with my own eyes how traumatic this entire business has been for you. That parasite nest must have dredged up some painful memories." He paused. "Memories of the parasite that killed Audrid's husband, unless I'm terribly mistaken."

Suddenly feeling defensive, Dax crossed her arms across her chest and leaned back in the pilot's seat. She knew it was useless to deny his assertions; he'd been at Jadzia's side five years earlier when Dax's equally painful suppressed memories of an ill-fated joining with the psychotic killer Joran Belar had resurfaced. Julian obviously knew the signs of mnemonic trauma. Still, she didn't have to like it.

"Well. This is all very 'who counsels the counselor?' isn't it?" she said.

"You're not a counselor anymore, remember?"

A deep frown sprang to her brow unbidden. "And you never were one. I love you, Julian, but I think you're straying a bit too far from your specialty."

He leaned toward her, taking her hand between both of his in an obvious effort to soothe her. Looking into his chocolate-brown eyes as his hands warmed hers, she had to concede that it was working.

"Listen, Ezri, I'm not trying to beat up on you. And I can give you three very solid, rational reasons why I should accompany you to Trill."

For the first time in what seemed like hours, she returned his easy smile. "All right. Let's hear them."

He began ticking off points on his long surgeon's fingers. "One: We haven't spent nearly enough time alone together since before this whole parasite business erupted. Two: I have entirely legitimate medical concerns about your current emotional state after observing your behavior here on Minos Korva."

Dax opened her mouth to protest, but he rode right over her words. "And three: I outrank you, my darling." His smile became an impish grin as he gestured toward the lieutenant commander's pips, two gold and one black, that adorned his collar.

Anger and affection wrestled for a protracted moment before calling it a draw. She disengaged her hand from his, turned her seat forward, and quickly entered several commands into the instrument panel. The *Rio Grande* rose swiftly into the gray Minos Korvan sky.

Julian grinned.

"You win, Julian. But just remember: I'm the only one here dressed in command red. And Kira placed responsibility for this mission with *me,* not you. So that extra pip on your collar doesn't mean all that much at the moment."

He dipped his head toward her in a fair approximation of a courtly bow. "I remain, as ever, your obedient servant."

As the runabout went into warp, Dax couldn't help but wonder if Julian would actually live up to that promise.

4

Julian Bashir was gratified that Ezri had relented and allowed him to accompany her on what otherwise would have been a solitary voyage to Trill. After having seen her obvious emotional distress back in the Minos Korvan parasite nest, he felt it prudent to keep an eye on her. Besides that, he simply wanted to spend some time alone with her, though he worried that he might have pushed a bit too hard in his efforts at persuasion.

Seated beside her in the copilot's seat, he watched Ezri as she flew the runabout and occasionally monitored its instruments. She spent most of her time looking silently through the transparent aluminum windows at the ever-changing star field, her gaze directed straight ahead.

Ezri had been uncharacteristically quiet and standoffish ever since the *Rio Grande* had gone to warp nearly an hour earlier. A glance at the instrument panel told him that she was pushing the runabout's engines nearly to their limit. *At this pace, we'll reach Trill in about three standard days,* he thought after performing a quick mental calculation.

It was easy to guess that much of her current mood stemmed from the parasite crisis and the fallout it was continuing to generate back on Trill. *Or perhaps my twisting her arm until she agreed to bring me along has something to do with it.* Either way, he knew that if she didn't unburden herself about it soon, the next three days would pass very slowly indeed.

Whatever Ezri might think of his counseling abilities, he

knew when it was prudent to back off. And whenever stimulating conversation wasn't an option, there was always the pursuit of knowledge for its own sake. Excusing himself, he quietly rose from his seat, fetched a few items from the pockets of his field jacket, then continued past the runabout's dual transporter pad on his way to the aft compartment. The sliding hatch hissed shut behind him, and he was alone.

Smiling to himself, he held up the small ceramic shard that Ezri had found in the parasite nest on Minos Korva. He studied the palm-size fragment carefully, turning it over and over in his hands as he wondered how and why it had come to be where it was.

Taking a seat before the computer console on the runabout's starboard side, he said, "Computer, show me the xenoanthropology database."

Dax heaved a relieved sigh a few moments after Julian left the cockpit. While she had to admit it was nice having the man she loved at her side during difficult times, she was less than eager to share this burden with him. She knew he couldn't be terribly surprised by her reticence. She was a Trill, after all, and he was already well acquainted with her people's penchant for keeping secrets, thanks to his role in discovering the Symbiosis Commission's systematic suppression of the fact that nearly half of her world's humanoid population were suitable for joining with the symbionts, not the one-tenth of one percent that was still the common belief.

Maybe it's that very secrecy that's at the root of all of our current troubles, she thought.

Putting aside her glum musings, she decided to take advantage of this solitary time in the cockpit to try to get a handle on the situation back on the Trill homeworld. Her hands moved with deliberation across the instrument panel, activating the runabout's subspace transceiver. She quickly keyed a personal subspace reception code within the Trill Defense Ministry.

A flashing amber light on the companel signaled that her subspace signal wasn't getting through. Carefully, she repeated the signal initiation procedure, trying once again to establish contact with Taulin Cyl's office.

Again, nothing. Muttering one of Curzon's preferred Klingon

curses under her breath, Dax made two more fruitless attempts. After the fifth try got her through to the Defense Ministry's general reception area—netting her a two-minute conversation with a junior information officer, who then transferred her to an even more junior-looking adjutant or assistant instead of to the evidently extremely busy General Cyl—she decided that she was getting precisely nowhere. Cyl evidently had his hands full, no doubt at least in part because of the Trill Senate's upcoming public hearings into the parasite affair.

Rising from her chair, she walked straight back to the *Rio Grande*'s aft compartment. When the hatch hissed open before her, she found Julian staring into the display at the computer station, studying a quickly scrolling text with an intensity that made her wonder if he even remembered that he was aboard a space vessel flying at many multiples of light speed—or that the rest of the universe even existed.

Or that I *exist,* she thought, smiling to herself. But wasn't that single-mindedness, that all-encompassing enthusiasm for knowledge one of the qualities that drew her to him?

"Hi, Julian," she said gently as she walked up behind his chair and placed a hand on its back. She was beginning to feel guilty about having driven him into solitude, though he hadn't seemed to mind much at the time. "Lieutenant Dax to Doctor Bashir," she added several beats after he failed to respond to her.

It took him another moment or two to react to her presence. When he paused the display and turned to face her, she wondered if he was going to ask if they had arrived at Trill yet.

Instead he smiled up at her and took her hand. His hands always felt warmer than any Trill's, and the sensation was almost electric. "Sorry. I thought I'd get started on a little research."

She gently squeezed his hand and returned his smile, and then he went back to his task. For Julian, doing "a little quick research" was often like having "a short conversation" with Morn while drinking at Quark's—in other words, it would most likely become an all-encompassing, completely attention-devouring endeavor. Over his shoulder, she could see odd images and snippets of text from the database he was so quickly scrolling through. Her brow furrowed briefly in puzzlement.

"When did you become so interested in exoarchaeology?"

Julian paused the display once more on a vaguely familiar-looking image. "Right after you made that rather odd discovery on Minos Korva."

She suddenly remembered that she hadn't given a thought to the ceramic shard since just after she'd picked it up from the cave floor. A momentary panic gripped her; she withdrew her hand from his and patted her uniform jacket in a futile search for the item.

Then she looked back at Julian, who was grinning and holding up the small pottery fragment. He gently placed it into her hand.

Her face reddened as she accepted it. She felt foolish for having forgotten that she'd given it to him. "Thanks for taking charge of this, Julian."

"I was more than happy to. You seemed to have a lot of other things on your mind at the time."

Dax decided to head off that particular conversational thread by discussing the artifact. "So, has your research told you anything important about this thing so far?"

"It's hard to say. The first thing I determined was that it's about twelve thousand years old. It didn't appear to be Bajoran, so I thought it was doubtful that Shakaar left it in those caves. There's absolutely no possibility that the piece is native to Minos Korva, and it seems rather unlikely that any of the other humanoid hosts taken by the parasites would have carried any such thing prior to their being attacked. So I started to wonder if the fragment might have had some significance to the parasites themselves. Then my tricorder detected this." He keyed a new image onto his screen, which Dax recognized as a layered molecular scan, presumably of the fragment, with its different constituent materials broken out by color. The dark outer glaze was represented in reds and purples; the inner ceramics by a bright blue.

In between was a small patch of green lines. A glyph?

Julian isolated the image and enlarged it. It looked like no language Ezri had ever seen before.

"From this, I've been able to determine that this object came from the planet Kurl."

"Kurl. That's the site of a long-dead civilization, isn't it?"

Julian nodded. "It is. What little we know of it is mostly by way of artifacts like that one, but our best guess has been that the

Kurlan civilization was at least tens of thousands of years old before it died out, five thousand years ago. And the planet is located hundreds of light-years from Minos Korva, well outside Federation territory. However this fragment ended up in that cave, it's gotten itself quite a long way from home."

Dax smiled, understanding his fascination. "Sounds like quite a mystery."

"A very nearly irresistible one." Julian returned her smile with a mischievous grin. "In fact, I can think of only one other thing I'd rather do to pass the time until we reach Trill."

As much as she enjoyed their infrequent intimate time together, Dax had to admit that not even Emony had ever whiled away three entire days doing *that*.

"Down, boy," she said with a grin as she examined the ancient and gracefully curved shard closely. Despite its great age, the fragment retained a smooth glaze. She wondered how anyone, even someone with a mind as brilliant as Julian's, could satisfactorily explain the thing. "I know how much you love puzzles, Julian. But I'm afraid you don't have very much to go on here."

He shrugged. "Neither did the Trill paleontologists who worked out the carnivorous habits of the extinct *Eomreker*. All they had to guide them was a fossilized rear claw and a single incisor tooth. But I'm quite a determined fellow, and I have three whole days to tease out some answers."

She looked once again into his brown, knowledge-hungry eyes and marveled at how easily he could transform himself from bantering adolescent to determined problem solver. It struck her then that it was at times like this that he was most attractive.

"I just had a thought," she said, taking his hand and squeezing it gently. "We *do* have three days. There's no need to wear yourself out." She grinned. "Studying, I mean."

Later, Dax watched Julian as he dozed beside her on the narrow bunk. His breathing made a gentle, repetitive susurrus, and his olive-tinted features looked slack and childlike.

Rolling onto her back, she stared up at the gray curvature of the ceiling molding, wishing she could feel half as relaxed as Julian obviously did.

After another few minutes, she rose quietly, gathering the pieces of her uniform as she withdrew from the sleeping compartment. Except for her boots, she was dressed by the time she reached the cockpit. All the instruments showed nominal; the *Rio Grande* remained on its heading for Trill, which now lay somewhat less than three days away. Leaning back in the pilot's seat, she suddenly realized that she was clutching the ceramic fragment tightly in her left hand; she had evidently grabbed it instead of her boots.

She set the fragment down on the panel and activated the communications system, hoping to reach General Cyl. Her luck was no better this time than on her first attempt shortly after leaving Minos Korva.

Rather than continue figuratively beating her head against the bulkhead, she entered another series of commands into the companel. A few moments later the rounded, stylized symbol of one of Trill's civilian newsnets appeared on her screen.

Her eyes widened involuntarily as watched the lead stories unfold. *No wonder Cyl's not answering.*

5

Stardate 53776.1

Trill's sun looked strangely orange and oblate as it dipped low on the horizon, its rays blazing an ocher and vermilion trail across the distant white slopes of Bes Manev, the planet's tallest mountain. The impending sunset cast lengthening shadows over the foothills even as it illuminated Manev Bay's deep purple waters. The *Rio Grande* arced past the bay and approached the capital city's dock district, descending toward the broad blocks of wide, shining reflecting pools and graceful copper towers that comprised the government sector. In the distance loomed the ancient sprawl of the Old City's core. From the pilot's seat, Dax took in the scene that was unfolding on the Trill capital's broad boulevards.

Never before in any of her lives could Dax recall having seen the city of Leran Manev in the grip of such palpable tension. Restive crowds milled behind barricades, held back by serried ranks of black-armored police. Behind the barriers, slogan-festooned placards waved. On the way to the landing concourse, Dax caught a glimpse of a sign that read SYMBIOSIS EQUALS DEATH, then another emblazoned with the words JOINING FOR ALL. A third said, more ambiguously, TIME FOR TRUTH.

She shook her head sadly. *What a mess of contradictions. Welcome to the homeworld, Ezri.* She felt a surge of gratitude that Ezri Tigan had actually grown up far from here, on the New Sydney colony. Even as the thought crossed her mind, she knew it was unfair; to the best of her knowledge, none of Trill's cities had ever experienced such sharp political divisions at any point during Ezri's lifetime. And she had to concede that the stories she had read on Trill's newsnets might have overstated the possibility of real social unrest.

"That's quite a gathering out there," Julian said dryly as Dax landed the runabout in one of the wide spots that was specially marked for official Federation visitors. A few moments later she was standing beside him on the landing pad, in the lengthening shadow of the immense Senate Tower.

Dax spied a pair of figures approaching briskly from the building's glass entryway portico.

"General Cyl," Dax said to the tall, white-haired man on the left as she and Julian closed the remaining distance between them. "Mister Gard," she said to the younger man beside him, nodding in greeting. Gazing at Gard, she hoped she'd managed to conceal her surprise at being received by the man who had actually carried out the assassination of Bajor's first minister. Perhaps the newsnet rumblings of Gard's forthcoming presidential pardon really was the done deal that some seemed to believe it was.

As perfunctory greetings were exchanged, Gard smiled disarmingly, though his dark, neatly trimmed goatee gave him an almost roguish aspect. "Please, Lieutenant, call me Hiziki. And that goes for you as well, Doctor."

Julian looked toward the broad boulevard that lay perhaps a hundred meters past the landing area. Beyond a handful of parked skimmers, hovercars, and small air trams, the milling crowds were clearly visible.

"It looks like a lot of people are becoming rather exercised over current events," he said dryly, apparently addressing no one in particular.

Eyeing the crowd with evident apprehension, Gard said nothing. Cyl nodded gravely. "The Senate's public inquest is already under way," the general said, meeting Dax's gaze. "Needless to say, there's been a great deal of popular interest."

"A lot of people across the planet are anxious to learn the truth about the parasites," Gard said. "It may be that secrecy is no longer an option." He sounded almost relieved at the prospect of setting aside Trill's long history of surreptitiousness; Dax wondered how many of his numerous lifetimes Gard had devoted to maintaining it.

Ushering the group toward the Senate Tower's broad, balustraded entrance, Cyl shook his head. "It's a pity we weren't able to keep the hearings entirely closed to the public. We could have decided later how much to reveal, and when to reveal it. But I suppose that wouldn't have been realistic."

Gard glanced briefly back at the crowd before returning his gaze to Dax. "At any rate, the Senate is particularly eager to hear *your* testimony, Lieutenant."

No pressure, she thought, hoping that the unalloyed truth about the parasites would serve to calm the restless crowds rather than inflame them further. Though she was well acquainted with her people's penchant for secrecy, she also knew that Trills, like all Federation members, were proud of their free and open society. She had to believe that her people would never throw away the latter because of an habitual attachment to the former.

"When does the Senate want Lieutenant Dax to testify?" Julian asked the general.

Cyl directed his reply to Dax, almost as though Julian weren't there. "Immediately, if that's all right with you. I'll be at your side throughout your testimony, just in case security considerations make it necessary to recommend that you answer any of the Senate's questions in a special closed-door session later."

Dax felt her stomach flutter slightly. She wasn't surprised at Cyl's evident reticence about what her upcoming testimony might make public. But she hadn't expected to have to leap into the thick of things so soon after landing on Trill.

"So, are you ready, Lieutenant?" Cyl asked, his dark eyebrows raised.

"I suppose so," she said at length, hoping she didn't sound quite as apprehensive as she felt.

"Lead on, then," Julian said.

Gard stopped at the gleaming transparisteel door, which was flanked by a pair of alert-looking, dark-garbed police officers. Turning to Julian, he raised a hand in a polite but firm gesture that clearly said "halt."

"If you don't mind, Doctor, we would prefer that you don't accompany us into the Senate Chambers themselves."

Julian looked astonished. "Excuse me?"

"You're welcome to walk around inside the building, of course," Cyl added. "Or tour the city. But the Senate has requested that no non-Trills be present at the inquest."

Dax saw that Julian looked peeved, his pride clearly wounded. Smiling, she said, "I did try to talk you out of coming along, Julian, remember?"

"Yes, you did at that," he said quietly, then put on a smile of his own a few seconds later. It was clear to Dax that her reminder hadn't helped matters.

He nodded to her. "I suppose I could go for a walk. I'll catch up with you in a few hours."

"Julian . . ." she said, trailing off as he walked away in stony silence. It was clear that he wasn't at all happy about being excluded from her mission. And that neither Cyl nor Gard wanted him to come along. *Dammit.*

"This way, Lieutenant," Cyl said, making a *follow me* gesture toward the Senate Tower's doors. For a moment, Dax was tempted to put up a fight on Julian's behalf.

But I'm here to help calm things down. Not to contribute more problems. With a sigh, she went where she was bid.

Secretive bastards, Bashir thought as he stalked away.

He was a little surprised at how quickly his initial feeling of pique evaporated as he made his way through the crowd that ringed the broad boulevards around the Senate Tower. Of course, he was well aware that he tended to be distracted fairly easily by interesting surroundings.

Political dissension was rare in recent Federation history, and as he passed through gaps in the placard-carrying crowd he found himself wondering about the substance of it. There were easily a thousand people lining the portion of the main thoroughfare visible to him, and a few minutes' study revealed that the only thing they all seemed to have in common was that they were unjoined Trill humanoids. It was a surprisingly diverse group, containing faces of every hue, from Ezri's pale tones to Captain Sisko's deep, burnished brown. Bashir's keen eye even discerned a handful of people whose faces were distinguished by graceful, upward-arching brow ridges instead of the facial spots more commonly associated with Trill humanoids.

He realized immediately that he shouldn't have been surprised in the least; after all, most of the Trills he had encountered until now belonged to a tiny minority of the populace.

The joined.

Judging from the signs carried by the largest clusters of people, at least three clear political viewpoints were discernible. One faction was demanding accountability from the Trill government regarding the parasite crisis; they carried signs suggesting that the genetic relationship between the parasites and the symbionts was quickly becoming common knowledge. Another group's placards vehemently denounced the entire institution of joining, offering the parasites as proof that the symbionts were in fact mind-controlling alien life-forms bent on the conquest and domination of Trill. A third group—which apparently equated symbiosis not only with upward social mobility, but also with a sort of immortality—demanded joining for all healthy Trill humanoids who requested it.

The sentiments of the joining-for-all contingent—which was comprised of adults of both genders and every age group from teens to the elderly—struck a chord of sympathy within Bashir's breast. *What would it be like to be denied something that so many of one's peers regard as so important?*

He walked south, approaching Leran Manev's graceful sprawl of reflecting pools. As the crowds receded behind him, he considered the demands of the third group of demonstrators, and recalled what the Trill Symbiosis Commissioner Dr. Renhol had said about the issue during one of Bashir's visits to Trill five years earlier. Renhol had begged him and Benjamin Sisko not to reveal their discovery that some fifty percent of Trill's humanoid populace could, in fact, qualify for symbiosis; she had argued that complete social chaos would erupt were the truth to emerge. Because the symbiont population had never been large enough to accommodate such a huge demand, the Symbiosis Commission had perpetuated the lie that only a tiny fraction of the humanoid population could join successfully.

Passing the reflecting pools and moving toward what the map on his tricorder identified as the periphery of the government quarter, Bashir wondered if the Trill people had finally begun

honestly challenging the restrictions to symbiosis. If so, would
Dr. Renhol's dire prediction actually come to pass?

He tried to push those concerns aside as he made his way into
what was clearly a far different sector of the city. Rather than
creating a skyline of vertical spires, the buildings were low and
broad, few exceeding four stories in height. Narrow, decorative
watercourses threaded between streets and buildings, crossed at
intervals by bridges of wood or metal. Bashir wondered if the
purpose of the clearly artificial waterways was to stimulate comforting thoughts of Mak'ala, the underground, aqueous caverns
where the Trill symbionts bred.

Turning his attention to the storefronts, office structures, and
apartment complexes, it struck Bashir that virtually every structure within sight was a landmark, a touchstone to some bygone
age or other. An ancient rococo library that resembled a me-
dieval Terran cathedral made entirely of glass and translucent
crystal beckoned to him with uncountable racks of data rings
and old-style hard-copy books. An old-fashioned, meticulously
hand-painted sign in the main gallery window touted a forthcoming personal appearance by a noted Trill author of an apparently highly regarded new work of serial biography. The book
concerned a figure from Trill history whose lives spanned the
period of warfare before the planet's political unification to the
uncertain years after first contact with Vulcan. The walls were
bedecked in swirling, colorful portraits, apparently actual wood-
framed canvas paintings mounted on easels rather than free-
floating holograms; the images, some of them old and cracked,
showed a wide range of visual interpretations of the biography's
evidently controversial subject, some heroic, others monstrous.

Bashir wandered on, eagerly drinking in the sights. Museum-
piece retail storefronts were being carefully shuttered by their
proprietors, while the operators of cafés and sidewalk restaurants appeared to be preparing for a busy evening. Bashir paused
momentarily to people-watch near a construction site where an
elaborately designed edifice was being erected; he was immediately taken by the confident bearing of the young woman—the
architect, Bashir presumed—who was directing a crew of workers. While the young woman carried herself without a hint of
trepidation, she also moved as though she was acutely aware of
anything that might conceivably endanger her. Only someone

with an extremely long view of life could control her body with such surgical precision, while at the same time making it look so casual.

She's either a very old soul, or she's joined. As he resumed walking, he wondered how many other lives echoed and reverberated inside her symbiont. Who but the most ardent anti-symbiont partisan could resist the siren song of such instantly installed, modular wisdom, which was in some ways so like his own genengineered abilities? How many clear advantages did those former lives confer upon their hosts—advantages that might be forever unavailable to the vast majority of the people now carrying signs outside the Senate Tower?

He walked on through the streets of the living Trill museum, troubled in spite of himself by what he had just seen. Though he certainly considered himself worldly enough to understand that Federation member worlds sometimes fell short of the UFP's social ideals—the planet Ardana's segregation of its intellectual and labor classes during the previous century sprang immediately to mind—he was still idealistic enough to be disturbed by it.

Trying to put such thoughts out of his mind, Bashir walked on for several more blocks, noting that the buildings he was encountering seemed increasingly ornate and baroque. A quick scan with his tricorder revealed that all of the structures around him were far older than any of the buildings in the government sector, though none betrayed any obvious signs of neglect or disrepair. A few dated back more than a millennium, a fact that would have been apparent only to a true expert in Trill architecture—or to the discerning eye of a Starfleet tricorder. Clearly, entire sections of Leran Manev had become gallery displays of cultural history. It was a vibrant, though chronologically arranged, metropolis.

Of course, he thought. *Joined Trill symbionts have serial lives that can go on for centuries.* It made perfect sense that the Trill people would have a tendency to revere memories, whether personal or architectural, and take great care to preserve as many of their cultural manifestations as possible.

The notion of Trill memories brought to the fore some poignant recollections of his own. Finding a vacant public information terminal, he tapped in an inquiry and determined that the source of his musings was in this very city. Within walking distance, even.

A small melancholy smile crossed his lips as he realized just how close he had come to the place he had avoided for nearly two years now.

Jirin Tambor entered the grand, crystalline foyer of the Najana Library and eyed the display of the new serial biography of General Tem.

The sight of Grala Tem's smirking visage set off yet another wave of chest pain. The joined newsheads on the nets seemed united in their praise of the old butcher. But Tambor always had to wonder if Tem could have risen to such prominence without standing on the shoulders of his symbiont's previous lives. What if he'd been among the faceless ranks of unjoined cannon fodder who had fought and died for him?

How hard could it have been to achieve apparent greatness with a built-in advantage like that?

Tambor suddenly became aware of the head librarian, who stood scowling at him, arms akimbo. Though she was young, her eyes were old. Joined eyes, he concluded. He realized with no small amount of embarrassment that she had been trying to get his attention for some time.

"I said, are you here to deliver the rest of the General Tem display for the art gallery?"

His chest hurting, Tambor nodded, abashed. "It's on the hover-truck outside."

"Fine, then," she said impatiently. "Bring it on down to the basement. The staff will unpack and assemble it tomorrow. And no antigravs inside the building."

"All right," Tambor said. Though he didn't relish carting his heavy cargo without the benefit of antigravs, he was thankful for once for the obsessive need to keep anachronistic technology out of their old landmark buildings. Because of that need, Tambor now had permission to place a large, sealed crate into the Najana Library's basement. He was confident that no one would notice that he was still in the basement along with it until after the library closed. By the time anybody did, it would be far too late.

The pain in Tambor's chest receded slightly. Soon, very soon, the joined would all begin to pay.

* * *

Dax found the quiet of the place almost deafening. Until this evening, she had made a point of avoiding this place. Memories could be treasured, after all, without having to dwell on them.

The sun had long vanished behind the ranks of low, ancient rooftops that dotted the edge of Manev Bay. Nearby, orderly rows of crystalline obelisks cast lengthy shadows over a lawn that stretched for kilometers. As with all cemeteries on Trill, the grave markers were a riot of color, even in the darkness. Illuminated subtly from within by remote-mediated photonics, each marker instantly told a story about the status of every interred person. The unjoined, who comprised the vast majority of the dead, were denoted by a simple, dignified yellow. The joined dead whose experiences were no longer being carried by a joined successor host—a fate that Dax knew awaited every joined Trill humanoid eventually—glowed a deep, mournful green.

The smallest group, representing only a tiny percentage of the forest of small spires, glowed a hopeful purple, the color of Trill's ever-regenerating oceans, the ultimate source of all life. These were the graves of once-joined humanoids whose symbionts currently lived on in other hosts, hosts who sustained their predecessors' memories in much the same way that Trill's oceans nurtured the planet's biosphere. *As Vic might say, these are the best seats in the house,* Dax thought wryly, uncomfortable in the presence of so much stark, immutable death. *Maybe it's not exactly* Mak'relle Dur, *but I suppose it's a pretty reasonable facsimile.*

A slender shadow, taller than any of the spires, fell across a grave marker bearing a name that was barely discernible in the waning light:

JADZIA IDARIS

Inscribed directly beneath the familiar name, in the same stark, simple script, were the words:

BELOVED DAUGHTER, SISTER, STUDENT, FRIEND
HOST OF DAX

Dax had the eerie sensation that she was standing at the edge of her own grave. At the same time, Jadzia was very much a stranger to her.

She moved quietly toward the still shape that now stood beside Jadzia's obelisk. "I thought I might find you here."

Julian didn't seem in the least surprised at her arrival. He continued staring straight ahead at the grave marker, and the darkness that framed it. "You could have asked the *Rio Grande*'s computer to locate me."

"Didn't think I needed to. Besides, I needed to take a walk, too. I guess I owed her a visit as well."

"Why? You never knew Jadzia."

"True. But in some ways I know her better than anyone," Ezri said, placing a hand on her abdomen. "Sometimes I wish I could have *really* known her. The way other people did, I mean."

"I think she would have liked you," he said, before trailing off into brooding silence.

Then he turned to face her. For a moment, Julian's grief shone through the darkness like a beacon. She felt a surge of relief when he changed the subject. "How did your testimony go?" he asked quietly.

Dax shrugged. "Bumpy, but survivable. Cyl seemed nervous about a few of the senators' direct questions about the parasites. He kept insisting that a lot of them be redirected to a closed-door session."

Julian nodded. " 'Security considerations,' " he said, using the general's words.

"Doctor Renhol seemed to be trying to make an issue of Cyl's need for secrecy," Dax said.

"That's rather ironic, coming from her."

"No argument from me. I think she's just positioning herself to run against Maz in the next presidential election."

"Why does Cyl feel the need to hold back so many secrets?" Julian asked. "Now that the parasite danger has been dealt with, what's the point?"

"I keep asking myself the same question. Senator Talris quizzed me about our mission on Minos Korva, and what we found there," she said, reaching into her jacket pocket. She raised the fragment of Kurlan pottery into the light of the cemetery spires. "When I mentioned this, and your theory that it came from ancient Kurl, he became pretty curious about it. And Cyl insisted that the whole issue be kept under wraps. Like you said, 'security considerations.' "

Julian stepped toward her, taking the shard and examining it in the near darkness. "Then I suppose he'll be doubly glad that I wasn't testifying beside you."

She felt a frown creasing her brow. "What do you mean?"

"Before we arrived at Leran Manev, I was still researching the historical records on both Kurl and Trill," he said, looking slightly embarrassed. "And I learned a bit more about the provenance of this thing."

"It would have been nice to have known that before facing the Senate, Julian."

"I'm not sure it has any significance. Besides, if your General Cyl hadn't booted me from the building, we might have been able to let the Senate make that determination."

"Or *I* could have. If you'd told me everything you'd learned before we arrived on Trill, that is."

His eyes narrowed and his jaw hardened, as though cast in iron. "Given Cyl's fondness for secrecy, I tend to doubt that, Ezri. Besides, I told you everything I thought was important at the time. Most commanders don't enjoy wading through too much extraneous information."

She regarded him in stony silence for a long moment. Was he questioning her ability to conduct the mission with which Captain Kira had charged her? Or was it something more basic and petty than that?

You really don't like being under me in the chain of command, do you, Julian?

Aloud, she said, "All right, what else did you find out?"

"Just that this piece is a fragment of the outer covering of an ancient Kurlan *naiskos*."

"A what?"

He handed the fragment back to her. "A *naiskos* is a ceramic figurine made in a squat, roughly humanoid shape. They stood about forty centimeters high, and they were designed to be opened. The inside was filled with dozens of smaller but similarly proportioned internal figures, illustrating the Kurlan people's belief that each individual is comprised of a diverse chorus of sometimes conflicting impulses and desires."

Though Dax found Julian's discovery interesting, she had to agree that it wouldn't have been of any intrinsic value during her Senate testimony. She immediately regretted having questioned his judgment, and wondered if she hadn't merely been projecting her own doubts about her ability to carry out the current mission.

Hold it right there, Counselor. You're on the command track now, remember?

She suddenly realized that Julian was still talking about the *naiskos*. "I find one thing particularly intriguing about this artifact."

"What's that?" she said, hoping he hadn't noticed her woolgathering.

"The philosophy behind the *naiskos* makes me wonder if the Kurlans might not have been a joined species, like the Trill."

"That sounds like a bit of a reach," Dax said, shaking her head.

"Maybe. Maybe not. We know that the parasites have a relationship to the Trill symbionts. The presence of this fragment on Minos Korva suggests that they also had some connection to the Kurlans. Maybe there's also a more direct relationship between Trill and Kurl."

Looking at the fragment in her palm, seeing it in the context of Julian's new information, Dax suddenly recognized what part of the humanoid form it represented: the mouth.

She heard a keening wail in the distance. Surrounded as they were by the remains of hundreds of the formerly joined dead, she found it impossible to suppress a shudder.

As if on cue, her combadge flared to life. The gravelly voice it carried needed no introduction.

"General Cyl to Lieutenant Dax. I'd like to see you back at the Senate Tower as soon as possible."

Dax heard the wail again, and realized it was coming from the government sector. Dropping the *naiskos* fragment back into her pocket, she quickly tapped her combadge. "What's going on, Taulin?"

"The transcript of your testimony has been leaked to the media. And the people down on the streets are starting to riot."

6

Moments later, the *Rio Grande*'s transporter deposited Dax and Bashir in the Senate Tower's expansive main lobby. A cacophony of shouts and screams from outside the building greeted them.

"Thanks for inviting me along this time," Julian said, still sounding miffed at having been denied entrance to the Senate Chambers a few hours earlier.

But there wasn't time at the moment to worry about that. Amid the crowd of office workers whose daily homeward journey had evidently been interrupted by the rioting outside, Dax noticed a tall, nattily dressed, silver-haired man directing a group of frazzled-looking young interns. He appeared utterly unruffled as he dispatched the cluster of young functionaries surrounding him to various tasks as though nothing at all remarkable were going on.

Julian had obviously noticed him as well. "Who's that?"

"Senator Rylen Talris," she said striding toward the man. "He had quite a few questions for me this afternoon. He also wasn't thrilled with Cyl's requests that I deliver some of my testimony in a special closed-door session."

And I'll bet he hasn't been shy about complaining about that to the media, Dax thought. She wondered if the crowd outside was reacting to Talris's contention that the Trill military was trying to cover up the entire parasite affair.

"I think I've read something about him," Julian said. "Quite a man of the people, and very sympathetic to the problems of the unjoined. Which I find surprising, considering his position in Trill society."

Dax frowned, hearing the tone of criticism beneath Julian's words. "Why?"

"Well, in addition to serving in the Senate, doesn't he also have a seat on the Symbiosis Commission?"

"Most joined Trill aren't out to oppress the unjoined, Julian. Remember, some of us never even *wanted* to be joined in the first place."

As the cluster of people surrounding Talris began to disperse, Dax noticed Cyl and Gard striding purposefully toward them from the bank of turbolifts that lined the gleaming black south wall. They came to a stop before Dax and Julian, just a few meters from Talris.

"How bad is the rioting?" Dax asked the general.

Cyl's expression was weary and sour. "Bad enough, and it's not just happening here in the capital. Unjoined agitators are coming together in large numbers at Mak'ala, and at some of the other symbiont spawning pools as well."

"We have already increased security accordingly in all those places," Gard said as they moved toward the senator. "No attacks on the symbiont pools have been reported as yet. But we can't afford to wait until something like that actually happens."

"At least we've found the right man to calm things down," Julian said, nodding toward Talris.

Cyl nodded. "Though I have little truck with the politics of the malcontents, I can't argue against Talris's credibility out there among the Great Unjoined. Working with Talris is our best chance to keep the police/protester skirmishes from getting out of hand."

"Our main concern is keeping everyone calm," Gard said. "In fact, President Maz has just announced that the rest of the Senate inquests will be placed on hold until some semblance of order is restored on the streets."

Dax wasn't surprised to hear that; Maz was a practical, no-nonsense politician who had a fairly low tolerance for unruly behavior. But if the developing situation was indeed as dire as the picture Cyl and Gard were painting, Maz's absence seemed conspicuous.

"Where is Maz?" she asked.

"She's quite busy at the moment, as you might imagine," said Cyl.

"Of course." *She's also probably less than eager to be seen with anyone as closely identified with Shakaar's assassination as the two of you are.*

Suddenly, they were in Talris's presence, and the senator was giving them his undivided attention. After Cyl facilitated a quick exchange of introductions, Talris gestured toward the building's broad entrance, beyond which a sizable crowd was visible.

"It's worse than I thought," Senator Talris said, his lined face taking on a melancholy cast.

Limned in the glare of the street lights, the angry mob outside was surging forward across the courtyard toward the Senate Tower proper, chanting, screaming, and waving placards. Through the floor-to-ceiling transparisteel lobby entranceway, Dax noticed that the police and security guards outside had linked their arms and raised their clear riot shields to form a skirmish line. She also noticed that many of the building's civilian workers remained trapped inside the lobby. She saw a small group of security guards enter the lobby, gesturing for the workers to vacate the area and to head for the relative safety of the stairwells and turbolifts.

"Senator Talris, please get to the turbolifts," Gard said, reaching through an opening in the center of his outer tunic and retrieving a slim phaser pistol, apparently from an underarm holster. "You'll be safest up in the office levels."

"All right," Talris said as the group entered the nearest lift. Dax noticed that the senator touched the keypad's third-floor control.

Cyl had evidently noticed the same thing. "Senator?"

"I need to address the crowd," Talris said in urgent tones as the lift began to ascend. "The speaker's platform is on the third level."

"Speaker's platform?" Julian asked.

"Just what it sounds like, Julian. It's a semipublic platform on a balcony overlooking the crowd," Dax said curtly, even as Cyl and Gard seemed about to question Talris's judgment.

"It's shielded against small arms, but it's visually open to the crowd," said Talris. "It's also equipped with dozens of holocams, for comnet-wide public addresses. And there's a viewer right outside the Tower that ought to make me large and loud enough to get everyone's attention."

The lift doors opened onto the third floor, and Talris pointed across the corridor toward a door that Dax surmised must lead to the speaker's platform. Several guards were already in place, and a pair of them were pushing a tarp-draped hovercart before them. Dax supposed they were present in anticipation of Talris's need to use the balcony, but they seemed genuinely surprised to have company. One of the guards even drew a weapon before anyone could take a step out of the lift; Dax was relieved to note that he wasn't aiming it at anyone.

Everyone's jumpy, Dax thought. *This is getting worse by the second.*

Cyl was the first to speak to the guards. "Lieutenant, what is your current assignment?"

One of the uniformed officers in the corridor moved into a ramrod-straight stance, then answered. "Sir, we are deploying protective countermeasures in case the building should be breached by the protesters."

"Do it with a few less men, Lieutenant," Cyl said, his stern voice crisply conveying the order. "I want three armed guards with Senator Talris at all times. He's about to address the crowd from the speaker's platform."

The guard nodded. "Understood, sir."

"I don't think this is wise, Senator," Cyl said as the sound of phaser fire reached them from outside the tower.

Dax hoped they were only warning shots.

Talris's face crinkled as he smiled, making him look like a beneficent grandfather. He chuckled as he said, "Given some of the risks you've taken lately, Taulin, some might question the wisdom of taking *your* advice as well." Dax supposed Talris was referring to Cyl's recent decisions with respect to Bajor. Cyl, who had evidently known Talris for many years, did not appear to be offended.

"I'll be fine, really," Talris told the general, his eyes twinkling. "Now let me go. I have a rampaging horde to calm down."

Talris stepped out of the lift to join the guards, leaving Dax and the rest of the group standing inside. Facing the lift, the senator touched the keypad on the wall, causing his confident face to disappear behind the lift's closing doors even as a trio of guards moved toward him.

"We need to get to the tower's security center," Cyl said, his sullen tone making it clear that he wasn't keen on leaving Talris's side, guards or no guards. He tapped a special code into the lift's keypad, and the conveyance began to descend. "From there, we should be able to track exactly what is going on topside."

"You mean outside the tower?" Julian asked.

Cyl nodded. "The security center has secure Z-twelve connections. We'll bypass the public comm channels and link directly to the defense grid. That way, we'll be updated about every location where there are major protest gatherings. We need to stay on top of the situation not only here, but at Mak'ala and elsewhere."

The lift descended below the first floor, then stopped at an unmarked sublevel. The doors opened on a wide, bustling room whose walls were covered with monitors. Uniformed military personnel swarmed throughout the chamber, punching keypads, reading data, watching the screens, or vigorously discussing the events now unfolding on the streets of Leran Manev and other locales with others not present in the room.

In all her lives, Dax couldn't recall having visited this place before. But she had been in other command centers like it—sprawling yet cramped control rooms filled from floor to ceiling with unbeautiful, solidly utilitarian computer keypads and monitors—both on and off Trill. She assumed that this was but one of perhaps dozens of similar security command centers located around the planet.

They quickly caught up with Cyl and Gard, who were already being briefed by an authoritative-looking female officer. Her head was nearly shaved clean, making the dappled purplish spots on her temples clearly visible. Dax immediately recognized her as someone to be reckoned with.

After casting a suspicious eye on Gard, the woman turned to Cyl.

"You have something to say, Colonel Rianu?" Cyl said gruffly.

"Permission to speak freely, sir?"

"I don't have time for parade protocol right now, Colonel. Out with it."

"Thank you, sir. I'm not sure it's such a good idea to bring that man down here, General." She nodded toward Gard with icy politeness.

Dax understood the colonel's apprehension. After all, Gard had killed the head of state of an allied planet. It was pretty hard to keep one's name and face out of the newsnets after such an incident. Gard's deed, as well as the official pardon that had apparently followed it, had arguably made him far better known than befitted a Senate security operative long accustomed to working in the shadows.

Cyl appeared a good deal less understanding. "Colonel, Hiziki Gard is my trusted right hand, at least for the duration of the current crisis. I expect you to give him whatever resources he asks for—and to obey his orders as though they had come directly from me. Do I make myself clear?"

"You do, sir." Dax was impressed at how impassively the colonel took the general's browbeating. She suddenly recognized her.

"That's Colonel Behza Rianu," Dax whispered to Julian. "She's supposed to be one of the best in the Defense Command."

"She certainly seems to have things well in hand here," Julian said.

"She has political ambitions, too. As well as a quick temper that's kept her from achieving a Senate seat so far."

"Are you sure she's not advancing because she's not joined?" Julian asked.

Even after everything she had witnessed so far today, Dax couldn't have been more surprised if he had suddenly lobbed a grenade into the room. "I can't even find the words to *answer* that, Julian." She glared at him for a moment, then attempted to resume listening to Colonel Rianu's briefing. But in the back of her mind, Julian's question echoed, and a small part of her knew it was relevant. *Especially today.*

In clipped, businesslike tones, Rianu informed them about the planetwide movements of various radicals, which she identified as anti-joining agitators associated with the neo-Purist movement, political radicals inspired by the late Verad Kalon's anti-symbiont Purist group. Consciously putting aside her unpleasant memories of Verad, who had briefly succeeded in stealing her symbiont from Jadzia, Dax listened, turning with the others to watch a cycle of images scrolling past on a large bank of wall-mounted monitors. The holoscreens showed other government buildings in Leran Manev and elsewhere, the Symbiosis Commission, the Caves of Mak'ala, and two other smaller symbiont spawning grounds. Around each of these places, throngs of obviously discontented Trill humanoids had gathered.

The military presence was heaviest near the Symbiosis Commission's copper-hued towers, though that structure was better protected than most of the other buildings in Leran Manev's government sector; after all, it was practically surrounded by a moatlike body of water, with only a few roadways and powered hover routes leading to it. Dax noted that the building's landing pads were filled with military defense craft, and that police were pushing the throngs slowly back away from the roadways that led directly to the Commission building.

Outside the Senate Tower, however, the situation was much worse. Protesters were throwing whatever was handy, and the guards were responding with force. Batons rose and fell, and the actinic flash of phaser fire split the air, some directed at the protesters, some aimed at the police. In the bunker, Dax noticed several people gathered near one monitor, each speaking into separate comm devices. On their viewscreen, she saw a flash of light as a soldier targeted a civilian sniper; the monitoring officers cheered momentarily, congratulating the soldier over one of the comm units. Dax assumed they had helped the shooter pinpoint his target. Though she was no stranger to combat, the sight of it occurring in the once tranquil Trill capital made her feel almost physically ill. After all, it was the living legacy of Verad, whose poisonous, invidious memories still lingered within her because of her symbiont's brief joining with him.

"There's got to be a way to resolve this without so much violence," she said. "Can't we release some neural gas in the plaza, or set up a phaser cannon for a wide-dispersal stun blast?"

"Either of those options could cause some deaths as well," said Cyl, shaking his head.

"I thought Talris was supposed to speak to the crowd," Julian said. "Shouldn't he have started by now?"

Dax saw a look of surprise flicker across the faces of both Cyl and Gard as each of them realized that several minutes had passed since they had left the senator on the tower's third floor.

She knew they were thinking the same thing she was: *What is taking Talris so long?*

"Bring up all cameras on level three," Cyl said to a nearby technician. "Focus the largest viewers on the speaker's platform." Dax could hear the urgency in his voice.

Multiple images came up on the screens, but none of them showed anyone at all. The speaker's balcony was completely empty. "Where is Talris?" Gard asked. "What happened to the guards?"

"Talris might have decided to exercise the better part of valor," said Julian.

"That doesn't square with his reputation," Dax said.

Cyl squinted at the viewers, studying them carefully. "Maybe they evacuated elsewhere because of the sniper activity."

Gard shook his head. "This doesn't add up. The balcony's shields would have stopped a sniper. And the guards around Talris would have known that."

Something about the images on the viewer was bothering Dax. Everything looked peaceful on and around the third-level balcony, as if nothing at all untoward were occurring a mere two floors below. *It almost looks too peaceful.*

A sudden realization struck her. "Magnify screen seven-Q, upper third quadrant," Dax said to the technician who was beside Cyl. The screen image quickly changed, showing the profuse greenery that ringed the speaker's platform. Above the dais was a red-plumed bird in flight.

Though its wings were fully extended, the bird was motionless, as though it had been flash-frozen an instant after takeoff

"Why is this image paused?" Cyl asked as he too noticed the discrepancy.

"It's *not*, sir," the technician said, his fingers sliding over a lit data panel. "This feed's coming in live."

Cyl pointed angrily toward the magnified and motionless bird on the viewscreen. "I see. So that *fenza* bird suddenly transformed itself into a fixed-wing aircraft. This feed is a still image!"

"Run the feed backward," Rianu said, as several more of the technicians began working the panels in front of the anomalous image. Although index numbers scrolled backward rapidly, the images on the third floor and speaker's platform viewscreens remained consistent—including the motionless bird. Finally, at minus nine minutes, the bird flew backward and returned to its perch. On another screen, a pair of guards pushing a tarp-covered hoverlift could be seen. One of them raised a hand from the hoverlift and aimed a small device directly at the cameras.

"Freeze it!" Cyl shouted. His eyebrows arched, and a look of anger flashed in his eyes. "These people are infiltrators. They sabotaged the feed before we even arrived."

Gard was moving toward the turbolift before Cyl had even finished speaking. He pointed at a pair of armed guards as he sprinted. "You two are with us."

Dax felt her adrenaline surge as she and Julian and Cyl moved toward the lift as well. Cyl tossed her a plisagraph, which she dutifully set for maximum scan before pulling the phaser from her hip to make sure it was fully charged.

"Set weapons to kill," Cyl said as the lift enclosed them. "Whoever these people are, we can bet they won't be very happy about being interrupted."

Dax did as Cyl bid, though she wasn't thrilled with the idea of killing. Then she turned toward Julian and saw that he had not switched his phaser past the "stun" setting.

Julian gave her a look that she wasn't sure she was reading correctly. His eyes seemed argumentative and imploring at the same time. Because she was the one in charge of their mission, she knew she could order him to change the setting on his weapon. But she also knew that he had disregarded Cyl's instruction because his primary loyalty was to Starfleet, not to Trill. That distinction set him apart not only from everyone else in the lift, but also from everyone else in the building.

Everyone on the planet, she realized.

He's not one of us, Dax thought. Suddenly the current clash between joined and unjoined conspired with the sometimes conflicting feelings of Ezri Tigan and Ezri Dax. Starfleet training warred with Trill loyalty, threatening momentarily to overwhelm her.

And then the turbolift doors opened.

His heart in his throat, Bashir flattened himself against the wall as phaser fire rained in on them, burning a hole through the lift's back wall. Cyl and Gard crouched near the floor, while Ezri and one of the security people Gard had brought along leaned forward to fire their weapons from the open, smoke-filled turbolift.

Another volley of shots passed back and forth before Bashir heard the sound of a pair of bodies crumpling to the floor in the corridor outside. One of the guards edged her way out the door, her weapon drawn and her stance defensive.

"Two down!" she said, her voice a low growl. Turning briskly with her weapon extended in a two-handed grip, the guard looked to either side, covering for the others. Suddenly, a phaser bolt shot her through the throat, half vaporizing her neck in a spray of wet matter. She immediately collapsed to the floor. Bashir instinctively started moving toward her, but restrained himself an instant later; the guard's wound appeared mortal, and he knew there was no way to examine her without being killed himself.

Cyl and the remaining security guard fired in the direction from which the fatal shot had come, down a side corridor. Though the adversaries returned fire, Cyl and the guard continued shooting. Bashir heard a distant cry of pain, followed by the sound of another body hitting the tile floor.

Bashir crawled over to the fallen guard, even as Ezri moved with him, crouching with her phaser drawn and her scanning device raised. Bashir turned the stricken guard over to inspect her wound and saw immediately that she was beyond all help. Though the heat of the phaser beam had nearly cauterized her wound, it had also blown out her trachea as well as a great deal of her spine.

"I read three more humanoid life signs in that direction," Ezri said, angling the small scanning device Cyl had given her toward the tower's east corridors, then toward the building's western side. Bashir recognized the palm-sized device as a powerful, Trill-specific bioscanner known as a plisagraph. "Three this way as well, including one that looks pretty weak."

Gard tapped the remaining guard on the shoulder, then pointed down a side corridor. "We'll take the east wing. Let's hope one of those life signs belongs to Talris."

Ezri shook her head. "I don't think he's here. I'm not reading any symbiont life signs on this floor. Other than our own, I mean."

"That weak humanoid life sign you picked up might belong to the one we just hit," Cyl said, frowning and nodding.

"He may not have taken a direct hit," Bashir said. He still wasn't happy about Cyl's insistence that they shoot to kill. And despite the horrible death the infiltrators had just inflicted on the security guard, he still hoped their adversaries wouldn't have to die unnecessarily.

Cyl gestured westward with his phaser. "Dax, Doctor, come with me. And stay sharp."

The team split up. Cyl, Dax, and Bashir moved cautiously down the wide corridor, hugging the walls and pausing to take cover behind alternating rows of support columns and large potted plants. Eventually, they reached a three-way junction, where the body of one of the impostor guards lay.

Crouching beside him, Bashir noted that he was dead—and that the phaser clutched in his hand was still warm from recent use. "No life signs here, weak or otherwise." He looked up at Ezri.

She consulted her scanner again. "My plisagraph is still picking up three Trill humanoid life signs, but that's all. One of the others must be hurt. They're down that way."

Even as Ezri pointed toward a windowless, unlit segment of corridor, the plisagraph in her hand exploded in a shower of sparks as a phaser blast hit it. She let out a cry and spun into the wall, then crumpled to the tile floor.

Cyl hit the ground instantly, returning fire. Using the dead attacker as a shield, he sent a volley of blasts down the darkened corridor, briefly illuminating it as brightly as the noontime sky.

Dropping to the floor, Bashir crawled quickly across the three meters that separated him from Ezri. The look of shock and pain on her face alarmed him, and he saw that her right hand was red and blistered.

"Let me do something about those burns," he said, reaching for the medical kit on his hip.

Using her uninjured hand, she grabbed his wrist, stopping him. "It's not that bad, Julian," she whispered, hissing through tightly clenched teeth. Her brave words didn't fool him for a moment; she was obviously in agony. "Besides, this isn't the best place for giving first aid."

As if to underscore her words, more phaser bursts pulsed over their heads, and Cyl responded with another volley. Bashir turned and saw that Cyl was taking aim at the edges of the wall, rather than shooting down the middle of the open corridor. Moments later, a large chunk of rubble fell away from the wall in a cloud of smoke and dust. Cyl strafed the area just beyond it.

Bashir held his breath for a protracted moment, but no further salvos came from down the corridor. Cyl turned to face Bashir and Ezri. "Stay here and cover me," he said, then pulled himself to a squatting position. A moment later he was sprinting down the corridor, zigzagging as he ran.

Despite the near darkness that surrounded Cyl, Bashir could see that the general had arrived unmolested at the corridor's end. Cyl beckoned them to follow.

Bashir helped Ezri to her feet, then gently took hold of her hand so he could look at it closely. She was right; there hadn't been much real damage. Just some redness, puffiness, and a few small blisters.

Dax withdrew her hand and gestured toward Cyl. "Hard to believe he used to be my darling daughter, huh?" She gave Bashir a wobbly grin.

Good to see she hasn't lost her sense of humor, Bashir thought. He was a great believer in using humor to overcome stress, and so far this day was one of the most stressful either of them had seen lately. *And it's not over yet.*

Moments later, Bashir and Ezri joined Cyl at the haphazard pile of rubble his phaser had created. Beneath it lay one of the "guards" who had greeted them when they had brought Talris to the third level. Cyl gestured toward a nearby door, and Bashir realized immediately that it must have been forced open from outside the building.

"That leads to most of the equipment that powers the speaker's platform," Cyl said, mopping the perspiration from his spotted forehead with the back of his hand. "The other two radicals must be trying to either commandeer or sabotage it."

"Is there another way in?" Ezri asked.

Cyl shook his head. "Not an easy one. And not if we want to get there in a hurry."

"Then we go in through the front," Ezri said, raising her phaser with her uninjured left hand.

Opening the door cautiously, they entered and found themselves inside a short, dimly lit hallway. Bashir could hear the hum of machinery, and heavy footsteps that sounded uncomfortably close.

At the end of the hallway, Cyl cautiously peered around the corner. He turned back toward Bashir and Ezri, a crestfallen look on his face. "Damn! It looks as if one of the radicals has got Talris. And he doesn't look good."

A question flitted through Bashir's mind. *Why didn't Ezri's plisagraph pick up Talris's symbiont?*

Then a booming voice rang out, echoing off the walls and machinery in the large chamber beyond the short hallway. "Whoever you are, show yourself. Come out and drop your weapons. Otherwise your precious Senator Talris will never get to deliver another one of his famous placating speeches."

Cyl scowled for a moment, then responded. "You'll just kill us all if we come out there."

"I admit it's a chance you'll have to take," the mystery voice said, taunting. "But really, I've already accomplished my mission. I just want to get out of here now. Safely, and without any more unpleasantness."

"The security people must have sealed off the doors leading to the outside," Cyl whispered to Ezri.

She nodded. "He must have just figured out that he's trapped."

He's desperate to find a way out, Bashir thought. *And desperate people are dangerous people.*

Bashir watched tensely as Cyl peered around the corner, then withdrew to safety. He had never seen the normally steel-nerved general look so agitated.

"He's got Talris in front of him," the general said. "Using him as a shield. Talris looks unconscious."

Fear twisted Bashir's belly into a knot. "I need to get to him."

"You can't do him any good if you get yourself killed," Cyl said.

"General, Talris isn't a young man. He may be in urgent need of medical attention."

"Our friend might not know how many of us are here," said Ezri.

Cyl appeared to apprehend her meaning instantly. "If the doctor and I go out there, you might be able to squeeze off a shot."

Ezri gave a short nod. "I suppose I've heard worse plans." She looked up at Bashir.

He thought things were going swiftly from bad to worse. And he knew that hostage rescues rarely went well for the hostages. But there seemed to be little choice. If he was going to help Talris, he had to get close to him. He slowly nodded his assent to Ezri's risky plan.

Cyl stepped out first, dropping his phaser noisily to the floor. "I'm unarmed now," he said. "My companion is joining me."

After taking a deep breath, Bashir stepped out of the shadows as well, dropping his weapon and then raising his hands. "I'm a medical doctor. If Senator Talris needs attention—"

"Don't worry about the senator," the provocateur yelled, interrupting. Bashir saw in the dim light that he was facing the "lieutenant" whom Cyl had assigned to guard Talris. It was no wonder that the general appeared so upset; he had to be blaming himself for delivering Talris straight into the hands of the insurgents.

"Where's the woman?" the "lieutenant" asked. "I saw her on the security recorders before you blew out that wall."

"Then you must have also seen your colleague shoot her dead," Cyl said coolly as he walked slowly forward. "She didn't make it."

Then Bashir saw to his horror that Cyl's lie was actually true for at least one other person in the room. Talris's head lolled limply forward, giving Bashir a glimpse of a telltale phaser burn that the senator's hair no longer covered up.

Obviously panicked by Bashir's startled reaction, the "lieutenant" raised his weapon.

"Ezri, shoot through Talris!" Bashir yelled as he pushed Cyl down, diving for the floor himself.

A bright burst of light sizzled through the air and struck Talris in the chest, coring a hole through him. The "lieutenant" behind him fell backward, and both crumpled limply to the floor.

Cyl sprinted across the room and dived on top of the fallen infiltrator, but the man's body was limp and lifeless.

Ezri ran forward as well, joining Bashir as he squatted to examine Talris. "Did I . . . ?" She couldn't finish her question.

Bashir shook his head. "No. He was already dead. I suspect that he died at about the time we reached the outer hall. Once my eyes adjusted to the darkness, I knew for certain." He pointed to the mortal phaser wound on the senator's right temple.

"You took one hell of a chance," Cyl said, his voice flinty. He paused to recover the phasers that he and Bashir had been forced to drop. "What if he wasn't dead?"

As Cyl brusquely tossed him his weapon, Bashir fixed the general with a testy gaze. Ever since his arrival on Trill, he had been either brushed off or ignored. He'd finally had enough of it.

"I don't *take* chances like that, General. I knew he was already dead. And I knew that his symbiont was gone as well, or its life signs would have shown up earlier on Lieutenant Dax's plisagraph."

Ezri stood, her attention diverted to something off to the side. "I believe we have another problem," she said, pointing. "I think that's a bomb."

Bashir and Cyl scrambled to their feet and looked over to where Ezri was pointing. There, atop the very same hovercart they had seen earlier, sat a two-meter-long metal cylinder. The tarp that had once covered it lay on the floor, demonstrating that stealth no longer mattered to the radicals. The device was connected via ODN cables to a bank of machinery set into a nearby wall.

Bashir followed Cyl and Ezri as they made their deliberate approach to the device. Unfortunately, a visual examination of the object revealed very little.

"So we don't know whether it's a bomb or not," Cyl said. Bashir could hear an edge in the general's voice; he clearly feared the worst.

"What else would it be?" Ezri said. "Think about it. If they bomb the Senate Tower, they could cripple the planetary government for months. Radicals and terrorists often see these sorts of actions as catalysts for whatever changes they want to bring about. And that dead man back there was awfully eager to get out of here."

Safely, and without any more unpleasantness, Bashir thought, recalling some of the dead man's final words.

Still, he searched for another explanation. "Maybe it's some kind of device designed to hijack the communications grid from the speaker's platform. If this facility is used for making planet-wide addresses, that might be a good way for the radicals to focus attention on their cause."

"Believe me, Doctor," Cyl said. "They already have almost

everyone's undivided attention. Besides, I don't think they'd go to this much trouble just to do that. They can already broadcast their own messages on the comnet, and they wouldn't have to kill a beloved senator to do it. Lieutenant Dax is right—our safest assumption is that this is a bomb."

"Okay, so how do you suppose it's triggered?" Ezri asked, pacing from one end of the device to the other. "If it's on a timer, how do we know how much time is left? And how do we disarm it?"

"I'm going to call for an evacuation," Cyl said, moving over to a wall-mounted comm unit. "We'll try to save as many lives as we can."

Knowing the loss of life could still be enormous should the object detonate, Bashir's mind worked to find a better solution even as the general barked orders through the comm unit. Sifting through his memories, the doctor could find very few that related to bomb threats. Such things were almost unheard of on Federation planets, especially bombings conducted for political purposes. It didn't escape him that conflicts were sometimes decided instead through large-scale engagements involving starships and phasers and cloned soldiers and shape-shifters and mind-devouring parasites; the idea of planting a lone bomb seemed almost quaint by comparison.

How would I get rid of a bomb back on the station? he asked himself. *I'd beam it into deep space. But we can't do that here.*

Or can we?

He turned toward Cyl. "Is this thing attached to any of the building's critical systems?"

Gard shrugged. Cyl snorted. "I wouldn't know for sure," the general said. "This isn't exactly my arena."

"Then I suppose there's no point in waiting any longer." Tapping his Starfleet combadge, he said, "Bashir to *Rio Grande.*"

"Rio Grande *acknowledging,*" the runabout's computer responded in an affectless female voice.

Ezri stepped closer. "Julian, are you sure this is a good idea?"

"I don't think we have a lot of alternatives, Ezri." *Or time to argue about it.*

She nodded, apparently having come to a command decision. "You're probably right. Go ahead."

He picked the combadge off the front of his uniform and

spoke quickly into it. "Computer, lock the transporter onto my combadge. Program a five-second delay, then transport the large metal object to which it's attached."

"Please specify transporter coordinates."

Setting the combadge atop the mystery device, Bashir said. "Deep space. Directly overhead. Maximum range."

As Bashir backed quickly away from the object, Ezri approached Cyl. "General, I think you'll want to warn your defense crew. They'll probably detect a good-sized explosion in orbit."

Cyl moved back to the comm unit and activated it. "This is General Cyl. Warn every orbiting ship to raise shields or break orbit. Immediately."

"Energizing," said the runabout's computer, speaking from the unknown object's hull. A moment later, a shimmering curtain of light enveloped the device, and it disappeared from view.

Bashir let out his breath in a whoosh. He hadn't even been aware he had been holding it. He opened his tricorder, swiftly entered some figures into the keypad, then raised the device to make its display clearly visible to Cyl.

"General, tell your ships to scan these coordinates for an explosion. If they don't find one, have them search for that device. And make sure they destroy it."

A grim smile came to Cyl's lips. "Well done, Doctor. We'll find out soon enough if—" He stopped and whirled into a crouch, his phaser raised and trained on the hall entrance from which they had originally emerged into the room.

Bashir saw a head peep around the wall just before a familiar voice called out. "Stand down, General. It's Gard and Trebor. We've eliminated or captured all the other infiltrators who'd gotten into the building."

At least the ones who were wearing uniforms or got caught committing assassinations or planting bombs, Bashir thought, wondering just how many unjoined radical sympathizers had quiet office jobs in the Senate Tower or countless other government sector buildings.

Cyl lowered his weapon, and moments later, Hiziki Gard and another military man stepped into the room. The second man—Trebor—was limping.

"What's the situation here?" Gard asked.

"We've neutralized all of them," Cyl said. "Including the man who was evidently leading this particular group." He paused, gesturing toward the senator's lifeless body. "They killed Talris, and installed what we believe to be some kind of explosive device here. Doctor Bashir used his ship's transporter to beam the device into space."

"Do we know what kind of bomb it was?" Gard asked.

"We don't even know for sure if it *was* a bomb," Ezri said. "But we couldn't afford to take any chances."

A beeping noise sounded from the wall's comm unit, and then a female voice spoke. *"General Cyl, Patrol Vessel TDM-one-twelve reports that a small device did just detonate above the atmosphere in the vicinity of the coordinates you specified. They report that it sent out some kind of electromagnetic pulse, but it dissipated before they could analyze it. They say it was more flash than substance, though."*

Bashir smiled grimly. Though the bomb apparently hadn't been all that powerful, his decision to dispose of it had been correct. Maybe he had finally earned some respect from Cyl and Gard.

"What's the status of the riot outside?" Cyl said, still speaking into the comm unit.

"The police are keeping the crowds back," the voice from the wall reported. *"But there have been a significant number of injuries and a good deal more violence than we expected."* She hesitated, then resumed. *"One of the neo-Purist leaders has sent out a planetwide message on the comnet. It's going out live right now. We're recording it and attempting to trace the feed back to its source."*

"I'll view it in one of the Senate offices," Cyl said. "In the meantime, send a security team to the prep room behind the speaker's platform, level three. Senator Talris was murdered here, and his body will need to be transferred to the coroner. Officer Trebor will be here to brief the team when it arrives. And send a general alert to all police and military units to be on the lookout for other bombs that might have been planted in public locations across Trill. Cyl out."

"If there *are* other bombs planted elsewhere on Trill," Bashir said, "they could detonate at any time."

Ezri nodded, looking glum. "And there's no way to be sure of finding them all."

The general clicked off the comm unit, then faced Bashir, Ezri, and Gard. Without commenting on Bashir's and Ezri's words, Cyl moved briskly toward the door and gestured for them to follow him.

Ezri and Gard followed the general out of the chamber and back into the hallway. Before following, Bashir took a moment to cover the slain senator's body—as well as the corpse of his killer—with the tarp that had formerly shrouded the bomb.

After walking into the corridor, he stepped over the rubble and the dead revolutionary trapped beneath it. He caught a glimpse of the man's face.

Bashir wondered what kind of person this man had been before the current unrest had engulfed his planet. *Is your cause worth dying for? Is it worth killing for?*

But the Trill man was dead and gone. He would never answer those questions. And Bashir had the horrible feeling that he would have to ask them many more times before he got a satisfactory answer.

7

President Maz was still unreachable via comlink, which wasn't surprising given the tremendous degree of disorder that had suddenly engulfed the city center. Many of the comm frequencies were jammed, though the emergency channels remained open.

Dax agreed with Cyl's assessment that there was little the four of them could do to alter the course of the riot, especially now that Senator Talris—who'd represented the best hope for a peaceful resolution to the crisis—was dead. Dax and Cyl entered the late legislator's sparsely furnished office, where Julian and Gard had already activated the desk computer.

"Let's see exactly what the neo-Purists have to say," Gard said as he patched Talris's computer into the newsnet, where it grabbed the broadcast that had been recorded moments earlier.

"Which one of the neo-Purist leaders issued this latest statement?" Julian asked Cyl.

"Does it matter?" Gard asked as he finished tapping the interface console. Clearly his sympathies toward the unjoined protesters who sought openness from their government did not extend to terrorists.

"My people inform me it was Nas Ditrel," said Cyl, his jaw set in a hard line. "She's one of the group's most prominent spokespeople."

A moment later a middle-aged woman appeared on the screen, her hard, angular face framed by a thick ring of dark brown spots. A simple blue drapery was all that was visible of the background behind her, making an assessment of her physical location essentially impossible. Though she appeared gaunt and haggard, her voice rang with strength and determination. Still, Dax thought she looked stressed almost to the point of physical and emotional collapse.

Ditrel began without preamble, speaking rapidly but precisely. *"Thanks to today's Starfleet testimony before the Senate—as well as long-classified government archaeological records that have recently come into our possession—we have verified that there is indeed a link not only between the symbionts and the parasitic creatures who recently attacked Bajor and attempted to attack our world, but also a close relationship between the parasites and the extinct civilization on the distant planet Kurl."*

Dax felt as though a great chasm had suddenly opened beneath her feet. She suddenly understood Cyl's impulse toward secrecy. *These people are acting on information I supplied to the Senate in a public forum.*

She realized suddenly that Julian was beside her, and had taken her hand. His brown eyes were brimming with compassion, as though he had read her thoughts. "It isn't your fault, Ezri. You were obliged to answer the Senate's questions."

She glanced at Gard and Cyl; their hard expressions made her wonder if they might not be quite so forgiving.

"President Maz's government has been concealing this from you," Ditrel continued, interrupting Dax's reverie. *"As has the Senate and centuries of their predecessors. The same power structure that uses symbiosis to keep the vast majority of us 'in our places' apparently doesn't want you to know that the Kurlans were in fact ancient Trill colonists."* The woman paused, as though allowing her listeners time to digest her last statement.

Dax found that statement patently absurd; from Julian's bewildered scowl, she gathered that he did as well. Gard and Cyl were stone-faced, essentially unreadable.

Have they heard this *before, too?*

"Can you pause the playback?" Dax asked Gard, who immediately entered a command into the terminal, freezing Nas's image and muting her voice.

"This proves that neo-Purists or other unjoined radicals have infiltrated the government pretty thoroughly," Cyl said, shaking his head. His stoic demeanor had begun to give way to a deeply troubled expression. "Somehow, they found out about the parasites' affinity for Kurlan artifacts."

"But the rest of it sounds like pure conspiracy-theory fiction," Gard said to Cyl. "Most people will find stories about ancient, forgotten Trill colonies pretty farfetched."

Dax nodded. "That's just what I was thinking."

"I'm glad to see I'm not the odd man out here," said Julian, releasing Dax's hand. "From my reading of Trill history, your people didn't make much use of warp technology until about three centuries ago."

"It was actually a little longer ago than that," Dax said. "Trill had already developed warp drive by the time Vulcans made first contact with us." She recalled that Lela, the Dax symbiont's first host, had been a little girl at the time of first contact. That initial visit by the Vulcans had generated a great deal of fear among the Trill populace, which had found itself divided on the issue of whether or not to accept alien interaction.

"But the Kurlans were already extinct millennia before that," Julian said. "Most exoarchaeologists believe they succumbed either to a plague or to biowarfare many centuries before the Trill became capable of interstellar travel. How could anyone believe the Kurlans are an offshoot of the Trill?"

"Let's find out," Gard said, then restarted the playback.

Ditrel resumed speaking, her gaze intense and locked directly on the visual pickup in front of her. *"For millennia, the joined ruling class has covered up the fact that the parasites originated on ancient Kurl, during a long-suppressed prehistoric era of early Trill interstellar expansion."*

" 'Prehistoric,' " Dax repeated.

Julian shrugged and spoke in a stage whisper. "I suppose any previously unrevealed era of ancient Trill space colonization would have to be prehistoric, by definition. Of course, that begs the question of how anyone could possibly know about it today."

"She mentioned old records of archaeological digs," Dax said. "Maybe someone discovered—"

Cyl made a shushing noise as the woman on the screen continued. Dax immediately stopped speaking, and Julian looked as though he wanted to bite off a sharp reply to the general before subsiding into silence.

". . . *cording to the documents now in our possession, five thousand years ago, Trill colonists formed an exclusive society on Kurl in which* everyone *was joined to a symbiont. There was no 'Great Unjoined' underclass among these people. The Kurlans therefore fancied that their 'joined-only' civilization would be better than that of the homeworld, where the unjoined have always been in the majority.*

"But this joined-only paradise failed. The humanoids of the Kurl colony used genetic engineering techniques on the symbionts, perhaps intent on increasing the symbiont population on their planet, or improving the rapport between host and symbiont. Instead, the Kurlans killed themselves off and released the parasites into an unsuspecting universe.

"The very same parasites that have been so determined to destroy us all—and whose genetic profiles match the few hundred thousand slugs who now quietly rule this world from the abdomens of their pampered and privileged humanoid slaves."

Ditrel paused in an apparent effort to collect her thoughts. Then she fixed her intense gray gaze back at eye level. *"The neo-Purist movement calls upon President Maz and the Trill Senate to stop trying to hide the truth about our world's past. To stop perpetuating the lies and secrecies that have now begun to engulf other worlds besides our own. To stop concealing the connection between the symbionts and the parasites, which has only left us vulnerable to the parasites' ancient vendetta."*

She's talking about the hijacking of the Gryphon, Dax realized. She knew that one of the parasites nearly succeeded in using the Akira-class starship to attack Trill, and that Kira was the main reason the attack had failed.

"Be warned: We will not permit any such thing to happen to our world again. We will stand vigilantly against the parasites and their so-called symbiont cousins. We will allow neither the joined nor the creatures who control them to lead us to destruction. In the defense of our world, we are prepared to take drastic measures."

The screen went dark then, and Dax found herself standing in silence, considering the neo-Purist's surprising revelations. Julian, Cyl, and Gard stood by, looking equally subdued and thoughtful.

"Do you suppose there's any truth to this?" Julian asked, finally breaking the quiet.

"The neo-Purists obviously know about the link between the parasites and Kurl," Dax said. "And that's something we've verified. Maybe there's something to the rest of their story as well." She truly didn't want to believe that the Trill government would conceal information of such vital importance to the homeworld's defense against the parasites. But she had too much firsthand experience with Trill cover-ups to dismiss the idea out of hand.

"But the time line doesn't add up," Julian insisted. "The *naiskos* fragment we found is twelve thousand years old. If the Trill colonized Kurl five thousand years ago, how could an artifact more than twice as old as the colony come from there, unless—" Julian stopped, his eyes narrowing.

"What?" Dax said.

"The *naiskos* were never native to Kurl," he said slowly. "They were Trill artifacts all along. Don't you see? All our assumptions about the age of the Kurl civilization were false, because so many of the artifacts we assumed were native to the planet were actually brought to Kurl by the colonists as treasures, works of art, keepsakes. They were imported!"

"Even assuming that's true," Gard said, "It makes me wonder how the neo-Purists came to their conclusions."

"It's pretty clear the radicals have infiltrated the government," Cyl reiterated. "Perhaps they've also found their way into some long-forgotten section of the classified archives."

"Forgotten?" Julian asked. "I thought the Trill revered and collected memories."

"We do," said Cyl. "But any society that collects and preserves its cultural and personal memories long enough can begin losing track of them. We Trill are no exception."

Though Dax had never spent much time considering the matter, she had to concede that Cyl was right; she knew that the physical records of Trill history occupied uncounted kilometers of winding catacombs beneath Leran Manev and other Trill metroplexes. How difficult would it be to misplace whole epochs of deep time?

"But there must be important gaps in the radicals' knowledge," Julian was saying to Cyl. "Otherwise, I think they might have told us more. For instance, more of the details of the Kurlans' alleged creation of the parasites. And why the government would want the story covered up in the first place."

"It seems likelier that the radicals have taken the sketchy Kurl information they gleaned from this afternoon's testimony and created embellishments out of whole cloth," Gard suggested. "If they're capable of planting bombs, they're certainly capable of planting lies and propaganda."

"Maybe," Cyl said, though he didn't appear entirely convinced. "But if part of their story checks out, then it's at least possible that they've stumbled onto information that even you and I aren't aware of. And if that's true, things may be even worse than we thought."

Dax was inclined to agree. Audrid's memories nagged at the back of her brain, telling her there was more to this mystery than even the neo-Purists suspected.

Before leaving Trill forever, Captain Christopher Pike was speaking softly yet insistently to Audrid. "Your people's secret, Doctor Dax. Is it that important? Was it worth all of those lives?"

Audrid silently considered everyone who had died as a result of the parasite's hate-filled rampage. Chin, Milton, and Juarez from the Tereshkova.

And poor Jayvin.

Tears came, and sobs wracked her shoulders. Pike waited patiently for the waves of misery to subside.

"I don't know," Audrid said after she finally recovered her voice.

"So we have to find out what the truth really is," Cyl was saying, the steel in his voice dragging Dax roughly back to the here and now. "That's really the root of our problem with these radicals."

Gard had crossed to one of the windows. Several stories below, the crowd and the police were engaged in violent clashes, masses of people spontaneously forming eddies and whirlpools of panic-fueled Brownian motion. Dax saw the flashes of police phaser fire. Bodies tumbled to the street, where they were trampled by panicked feet, either advancing or retreating. Though the police weapons were no doubt set on stun, people were going to die anyway.

And all for want of a little bit of hard truth, and equal footing in our society, Dax thought, feeling hot tears begin to sting her eyes.

"*That* is our main problem with these radicals," Gard said, indicating the riot. "Putting a stop to the violence. Not plowing through some antediluvian archive looking for something that might not even be there."

"I agree completely," Julian said to Gard. He sounded impatient to get busy doing something. Beginning to experience some restlessness herself, Dax didn't blame him a bit for feeling that way.

"If we don't get to the bottom of this Kurl business soon, *that* might just prove unstoppable," said Cyl. He, too, gestured toward the violent tableau outside.

Dax thought all three of them were right. Though she wished she could quell the riot simply by wading into the thick of it, she knew better. The match had been lit and the fire was already burning bright and hot. They had to find a way to snuff it out without inadvertently fanning the flames—or being consumed by them.

"I think we might have a shortcut to some of the oldest information about Kurl," Dax said before she realized the words had slipped out. Looking into Cyl's eyes, she saw a glimmer of understanding there. The ghost of little Neema's smile lingered at the corners of his mouth.

"The Guardians of Mak'ala," he said.

Bashir could hardly believe what he was hearing. Just outside the building, people were being injured, perhaps even killed. Now hardly seemed an appropriate time to stop by the underground breeding pools merely to chat with the symbionts' unjoined humanoid caretakers.

Ezri and Cyl were already crossing to the door. "I'll take the runabout straight to Mak'ala," Ezri said over her shoulder. "Julian, I want you to report to the government's Emergency Response Med-Center and assist with the injured."

He nodded, but still felt completely confused about what they were doing. "Of course. But why make the trip to Mak'ala now? Are the symbiont pools in any direct danger from the rioters?"

Ezri and the general paused in the doorway. "There *are* large numbers of protesters massed outside the caves," Cyl said. "But the additional security troops I deployed earlier today seem to be discouraging any untoward activity. So far, that is."

"Then why go there now?" Gard asked, repeating Bashir's question.

"Because the monks who watch over the symbionts have been doing that job for upwards of twenty-five thousand years," Ezri said.

That struck Bashir as a complete non sequitur. "So?"

"So if anyone on Trill, outside of the most inside of government insiders, knows our people's ancient past," said Cyl, "it's the Guardians."

Bashir recalled that orders similar to the Guardians had preserved many important texts during the cultural self-lobotomizations that characterized Earth's Dark Ages. But managing the current crisis still seemed a far more urgent priority than delving into the Kurlan mystery. And there was another consideration as well.

"I remember a Guardian named Timor from our visit here five years ago," Bashir said. "He wasn't terribly interested in the outside world, except for the occasional weather report. And he also wasn't very forthcoming with information—even when we needed it to save Jadzia's life."

"Under the current circumstances, I don't think it'll be too hard to convince the Guardians that the stakes are a bit higher today than they were back then," Ezri said.

"And if they agree to let us reveal some additional information about the Kurlan/parasite connection," Cyl said, "some of the neo-Purists might take that as a gesture of good faith from the joined. The ones that aren't completely crazy, that is."

Bashir was well aware that continuity of memory was of supreme importance to most Trills, joined or unjoined. A reverence for the accurate accounting of history was an ingrained Trill characteristic that probably motivated the radicals as much as it did Ezri and her colleagues.

Still, he wasn't at all certain that Ezri and Cyl were doing the right thing under the current circumstances.

"Have you considered that you might turn up some information that further vindicates the radicals' paranoia?" he asked, now concerned that Ezri might well face dangers far greater than the mere wasting of time.

She sighed impatiently, and Bashir could sense her rising anger—and perhaps a hypersensitivity to being second-guessed as the one in charge of this mission.

"I don't have time to debate this with you right now."

Whatever she finds at Mak'ala, he thought, *she'll have to decide afterward whether to reveal it—or to bury it again, the way Audrid helped cover up the initial discovery of the symbiont-parasite connection.*

Having kept his genetically engineered nature carefully hidden for so many years, he felt he could speak authoritatively about the keeping of secrets. "Please, Ezri. Think for a minute about what you're about to do. Suppose you discover some entirely new unknown horror from your people's past. What will you do then?"

He couldn't help but consider the past horrors unleashed by ill-considered genetic engineering. Such techniques had not only essentially created Bashir himself, but had also spawned the Eugenics Wars. Khan Noonien Singh. Ethan Locken. The Jem'Hadar.

And, apparently, the parasites of Kurl.

"What will you do then?" he repeated. Softly. Imploringly.

Ezri regarded him in silence for a protracted moment, her cerulean eyes smoldering with anger.

"Report to Emergency Response, Doctor," she said in by-the-book tones, ducking his question. "Ask Mister Gard to help you if you have trouble finding your way around."

"At least let me treat those phaser burns on your hand before you leave," Bashir said. Since the firefight near the speaker's platform balcony, she hadn't slowed down enough to receive any real first aid.

"I promise to take care of it on the way to Mak'ala," Ezri said coolly, obviously unconcerned with her admittedly minor injury. Without another word, she turned and exited the office, with General Cyl at her side.

It's your mission, Ezri, he thought, his ire rising at the brusqueness of her rebuff. *I sincerely hope you haven't just completely fouled it up.*

8

The emergency medical kit shimmered into solidity on the floor of Talris's office, and Bashir bent to retrieve it. Popping open the top, he made a quick inspection to make sure Ezri hadn't left anything essential on the runabout; at the same time, he hoped she'd taken a moment to treat the burn on her hand before depleting the *Rio Grande*'s medical supplies. He was almost glad in a way that he no longer had his combadge; he felt such frustration with the woman he loved just now that he didn't imagine any further immediate conversation was going to help matters between them.

Using a comm unit in the late Senator Talris's office, Gard informed Ezri and Cyl that the medical equipment had arrived safely. "Good luck," he said, and then hesitated a moment. Finally, he added, "Doctor Bashir wishes you both the same." Then he tapped the console, ending the transmission.

Over his shoulder, Bashir shot Gard a petulant look.

"You seem to be taking her actions personally," said Gard. "I can understand your position. But you must understand hers."

Bashir stood, hoisting the medical kit over one shoulder. "What I understand is that she and the general seem more concerned with ancient Trill history than they are with dealing with the violence on the streets."

"You're probably right. But General Cyl is also trying to get to the bottom of what the neo-Purists are agitating about. He's trying to get at the truth."

Bashir felt his ire steadily rising. "The truth? The only truth I'm interested in at the moment is that the streets are becoming drenched in blood."

Gard nodded solemnly. "The truth is a complicated thing sometimes, isn't it? Haven't you ever had a secret you felt you couldn't share with anyone, because you knew . . . you *knew* that it would change *everything?*"

Bashir attempted to control his reaction. *Does Gard know about my genetic enhancements?* Had Ezri told him? Or Jadzia? He had indeed concealed the fact that his parents had resequenced his genetics decades earlier, and keeping that secret had cost him dearly over the years.

Whether he knew Bashir's secret or not, Gard's tone contained no condemnation as he continued. "Even if you haven't covered up aspects of *your* life, surely you've kept confidences in the course of your duties as a Starfleet officer. Surely you've concealed actions or decisions that could have caused grave damage if they were revealed."

"You seem to be talking about yourself, Mister Gard."

Gard nodded, allowing that. "As you've no doubt already learned from Dax, I'm not like most joined Trills. Rather than redefine my life with every new incarnation, my existence has always been about one thing: neutralizing aberrant joinings."

"Like Joran."

"He wasn't the first," Gard said. "And it's important to understand that while Joran Belar was troubled, neither he nor Dax were dangerous individually. Had he never been joined, or perhaps if he'd been matched to a different symbiont, Joran might have lived a long, full life without ever having harmed anyone. It was the unique combination of Joran and Dax that made them violently unbalanced. Such things are rare and unpredictable, even given the rigorous tests and screenings of the initiate program. But every so often, despite the Commission's best efforts, an apparently healthy joining unexpectedly gives rise to a monster."

Though Bashir was familiar with the unfortunate story of Joran Belar, he found that his curiosity was becoming roused. "How often does that happen?"

Gard shrugged. "Centuries can pass between such aberrations. Spotting them requires constant vigilance."

"And you're the one who maintains that vigilance? You alone?"

"Not exactly. A number of us keep watch. But whenever a threat comes to light, I'm the one who deals with it. It's what I've always done."

Bashir felt he was beginning to understand. Still, he didn't much like it. "I imagine that's why you maintain such a low profile most of the time. When you're not assassinating heads of state, that is."

Gard appeared oblivious to the jab, making Bashir wonder what sort of person could pursue a career of this sort and remain sane—and for multiple lifetimes, no less.

"Maintaining secrecy is important," Gard said. "For reasons I'm sure you can imagine, the aberrations have to be contained before word of their existence can get out. That's the only way our society can maintain faith in the system that enables us— even a tiny minority of us—to enjoy the serial immortality of joining."

"That's why there aren't more like you," Bashir said, and Gard responded with a silent, affirmative nod.

Bashir released a long, frustrated breath through his nose; he found that his disgust with the ingrained Trill propensity for cultural secrecy was becoming harder to conceal. And the most damnable thing about it was that the reasons for concealing aberrant joinings seemed so eminently sensible. He already knew that the Symbiosis Commission feared the symbionts would become slaves or black-market commodities if it ever became generally known that joining was possible among half the Trill humanoid population instead of the official one-in-a-thousand figure; what might some Trills do if they were to learn that some apparently healthy joinings could produce lethal sociopaths, however rare their occurrence might be? Unscrupulous opportunists might seek to investigate and exploit that potential, while others might turn against the symbionts entirely.

So the Commission keeps it a secret. They lie. Bashir knew better than most how naturally lies could come. Especially when they came to be regarded as necessities of survival.

"What about your previous hosts?" Bashir asked. "Other Trill symbionts are guided by the needs, ambitions, and desires of the humanoids they join with. But you're telling me that your hosts set all that aside to pursue the goals of the Gard symbiont."

"It's entirely voluntary, I assure you," Gard said. "The screening process for my hosts is even more stringent than that of the regular initiate program. When the Commission finds the right match for Gard, that potential host is brought into the loop, and is allowed to make an informed decision."

Bashir felt the hairs on the back of his neck stiffen; Gard's story brought to mind uncomfortable recollections of Section 31's periodic efforts to recruit him into their unofficial—and ethically questionable—intelligence operations.

"Have any of Gard's potential hosts ever declined the honor?"

"Only once," Gard said.

"And what happened to the candidate?"

Gard's eyes narrowed at the unspoken accusation. "What makes you think something happened to her?"

"Because, given your people's obsession with secrecy, I have to assume either that her memories were wiped, or that she was killed. Which was it?"

Gard didn't answer. But he didn't avert his eyes from Bashir's hard stare.

The moment stretched, until Bashir said, "All right. Let me ask you something else, then. How many hosts have you had?"

Gard displayed a small, enigmatic smile. "Let's just say the number is a good deal higher than any other joined Trill you've ever heard of."

Bashir nodded. "And you remember all of them?"

Gard hesitated, then made an admission that Bashir found surprising. "No. Beyond a certain point, I can't remember anything. Whether that's a consequence of my symbiont's longevity or a security measure I've never been briefed about, I'm not certain. Nor do I care. My role, my function, is all that matters. In fact, I can't remember ever doing anything else."

Bashir found the idea of an existence that stretched so far back into the depths of time both exhilarating and frightening. He wondered what it would be like to have personal origins as ambiguous—and perhaps even as ancient—as the earliest joined Trill.

Or as ancient as the parasites. The insight came to him with the suddenness of a lightning strike.

"Then, is it possible . . . ?" His voice trailed off as he struggled to formulate his inchoate question.

"Yes?" Gard's mild expression betrayed the patience of the ages.

Bashir caught his breath. "If these aberrant joinings are truly as rare as you say, might your role have originally come into existence for an entirely different reason?"

"What are you suggesting, Doctor?" Gard asked, in a manner that made it clear he knew exactly what Bashir planned to say next.

"I'm wondering if you were created originally to detect and deal with joined parasites. Like Shakaar."

"That would imply a very ancient connection to Trill," Gard said, nodding thoughtfully. "And equally ancient knowledge about the threat the parasites pose."

Bashir adjusted the medical kit on his shoulder. The faint sound of screams and phaser blasts outside reminded him that he needed to get moving. "Yes, it would. Do you think it's true?"

Again, Gard smiled his enigmatic smile as he escorted Bashir back to the foyer door that fronted Talris's office. "I think, Doctor, that some things should never be forgotten."

After giving Bashir directions to the hospital, Gard excused himself, saying he needed to return to the security center. He gave Bashir his personal comm key in case the doctor needed to reach him. The night-shrouded streets in front of the Senate Tower were still in the grip of pandemonium as Bashir exited the building.

Bashir hadn't gone twenty meters before a police officer tried to turn him away. After he displayed his medical equipment— and made loud mention of his Starfleet credentials—he was free to proceed. Fifty paces later, after skirting a police blockade, he was stopped again by another contingent of officers.

"I am a Starfleet medical officer," Bashir said in mounting exasperation. "And I'm needed right now at Manev Central Hospital's Emergency Response Department."

The burly officer who seemed to be in charge squinted disapprovingly at him, as though he were a six-foot talking bug. "I don't know why Starfleet would be here. This situation is Trill business."

Maybe if the Trill government had done a better job of managing its "business," then Starfleet wouldn't need to be here, Bashir thought.

Aloud, he said, "I told you, I am a Starfleet medical officer, and I'm expected at the hospital. Why don't you call there and see if they want you to turn me away?"

The police officer grunted, then turned away and spoke into a wrist-mounted communications device. Less than a minute passed before he turned back to Bashir. "Apparently they *are* expecting you," he said, his voice sounding no friendlier than it had before. "You evidently have some friends in high places. I'm supposed to assign a member of my unit to escort you there."

"Thank you," Bashir said acidly, though he was sorely tempted to tell the man he could find his own way. He waited, impatient.

"Asal, make sure that this doctor gets to Manev Central," the commander said to one of the other nearby officers, a solidly built woman outfitted in scuffed black body armor.

"Yes, sir," Asal said.

Moments later, Bashir was following Asal through a side alley. They continued for some time, weaving in and out of dark alleys and dimly lit side streets, avoiding any further crowds or major obstacles.

Asal nodded, then pointed forward down the alley toward the warm glow of nearby street lamps. "A few more blocks and we'll be coming out near the hospital."

"Good, thanks," Bashir said. He followed the officer silently, his mind processing her comments along with the cacophony of tonight's uprising.

They rounded a corner and saw three figures slumped in the shadows. Asal leveled her phaser at them. "You there. Stand and identify yourselves!"

One of the figures rose haltingly, and in the dim light Bashir could see it was a young girl, perhaps eleven years old. "I'm Dula Seng, and this is my mother and brother. They're both hurt. They *can't* stand up."

Bashir began to approach, pulling his medical tricorder out. "I'm a doctor. I can help—"

"Wait, Doctor Bashir," Asal said, interrupting. "We don't know if they're armed."

"Please," the teenage boy on the ground pleaded. "They wouldn't help us at the hospital. My mom is very sick."

Bashir looked over at Asal. "I'm going to help them." She nodded curtly, still holding her weapon at the ready. He crouched to begin scanning the scarcely breathing woman.

"What happened?" he asked the girl.

"We were at the Najana Library when all the yelling started outside. Mama was trying to get us home, but we kept getting caught in the crowds. They sprayed something on the protesters, and Mama started having a hard time breathing." She gestured toward her brother. "Dapo couldn't walk very well either."

"They turned us away from the hospital because Mama isn't joined," he said, his tone almost venomous.

After running a quick tricorder scan to check for possible drug incompatibility reactions, Bashir deftly withdrew a hypospray from his medical kit and set it for lectrazine.

"Are you sure it wasn't because they thought you might have been with the protesters?" he asked as he worked.

The boy was silent, regarding him with baleful eyes. Bashir crouched beside the mother, pressing the hypospray gently against her neck. The drug hissed home, and the woman gasped loudly in response. A moment later her breathing began to steady.

Bashir turned to the boy. "Your turn. Seems like you might have a touch of your mother's allergy to anesthezine. That appears to be the active ingredient in the gas they sprayed on the crowd." He wondered how many other Trill in the crowd had experienced similar seizures.

The boy winced as the hypo hissed into his neck. Then he looked surprised. "Hey, that didn't hurt much at all."

Bashir gave him a slight grin, then turned back toward the mother. Her eyes were now open, and she appeared to be trying to get her bearings. "You'll be all right, ma'am. You were having a reaction to the gas the police were using. Your children tried to get you help." *And were refused,* a small voice inside him shouted. "Luckily, we happened to come along."

"Thank you," the woman replied in a weak stammer.

"You should be able to walk in a few minutes," Bashir said, putting the hypo back into his kit.

"Have the bombs gone off yet?" the woman asked, her voice barely above a whisper.

"*What* did she say?" Asal asked sharply, moving in closer.

Bashir felt his blood chill. "The bombs?"

"I heard some people talking about bombs while I was at the library," the woman said, distress evident on her face. "That's why I tried to get my children out of there."

"Why didn't you inform anyone?" Asal asked.

"She *tried* to, but the police wouldn't listen," the little girl said. "They sprayed the gas on us right after that."

"I've got to report this," Asal said, tapping her wrist comm unit.

"How many bombs were there?" Bashir asked. "And did you hear where they were?"

"No," the woman said. "They just said 'bombs.' And that the joined would be sorry when they went off."

"I can't get a signal here," Asal said. "I've got to get out and warn the other units. Just in case there's anything to this."

Bashir's mind whirled as he stood. He pulled Asal aside and whispered. "I'm almost certain there is. We already disabled one bomb, in the Senate Tower."

"I'd better go," Asal said emphatically, evidently taking him at his word. "The hospital is that way," she said, pointing. "You should be able to get there from here without a lot of trouble."

"Good luck," Bashir murmured as Asal began running back in the direction from which they had come.

He crouched again, and performed another quick scan of the boy and his mother with the tricorder. "You should be able to walk in a few minutes. I'd hurry home as soon as possible if I were you. And thank you for the information."

"Thank *you*," the woman said, and the boy and girl both immediately echoed her grateful sentiment.

Bashir sprinted down the alley, turned a corner, and exited onto a street. Ahead, he could barely make out one of the emergency entrances to Manev Central Hospital, though the street was clogged with hovercars and limping, wounded, or angry people. Limned in the vehicle headlights and overhead street lamps, a handful of police were attempting to direct the traffic, unsuccessfully.

Before attempting to dash across the street and into the nearest hospital entry foyer, Bashir found a public comm terminal on the opposite side of the boulevard. He swiftly entered commands into its flat touchscreen. Gard's face appeared on the small screen a moment later.

"What can I do for you, Doctor?" Gard said, an expression of studied patience on his face.

"I've just learned some potentially important information, Mister Gard. One of the people in the crowd overheard somebody talking about several more bombs."

" *'Several'?* "

Bashir nodded. "The woman who overheard this was at the Najana Library. She said that the bombs were somehow targeted specifically at the joined."

Gard frowned. *"Thank you, Doctor. Is there anything else?"*

"I think we should call for additional help from Starfleet. This situation is quickly getting out of hand." Bashir glanced up to see a large group of rowdy-looking teens moving quickly out of the darkness toward him. All of them were dressed in baggy, dark clothing, and they seemed to have been roughed up in the protests.

"I suspect President Maz won't support that idea," Gard said, shaking his head. *"But I promise to pass it along when I find her."*

Bashir wondered if he heard a hint of derision in Gard's voice. "Can you patch me through to Lieutenant Dax?" Bashir asked, turning slightly and stepping back against the wall to allow the group of teens to pass.

"Not now. I've got larger concerns," Gard said. Then the screen went blank.

"Of all the—" Bashir was about to curse Gard, when a fist connected with his jaw, knocking him back against the wall. Before he could react, he felt a second fist strike his midsection, while another blow glanced off his ear.

Dazed, he was barely aware that the teens were grabbing his medical kit and tricorder. Red stars burst across his vision after one of them kicked him in the ribs. He doubled over in pain, coughing and spraying blood onto the sidewalk.

Barely conscious, Bashir heard the gang members laughing as they ran away, melting back into the shadows.

9

"Of *course* I've questioned it," Dax said. "Even if my symbiont hadn't lived through nine hosts, two of us have been Starfleet officers, and one of us was a Federation diplomat. It's inevitable that we'd have a wider view of things than most. That we'd question the status quo more." She was sitting behind the controls of the *Rio Grande,* one hand guiding the vessel on a swift suborbital trajectory over the Ganses Peninsula toward the Caves of Mak'ala. Her other hand, the one that still sported an angry red phaser burn, absent-mindedly played with the fragment from the Kurlan *naiskos.* The pain in her hand was tolerable, though she wished she'd taken a moment to treat it with a dermal regenerator before beaming the runabout's medical equipment down to Julian.

"So what makes you different from the protesters?" Cyl asked, sitting next to her. He appeared more relaxed than he had back in Talris's office. But Dax knew he was a military general, and therefore a soldier. She surmised that he was really as tense as she was, if not more so.

"Questioning and exploring aren't quite the same as anarchy and outright defiance of authority," she said, a touch of defensiveness rising within her. She was reminded briefly of Curzon's wry observation that anarchy is better than no government at all.

Cyl nodded, his mouth forming a small smile. "So it's a matter of degree, not necessarily a question of the goal. And you would never defy the authority of accepted morality by say . . . reassociation?"

Dax's eyes narrowed as her mind flashed back to the brief time that Jadzia Dax had met Torias Dax's previous wife, Nilani Kahn, whose symbiont was then hosted in the body of Dr. Lenara Kahn. Dax had been willing to break the taboo forbidding reassociation between joined Trills who had been intimate with one another during previous lives. Kahn, however, decided ultimately not to pursue their renewed relationship.

"Point taken," Dax said after a moment of reflection. "But it sounds to me that you're either finding reasons to excuse the actions of these neo-Purists, or you're painting anyone who disobeys the rules with the same broad brush you'd use on the radical fringe."

Cyl's smile widened. "I'm doing neither, Ezri. Or maybe both. This is a confusing time for Trill, and no matter what comes in the next days and weeks, we are *all* going to have to reexamine our values and beliefs. Our traditions and laws may be open to change, and we'll be forced to decide if our society *should* change, or if we should remain anchored to the past. Evolution itself is about change, after all. Do we allow our society to evolve? And if we examine the mistakes and secrets of our past, how will that affect the evolution of our future?"

Dax checked the course of the runabout on the instrument panel, then looked back over at Cyl. "You're certainly not Audrid's little girl Neema any longer. You've become quite the warrior-philosopher."

"The accumulated experiences of six hosts tend to do that sort of thing to a person," Cyl said. "Not that I need to tell *you*, Para."

The word hit Dax harder than she thought it might have in any other context. "Para" had been Neema's childhood name for her mother, Audrid Dax, lifetimes ago. Now Dax was a part of a twenty-seven-year-old Starfleet officer, and Cyl existed as a fifty-something-year-old military general. The familial bond they had once shared remained strong in Dax's memory, but the physicality of their current hosts made such recollections feel strange and confusing. Such mnemonic turmoil no doubt accounted, at least in part, for the Trill people's cultural taboo against reassociation.

Dax looked at the Kurlan fragment she was holding and turned it over in her hands. "I don't regret it, you know. Reassociation, I mean. I don't regret what happened with Lenara Kahn. Just as I don't regret my decision to reconnect with my friends on Deep Space 9, or getting reacquainted with you."

"Maybe not yet," Cyl said, a wry grin appearing on his face even as his eyes grew sadder and older. "Give it time. I can be quite the tyrant."

Dax returned the grin. *So could Neema.*

She looked up at Cyl. "Do you suppose that a part of the taboo against reassociation is to keep the joined from sharing too much of the past? I mean, it seems as though that concept is against everything we're taught about revering memory and history. Did we decide somewhere along the line that reassociation could spark some kind of . . . atavistic racial recollection of early Trill?" She held up the Kurlan object so that Cyl could see it clearly. "Or of some horrible truth we've kept buried deep in our past?"

"Why don't you ask Audrid?" Cyl said. "True, the Cyl symbiont is older than Dax, but Audrid was the head of the Symbiosis Commission for over fifteen years." He hesitated, then looked away. "But then, Audrid always excelled at keeping secrets."

Dax and Cyl had danced around that subject time and time again. How Jayvin Vod, Neema's father and Audrid's husband, had been taken over by one of the parasites, in the icy interior of a rogue comet. How Jayvin had been allowed to die because of the irreversible psychic damage the Vod symbiont had suffered. How, in order to keep the existence of the parasites quiet, Audrid had lied to her children about the actual circumstances of Jayvin Vod's death, thereby estranging Neema from her for years. How Audrid had eventually told Neema the complete truth about her father's death, including the facts about the parasite, a creature supposedly stricken from Trill's earliest historical records, buried and forgotten.

More than a hundred years and a lifetime later, the pain of Audrid's betrayal of her daughter's trust evidently remained an open wound for Taulin Cyl.

Dax reached out and took Cyl's hand, squeezing it. He looked at her, his eyes uncharacteristically soft and imploring. "I'm sorry, Neema," Dax said, her voice taking on Audrid's measured cadence. "I would give anything to change what happened that day."

"And that is the difference between us and the powers that we serve," Cyl said, nodding. "We should not reassociate. We should not remember the bad. We should cover up our sins. That is what the governing body of Trill wants." He chuckled slightly. "Perhaps neither of us is really very different from the people who are crying out for radical change."

Dax offered him a grim smile. "There's that broad brush again. Not everyone crying out for change wants what the neo-Purists want. The neo-Purists aren't agitating for equal access to symbiosis. Sure, they want to eradicate the boundaries between the joined and the unjoined—but they're trying to eliminate the joined in order to do that."

Dax again raised the *naiskos* fragment. "What do you think the truth really is behind the neo-Purists' revelations about the parasites? About Kurl?"

Cyl sighed as he took the ceramic shard from Dax and inspected it. "My people have found similar Kurlan artifacts in some of the other parasite lairs we've investigated. At first, we thought they might constitute some kind of message, or function as calling cards. But we decided that neither idea made sense. The parasites never expected their lairs to be invaded. Why would they leave messages there for outsiders? Now I suspect they hung on to them as artifacts of memory. Perhaps they revere their history as much as we do ours."

Cyl handed the shard back, and Dax shuddered involuntarily in response. It was bad enough to have to accept that the symbionts and the parasites shared genetic characteristics. But today's revelations also suggested that the two species might have deep cultural commonalities as well. Dax was profoundly disturbed by the notion that the Trill might share any behavioral traits whatsoever with such lethal, implacably hostile creatures as the parasites.

She blinked, and in the nanosecond of darkness saw Jayvin Vod deep inside that icy comet, his speech jangled and incoherent and enraged, his eyes cold and murderous. He was no longer her lifetimes-ago husband, but was "the taker of the gist." Though the creature had worn Jayvin's form, it was intent on destroying all that was Jayvin Vod. And all that was Trill.

And then her eyes were open again, and she focused on the *naiskos* fragment in her palm. She squeezed it in her fist and impulsively threw it against the aft bulkhead. It shattered as though shot from a cannon, clattering to the deck in countless tiny shards.

"Feel better now?" Cyl asked after a lengthy silence, one eyebrow raised.

"For now," Dax said, nodding. A blush of color rose to her cheeks as she realized how silly she must look. A sudden, insistent beeping from the instrument panel seized her attention. Embarrassed by her inattention, she quickly turned to check the cockpit readouts. Then she began guiding the runabout into a rapid controlled descent. Through the front windows, she could see dawn glimmering against the distant white-topped crags of the vast Ayai'leh-hirh mountain range.

"We're only a few dozen klicks from the caves," she said, forcing her words into a businesslike cadence.

Cyl settled back in his seat. "So, we've managed to voyage nearly halfway around the planet without *once* discussing the problems in your relationship with the doctor."

Dax shot him a look that was equal parts surprise and annoyance. "What? I don't think— I don't— We aren't having any problems."

"Oh." Cyl stared straight ahead at the rapidly approaching countryside. Its luxuriant carpet of greens and browns was punctuated by jagged gray volcanic buttes, leftovers of the ancient geological processes that had also carved Mak'ala's network of subterranean caverns.

"What is *that* supposed to—" Dax was interrupted by a beeping from the console and several flashing lights. "I'm detecting weapons fire at the caves."

Moments later, the cliffside entrance to the Caves of Mak'ala hove into view through the front windows. Several hundred people had gathered outside. Unpowered hover vehicles lay overturned on the rough ground—one was afire, belching clouds of thick, black smoke—and phaser fire came both from the military troops lined up behind barricades near the caves and from the protesting crowd.

"Why haven't we gotten any distress calls?" Cyl asked, leaning forward.

Dax punched several buttons on the panel. "Incoming transmissions are being jammed from outside. Looks like the

Guardians couldn't raise anyone over any of the comm channels."

Cyl breathed a quiet curse. "Can you set the ship's phasers on stun, as you suggested back at the Senate Tower?"

Dax nodded. "Yes, but the wider the dispersal, the less effect it will have on the crowd. A runabout's phasers aren't exactly built for crowd control. It might knock them down for a few minutes, but not for much longer than that. And I can't guarantee that some of your guards won't get caught in the beam."

"Do it," Cyl said. "In the meantime, we've got to call in some reinforcements." He tapped on the console, evidently well versed in Starfleet communications protocols.

"I don't know if this message will get through either," Dax said, nodding. "But it's worth a try."

As Dax gingerly maneuvered the *Rio Grande* a few meters over the heads of the crowd, she saw many of the people below look up, some pointing. She quickly entered several commands into the instrument panel, then swiped her hand over the phaser controls.

Moments later, the phasers had created a wide swath in the crowd as hundreds of people fell to the ground, unconscious.

Let's hope that's the worst violence we're going to see here today, Dax thought as she sought out a safe landing space.

Brushing his long, dark hair back from his high, spotted forehead, Ranul Keru emerged from one of the heavily fortified cave entrances just in time to see a *Danube*-class Starfleet runabout turn its phasers on one of the most unruly portions of the protesting crowd. He was momentarily appalled, until he observed that no one had been burned or vaporized; the vessel's weapons had been fired at low power—just enough to stun.

Moments later, the runabout landed near the caves' main entrance, as guards moved aside. Keru joined the captain of the guard as he waited for the runabout's occupants to emerge. The craft's hatch moved outward, and two figures stepped onto the rocky ground. One was a diminutive woman in her twenties; she was dressed in a Starfleet uniform, and her dark hair was cut short. The other was older, an iron-haired man wearing a Trill military uniform. Keru recognized him at once.

"General Cyl, I'm Captain Doyos," the leader of the gu

said. "We've been calling for backup for an hour now, since things began getting ugly. More protesters have arrived since then, and some of those brought vehicles and weapons."

"Someone's been jamming your communications. Probably neo-Purist agents who have even more dirty tricks up their sleeves," Cyl said. "We didn't know." He turned to the woman. "Ezri, I will leave the historical research in your capable hands. I need to strategize with my people out here to keep the caves protected."

"All right, General," the woman said.

As the general and the captain began conversing, the woman turned to Keru and presented her hand. "I'm from Starfleet, and I've come to ask for the help of the Guardians."

Keru smiled warmly and shook her much-smaller hand. A jolt of recognition struck him as their flesh came into contact, filling a portion of his mind with new awareness. A name.

"Dax. You're hosting the Dax symbiont."

Scowling slightly, Dax withdrew her hand. "You know, I don't think I'll ever get used to you Guardians doing that."

Keru had to shake himself out of the euphoria of indirect symbiont telepathy. "Forgive me. I haven't been doing this quite as long as some of the other Guardians here. It takes some getting used to." Joining the Order had not only made permanent Keru's desire not to enter a traditional symbiotic joining, it had also opened up within him a privileged channel of communication with the intelligent, sluglike creatures; he supposed it was probably as much a consequence of the Order's assiduous training regime as it was of prolonged exposure to the unique environment of Mak'ala's underground pools, which some said directly tapped the vital living heart of the planet itself. Though every fully initiated Guardian shared this rapport with the symbionts at least to some extent, no humanoid host seemed fully able to understand it. This wordless concord, evolved over the forgotten eons the unjoined Guardians had spent caring for the helpless symbionts, was arguably in some ways even more intimate than Trill symbiosis itself.

"You've got me at a disadvantage, Mister . . ." Dax said, trail-
--- as she eyed him with apparent suspicion.
------- moment, he stroked his capacious mustache, a nervous
------- -emed to grow worse the longer he lived in the cav-

erns. "Keru," he said. "Ranul Keru. Lieutenant commander, *U.S.S. Enterprise.*"

"You're Starfleet?" Dax said with a smile.

"I'm on extended leave." Keru explained. "I had some . . . personal things to work through." He'd stayed on the *Enterprise* for some time after Sean's death three years ago, but found little joy in stellar cartography anymore. The entire ship had become too painful a reminder of all he had lost.

Keru saw no need to share any of that with Dax, however, especially given the present circumstances.

"Well, I'm glad you're here," Dax told him. "You might make things go easier. If you don't mind, I'd like you with me when I speak to whoever's in charge here."

"I'll be happy to provide any help I can, especially if it'll help rein in the madness out there." He swept his arm to the side, ushering her toward the cave entrance.

As she descended the winding stone stairs alongside Keru, Dax reflected that it had been five years since her last visit to the winding catacombs of Mak'ala. *No, not* my *visit,* the part of her symbiosis that was Ezri Tigan reminded her. Despite the familiar sights, sounds, and smells of the dark, rough-hewn rock faces, the high, igneous stone ceilings and dripping stalactites, and the bubbling, geothermally heated pools of mineral-rich water, she knew that all her memories of this place had come from Jadzia Dax and previous hosts.

The thing that struck her most viscerally was the tomblike darkness of so much of the place, which was lit only in the most strategic and necessary places, mainly along the stone stairways and near the frothy gray symbiont breeding pools. The blackness that enclosed the rest of the vast underground spaces felt oppressive and tomblike. Ben Sisko had angrily confronted her shortly after Ezri had become joined to Dax, telling her she could always retreat to this place to live out a challenge-free existence should life in Starfleet prove too difficult for her.

But it was clear to her now that the oppressive nature of Mak'ala, along with the obvious stolid toughness of the Guardians to whom Keru had introduced her—they were single-mindedly dedicated people who seemed to spare no effort in the constant monitoring and testing of the nutrient and mineral · ·

tent of the symbiont breeding pools—demonstrated that this was no place for the weak. As Keru conducted her to a small natural dais near one of the larger pools, she reflected that it must take a special sort of person indeed to devote his entire life to the care of the symbionts, while at the same time being forever denied the benefits of joining.

When was the last time any of these people went outside and got any sun? she wondered as Keru briefly excused himself to summon his order's leaders. While waiting for her guide to return, Dax watched as a pair of younger Guardians received a patient lesson in acidity adjustment from an old woman who knelt beside the nearest pool, dipping sampling tubes into the gently lapping gray waves. Several unjoined symbionts breached then, momentarily sending crackling latticeworks of energy across the rippling surface before disappearing once again down below. The old woman smiled in evident satisfaction, as though the symbionts had just spoken directly to her, peer to peer.

It occurred to Dax that maybe they had. Maybe the Guardians enjoyed a relationship with the symbionts that the joined could never understand. As far as she knew, no joined person had ever served as a Guardian. Perhaps after communing with the symbionts as the Guardians did, one lost all desire or capacity for joining. Perhaps selecting one path—either joining or the Order of the Guardians—forever rendered the other inaccessible.

Her reveries were interrupted by the return of Keru, who accompanied six pale, dour-faced, robed men and women ranging in age from late middle age to elderly, whom Keru introduced generically as the Order's senior leadership. They seemed preoccupied and unwilling to spend much time in conversation, as Timor had been five years earlier. Just as she had feared, the Guardian leaders were hesitant to answer direct questions about the early history of Trill joinings, the parasites, or the lost joined Trill colony that the neo-Purists claimed had once existed on Kurl. Her explanations about the unrest that was flaring up across the planet and the government cover-up allegations recently broadcast by the neo-Purists didn't seem to move them.

What are they so determined to hide? she wondered. Well ... of how ingrained Trill secrecy was, she had to consider ... ility that they might not even know the secrets they ... ermined to protect.

Ranul Keru, with the assistance of a young male Guardian who introduced himself as Rantic Lan, took up the pleading on her behalf, conferring with the senior Guardians on one of the cave plateaus out of Dax's earshot. The other Guardians kept a wary eye on her from a distance, as if afraid she might suddenly jump into one of the pools.

I wonder what Timor told them? she thought. He had been the one who had allowed Jadzia to enter the pools five years ago, after she had learned the truth about the Dax symbiont's temporary joining to Joran more than a century earlier. It occurred to her that she hadn't seen Timor among the Guardians gathered here today. Had he been fired or transferred for aiding Jadzia?

Several silent minutes later, Keru and the senior Guardians approached her. The eldest of them, a woman whose face and spots were almost indistinguishably pallid from lack of sunlight, approached Dax closely.

"What you have told us is troubling, Ezri Dax," she said. "Troubling not just because of the unrest it causes our people now, but also because it incites a distrust between Trill humanoids and symbionts. Our memories, our history, our truth . . . these are the foundations of our society, and of joining itself."

The old woman paused, looking uncomfortable, then continued. "But we cannot help you. We cannot concern ourselves with anything other than caring for the symbionts."

"Do I really have to point out that it'll be impossible for you to keep doing that—caring for the symbionts, I mean—if this place gets overrun by neo-Purist radicals?" Dax said dryly.

Dax noticed that Rantic Lan's expression was downcast and defeated. Keru walked away from his superiors, coming to a stop facing the nearest pool, his back turned. *Damn. Even he's given up.*

Then, as the six Guardian leaders began to disperse to their various tasks, the normally placid back-and-forth wave action of the pool suddenly became tumultuous. Three, then four symbionts breached the pool's gray surface simultaneously, followed immediately by a dozen more. The senior Guardians stopped in their tracks, transfixed. Jagged forks of lightninglike discharges sprouted, connecting each of the symbionts to one another. And to Keru.

The big man turned to face Dax again. "It seems my superiors have just been overruled. I think your questions are going to be answered."

Dax's heart leaped into her throat. "What do I have to do?"

A beatific smile spread across Keru's lips. "Just swim to the very bottom of the pools. Where nobody's ever gone before."

Fifteen minutes later, Keru stood by the side of the pool, checking the seals on Dax's environmental suit, retrieved from her runabout. He knew the suits were rated for marine operations and considerable pressures, but he had never been involved in putting those claims to the test. "You know this might not work, right?"

"I have to try," she replied.

"That sounds like something my partner used to say just before doing brave but foolish things. Be careful," Keru said. Before his death during a Borg attack, Sean had been utterly fearless, whether facing holodeck pirates, scary alien cuisine, cloaked Romulan weapons, or the Borg.

Dax smiled back at him. "Speaking of which, if I don't make it back, you'll give Julian my message. Right?"

Keru felt a lump forming in his throat and his eyes misted involuntarily. "You'll come back. . . . Just watch the time. As you make your descent, you'll be racing against your air supply and the rising water pressure—not to mention whatever besides the symbionts might be living down there in the deepest pools."

Dax took a deep breath, then waded knee-deep into the grayish murk of the pool. "Okay. I'm ready."

"Hurry back. I'll be waiting."

"I've got a better idea. Since you've got a Starfleet background, I suggest you get out there with Cyl and make sure these caves are well defended for my triumphant return." She gestured to the phalanx of Guardians that ringed one side of the pool, watching her intently. "And try to make sure none of the protesters out there get hurt too badly."

"Yes, *sir*," Keru said with a grim smile. Then he watched Dax move deliberately toward the center of the pool.

10

Dax waded slowly out into the pool's grayish-white, almost milky water, allowing it to engulf her environmental suit. The nutrient-rich fluid soon splashed against the faceplate of her helmet as she moved deliberately forward, and moments later the water rose to cover her head entirely. After she was fully submerged, the ragged sound of her own breathing reverberated within her bubble helmet—much too loudly, she thought.

As she drifted free in the murky water, she could see at least half a dozen symbionts swimming energetically near the pool's surface, while several arced gracefully about her body. Their tranquil blue static-electrical discharges linked each of them together every few seconds, and provided illumination as the cavern lights faded quickly with the increasing distance of the pool's surface. Occasionally, one of the symbionts' static bursts would gently reach out to her abdomen, no doubt speaking directly to the Dax symbiont on some level that bypassed symbiosis itself. Though the communication was entirely wordless, these brief psionic touches filled her with feelings of peace and reassurance, and evoked flashes of comforting colors, sounds, and even smells and tastes. If the Guardians experienced such things regularly, she could certainly understand why they showed such dedication to their charges.

Placing a gloved hand near her suit's neck ring, she opened up a comm channel. "Dax to Cyl," she said, her voice echoing strangely inside her helmet.

"Cyl here," came the general's static-laced reply. Evidently the jamming signals that had disrupted the runabout's communications weren't extending into the depths of Mak'ala, at least at the moment. *"How's your descent going, Lieutenant?"*

She glanced at the glowing display on the tricorder mounted on her right gauntlet. "So far so good, as long as 'down' is the right general direction." A loud rush of static assailed her ears for a moment, then abruptly faded to the background. "But I'm not sure how long I'll be able to keep this channel open."

"Understood. I guess I don't need to remind you to be careful."

After she signed off, Dax's boots came to the edge of a steep drop-off. She stepped over it, pushing her legs hard against the precipice to ensure that her body would fall well clear of it. The bottom of the submerged cavern fell away beneath her, prompting a momentary surge of fear; it was as though she were tumbling, untethered and in slow motion, into one of the icy crevasses on Minos Korva. She was surrounded by an all-encompassing darkness broken only by the navigational data scrolling across her tricorder's display. She recognized the silence that enfolded her as the absence of all sound, both inside and outside of her helmet.

The symbionts who were escorting her began to withdraw, but before they moved back toward the surface, each of them touched her with an electrical tendril. A moment later she was alone, floating in the stygian gloom.

In spite of the darkness and the isolation, she wasn't afraid. Although the symbionts had not communicated with her verbally, their meaning seemed crystal clear to her. *They aren't abandoning me. They want me to continue downward, but they can't—or know they mustn't?—go below this point.*

Another thought, less benign, occurred to her: *They don't know what's down here any more than I do.*

As the weighted belt that encircled her waist drew her steadily downward, she tried to draw some comfort from the fact that the water was far warmer than the Minos Korvan caverns had been, no doubt because of the upwellings of the underground hot springs that helped sustain the symbionts.

She also noticed that the increasingly viscous water seemed to be fighting her, almost as though Mak'ala itself were trying to reject her presence, like a Trill humanoid entering the throes of neural shock following a badly executed symbiosis.

She glanced again at her wrist-mounted sensor display. As far as she could tell, the dark cavern into which she was descending was bottomless; she knew that at some point her suit would no longer be able to take the pressure.

Keep breathing, she thought, concentrating on taking normal, shallow breaths. Not for the first time, she wondered if Julian hadn't been right when he'd tried to tell her that she was embarking on a fool's errand. Why did he have to be right so damned often?

Just as she was about to activate her suit's wrist lights, she glimpsed a dim, orange-green glow lining a nearby cavern wall. Her tricorder identified it as a colony of bioluminescent microorganisms, evidently growing out of a side channel that appeared to be an ancient, partially collapsed lava tube. As she watched the mat of glowing microbes, the pool's currents carried some of its tentacle-like fronds away from the wall and toward the surface. *Maybe this is what they eat when they're living down here unjoined,* Ezri thought, finding it curious that she couldn't recall the Dax symbiont's experiences in the caverns with any degree of detail. *Maybe the symbionts don't share* everything *when they join with us.*

That thought made her more determined than ever to continue her descent. To get to the bottom of things, as it were.

Ignoring the protest of the burned skin on her hand, she checked her navigational data again, then touched her comm button again. "Cyl, I'm continuing my descent. I think I'm finally getting close to the cavern floor."

She heard only hissing and crackling in response as her comm signal tried and failed to negotiate the magma-fed, ion-rich water and Mak'ala's fistrium-laden cavern walls. *Looks like I'm on my own down here,* she thought, swallowing hard.

Her boots suddenly found purchase on the stony and steeply sloping bottom, and Dax finally activated her suit's powerful helmet lights in the hope of actually seeing where she was headed, as opposed to relying entirely upon her tricorder. The soupy miasma all around her swallowed most of the light before it got more than a few meters away in any direction. Despite the limited visibility, Dax caught glimpses of the pool's rocky walls, and noted that they were narrowing as the passage descended ever deeper through Trill's volcanic crust.

As she dropped slowly into the increasingly claustrophobic passage, she recalled the Dax symbiont's experience inside the mysterious "cathedral artifact" the *Defiant*'s crew had discovered in the Gamma Quadrant. Ezri and Dax had been separated for a short time, and the unjoined Dax symbiont experienced a horrific, solitary vision that Ezri Dax now recognized as a premonition of the recent parasite attack on Trill. This unsettling encounter had brought the symbiont face-to-face with all of its previous hosts, each of whom had carried dire, oracular warnings—and had accused Dax of negligence in preparing for what was to come. Dax had surmised that the mystical, almost nightmarish experience had been precipitated as much by symbiotic interruption as by Audrid's painful memories of the alien thing that taken the life of poor Jayvin.

Dax's boots settled at last to almost level ground, and she saw that the passage had narrowed to the point that her suit lights had no trouble illuminating the walls in any direction; every crack and crevice stood out in sharp relief. As she moved forward, half walking and half swimming, the passage wound and twisted and narrowed until she thought the wide upper portion of her environmental suit might get her stuck.

Any symbiont that manages to make it this far down has got to be hunchbacked, she thought with no small amount of gallows humor. Even if she were able to raise Cyl or the runabout's computer, she knew that an emergency beam-out to the *Rio Grande* would have a very low probability of success. The very geological features that protected the symbionts in the caverns from long-distance transporter kidnappings would kill her if she were to become trapped down here.

Dax continued following the tunnel's gentle downward slope for perhaps another twenty minutes, her suit's metal-ribbed shoulders scraping disconcertingly from time to time against the sides of what had become a nearly horizontal tube of fluid-filled rock. For several minutes, she was literally crawling on her belly through yet another ancient lava tube. On top of this difficulty, the steadily increasing water pressure was pushing relentlessly against her suit, making its joints stiff and unyielding. Her thighs and arms ached with exertion, and exhaustion was threatening to overwhelm her. Still, her suit sensors indicated that something—something alive and symbiont-like—lay an indeterminate distance ahead.

Fortunately, one of her helmet lights revealed what appeared to be a ledge only a few meters ahead. Beyond that ledge lay what looked like another one of Mak'ala's large, open pools. A gentle current seemed to be pulling her in that direction. She heaved a sigh of relief at the prospect of getting out of the narrow passage soon.

Wrunch.

Once again, both of her shoulders had come into sharp contact with the alarmingly tight rock walls that bracketed her. Fortunately, the suit wasn't pouring oxygen bubbles into the water, so its seals hadn't been compromised. Then she noticed the true gravity of her predicament.

Stuck. Damn!

Fear kicked her hard in the belly; she knew that the intense pressures at this depth made it extremely doubtful that a symbiont would notice her plight and carry word of it back to the Guardians. And even if the Guardians somehow did become aware of her problem, they wouldn't be in a position to do anything about it.

Forcing down an impulse to make matters worse by hyperventilating, Dax simultaneously called upon the expertise of two previous hosts: Emony, among whose skills were agility and deep-breathing exercises; and Curzon, who'd been *nonpareil* in the fine art of complex extemporaneous cursing.

Neither was of much help. She was jammed in tight. And her injured hand felt like it had caught on fire.

After perhaps a minute of fruitless pushing and disciplined breathing, she recalled the time Torias had performed an EVA to repair some meteor damage to a shuttle he'd been piloting in low Trill orbit. Matters had gotten very complicated and interesting when his environmental suit malfunctioned, causing portions of it to expand like a balloon. In pretty short order, his suit had become larger than the shuttle's hatchway, trapping him in the airless void outside. Ezri realized she had no choice now other than to employ the very same risky-but-elegant solution Torias had improvised that day.

She felt around on her chest-mounted keypad until her gloved fingers came into contact with her suit's manual valve control. A few seconds later, a spray of bubbles flooded the narrow stone tube. She heard another sharp *wrunch* as her suit contracted slightly and her shoulders came loose. Moving her feet in tandem in a flukelike motion, she quickly developed enough forward momentum to traverse the two meters or so that separated her from the end of the passage. Then she tumbled languidly into the vast pool that lay beyond it.

As she scrambled to close the valve before too much of her air supply bled away, she was relieved to find herself descending into a much larger chamber, though her lights told her little else about her new environment. Her weighted belt drew her steadily downward, and she noticed a conspicuous lack of both symbionts and their conversational energy discharges. It was as though she were floating in the same featureless white void Benjamin Sisko had described to her when he had recounted his "visions" of the wormhole aliens.

Then her boots once again made contact with a hard, irregular surface. Because her lights were revealing little of value about her surroundings, she turned them off, just as Taran'atar had done back in the frigid cavern on Minos Korva. Whiteness instantly gave way to blackness; Mak'ala's weak but persistent currents and the stone beneath her feet were the only proof that anything in the universe existed other than herself.

Eventually her dark-adapting eyes picked up the slender flicker of blue-white energy in the distance. It looked distinctly like the communications impulses that the symbionts passed between one another. But these exchanges lasted significantly longer, almost like lightning magically trapped in amber. The colors of these energy spikes were subtler than the discharges of the symbionts, layered in countless variegated hues.

Unsure how far away they might be, she moved toward them, trying not to dwell on the ever-burgeoning pressure at these depths; the fluid that surrounded her seemed increasingly intent on crushing her environmental suit flat.

After an interval that might have lasted ten minutes or an hour, she felt she had come nearly close enough to grab the slow, stately energy discharges in her gloved hands. The rocky surface upon which her boots had settled took on a smooth, almost paved feel, ending at a gracefully curving section of rough stone wall that rose several meters over her head and curved away into the darkness. The stone wall had an almost scaly texture, and exhibited an eerie greenish glow that brought to mind recollections of Minos Korva, as well as memories of the ice comet that had brought Audrid such pain and horror.

Spying a sudden, furtive movement on the periphery of her vision, Dax turned toward it. Her jaw dropped in incredulity as she realized she was standing perhaps a meter away from the largest symbiont she had ever seen. Though the creature had the same overall vermiform shape of the symbiont that dwelled within her, it was nearly two meters in length. Lit by Dax's wrist lamps, the giant symbiont's bulk reminded Dax of a Tenaran seal, or a manatee that Emony had seen during a visit to one of Florida's Gulf Coast estuaries on Earth. Somehow, Dax maintained the presence of mind to run a quick scan of its RDNAL profile, which revealed it to be a good thousand years older than any other known living symbiont.

Dax was startled further when a flash of blue light lanced from one end of the creature and into her abdomen. Simultaneously, a voice, filled with equal parts indulgent humor and idle curiosity, sounded inside her head and seemed to reverberate all the way down through her midsection.

<<*The Annuated have already been told to expect you. The Annuated understand the danger Trill now faces. The Annuated have consented to interrupt their isolation in order to help.*>>

Annuated? Dax thought.

The creature began swimming, circling Dax in a graceful arc. <<*The Annuated. The eldest of the Interior People. Their progenitors, and the keepers of their most ancient memories.*>>

Even though the water was a superb sound conductor, the creature certainly couldn't have been employing actual words, given the symbionts' distinct lack of any humanoid-type speech apparatus.

Telepathy, Dax thought, theorizing that the creature's energy discharges were connecting it directly with the Dax symbiont inside her. She wondered if she was beginning to lose some of her capacity to be surprised.

Aloud, she said, "My escorts must have warned you that I was coming,"

<<And why.>>

"So you can tell me the truth about Trill's relationship to the parasites? And what happened to the ancient Trill colony on Kurl?"

<<I cannot.>>

Dax blinked several times, temporarily at a loss for words. "But you said that the Annuated are the keepers of the oldest memories."

<<Yes. But I do not yet qualify as Annuated. That is for some eon yet to come.>>

That made no sense whatsoever to Dax. "As far as I can tell, you're the oldest symbiont anybody's ever encountered."

A light, buoyant sensation tinged with flashes of pastel colors flashed through Dax's mind. She realized belatedly that it was laughter.

<<I am but young,>> the creature said. *<<I tend to the material needs of the Annuated, and ensure that their eggs reach the Shallows whenever one enters an interval of fecundity. I also assist the Annuated in assimilating the memories of those symbionts who come here to die. It is the memories kept by the Annuated that you seek.>>*

Though her brain spun with questions—not least of which were those surrounding the issue of symbiont reproduction, about which even joined Trills knew next to nothing—she struggled to keep herself focused on the topic at hand. Assuming she survived the current mission, there would be time later to return here to satisfy her curiosity about the Annuated, their mysterious life cycle, and their relationship not only to the younger-yet-still-venerable symbionts who dwelled in Mak'ala's depths, but also to the general symbiont population at large.

"All right," Dax said. "Where are these . . . Annuated?"

The creature suddenly released an intense bioelectrical discharge, which struck the wall with the apparent intensity of a phaser blast. Curiosity drew Dax to place her hands on the spot where the bolt had impacted, which she was surprised to see hadn't been marred by the release of energy.

<<You are among them already.>>

The scaly stone surface began to move beneath her gloves, writhing sinuously like a serpent's belly. Several meters directly overhead, brilliant multicolored energy discharges began flashing in all directions.

It's alive, she thought, withdrawing her hands. *This thing's alive, and it's waking up.*

Fear reached straight into her chest and clutched her heart when she noticed that her boots had suddenly left the ground. It was as though she had been caught in a sudden upwelling or deepwater current, and it propelled her inexorably upward and past the stone wall, until she was nearly smack in the middle of the overhead electrical display. Just as she became concerned that one of the energy charges might strike her, leaving her either dead or dying within a nonfunctioning environmental suit, she began to descend. Looking down, she saw that what she thought had been a wall was actually a rounded, streamlined form that might have been thirty meters long and eight meters high. Its shape was entirely familiar.

It was a gigantic symbiont, one of many that Dax could now see limned clearly in the ambient glow of what was undoubtedly a bioluminescent effect similar to that of the parasites. Tentacular projections issued from along their bloated sides, disappearing into meter-wide cracks in the cavern floor, like taproots extending from a plant into the life-giving heart of the planet. Dax assumed that the massive creatures drew their sustenance from the same mantle-deep, nutrient-rich hot springs that sustained Mak'ala's entire vast network of submerged channels, tunnels, lava tubes, and pools.

Dax arced over the awe-inspiring creatures, then slowly descended back toward the cavern floor. Moments later, her boots once again made contact with a stony surface, evidently ground smooth by eons of occupation by these ancient, massive, bottom-dwelling creatures. Other, similarly massive shapes were visible in the distance, conversing with one another in long, eerily beautiful bioelectrical discharges, sharing their impossibly ancient, ineffable thoughts.

Enthralled, Dax consulted the glowing display of her suit's tricorder. If these gigantic things were indeed symbionts, they were far older than any she had ever encountered before, or had ever even heard about. She quickly determined that the one nearest to her was nearly twenty thousand years old. At least five others lay nearby, though not near enough for her to make an accurate determination of their ages.

She wondered momentarily if she had discovered the literal truth behind the myth of *Mak'relle Dur,* then brushed the thought aside as useless; too many of Dax's hosts had pursued careers in the hard sciences for her to permit metaphysics and mythology to cloud her judgment. What she was seeing was merely a group of extremely old—not to mention large—variants of the more familiar Trill symbionts, rather than figures out of some unverifiable myth.

It occurred to her then that very little was definitely known about the extreme latter end of the symbiont life cycle, other than that most of them apparently ceased to be capable of joining after several centuries of symbiotic existence. *Is this where the Dax symbiont will eventually end up?*

<<*Perhaps,*>> said the smaller caretaker creature, who suddenly swam past Dax. For the first time, she noticed small immature nubs along the sides of the caretaker, matching the tentacular projections of the Annuated. <<*If you take great care not to get it killed in the meantime.*>>

A rivulet of sweat ran from Dax's scalp into her eyes, making her wish she could open her helmet long enough to wipe her face. She also noticed a discordant electronic background hum; it told her that her environmental suit's heat exchangers were being strained to the limit. A glance at her sensors informed her that the water temperature outside was already close to three hundred degrees Celsius; were it not for the intense pressure at these depths, the close proximity of Mak'ala's life-giving geothermal heat sources would have transformed the water down here into superheated vapor. Whatever these elder symbionts' hides were made of, it was sterner stuff than her suit.

"Speaking of not getting killed prematurely, I think we had better get started soon."

<<*Impatient youth,*>> the caretaker said.

Dax chafed at that, even though she was well aware that the long-lived Annuated, and probably their much younger attendants, would necessarily have a unique perspective on time. Eight prior lifetimes had taught Dax herself more than a little about patience, after all. But the actions of the neo-Purists—to say nothing of the strain being placed on her environmental suit at the moment—made patience a luxury she could scarcely afford.

"Look," Dax said, trying not to sound as impatient as the creature had accused her of being, "I'm running out of time. Just how long—"

The nearest of the gigantic elder symbionts answered with a powerful bioelectrical blast that took her full in the face.

The group of Annuated and their caretaker abruptly vanished, as did Dax's environmental suit. She was suddenly falling naked through a void that was like nothing she had ever experienced before. It wasn't filled with the crushing gray water of the deep pools of Mak'ala, nor was it a vacuum like empty space.

A sudden recollection of a therapeutic mind-meld Curzon had once shared with the late Vulcan Ambassador Sarek made it clear what she was experiencing: a freefall tumble into an ocean of pure experience—the vast storehouse of memories of the Annuated.

Her mind quickly converted the disorienting mindscape into something concrete, a white backdrop filled with an apparently infinite number of spheres, each one bearing an absolutely unique color. Intuitively, she understood that each sphere represented a discrete package of stored memory and experience. The motley assignation of colors made it appear that each of these was gleaned from the memories of a different person.

Of course, she thought, angling herself toward one of the closer spheres with an effort of pure will. *The Annuated have been isolated down here for ages. The only way they'd be able to stockpile memories is if those memories came to them from others on a fairly regular basis.* It was a sobering thought. The Annuated stored the knowledge retained by dead symbionts, at least the ones who made it down here into the deep waters before expiring.

The nearest of the spheres made a close approach. Though it

had to be over a meter in diameter, she threw her arms around it—

—and became Dhej, a symbiont who had descended to this place of remembering more than six centuries ago. Dhej's eleven hosts had distinguished themselves in fields ranging from medicine, cybernetics research, poetry, and criminal law. This symbiont's hosts had experienced motherhood, fatherhood, exultation, grief—

Dax released the sphere and thrust it roughly away, unwilling to risk losing focus on her mission by becoming caught up in the minutiae of a serial existence as rich as her own. She reached for a second sphere—

—and became one with Liak, a symbiont whose fourteenth host expired nearly fifteen centuries earlier. Dax ached in sympathy as the dying, senescent symbiont swam laboriously into ever deeper, denser, and hotter waters, desperate to leave its enormous burden of memory in a safe resting place, as though it were carrying a clutch of eggs—

Again, Dax pushed the mnemonic orb away and clutched at others, spending momentary eternities with a whole series of them. Though she wasn't certain how much objective time she had spent in this pursuit, she realized that a pattern was gradually emerging: Each successive batch of memories hailed from farther and farther back in the long history of Trill.

Even as this realization struck her, the encounters began coming with steadily accelerating frequency. The successive touches of multitudes of other memory-laden symbiont minds quickly ran together in a dazzling mnemonic blur, a rapid experiential torrent that submerged both Ezri and the Dax symbiont, washing them swiftly backward in time. Like an unprotected swimmer caught in the rapids, Dax reached out frantically with her mind, seeking anything that might slow the dizzying motion. Nothing worked; her course seemed as unalterable as that of Trill itself as it made its stately, eternal freefall around its sun.

Shutting her eyes tightly, Dax felt her abdomen begin lurching crazily from the sensations of acceleration and falling. *Oh, pleasepleasepleaseplease don't let me yark inside my helmet,* she thought even as she realized that her closed eyelids posed no barrier to the telepathic kaleidoscope that assailed her.

Time passed in reverse even more quickly, and her perception of falling reached what felt like terminal velocity. She tried to calm herself by getting analytical; she reasoned that the oldest stored memories must lie closest to the center of this weird mindscape, like the pungent, meaty nut found at the heart of a *syto* bean.

More glimpses of the lives of other symbionts and humanoids entered Dax's consciousness, vanishing almost as quickly as they arrived. Shards of millennia-old memories that seemed as broken and worn as the piece of Kurlan sculpture she had found on Minos Korva came and went, briefly grafting themselves onto her consciousness as they passed. For a few moments, Dax became—

—a nearly naked humanoid male named Hodak. As Healer, it fell to Hodak to use the valley's plants and animals to try to restore health to those members of his tribe who fell ill. After lifting the riverworm over his head in supplication to the gods of healing, he brought the wriggling brown creature down onto the abdomen of the fever-stricken young woman who lay unconscious before him.

Hodak had seen the riverworms attach themselves to other animals, and noted that both had seemed strengthened by the contact; perhaps a similar effect would save this woman from the fever that was consuming her. As the villagers looked on, hope and apprehension etched across their painted, spot-framed faces, the eyeless riverworm found the opening of the woman's empty abdominal pouch. The pouch not only allowed males and females alike to provide postbirth incubation for helpless newborns, it also served Healers as a conduit for their cures and medicaments.

The riverworm worked its way into the pouch. The woman's eyes opened moments later, and a beatific smile split her face. Hodak thanked the gods and—

*—*disappeared. The village and everything in it were swept away, replaced by darkness. But the darkness was filled with sensation, warmth, and even flashes of wordless conversation. Dax—

—became Sef, one of the first of its kind to gain the sense known as "sight." On numerous occasions, Sef had used the mind-tendrils it customarily used to converse with its fellow Swimmers to entice various four-legged beasts to the Pool's

edge. Some of those creatures had bolted at the last moment, but others had permitted Sef to "ride" them, sharing their sensory experiences, sometimes for lengthy periods.

And what experiences the Fourlegs had to share! To see! To hear! To run across the Aboveworld, basking in all its light, glorying in the variegated colors and tastes and smells. Few Swimmers had any real knowledge of these sublime sensations, for only a handful had ridden on the Fourlegs. And like those others, Sef wanted more.

Many had been the times that Sef had wished to share the experiences of a creature whose subtlety of intellect equaled Sef's own. But did any such creature exist anywhere on Trill?

Then the first of the two-legged Walkers approached the Pool's rocky edge, in answer to one of Sef's mind calls. Of course, Sef did not know what a Walker was until after riding the creature for the first time and examining its sleek, furry coat and feeling its steeply ridged brow with the being's own graceful, long-fingered hands. The Walkers had bigger brains than any of the Fourlegs, and quite subtle intellects—at least in comparison to the Fourlegs. The creature's initial fear response had been quite intense, and might take some time to counter. The Fourlegs have taken us far from the Pool and back again, *Sef thought, gazing wonderingly at the beetle-browed face reflected in the Pool's surface.* Who knows how much farther the Walkers might take us?

The reflection of Sef's host vanished, replaced by several other vignettes of stored memory. Like the previous encounters, some of these related the experiences of long-dead symbionts, while others belonged to hosts who had become dust eons ago. Like the experiences of Hodak and Sef, many of them seemed to go back to the very genesis of Trill symbiosis, an event that might have occurred as long as twenty-five millennia ago—and had been completely obscured by the passage of time. Whenever Dax had considered the conundrum of the origin of Trill symbiosis, she concluded it was as unfathomable as the Big Bang itself.

These must be memories of memories, Dax reasoned in between the ancient, mutually exclusive encounters. *Or maybe memories of memories of memories. Of other memories.*

She recalled her earlier tricorder readings. Despite their great age, she tended to doubt that any of the Annuated were quite old enough to possess anything like an accurate, firsthand recollection of the very first instance of symbiont-humanoid joining, or the precise circumstances surrounding it. But they certainly *could* carry within them many mnemonic echoes from long-dead symbionts born eons before they were. And thanks to Joran, whose existence the Symbiosis Commission had concealed from her for nearly a century, Dax knew very well that memory was a very malleable thing; because of this, all of the "first symbiosis" memories she had glimpsed might be false to a significant degree—or true, at least in certain respects.

She noted wryly that asking questions about such things always seemed to leave one with more questions than one started with. As a person whose mind had a decidedly problem-solving bent, she found the idea of increasing the universe's net question-content somewhat distressing.

Dax suddenly noticed that something had changed yet again in her surroundings. She was back in her environmental suit, and yet she was also floating in the void that contained the moving mnemonic spheres. But the spheres were altering their speed and direction. Her headlong plunge into the mnemonic past seemed to be reversing course.

Of course. I'm inside an Annuated's head, so to speak. And I've zipped all the way to the oldest fragments of its memory. So there's no place else to go but forward.

Her reverie was interrupted by yet another sudden change of scenery. All at once—

—her environment suit was gone again, and she stood on what appeared to be the deck of a space vessel. She was in a brightly lit, low-ceilinged control center filled with consoles, screens, and other instruments. The consoles bore markings that resembled some archaic form of the Trill written language, and she found she could read none of it.

This sure isn't Starfleet issue, *Dax thought as she looked around the narrow control center, where several green-uniformed Trill humanoids of both sexes were intent on various consoles and readouts. Dax noted that she, too, was wearing similar garb.* None of this looks very much like anything the Trill Defense Ministry has at the moment, either.

Someone activated a large forward viewscreen, which dis-

played a half-lit blue planet. The serene-looking world was swiftly growing in size, as though the ship had just dropped out of warp and was making its initial approach.

"There it is," said one of the Trill humanoids, a male. *"The first other world we've ever found capable of supporting both humanoids and symbionts throughout the entirety of both species' life cycles. Or so the survey reports say."*

"It took us long enough to find it," another crew person answered, this one a female. *Behind the woman was a circular conference table, the centerpiece of which Dax had never seen before—not in its entirety, anyway—but which she recognized at once: a naiskos. "Let's hope we don't have to travel as far or search as long before we locate the next one,"* the woman said.

Kurl, Dax thought as the crew members continued making small talk about their mission, which was evidently to drop a large contingent of colonists off on this planet, along with sufficient agricultural resources and machine tools to allow them to establish permanent habitations here. Though she still believed Kurl was so distant that it made an improbable site for an early *"lost Trill colony,"* she thought its selection might make perfect sense if the exacting environmental requirements for maintaining both humanoid and symbiont populations were taken into account.

Though Dax found the crew's grammar, vocabulary, and syntax strange—*archaic, in fact*—she had no problem understanding their speech. *More Annuated telepathy,* she thought, realizing with no small amount of wonderment that at least part of the recent neo-Purist manifesto was apparently true: there evidently really had been a previously undiscovered ancient period of Trill interstellar exploration—an era that had been all but forgotten millennia before the time of Dax's first host, Lela.

As though the Annuated with whom she was linked were now satisfied that Dax's remaining questions were best answered elsewhere, the scene shifted again.

The starship and the blue planet vanished, to be replaced by a sterile white room whose tightly sealed windows looked out over a placid blue lake. A few pleasure craft skated slowly across the azure water, and homes dotted the lake's far side.

Somehow, Dax knew she was on Kurl—and that centuries had passed since the initial colony ship had deposited its living cargo here to form the very first society to be composed entirely of joined Trills.

And she also knew with certainty that something had been going horribly wrong with that society lately.

Dax turned from the windows and found herself inside what appeared to be an extremely well-equipped research laboratory. A pair of white-smocked Trill humanoids, a man and a woman, were intent on an experiment. A Trill symbiont sat on a table before them, its brown, wrinkled skin slick and shiny from the shallow nutrient bath in which it sat.

"It's so peaceful out there," Dax said, indicating the lake behind her.

The female scientist made a harrumphing sound. "It won't stay that way for long. Not unless we find a way to neutralize this damned virus, and quickly."

The virus. Yes. Dax was aware that the virus, perhaps the accidental offspring of a misfolded protein molecule produced by some of the indigenous biota, had already killed more than ten percent of the colony's fifteen million people. Images of horrendous, blood-spattered deaths from hemorrhagic fevers, isoboramine starvation–induced symbiotic interruptions, and complete RDNAL breakdowns flashed unbidden across her mind—an extraordinarily vivid memory-within-a-memory that Dax found highly disconcerting. Obviously not everyone on Kurl had succumbed as yet, otherwise the original owners of these memories could never have found their way to the deep pools of the Annuated.

She also knew that so far, the symbionts had been the most vulnerable to the virus, though no one had yet discovered precisely how or why the infections were occurring. But hope remained that a cure would come soon.

And Dax knew that this lab was one of the brightest sources of that hope.

She watched as the man prepared a hypo and injected the symbiont with it. The small vermiform entity twitched several times as the woman ran a handheld scanner over its length. She studied the device's readout for a moment, then smiled up at the man and at Dax.

"The RDNAL sequences are strengthening and repairing themselves, just as we saw in the simulations," the woman said brightly. "With a few more adjustments to their genome, I think

the symbionts will be toughened up enough to make them completely immune."

The man returned the woman's smile, though he powered it
with somewhat less wattage. "Let's hope so."

The white-smocked duo vanished, and—

—Dax was suddenly in another room.

She recognized the young man lying on the medical theater's
operating table as an initiate being prepared for his first joining.
A pair of physicians dressed in surgical tunics carefully lifted a
symbiont toward not the initiate's abdomen, but his waiting
open mouth. The Kurlans' experiments had led them to believe
that symbiosis could be achieved more effectively by direct connection to a host's brain stem.

Then Dax noticed that the symbiont looked . . . strange. Its
overall vermiform shape was no different from that of any other
symbiont she had ever seen, but the creature's body was much
paler. Small barbed feelers extended from its "head." It would
need those, Dax knew, to burrow its way gently through the back
of the host's throat . . .

Minutes later, the joining was done. The initiate sat up. He
smiled. Then he opened his eyes.

The light of pain and madness burned there, and a long
string of drool looped from his mouth. Something had clearly
gone wrong with the symbiont's new immune-system modifica-
tions . . .

Before Dax could recoil in horror, the scene changed once
more. The memory vignettes to which one or more of the Annuated were treating her were now becoming briefer and more fre-
quent, much as they had been during the earlier part of her
mnemonic journey. And they were moving steadily forward in
time, as though the elder symbiont had looked inside her, had
anticipated her every question, and was deliberately trying to
spin his memories into a coherent narrative in order to furnish
the answers she sought.

Dax saw more labs, more researchers. Some were devoted to
the continued enterprise of artificially enhancing the symbiont
genome to make it more resistant to the disease. Others had the
task of devising direct attacks on the virus whose extraordinarily
high mutational rate was bringing continued devastation to
Kurl's symbionts. It even appeared that some of the symbionts'

genetic enhancements had accidentally crossed over to the virus, rendering it that much harder to kill.

The race against the virus continued for a decade or more. And the Kurlans were losing ground, their crash program to heal the symbionts leaving them diseased and insane instead. More disturbing still, the altered symbionts had begun taking control of their hosts, closing themselves off to the Kurlans' long-term memories in order to dominate where once they had shared.

Dax once again found herself aboard a starship, watching the planet Kurl from low orbit. This time, however, the planet appeared anything but serene. Ugly plumes of brown-gray smoke rose in crooked columns on the day side. Fires raged at the edge of the southeastern continent, visible just beyond the darkness of the night-side terminator.

And this vessel carried people whose dark uniforms and serious bearing told her that the current mission did not involve establishing a new colony.

From a duty station on the port side of what could only be the bridge of a military vessel, Dax watched as a stern-faced middle-aged woman gave orders to a disciplined crew of six of her fellow Trills. From the way they carried themselves, she could tell immediately that most of them were joined.

"Have they launched any of their ships?" the captain asked.

A young male science officer responded crisply. "Not since we got here, Captain. However, some of them could have broken the planetary quarantine and gotten offworld before we arrived. There's really no way to know for certain."

Of course, Dax thought. The Kurlan memories I've been experiencing, or at least their echoes, had to have gotten off Kurl and back to Trill somehow.

The captain nodded grimly at the science officer. "How many are still alive down there?"

"Almost four million. All infected."

Dax saw a light flash on her console. Though she couldn't actually read the text on her display, she somehow understood its meaning. "Someone on the surface is hailing us, Captain. It's coming from a high-level official address."

"Put it on the screen," said the captain.

The face that appeared on the central viewer was that of a

fortyish Trill humanoid male. He was joined, no doubt, as was every adult on Kurl. But the creature that shared his existence had obviously been so greatly altered to resist the virus that it was clearly no longer fit for joining—at least not in the mutually beneficial manner that had always been the very essence of Trill symbiosis.

Dax, or rather the person whose memories she was experiencing, recognized him as the current Kurlan president. And she saw the same fires of madness that had illuminated the young initiate's eyes in this man's intense gaze.

Just like Jayvin, Dax thought. She no longer had any doubt that yet another of the neo-Purists' assertions was true: the ancient Trill colony on Kurl was indeed the source of the parasites, or at least had spawned their remote ancestors.

"So you've finally come to kill the rest of us," the man on the screen said, his eyes fixed upon the captain's.

"You've already done a pretty thorough job of that yourselves," the captain responded, apparently referring to the smoke and fires that were visible from orbit. "We've been sent to maintain the medical quarantine," the captain continued. There was sympathy in her tone, but also cold, hard duranium. "By any means necessary."

"You have failed to heal us. You have betrayed our symbiosis. You have forced us to take charge of it, rather than allowing you to inflict further harm upon us. You can no longer contain us. We have vessels ready to launch even now."

"Contact them. Tell them they have to power down and remain on the surface."

The president laughed, a hard, braying sound. "You do not command here."

"Captain, I'm reading several vessels leaving the surface," said the science officer, alarmed. *"They all read as transluminal configurations."*

The captain turned and addressed Dax directly. "Private Memh, can you target all four of them simultaneously?"

Somehow, Dax knew that she could. Such things seemed to be Memh's specialty. "Yes, Captain."

Approximately two and a half minutes later, nothing remained of any of the other ships save orbiting fragments of superheated metallic debris.

And dozens of Kurlan Trill, both humanoids and symbionts, were dead. Dax felt physically ill, but remained at her—at Memh's—post.

"They can still launch a lot more ships, Captain," the science officer said, breaking the dolorous silence that had enveloped the control center. "We can't possibly chase down every last one of them."

"We might," the captain said. She clearly did not like the direction the conversation was taking. Neither did Dax.

The science officer was almost in tears, but he held his ground admirably nevertheless. Like everyone else here, he was a creature of duty. "We can't rely on that, Captain. The risk to Trill is too great."

The captain settled back in her chair, staring straight ahead quietly. "You're right, Mister Lev," she finally said at length. "Womb help us all, you're right."

Turning her chair until she once again faced Dax, the captain said, "Private Memh, deploy the biogenics, along with the incendiaries."

Dax was surprised at how little she hesitated after hearing that order. Memh must have anticipated the very real possibility of having to do this. Perhaps it had become second nature to her.

After Dax entered three brief commands into her board, a console light's telltale flash confirmed that the network of satellites had left the ship's belly, the individual pulse launchers already well on their way to their optimal firing positions.

Fourteen minutes later, the first of the rhythmic flashes appeared on the forward screen. First, the spaceports and landing fields erupted in orange flames that consumed hangars, terminals, spacecraft, and people indiscriminately. Moments later, the flames were eclipsed by multiple nimbuses of dazzling golden-white light as the biogenic detonations struck each city in turn. The individual pulses faded almost as quickly as they had registered on everyone's retinas, though the effects were actually still propagating throughout the entire Kurlan biosphere.

There would be no more ships launched from anywhere on Kurl. Though the cities were largely intact, no one on the surface would now be in any condition to pilot a vessel, even if the planet's spaceports hadn't been leveled. Within a few short hours, every trace of the virus would be gone. All four million or *so of the planet's inhabitants would be dead as well, thanks to a biogenic weapon that no one on either Trill or Kurl had expected ever to be put to use.*

The sheer horror of what she had just witnessed made Dax want to scream. But all she could do was look at the forward viewer with a disciplined gaze, her larynx all but paralyzed. That's how nightmares go, she told herself.

But she knew this was no nightmare. She understood on some fundamental level that what she had just witnessed was absolutely real. Trill's penchant for secrecy had evidently begun here, some five millennia in the past, during a lost age. Kurl had been sacrificed in an attempt to contain a lethal disease and prevent it from spreading to Trill—just as a host is sometimes sacrificed to save an ailing symbiont.

No wonder the parasites hate us, *Dax thought.* We created them, then we tried to wipe them out. Thousands of years later, the children of the survivors came back looking to even the score.

She couldn't really say she blamed them for feeling that way. And she had to marvel at the intensity and longevity of the creatures' hatred; it had evidently outlasted the virus that had brought it into being in the first place.

More images, obviously gleaned from still other, later memories, followed in rapid succession: Back on Trill, important, influential people held closed-door meetings. They made clandestine decisions, as important, influential people were often wont to do.

Cover stories were crafted, for no one in the circles of power wanted it known that the benign Trill symbionts could be perverted into such a terrible menace—a menace whose destruction had required nothing less than an act of mass murder to avert.

The cover-up took on a momentum of its own. Overly talkative military officers and politicians died under mysterious circumstances. Computer files were erased. Paper documents were shredded, except for a few that had been hidden away without official sanction, then ultimately lost in the ever-expanding records-storage catacombs beneath Leran Manev.

Trill turned inward, withdrawing from space, isolating itself, eventually abandoning space travel and alien contact until such knowledge was all but purged from its collective memory. Conceal-

ing the symbionts and Trill symbiosis from outsiders, they reasoned, might help keep the ghosts of Kurl from rattling their chains. The planet's extreme distance from Trill took care of the rest.

Kurl was effectively buried.

The usual ebb and flow of history followed as the centuries piled up like drifts of snow over the Tenaran permafrost. Governments, nations, languages, and whole Trill societies rose and fell over the next five millennia. Even Trill's first period of interstellar colonization became lost to antiquity, though by rights it should have been revered as a golden age, a time when the Trill people had reached across the stars.

But it wasn't. Kurl was not only buried, it was forgotten.

Almost.

Dax knew now that this terrible secret had to be part of the full accounting of Trill's deliberately buried past that the neo-Purists were demanding. She wondered how the radicals—along with their sympathizers and the networks of discontented unjoined who were protesting all over the planet—would react to the revelation of ancient Trill's shameful act of genocide.

Julian's parting words echoed in Dax's mind: "Suppose you discover some entirely new unknown horror from your people's past. What will you do then?"

She had absolutely no idea.

Dax suddenly became aware of the physical world once again. She was sweltering inside a standard Starfleet environmental suit, floating limply before what might well be the oldest symbiont on the entire Trill homeworld. The smaller caretaker symbiont cut a slow, repetitive circle in the water beside her, evidently the symbiont equivalent of nervous pacing.

Dax's exhausting mnemonic journey was at an end. She was glad; she felt spent, both physically and emotionally.

<<*You have found what you sought,*>> the caretaker said amid small crackles of energy. It was not asking a question.

Dax nodded, though she knew the creature couldn't see the gesture. "Yes. In fact, I think one of the Annuated took me straight to what I needed to know."

<<*Your needs and desires are not nearly so difficult to parse as you might think.*>>

"Thanks. I think." Dax felt too fatigued to react to the caretaker's barb, if that's what it was.

<<*Your ancestors did what they thought they had to do, Ezri Dax,*>> said the caretaker, prompting Dax to wonder if the creature had eavesdropped on the memories the Annuated had shared with her. <<*You must try not to judge them too harshly. They discovered that our kind can be tampered with, and perverted into a thing of horror. They sought to keep others from discovering this.*>>

"They killed four million people, then covered it up," Dax said sharply, wondering if she was channeling Curzon's temper again, her fatigue notwithstanding. "That's a little hard for me to write off as a mere youthful indiscretion."

<<*Yes,*>> the caretaker said. <<*They covered up their embarrassments. Just as Audrid Dax did. And so many others before and after, both Swimmers and Walkers.*>>

Before Dax could compose a rejoinder, the caretaker made an impatient noise and added, <<*The Annuated are not accustomed to thinking at speeds compatible with extreme youth. You must leave now, Ezri Dax, and allow them their rest.*>>

Dax thought that was a good idea. Why stay down here and argue? Then she wondered how she was going to substantiate what she had learned here. After all, it wasn't as though these elder symbionts had given her an isolinear chip filled with information that could be objectively examined. On the other hand, nobody would have time to study any such document anyway. Events had already begun moving rather quickly before she and Cyl had come to Mak'ala; she could only imagine what was going on now in the streets of Trill's cities.

Dax suddenly noticed that the whine of her suit's overstrained heat exchangers had risen about half an octave in pitch, which wasn't a good sign. But at least she had what she'd come for. Now she just had to get back to the surface to report her findings to Julian, Cyl, and Gard. Together, the four of them would figure out just what to do with her discoveries. And how to substantiate them if necessary, perhaps with the help of the Guardians.

Then she heard a sharp click, coming from somewhere inside her suit. The whine of the heat exchangers ceased at once, and the acrid tang of ozone assaulted her nostrils. A key circuit or relay had probably burned out, and there was no way to change it down here, or even to reach it.

A glance at her sensor display confirmed the worst. Her suit couldn't sustain life support for even a fraction of the time it would take for her to swim back to the surface. Soon, she would literally cook inside her own environmental suit. And she still couldn't call Cyl for a rescue. This excursion and the revelations she had experienced had all been in vain.

Clenching her burned hand into a fist, she decided that this was a perfect occasion for one of Curzon's highly inventive curses.

12

"What do you *mean* no one has been able to find President Maz?" Gard yelled into his communicator as he dashed down the corridor.

"Exactly what I said, Mister Gard," Colonel Rianu said, her voice sounding slightly tinny as it issued from the comm device's small speaker. *"We're having more and more communications blackouts. We lost contact with the president's contingent five minutes ago."*

"Was she warned about the bomb threats? Is she en route to one of the emergency bunkers?" As Gard neared the turbolift, he held his phaser in his free hand, his finger hovering over the triggering button just in case anyone else had infiltrated the Senate Tower.

"We tried," Rianu said. *"We think Commander Grekel heard our warnings before we were cut off. We— Hold on."*

Gard saw the colonel's face turn from the tiny monitor, and heard her conversing in low tones with her subordinates. Her brows knitted in anger as she turned back to him.

"Two search teams have found additional bombs in the vicinity. One was in the Najana Library, and another one was near the shuttle docking station on Maran Avenue. They're attempting to disarm them now."

Gard pressed the button for the turbolift. "Do we know what kind of bombs they are?"

"Negative," Rianu said, shaking her head, her gaze focused off-screen. *"The scans have been inconclusive so far."* She

paused and listened for a bit. *"I'm told there are traces of some kind of radiation, but we can't analyze it on the spot. We're going to try beaming them out as soon as we can get site-to-site transporter stanchions in place."*

The turbolift doors opened, and Gard prepared to step inside. "I suspect more of these devices have been planted around Leran Manev. Until we know what they can do, it might be best to evacuate as many people as possible from the central districts. We should get key officials to radiation-shielded facilities as quickly as possible."

Colonel Rianu's reply was lost in a sudden haze of static.

Jirin Tambor checked his chronometer for the eighteenth time in the last few minutes. The pain suppressants in his system were doing a good job of keeping him from noticing the progress of the bloodborne malignancy that was attacking his heart muscle, consuming him layer by layer from the inside. But they did little to quell the nervousness and trepidation he was feeling at the moment.

He paced in front of the neurogenic device quietly, careful not to let his footfalls be heard. Though the building was closed to the public for the night, it was still possible that someone might happen upon him in time to stop what he was doing. The other members of his cell had already left. He didn't blame them; he had *chosen* to stay behind.

My life is over anyhow. Weeks or days or minutes. It doesn't matter now. He had already said good-bye to all of his friends and what family he had left. Most of his family would no longer communicate with him, ever since he had told them he was joining the neo-Purist movement. They, too, were members of the unjoined majority, but had always appeared content with their lives despite the chronic lack of opportunity Tambor now saw as their unjust lot. They hadn't even been permitted the wherewithal to earn university degrees. Given that, why couldn't more people see what was so glaringly obvious?

"Why involve yourself in all this protest?" his mother had asked him. "What good does it do you to provoke the government? The joined aren't purposely discriminating against us. You've just chosen to interpret every bit of bad luck in the worst possible way."

But Tambor knew better. His family knew he was sick, but not *how* sick. They didn't know what he had learned from his doctors, one of whom had broken a sacred vow to tell him the truth. His chances of survival would be greatly increased if he were joined. A symbiont living in his abdomen could, at least potentially, stop the cancer that was eating him alive. The doctor had tried to backpedal, saying that even joining was no guarantee of recovery. But he couldn't hide the fact that the joined almost never suffered from this particular condition. And on those rare occasions when they did, no expense seemed to be spared in restoring them to health. Medicines and radiation treatments had already failed Tambor; he knew with bedrock certainty that the slugs would have saved him.

But the Symbiosis Commission would not grant him the right to join, even as an emergency measure to save his life. They had repeatedly denied his requests, until he had exhausted every avenue of appeal.

The malignancy within him was consuming more than his organs; it had removed his inhibitions, chilling a lifetime of carefully observed morality into a glacier of cold rage. Increasingly over the past year, he had noticed the inequities practiced by his government, by the university he attended, and even by the people on the streets. Every advantage possible in life seemed to flow effortlessly toward his world's charmed few: the joined.

Then he found the neo-Purist movement, and the arguments of its members made sense. As they uncovered more and more hints about Trill's history, and the past horrors those ancient records had hinted at, he came to understand that something radical would have to be done to right his world's ingrained wrongs.

Tambor's cell had received a great deal of information—including rudimentary plans for the neurogenic bombs—from a neo-Purist operative within the government archives. Tambor believed implicitly, as did his fellow revolutionaries, the records claiming that similar neurogenic devices had been used before, in the depths of Trill's all-but-forgotten past.

And now they will be used again.

Tambor knew his family would be safe, since none of his relatives lived anywhere near the bomb sites. Everyone he cared about would be safe. The bombs were supposed to have little effect upon unjoined persons anyway, except for those unlucky enough to be at extremely close range when the devices deto-nated. Tambor had decided to take luck out of the equation en-tirely by remaining at ground zero until the clock ran out.

He checked his chronometer again, then set his hand phaser down on the floor.

Even if somebody were to try to stop me now, there wouldn't be any time for a fire fight.

Julian Bashir stumbled into the intake room at Manev Central Hospital, holding his tunic sleeve up to his nose to stanch the blood flow.

The place was overflowing with people, though most of them appeared to have suffered relatively minor injuries. The nurses and trauma teams seemed to be doing their best to divide people into groups depending on their needs, ushering the worst cases down the hallways toward what he assumed were medical al-coves and emergency treatment facilities.

He started to approach one of the nurses, then felt woozy. Nearby, he noticed a just-vacated chair, and he moved toward it, sitting down heavily.

Just breathe, Julian. You can't do any good for anyone else in this condition. He closed his eyes for just a moment.

He heard a noise then, and opened his eyes, focusing as a thin nurse stepped in front of him. "Sir, can you hear me?"

Bashir was perplexed by the question. "Of *course* I can hear you. I was just mugged, but I'm going to be fine. I'm a doctor—"

She crouched beside him, pulling gauze and bandages out of the medkit that was slung over her shoulder. "You were *uncon-scious,* sir. Let me see that."

Unconscious? Bashir didn't recall having passed out. But then how could he?

"The good news is, I think you look to be in worse shape than you really are," the nurse said, smiling grimly as she used a white cloth to wipe away some of the caked blood under his nose.

She dabbed an acrid-smelling ointment under his eye. "Thanks for the inspiration," he said, wincing as the ointment stung him. "You've got a great bedside manner."

"We're a bit busy here, as you can see," she said. "No time to be excessively sweet." She removed a hypospray and tapped a combination of codes into it as he watched.

As she touched the hypo to his neck, he felt a surge of energy. *Sakarnel,* he thought. *Not what* I'd *have used, but it'll get me back on my feet.* "I'm a doctor with Starfleet. I can help you here."

"That was just what I was thinking," she said. "I recognized the uniform." She pointed to his face. "None of your injuries are life-threatening, but you'll probably have some bruises for a few days."

"How long was I out? Has there been any word from the police about the bombs?" Bashir asked.

The nurse gave him a guarded but quizzical look. "Bombs? I don't understand."

Then there's still time, Bashir thought, his pulse quickened by both hope and fear.

"They've now found three *devices,"* the lieutenant said, his voice competing with the static issuing from Gard's comm device.

Gard frowned. "They're all near the Senate Tower?"

"Yes, sir. Each was discovered within half a kilometer of the Tower."

Gard's mind whirled. *Short-range bombs, then. Low-yield devices probably intended to saturate the area. They've targeted the government. And probably the Symbiosis Commission as well.*

"Lieutenant, make certain the guard units at the SymCom are aware that—"

The comm device flared up into a loud hash of static, just a split second before the lights inside the command center's turbolift blinked out. Gard fancied he could feel the blast strike him and pass entirely through his body, even though he could neither see nor hear it. Even though he was in a shielded building, he felt certain that whatever had just happened out there had passed through the thick, rad-shielded walls, at least partially.

His symbiont lurched and scrambled within him, and Gard dropped to the turbolift floor, writhing in agony. Holding his belly, he tried to calm himself, his *whole* self.

We're not going to die in the dark. We're not going to die in the dark. He thought it again and again, repeating it like a mantra.

Gard raised his phaser and pointed it at the turbolift entrance, praying that the lift wasn't stalled somewhere between the reinforced floors.

The beam began melting an aperture in the doors, the glowing metal and phaser burst providing a temporary brilliance.

We're not going to die in the dark.

The door gave way. Outside he could hear people screaming and equipment tumbling and crashing.

Jirin Tambor heard a chime, and in a nanosecond, he was flooded with memories, even as he felt the energy wash over and through him as the bomb exploded.

The neurogenic radiation blasts would sever the links between the joined and the strange creatures that dwelled in their pouches.

He remembered playing in the snow with his baby brother Kal, who had made an art of falling down.

The joined would soon be in excruciating agony, and their stranglehold on the planet would be broken.

He saw his first love, Hennene, emerging from the cold wavelets of Lake Devritane, water beading on her skin, her smile radiant despite her shivers as he rushed toward her with the towel.

The unjoined would be mostly unaffected. A very few would be hurt due to the electromagnetic pulse that would accompany the radiation dispersal. But the lives of the survivors—of the majority of Trill—would be much improved by their sacrifice.

He saw Hennene lying cold on the hospital bed, the doctor standing nearby ready to tell him that their baby had also died.

The pulse would destroy most of the government's communications capabilities, would wipe its files, drain the power from its hovercars and its weapons.

He heard the Commission doctor tell him again—emphatically this time, as if he'd been talking to a recalcitrant child—that he was not qualified to carry a symbiont, even if that denial meant certain death from the malignancy that was spreading throughout his body.

Trill society would begin again tomorrow, but he would not be there to greet it.

Hennene. He tried to speak her name aloud, but his proximity to the blast had ravaged his body too badly. Light and darkness came in equal measure, a final sunset in the depths of the night.

Dante could not have crafted a more explicit version of hell than the one that existed in this place. As a doctor, Julian Bashir was used to trauma and suffering—he had dealt with severe episodes of both during the Dominion War—but those chaotic, bloody moments had not been entirely unexpected.

Here, however, in the bedlam of Trill's Manev Central Hospital, things seemed very different. As the overflowing triage center filled with cacophonous screams and tortured wails, Bashir and the other physicians and medics struggled against a tide of death whose source had been both surprising and invisible.

And though Bashir's medical conscience did not want to admit his own personal fears, the worst part for him was having no way to know whether Ezri had survived the initial bioelectric attacks—or even if she was in danger at all. But as Trill society continued to collapse around him, and reports kept coming in of hundreds—or maybe thousands—more casualties, he could only respond to the unfolding crisis as best he could, while striving to avoid considering the personal loss he might have to face in the very near future.

The little boy with the spinal injury was going to live. He might even make a full recovery. *No thanks,* Bashir thought bitterly, *to people like Doctor Torvin, who keep putting the joined patients at the head of the line whether their injuries warrant it or not.*

But he also knew that dozens of joined patients here tonight were in extremely grave condition, obviously because of the bombings. And it was equally clear to him that the way to save their hosts was not to be found in the hurly-burly of Manev Central Hospital's trauma unit.

It might, however, be found among the files relating to an incident Bashir himself had become caught up in, on a visit to Trill four years prior. . . .

Shortly after finishing surgery on the boy, Bashir edged his way down a hallway on the hospital's seventh floor. This upper level was relatively quiet, mainly because the staff was refusing to take the sometimes malfunctioning turbolifts, and it was too difficult to get the hover-gurneys up the stairwells. There wasn't much on this floor that could help anyone process or treat the dying patients anyhow; it was mostly reserved for the private offices of the doctors and administrators, in addition to break rooms for the support staff.

Bashir stopped at the door to one of the administration offices, trying to open it. It wouldn't budge. He saw that it required an identification badge, and noted that the reader was dark. *Probably not working, like a lot of things around here.* He wondered if whatever shielding had protected most of the hospital from the blasts was thinner here on the upper floors. That would certainly give the besieged staff another reason not to bring the joined up past the first few levels.

Looking up and down the halls to make certain he was alone, Bashir grabbed the lid from a trash receptacle and smashed it into the glass of the office door. Despite the loudness of the sound, he didn't hear any footfalls or cries of alarm.

Gingerly he reached inside and opened the door, then let himself into the offices. He quickly settled in behind one of the desks and activated the computer system. For a moment, the viewscreen was dark, and he felt stupid. *If the door reader wasn't working, what made me think the computers would still be running?*

But then the screen flickered to life. The interface was different from most of the designs he was used to, but at the Academy he had become familiar with a multitude of diverse computer systems.

He began the obvious search patterns, trolling both the Trill medical database and the Symbiosis Commission database. Bethan Roa. Roa, Bethan. Roa symbiont.

No records found within the search parameters. Ignoring the on-screen message, he considered others who had known Roa.

Verad Kalon. Kalon, Verad.

No records found within the search parameters.

Duhan Vos. Vos, Duhan. Vos symbiont.

Finally, a pair of records came up, and Bashir read them quickly. The symbiont Vos had been joined to Duhan Weckna some twenty-five years ago, then the joined Trill had ascended to the Symbiosis Commission in 2373. Just as Dr. Torvin had already told him, Vos had been removed from his post about a year later, while under investigation for financial improprieties. His file ended abruptly, as though Vos had ceased to exist at that time.

Bashir cursed. Unless he could find some other link to Bethan Roa's apparently lost research, there would be no help for hundreds of joined Trills whose connection to their symbionts had been sundered by the radiation blasts.

Wearily, he stood up from his seat and exited the office, glass crunching beneath his boots.

Dr. Torvin had said that Bashir's medical help would be useful elsewhere in the hospital, and every second he spent looking for the evidently nonexistent research of Bethan Roa, another life might be lost. *And Trill cannot afford to lose any more than it has already lost today,* he thought, his spirits downcast.

Bashir stepped into the cool stairwell and began his descent back into the hell that waited below.

The morning sun blazed across the distant, snow-capped mountains as Ranul Keru stood just inside the cavern entrance, watching the gathering on the rocky plain below with increasing trepidation. The crowd had become boisterous in the half hour since Keru had watched Ezri Dax descend into the symbiont pools.

"What's riling them up now?" he asked General Taulin Cyl, who stood nearby on a rocky outcropping that led to the entrance to the Caves of Mak'ala. The general was conferring with one of the military guards.

"We don't know," Cyl said. "We have managed to target some of the ringleaders, and from the way they've been checking their chronometers, they're expecting something to happen soon."

"Coordinated attacks?" Keru asked. "Could they be moving against other spawning grounds or the Symbiosis Commission?"

Cyl scowled. "Unfortunately, all communications out of here are still being jammed. We don't know what's happening elsewhere, and I doubt anybody outside of the caves is hearing the signals we're broadcasting either."

Keru surveyed the crowd. Some of them certainly fit the profile of the disheveled, wild-eyed unjoined revolutionary, but more than a few didn't. A few protesters displayed placards emblazoned with such slogans as JOINED FOR UNJOINED RIGHTS and MY DAUGHTER DESERVES A SYMBIONT, TOO! He was only mildly surprised to see that joined Trills had rallied to the cause of the disgruntled unjoined majority. Like every Guardian who made it through the Order's probationary period, he understood the intrinsic unfairness of the way the benefits of symbiosis were distributed among a populace taught since birth to strive to become respected links in a great mnemonic chain. He simply had never seen a better alternative. There were many humanoids who wished to be joined, and only a relative handful of available symbionts. And those symbionts required his protection, now more than ever.

It's not the symbionts' fault that our society has flaws. It's our fault. If we want a fairer world, then we humanoids will have to build it ourselves. Keru knew that he wasn't unique in holding this opinion; many of the protesters gathered here at Mak'ala, as well as those congregating in the cities, were indeed working to change Trill society; Keru took issue only with some of the means being employed, rather than the ends.

He heard a faint clattering sound coming from the rock face that extended to the summit of the mountain from which Mak'ala was carved, and turned to see some small stone fragments tumble onto a nearby overhead ledge. He looked up, the hairs on the back of his neck bristling.

"General! Above us!"

Keru did a quick count. Eight people, men and women garbed in utilitarian gray paramilitary garb, were rappelling down the cavern wall toward them, descending rapidly on whip-thin cords. Several of them were conspicuously armed. Keru assumed that they must have had themselves surreptitiously beamed onto the mountain's summit, or to some discreet place nearby. Evidently their unexpected entrance had also enabled them to overcome the small contingent of guards Cyl had assigned to the high terrain.

Even as the general and his guard drew their phasers, three of the intruders opened fire from above. Keru ducked and rolled into the cover of the cave entrance, shouting to the other Guardians as he moved. "We're under attack! Eight intruders, from above!"

Rantic Lan, one of the youngest members of the Order, threw him the Starfleet phaser that Dax had left behind. Keru caught it one-handed, then whirled back toward the entrance. He saw booted feet descending from above and waited, timing his shot. A moment later, when the first torso became visible from inside the shelter of the cavern entrance, he fired, sending the attacker spinning off the ledge; stunned, the intruder dropped his weapon and swung limply, entangled in his own rappelling line.

Keru rushed toward the ledge as the Guardians arrayed themselves behind him. He could hear shouts and sounds of fighting coming from the direction of the crowd outside; apparently the demonstrators had begun openly clashing with the Trill military contingent as well.

Before he could determine what had happened to Cyl and the other soldier, several more attackers leaned around the cavern entrance, firing particle weapons into the cave. Keru felt one blast singe his shoulder, and then heard a cry from one of his fellow Guardians behind him. Ducking behind an outcropping of the stony wall, Keru returned fire, but he knew it wouldn't be long before his position was pinned down. *And I'm the only one down here with phaser.*

A barrage of fire rained onto his position, confirming his fear that his time was quickly running out. Then, he heard the sound of more phaser fire, this time from well outside the cave entrance. Keru peeked around the rock formation before him to see a second attacker fall, even as the remaining six spilled into the passageway a few meters away.

Keru tried to get a bead on the nearest of them but was distracted as a dozen or so other Guardians moved into offensive mode. Armed with nothing more than wooden staves, knives, and fists, they ran to defend the caves and the helpless symbionts in their charge. But the interlopers apparently had both phasers and disruptors—as well as no apparent compunctions against hitting one of their own.

These bastards are on a suicide mission. That thought turned Keru's heart to ice, but also galvanized him into action.

Keru tucked the phaser into his tunic, having decided that the odds of hitting another Guardian were too great to risk trying to take another shot. Running across the dimly lit, rocky chamber, he tackled a man who was stabbing Pran Sevos with the elderly Guardian's own knife. They rolled to the side of the wounded Pran, but Keru couldn't get a firm grip since his foe was slippery with his victim's blood. The attacker grimaced as he raised the knife, but Keru drove a knee hard into his attacker's abdomen, forcing the air from his lungs and sending his knife skittering across the cavern floor. Rising to his feet, Keru slammed his adversary's much smaller body into a rocky wall, knocking him senseless.

Then Keru heard a phaser burst, and saw that Pran's attacker had crumpled at the base of the wall.

Turning, Keru saw Cyl standing with a phaser in his hand. He was a bit bruised and bloodied, but didn't appear to be seriously injured. He noticed that the fighting that had begun so quickly in the entranceway was mostly over already. The intruders apparently weren't used to fighting in close quarters inside a darkened cave. The surviving Guardians were already moving to administer first aid to Pran and several other wounded Guardians, after having subdued the remaining five attackers.

Six, Keru thought with a start. *There were* six *of them!* He scrambled down the passageway toward the interior of the caves and saw a female Guardian named Nelenne Lef lying prostrate on the ground ahead. After stopping to confirm that she was merely stunned, he moved beyond her as quickly as he could. *Luckily, I know the passageways better than this intruder does,* Keru thought, trying not to be distracted by worry over his fallen friend.

A moment later he turned a corner and saw a gray-garbed man ahead of him, running down the passage toward the pools. Keru skidded to a stop and grabbed a loose piece of flattened rock from the cave floor. As a child he had been a champion rock-skipper at the Lake Ograls Celebration Days Festival; the aim and skill he had acquired in those carefree days had later made him a formidable velocity opponent during his time in Starfleet.

Keru took a breath and drew his arm back, then brought it forward again in one seamless, fluid motion. The rock whizzed through the air and struck the running man squarely at the base of his spine. With a hoarse cry, the attacker dropped to the ground as though poleaxed. Keru didn't need to check; he knew the invader wouldn't be running anywhere anytime soon.

Rejoining the others, Keru informed them of the injured attacker back in the passageways, then turned to Cyl. "It sounds like they're mounting a full-scale attack outside."

"Yes," Cyl said. "And my men are severely outnumbered."

With some of the Guardians trailing behind them, Keru and Cyl ran back to the outer cave entrance to survey the scene below. The military men were just barely holding the line, but the crowds were steadily pushing them closer to the base of the cliffs—and to the pathways leading to Mak'ala's entrance.

Speaking in clipped military tones, Keru and Cyl briefly discussed their options. There weren't many. Even if the military detachment were to set their weapons to kill, the vast majority of the survivors would quickly overwhelm the skirmish line. Mak'ala would then fall to the angry throngs, and the symbionts would be at their mercy.

Prompted by his Starfleet training, Keru considered another option. He pointed to the Federation runabout that was parked about ten meters behind the skirmish line. "If I can get down to the *Rio Grande,* General, I think I might be able to do something about this."

Cyl nodded, his own thoughts apparently moving in precisely the same direction. "Let's do it."

Moments later, after having left the Guardians armed with the particle weapons taken from their attackers, Keru and Cyl had reached the cover of a rocky outcropping only meters away from the runabout. The igneous stone formation formed a low escarpment that rose perhaps three meters above the spacecraft's dorsal surface.

"If we try to reach the hatch, we'll be directly in the crowd's line of fire," said Cyl.

Keru had noticed the same thing. "Give me some cover fire. I think I can get inside."

Cyl checked the charge on his phaser. "What exactly are you planning on doing?"

Keru grinned. "I'm going to put up an electric fence—Starfleet style."

Cyl nodded, a grin of his own slowly spreading across his weather-beaten face. He raised his phaser. "I'll give you some covering fire. Ready when you are, Mister Keru."

Keru nodded, took a deep breath, and stepped back three paces, his heart racing. *You don't know how much you miss the adventure until it's gone,* he thought. Sprinting forward, he launched himself off the ledge and into the cool morning air.

Even as he heard the whine of Cyl's covering fire, Keru landed in a crouch on top of the runabout, skidding forward to a point just behind the cockpit. Flattening his body as best he could, he spider-crawled his way toward the center of the craft, where—in response to the authorization code he tapped into a discreetly concealed keypad—a round access hatch opened into the Jefferies tube that connected with the runabout's interior. He felt the vessel rock slightly in response to a few quick pulses of phaser fire; fortunately, none of the hits appeared to have had any great effect on the runabout's hull. *Well, they know I'm here,* Keru thought with a grim smile. *But they probably don't know what's coming next.*

Quickly making his way forward to the cockpit, Keru sat down at the aft port system chair, where he activated the tactical systems.

He studied the readouts for a moment, his mind racing to try to figure out exactly how he was going to accomplish what he needed to do. *It's been too long since I've piloted so much as a simulator,* he thought, finally beginning to doubt his chances of success. He knew that Sean, a career conn officer, would have been able to do this blindfolded. *What would* he *have done?*

A minute passed, then two. And then, as though guided by the hands of his dead lover, Keru knew exactly what he needed to do.

Once Keru had reached the top of the runabout, Cyl scrambled down the slope, barely managing to avoid a rapid volley of blasts. He'd made himself a target, hoping to divert the radicals' attention from the massive Guardian.

Cyl felt safe for the moment, crouched behind the portable duranium blast shields that the small military unit had erected between themselves and the mob. Still, he was saddened to see that several of his soldiers had been captured by the protesters during the skirmishes.

He caught the attention of the highest-ranking person he could find. "Lieutenant, when I give the command—which I'm hoping to do within about two minutes—I want all of our troops to retreat by twenty meters."

The young female officer looked bewildered. "Twenty meters? Sir, we'll literally be up against the cave entrance. We'll be giving up all our maneuvering room."

"You won't need it if what we have planned works. If it doesn't work, I won't give the signal. Just tell the troops."

With a worried glance, the lieutenant began relaying the order down the line.

Cyl kept his eye on the runabout, trying to clear his mind of the shouts and shots that rang through the air. The seconds ticked by. *One minute.*

He realized that he was holding his breath, and exhaled. *Two minutes.* Another thirty seconds passed.

A beam of pale, bluish light suddenly flashed out of the forward viewport of the spacecraft. "Now, Lieutenant!" Cyl barked.

"Retreat!" the lieutenant yelled, and the embattled soldiers stepped backward.

For a moment, the crowd was unsure what was happening, and then they surged forward *en masse*—and were just as quickly stopped, their bodies bouncing off an immovable object. Their phaser blasts ricocheted in midair, as did several rocks and other projectiles the protesters threw.

The lieutenant and several of his men looked over at Cyl, puzzled expressions on their faces. Cyl grinned and pointed to the runabout. "Our Guardian friend modified the ship's force fields to enclose everything from the skirmish line to the cave's entrance. Nobody is going to get into the caves *now.*"

The soldiers cheered, some of them pounding each other on the back. Almost all of them, Cyl was pleased to note, remained vigilant.

Then one of the nearby troopers pointed into the crowd, calling to the lieutenant. "Sir! The hostiles are driving a vehicle toward us!"

Cyl turned to see that someone had indeed driven a cargo skimmer into the crowd, which was now stirred well toward panic. The general hoped that common sense would entice the gathering to disperse before anyone was seriously hurt.

"Don't worry," Cyl told the lieutenant as he watched the skimmer make its herky-jerky approach through the crowd. "They can't get that thing through the force field." He felt reasonably certain that the Starfleet shields would hold easily against such a relatively unsophisticated attack.

But the driver didn't seem intent on continuing his approach to the shield boundary. Instead, he stopped, exited the skimmer, and scrambled onto the vehicle's roof.

Cyl couldn't hear what the driver was shouting, but in a

blink, the skimmer exploded with light, forcing him to avert his eyes. Cyl's dazzled eyes could barely make out the multicolored disturbances in the runabout's force fields, punctuated by tiny, short-lived conflagrations that resembled thousands of glowing, flame-loving *mun'ika* bugs stupidly immolating themselves in a fire.

Then his vision went white. Inside his abdomen, the Cyl symbiont spasmed in agony, sending waves of pain through every system in his body.

What have they done? Cyl thought just before a blanket of darkness mercifully replaced the excruciating white light.

His vision still slowly clearing perhaps a minute after the dazzling light-pulse had come and gone, Keru found he had to open the runabout's hatch manually, since some of the ship's electrical systems seemed to have failed. Luckily, a backup console confirmed that his improvised force field was continuing to hold. Not that it mattered much at the moment, since everyone outside was either writhing on the ground or not moving at all.

The runabout's sensors could tell him precious little about the detonation. Though the blast wave had consisted primarily of a fairly standard electromagnetic pulse, it also had apparently carried some unknown type of fast-dissipating radiation. The radiation evidently hadn't penetrated the runabout's hull, where its shields were strongest, but might well have pierced the force fields nearest the cave entrance, where the fields would have been at their most attenuated. Fortunately, the readings confirmed that there was little if any danger now of his being exposed to lingering radiation. Hoping no other bombs were present, he opened the force field where it surrounded the hatch and clambered outside.

As he approached the soldiers, Keru was grateful to see that most of them appeared to be either temporarily stunned or dazzled by the flash. None of them seemed to have been hurt nearly as badly as had those on the other side of the force field.

Except for one. Taulin Cyl.

The general lay on his back, and Keru could see that his abdomen was roiling beneath his uniform jacket. *His symbiont is going into shock.* Keru had only seen this happen twice before during his brief tenure as a Guardian. On both occasions, they had tried to save the symbiont by returning it to the pools; only once had their efforts succeeded.

Keru yelled over to two of the soldiers who seemed the least affected by the blast. "Come help me with General Cyl! We've got to get him into the caves!"

Minutes later, they had managed to carry him down from the rocky outcropping that overlooked the plain and up into the cavern's mountainside entrance, where it seemed that the majority of the Guardians were also mostly unaffected by the blast; only those who had been nearest the entrance during the detonation were partially blinded, and none showed any other ill effects. But as they brought Cyl nearer to the pools, Keru heard a mournful keening issuing from deeper in the caves.

Keru saw several of the Guardians standing near the closest of the pools, watched them screaming and thrusting their hands into the murky water, witnessed the shock and despair etched into their faces as they turned and regarded their equally horrified brethren. And then he saw why they were wailing.

The surfaces of the pools were clotted with floating symbionts, but the only movements they made were either the result of the Guardians trying vainly to assist them, or were caused by other symbionts floating up from below, jostling the small lumpen bodies that bobbed on the surface like so many rotting bogblossoms.

Keru and the others fell to their knees as the enormity of the situation became apparent. *They've killed the symbionts.* The thought came as a scream in Keru's mind, and he couldn't be certain that he hadn't shouted it aloud.

Cyl groaned and reached up to clutch his arm. "Something's . . . wrong with . . ." He seemed too fatigued and distressed to finish his warning.

Knowing that the time to grieve would have to wait until later, Keru stood and dragged Cyl toward the largest of the pools, the one that Dax had dived into just an hour or so earlier. Many of the floating symbionts had already begun to sink again, like balloons that were losing their air.

"We need to extract his symbiont," Keru shouted to a pair of Guardians who stood nearby, looking stunned. "It's still alive." He removed Cyl's jacket and pushed him into the water, entering the pool with the general. He held Cyl's arms to keep him from flopping face-first into the water.

And then, miraculously, a silver discharge arced across the water toward Cyl. Moments later, a weaker discharge came from the general's bloated abdominal pouch, and Keru saw dark, indistinct movement underneath the pool's gray surface.

"They're communicating!" one of the Guardians shouted. "They're not dead, at least not all of them."

Cyl rolled in the water and looked toward Keru, his eyes ablaze with a light that resembled insanity. "I need to go down there. Dax is in trouble."

"What?" Keru was unsure he had heard the general correctly.

"Dax is still down in the deep pools. She needs my help. Fal told me. Get me an environmental suit."

"Sir . . ."

Cyl's eyes met his with an imploring look. "Get it now, Mister Keru. Please. We haven't much time."

Two Guardians held Cyl in place as Keru climbed from the pool and ran out of the caves into the gathering night. He was out of breath and shivering by the time he reached the runabout to fetch the remaining two environmental suits, but he didn't allow himself to pause for breath. By the time he got back to the pools, he felt as if his lungs were on fire.

Keru saw that the general was sitting on the rocks at the side of the pool. Though he looked as pale as death, Cyl wore an expression of defiant determination.

"I haven't been affected by the blast, General," Keru said. "I ought to go with you." *Or instead of you,* he thought.

"I'm perfectly capable of handling this on my own, Mister Keru." Cyl took one of the suits from Keru's big hands and started donning it.

Keru scowled, not fooled for a moment by the general's brave show. He reached for the other suit and began putting it on. Cyl laid an unsteady hand on his shoulder, stopping him.

"No. Stay here, Mister Keru. You have injured friends who need first aid. More importantly, you have to tend to the symbionts. The few who've survived are going to need your help badly."

"You're . . . not well, General."

"That's not as important at the moment as making certain that Lieutenant Dax fulfills her mission."

Finally accepting the inevitability of Cyl's decision, Keru set his own suit down and began to help Cyl finish suiting up. As he worked, Keru heard volitional movement from at least one other symbiont in the pool, a sign that both buoyed his spirits and confirmed that the general was right. *The symbionts are going to need my help more than they ever have before.*

As he locked the helmet to the environmental suit's neck ring, Keru noticed that Cyl now seemed calmer, more in command of himself. But intense pain remained evident in the general's eyes, and was betrayed by the random, spasmodic twitches of his forehead and jawline.

"Thank you for everything you've done here today," the general said, once again placing his gloved hand on Keru's shoulder. "And neither Cyl nor I blame you for what has happened. Without your help, many more of us would be gone."

It didn't escape Keru that the general had referred to the symbiont within him as though it were a separate entity. He wondered if the words the general had spoken hadn't come entirely from either Taulin or Cyl. *His symbiosis is dissolving,* he thought, and a profound sadness settled across his soul.

"If you're not back in two hours, I'm coming after you," Keru said.

Fully suited, Taulin Cyl stepped into the pool and slipped beneath the murky, corpse-strewn waters. Keru watched him vanish, leaving not even a stream of bubbles in his wake. He wished he'd asked the general if he had any messages he wanted relayed to his loved ones.

And hoped he wouldn't have to fulfill that same promise for Ezri Dax.

Stardate 53777.6

Bashir rejoined the busy trauma teams mere minutes before a veritable flood of new injured patients entered the already bustling triage center. Except for a few dozen unjoined individuals who had suffered grievous injuries—apparently as a result of hovercar failures and the like caused by the bombs' radiation pulses—virtually all of the first hundred or so patients to be carried, dragged, or gurneyed into Manev Central Hospital were joined Trills.

Though the sudden influx of ailing and dying joined had stretched the hospital's already strained resources well past their limits, Bashir knew that he and his medical colleagues had no choice but to soldier on. He tried his best to attend to the unjoined who seemed a secondary priority to the staff. Over the course of the next hour or so, he came to understand clearly that the joined *had* to be bumped to the head of the line. The sight of the lifeless body of Dr. Renhol—the woman from the Symbiosis Commission whose desire for Trill secrecy he had accommodated five years earlier—brought that realization home with brutal finality. Her symbiont had been removed and transported either to a symbiont-specific care facility, or back to Mak'ala or one of the other breeding pools. Nobody seemed to know whether or not it had survived.

It occurred to him that Renhol had been the prominent commissioner who'd been gurneyed into the trauma room while he was preoccupied with saving the life of a grievously injured small boy. Though he didn't regret the choice he'd made, Renhol's passing pained him nonetheless.

Another thing that bothered him was that nearly all the medical personnel here—joined and unjoined alike, from Dr. Vadel Torvin on down—seemed far too quick to sacrifice the hosts of those injured symbionts. The hosts whom Dr. Torvin had declared beyond saving—despite the fact that most of them had sustained no life-threatening injuries—received about as much regard as had the hospital's backlog of unjoined casualties.

Which was to say they were being ignored completely.

Now bereft of their symbionts, fourteen former hosts were currently being left untended even as the medics carefully transferred their symbionts into nutrient-rich, hyronalin-saturated mobile symbiont pools in preparation for their transportation to Mak'ala or one of Trill's other natural symbiont habitats. In this way, the Trill doctors hoped to save the symbionts' accumulated memories and experiences, though the hosts that had carried the creatures were to be sacrificed to accomplish this.

But Bashir knew that there was no guarantee that the symbiont pools would be of any help to the creatures. Many of them seemed simply too far gone from the radiation their delicate and extraordinarily complex neural tissues had absorbed. And he wasn't even sure that the very same terrorist weapons that had detonated in central Leran Manev hadn't also been placed elsewhere. Who was to say that other such devices hadn't also irradiated the Mak'ala pools?

Still, he had to concede that he could suggest no workable alternative to the removal of the symbionts—at least not yet, though he hadn't stopped querying the hospital computers about alternative methodologies. And despite the megadoses of isoboramine and other symbiogenic neurotransmitters he had injected into scores of other dying joined people, they were growing progressively weaker, expiring right before his eyes. Their symbioses inevitably grew tenuous, rapidly dissolving as each of the symbionts went into convulsive neuroleptic shock. The joined who had taken the brunt of the neurogenic pulses were experiencing extreme autoimmune reactions, rejecting their symbionts as though the creatures were foreign, invading bodies.

It struck Bashir as ironic that this was precisely how the symbionts were regarded by the neo-Purist radicals, who were the only really likely culprits behind the radiation attacks.

One of the hardest things for a doctor to do was to watch a patient die. But Bashir seemed to have little choice in the matter. He knew all too well that a joining between a compatible host and a symbiont would become permanent after the first several days, after which time the host would be incapable of surviving without the symbiont. After crossing this physiological threshold, the two effectively merged into a single, indissoluble being. To separate symbiont from host past that point was to kill the host, just as surely as a terrestrial human would die following the removal of his or her liver, even though the organ might live on via transplantation to another person's body.

From the severity of their autoimmune reactions, Bashir expected most of these hosts to take an hour or less to die once their symbionts were extracted. A few expired almost instantly after the removal of their symbionts, despite his best efforts to save them.

Such is the Trill reverence for the preservation of memories, he told himself as yet another host, a middle-aged woman, slipped away from him. He hoped that her radiation-plagued symbiont would somehow find a means of regenerating itself in the network of aqueous subterranean caverns where the unjoined symbionts spawned and recuperated between joinings. At least the dead woman's experiences would live on in the symbiont, assuming it survived.

As always, he found it difficult to wrap his mind around the alien notion that some sentient beings were valued more highly than others, merely because of their lengthy life spans and backlogs of memories. It was an idea antithetical to his way of thinking, his tolerant and egalitarian Starfleet training notwithstanding. Indeed, he was beginning to find the entire concept repellent, whatever societal necessities might underlie it.

Worst of all, he remained certain that a remedy of some sort existed—if not for the symbionts specifically targeted by the neurogenic weapons, then for the Trill humanoids who were dying because of their dissolving symbioses.

There was no question that a drug possessing the latter property had been developed. Based on what Benjamin Sisko and

Jadzia Dax had told him four years earlier, a drug of this sort had been perfected by a now-deceased joined Trill scientist named Bethan Roa, and had in fact been used successfully by the late unjoined Trill malcontent Verad Kalon. Bethan Roa's serum had enabled Verad to steal Trill Symbiosis Commissioner Duhan Vos's symbiont without killing its host, and later enabled the removal of both the Roa and Vos symbionts from their respective unauthorized hosts, without bringing significant harm either to humanoid or symbiont.

Unfortunately, Bashir himself had never had an opportunity to make a firsthand appraisal of Bethan Roa's pharmacological work. When Bashir had asked Dr. Torvin about it, the Trill physician not only had insisted that no such serum existed, but also was adamant that no such thing was even possible.

And if Bashir's initial cursory search of the official Trill medical database was to be believed, Dr. Roa himself might as well never have existed.

Though Bashir had no way to prove it, he smelled yet another cover-up. Not for the first time, he wished Ezri were here to help him get to the bottom of it. After all, she knew the peculiarities of her own homeworld's record-keeping systems far better than he did.

As had been his practice ever since the first wave of dying joined patients had arrived at the triage center, Bashir tried to avoid considering what had become of Ezri. Though he hadn't heard from her—or succeeded in getting a signal through to her—since she had departed for Mak'ala, he had picked up some fragmentary reports of neurogenic blasts in other locales around Trill. Neurogenic attacks had even been reported near some of the symbiont spawning grounds.

Is Ezri even still alive? he wondered yet again before forcibly pushing the thought aside. He had other, more immediate things to consider.

Bashir and Torvin had just finished making the rounds of a cramped, makeshift "joined ward," where more than sixty joined Trills lay dying, though their symbionts had yet to be extracted. The unconscious had been placed on cots, gurneys, improvised tables, or even the floor. Several of the stricken appeared to be awake, though their eyes were unfocused and staring, the smooth melding of symbiont and host that characterized a healthy joining utterly disrupted. A few issued intermittent but piercing shrieks.

Each of these incoherent madhouse cries made Bashir wonder whether the host or the symbiont was screaming.

"We've waited long enough," Dr. Torvin was saying, shaking his balding head sadly as they moved through the crowded ward, surveying the hapless patients.

Bashir's stomach went into free fall as he walked beside the tall, gangly Trill physician. "What are you saying, Doctor?"

Torvin scowled as he brought the peripatetic appraisal of the ward to a halt. "I think you know what I'm saying, Doctor Bashir. We have to begin the wholesale extraction of the symbionts carried by these hosts, immediately. If we wait much longer, it may be too late."

"Doctor Torvin, if we remove the symbionts, these people will die, just like the others. We can't go on sacrificing people this way."

"We have no better options," Torvin said, shaking his head. "You've seen that. Sometimes a host must be sacrificed so that a symbiont can live on."

"But not if an alternative exists. If we could find some record of Bethan Roa's work on nonlethal symbiosis dissolution, we could at least—"

"Roa again," Torvin interrupted, his frown taking on more ferocity since the last time Bashir had tried to discuss this subject with him. "I thought we'd been through all this before, Doctor. I've already explained to you that no such thing exists."

Bashir had finally had enough of Trill denial. "Yes. You have. And I don't doubt that you're right, at least as far as Roa's files are concerned."

"What are you saying?" Torvin asked guardedly.

"I'm saying that Roa's work appears to have been the subject of yet another whitewash by the Trill Symbiosis Commission."

Torvin's frown gave way to an amalgam of pique and bewilderment. "Why would you say that?"

Bashir tried to tamp down his rising anger, with only limited success. "Because your society is at war with itself at this very moment, apparently as a direct result of your government's rather checkered history with regard to such things. Because your world's official database contains no references to Roa's work—work whose results other Starfleet officers can verify independently. And because the Trill Symbiosis Commission's joining registry does not reveal the current status of the Roa symbiont.

"Let me speak plainly, Doctor Torvin: I believe that the Commission doesn't want anyone to interview Roa's new host, assuming there is one, about Bethan Roa's symbiosis dissolution serum."

Torvin gestured broadly at the dozens of people who lay suffering all about the small, curtained-off section of the room. His expression took on a desperate cast. "A drug that would allow us to remove symbionts for radiation treatments without killing these people would be a great boon, I should think. We're not monsters, Doctor Bashir. If such a thing really *did* exist, then why would anyone want to see it suppressed?"

Based on Torvin's reaction, Bashir was now willing to bet that the Trill doctor wasn't a direct participant in any Symbiosis Commission cover-up of the Roa formula. In Bashir's eyes, Torvin genuinely did not seem to be a political animal.

But that didn't mean he couldn't have been duped and manipulated by others who were highly motivated to bury Roa's work, and keep it buried.

Bashir held up a hand in a gesture of truce. "Doctor Torvin, imagine what might happen if it became known that symbiosis could be undertaken on a temporary basis. That the bond between symbiont and host could be established, then broken, then established again just as easily with a new host. The symbiont population is relatively small as it is, They would become a sought-after black-market commodity if Roa's drug were to become common knowledge."

Torvin looked horrified for a long moment, then began nodding slowly. He actually seemed to be considering alternatives to simply letting more hosts die, giving Bashir a surge of renewed hope.

Then the Trill physician sighed, looking downcast and shaking his silver-fringed head yet again. "Unfortunately, when the Commission decides to bury something, it tends to stay buried."

Bashir thought bitterly of the unrest that had spilled onto the streets of Leran Manev and so many other Trill cities prior to the bombings. And the secrecy that had caused it all in the first place.

Then a sudden inspiration seized Bashir's imagination. "Not always, Doctor Torvin." He turned toward the main section of the triage center, intent on finding the nearest computer terminal.

More perplexed than ever, Torvin took a step toward him. "Doctor Bashir! Where are you going?"

Bashir paused at the curtain that separated the makeshift "joined ward" from the rest of the triage center. "Can you keep these hosts and their symbionts joined and alive for, say, another hour without endangering the symbionts?"

"Perhaps, at least with some of them. But the sooner we remove the symbionts, the better their chances for survival."

Bashir smiled, his mind already racing. "Then please hold off for as long as you can."

He left the ward at a run.

Bashir focused his attention on the computer terminal before him, tuning out the shrieks and screams of the dying as best he could.

As in his previous round of computer queries, no record remained of any relevant pharmacological work by anyone named Bethan Roa. Reasoning that Roa's serum would have been present in trace amounts in his symbiont's neural fluids, Bashir accessed the database of Gheryzan Hospital. He knew that the state-of-the-art facility's symbiont trauma center had treated the Roa symbiont after Jadzia Dax's sister Ziranne had rescued it from a ring of symbiont thieves. Working quickly, he searched for the symbiont's confidential medical records. As he navigated through the database, he began making plans to crack Roa's files open, recalling a few "hacks" he had learned from his holoprogrammer friend Felix.

Damn. Bashir's heart sank. Whatever medical records Gheryzon Hospital might have had on the Roa symbiont had apparently been either deleted or sealed. The Commission had been thorough indeed in its cover-up—a whitewash for which he now felt partly responsible. *I should have demanded that the Commission allow me to study Roa's formula five years ago. People are dying because I thought it better to let them keep their damned secrets.*

He sat in silence for perhaps a minute, despair threatening to overwhelm him.

Then it occurred to him that Roa's formula would also have been present in at least one other place.

His hands moving with preternatural speed, he made a second query.

A few moments later, a jubilant grin spread across his face.

Torvin waited as long as he felt he could. But less than twenty minutes after Dr. Bashir had left the room, four of the afflicted joined Trills in Ward C suddenly took an abrupt turn for the worse. With the assistance of a trio of other surgeons and several medical technicians and nurses, Torvin removed a quartet of radiation-injured symbionts from their convulsing, screaming hosts. Although Torvin was trained to maintain an emotional distance from his patients, the sight was almost too horrible to behold.

Two of these hosts, both of them males, died with what Torvin could only regard under the circumstances as almost merciful swiftness. The third, an elderly woman, hung on for nearly ten minutes, shrieking in agony until the very end. Torvin pronounced the fourth host, a comatose young woman who had never regained consciousness, dead not six minutes later.

One of the dying joined patients who lay restrained on a nearby table suddenly screamed. The haggard middle-aged woman's eyes were wide open, gray-clouded and sightless. Her limbs strained against their restraints as she began to convulse vigorously enough to break her own bones. Torvin took a quick step backward, then directed a pair of med-techs to prepare to remove her symbiont as well.

A scant two minutes later, Torvin held a laser exoscalpel over the struggling woman's bare abdomen, preparing to begin the extraction process.

"Stop!" barked a voice from behind Torvin. It startled him, almost making him drop the scalpel.

He turned angrily toward the source of the sound, only to be greeted by an incongruously ebullient Dr. Bashir. The human physician was holding up a loaded hypospray as though for inspection.

"I've reconstructed Bethan Roa's formula," he said.

Torvin felt his eyes narrowing involuntarily. He couldn't afford to permit himself to believe that it might be true. He realized for the first time that he hadn't even considered the possibility that Bashir might actually succeed in his quest.

"Where did you find it?" was all Torvin could think of to say.

"Roa wasn't the only symbiont whose tissues would have carried traces of the formula," Bashir said quickly, his words tumbling out in a rush. "It was also present in Duhan Vos's medical records. Apparently, the Commission opted merely to seal the records of his admission to Gheryzan Hospital rather than to delete them altogether."

Torvin's eyebrows shot skyward, and he noticed that several nearby nurses and medics had paused to stare. This was not a conversation he wanted to have in front of them. He felt his skin redden with anger at the violation of his fellow commissioner's confidential records. And though he was curious about exactly *how* the Starfleet doctor had managed to do such a thing, he decided the question was moot. The human obviously possessed considerable talent in fields other than medicine, and the deed had already been done.

"You had no right to break into Vos's files," Torvin said, suddenly realizing he was gripping his exoscalpel almost tightly enough to shatter it.

The human's smile gave way to a look of quiet determination. "You may, of course, feel free to file an official protest with Starfleet Command. In the meantime, we have lives to save." He approached the patient who still lay restrained and convulsing on the table.

Torvin stepped into his path, raising the scalpel in a gesture of warning. It occurred to him only then that its glowing orange blade was still active. "I'm sorry, Doctor. I simply can't allow you to put this woman's symbiont at risk with an experimental procedure."

Bashir took another step forward, as though daring Torvin to use the scalpel as a weapon. The hand that carried the hypospray didn't waver. But then neither did Torvin's scalpel.

Torvin began to repeat himself. "Doctor Bashir, I'm afraid I can't permit you to—"

Moving more quickly than Torvin thought possible, Bashir weaved around him, evading not only the scalpel but also the grasp of a burly male med-tech who had evidently tried to run interference for Torvin.

With a loud hiss, Bashir's hypo deposited its contents directly into the convulsing woman's abdominal pouch. Cursing, the med-tech grabbed Bashir in a wrestler's hold and began dragging him bodily toward the door. Though the human doctor was a good deal smaller than the medic, he was clearly determined not to be moved quickly or easily.

Anger seared Torvin's breast. Though he shared Bashir's compassion for the unfortunate hosts who were losing their lives, such blatant interference with his medical practice simply couldn't be tolerated. "You'd better believe I'll be telling your superiors about this, Doctor Bashir. Your Starfleet career is *finished.*"

"Maybe," Bashir said, still struggling against the med-tech's grip. "But that hardly seems as important as all the lives you're prepared to sacrifice merely for expediency's sake." He gestured with his head toward the woman who lay on the table. Torvin spared a glance at her.

And noticed that she had stopped convulsing. His first thought was that Bashir's unauthorized treatment had killed her. Then he noticed that she was beginning to take deep, regular breaths.

"Let him go," Torvin said. Bashir fell unceremoniously to the floor.

"I think it's clear that you don't want these hosts to die any more than I do, Doctor Torvin," Bashir said, still sprawled on the floor while the med-tech continued eyeing him warily. "I also think you realize that your world's 'symbionts first' ethic is what's largely to blame for all the upheaval your people have been experiencing lately."

Torvin quickly examined the woman, his plisagraph reporting that her vital signs now appeared unaccountably stronger. The symbiont still needed to be removed for radiation treatment, of course, but doing so didn't appear to pose a mortal threat to the host. It was the closest thing to a miracle Torvin had ever seen.

Torvin's earlier anger at Bashir quickly yielded to a flash of self-loathing. Had his own loyalty to the Symbiosis Commission made him lose sight of what was right and what was wrong? Had he forgotten what it meant to be a doctor? *If I had taken the cost of the Commission's secrecy into account, then perhaps Doctor Renhol would still be alive.*

Within seconds his self-disgust was eclipsed by hope. Hope that Bashir's wild idea might actually work on the other patients who lay around the room, dying.

Torvin approached Bashir. Extending a long, wiry arm, he helped the human doctor back to his feet. Warm tears suddenly stung Torvin's eyes; he realized he had never before been so delighted at having been proved wrong.

"I think you and I have a great deal of work ahead of us, Doctor," Torvin said. "Don't you agree?"

Grinning, the human held up his now-empty hypospray. "Give me a few minutes with one of your pharmaceutical replicators. And alert your nurses and medics to get ready to start distributing the drug immediately."

15

"Is there another way to the surface?" Ezri Dax asked.

<<*There are many ways,*>> the caretaker symbiont said. <<*The Annuated would prefer that you return the way you came, however.*>>

"My equipment has malfunctioned. The pressure down here has put too much strain on it." Dax felt awash in sweat as her environmental suit's temperature quickly and steadily climbed. She did her best not to let the onset of panic affect her respiration or heart rate; there was nothing to be gained by wasting her few remaining life-support resources, even if she was slowly cooking inside her suit.

<<*You require rescue.*>>

There was no point trying to hold anything back from the telepathic creature, Dax realized. "That's a pretty fair observation."

<<*And none is forthcoming.*>>

"Right again."

The caretaker symbiont went silent for a protracted moment before speaking again inside Dax's mind. <<*I regret that I cannot help you. Nor can the Annuated.*>>

Of course, Dax thought with a growing sense of resignation. *This creature has to tend to these giant superslugs. They probably need constant care, so it can't just abandon them. Not even to return me to the surface.*

But she couldn't simply give up. Aloud, she said, "If I don't get back safely, the Annuated will have shared their memories with me in vain. I'll die down here, along with my symbiont. And this entire mission will have been an utter waste."

An unsettling thought occurred to her: What if the Annuated had never intended that she succeed in her quest to reveal the truth about Kurl and the parasites? Certainly, they had been generous about sharing with her thus far. On the other hand, it was hard for her not to conclude that everything that Trill humanoids knew about the symbionts was what the symbionts had decided to reveal to them, symbiosis notwithstanding. What if they had decided that Trill's deepest secrets needed to remain buried?

The caretaker's telepathic "voice" reverberated reassuringly through Dax's mind. <<*Were your symbiont to die, I would see to it that its memories are absorbed into the experiential storehouse of the Annuated.*>>

"Wonderful." The heat inside Dax's suit was rapidly growing intolerable.

Sensing sudden movement behind her, she turned to see another nearly two-meter-long symbiont swimming ponderously toward her from the direction of the monolithic, apparently slumbering forms of the Annuated. Several long, whip-thin, cilia-like tentacles streamed from its body, which was more rust-colored than the first caretaker symbiont.

The ruddy creature undulated and turned one end toward Dax. She couldn't tell whether that end was its head or its tail. <<*Vah is not the only caretaker of the Annuated, youngling. Hold fast to my appendages, and I will conduct you surface-ward.*>>

Dax reached forward and grabbed two of the tentacles. "Thank you," she said, ignoring the surge of pain in her burned hand as she established a firm grip.

The giant symbiont moved quickly forward, its armored body rippling as it swam. Dax was pulled along behind it, concentrating all her energy on controlling her breathing and keeping hold of the tentacles. Sweat streamed into her eyes from the intense heat that was flooding her damaged suit.

As they swam forward and upward, Dax noticed that she didn't recognize the cavern walls her wrist lights were illuminating, as if they were taking an alternate, more expansive route. It made sense that the larger symbionts would use larger travel arteries than would the smaller ones; no matter how slippery their hides, she couldn't imagine that either of these caretaker symbionts could have passed through the narrower lava-tube channels she had been forced to squeeze through during her initial descent.

<<*Did you find the experiences the Annuated shared with you surprising?*>> The creature asked as it knifed through the hot, murky water.

"More than you can imagine. I just hope that all the secrets I've dredged up will calm down some of the chaos that's going on now up on the surface."

The caretaker's psionic "voice" was a study in perplexity. <<*Secrets? Why would the experiences of the Annuated be secrets in the Aboveworld?*>>

The question sounded strange to Dax. "Apparently because my ancestors decided they needed to be kept that way. The destruction of Kurl was stricken from our collective history long ago."

<<*I know nothing of the history since then,*>> the symbiont said. <<*My last host chose to end her life after the Kurlan civilization was ended.*>>

Dax saw an image then, in her mind, similar to those she had received from the Annuated. This time she saw the woman who had been Private Memh, one of those who had deployed biogenic weapons on Kurl, but she was not wearing her dark military uniform. Instead she was dressed in a crimson-stained robe and was praying in her home, her blood flowing freely from the slits on her wrists as someone behind her screamed.

It wasn't *second nature to her to deploy those bombs,* Dax thought, correcting her earlier misperception. *She was numb when she pressed the button that wiped out the Kurlans. And once she could no longer lie to herself about what she'd done, she killed herself.*

"I'm sorry for you," Dax said quietly.

<<*I never joined with a Walker again,*>> the symbiont said. <<*I have stayed below, tending to those who preserve all the memories of my time. Perhaps now is the moment to bring those memories forward into your time.*>>

Dax was finding it hard to concentrate; her breath was coming in increasingly shallow gasps, and the acrid smell of her suit's burned-out heat exchanger stung her eyes. "We need to go faster. I can't last much longer." She wondered if death by asphyxiation, heatstroke, or the bends were the only options left to her.

The symbiont slowed to a stop and floated nearly motionless, and Dax thought she might have offended it somehow. "I'm sorry. I didn't mean to pressure you. But if I don't surface soon, I promise you I'm going to die," she said, her voice raspy from the oppressive heat.

The symbiont's thoughts suddenly became alarmingly discordant and jangled. <<*Something has happened above us. Something terrible. Many voices are raised, yet many more have gone silent.*>> The creature surged upward again, its pace even faster now. Dax nearly lost her grip, surprised at the sudden acceleration.

She looked up as something soft bumped against her shoulder. She saw a symbiont—an ordinary, garden-variety symbiont, she noted—brush against her hand as it swam downward. Then she realized that it was *sinking* rather than swimming. Angling one of her wrist lights upward, she craned her head back to see what was happening closer to the surface.

Above them, the hot gray water was clotted with symbionts, some moving of their own accord as they fled to the lower depths, others barely fluttering as they were carried by the currents generated by the swimmers. But she could see that many of them were not moving at all, their bodies lifeless, contracted into curls and spirals as though they had died convulsing in agony. Some of the plunging bodies emitted weak bioelectric flashes, a few of which came into direct contact with Ezri's abdomen, and the Dax symbiont that dwelled there.

Now Dax wasn't at all certain that she *should* return to the surface, though she knew her survival depended on it. The snippets of information she gleaned from the passing symbionts were scattered and garbled; even so, it was clear to her that something located near or on the surface had just brutally struck these creatures down en masse.

<<*The Walker needs help.*>> She "heard" the voice but wasn't sure whether it had come from the caretaker or one of the countless injured and dying symbionts that tumbled past her into the stygian depths.

Dax felt lightheaded. She tried to speak, but found her throat so parched that she couldn't. Then words no longer mattered, and her numb fingers released the caretaker's cilia.

She drifted downward into the rain of small corpses, enfolded by heat and sweat and stifling darkness.

"Ezri?" The voice was familiar, but sounded as if it were coming from behind the thick duranium hatch of an airlock.

So far away. Let me sleep.

"Ezri Dax?" The voice was back. Insistent. Closer.

Ignore it. Go away.

"Para!"

Dax felt an electrical jolt course through her body, and she thrashed to the side. Her movements were slowed as if she were adrift in deep water. Then, as her senses returned, she realized that she *was* in water. She was still deep in the pools below Mak'ala, where an outsize, millennia-old symbiont had been ferrying her back to the surface.

But someone else was here with her now.

"You're awake," that someone said, and she finally recognized the voice.

Taulin. She could make out his form in the darkness as her eyesight returned, and she saw that he, too, was clad in an EV suit. He floated about a meter away from her. But something was wrong with him. His face, clearly visible through his bubble helmet thanks to the glare of her own suit lights, was etched deeply with lines of pain.

"What's wrong?" Dax asked, her tongue thick, her words coming with frustrating slowness.

A small, ordinary-looking symbiont swam near Cyl, It orbited him almost protectively, although it, too, seemed to be in pain. Cyl reached out his gauntleted hand, touching the side of the faceplate on Dax's helmet. *"They set off some kind of radiation-dispersal device on the surface. It irradiated all the joined Trill there, as well as the symbionts in the upper pools. Must have killed hundreds of symbionts."* He gestured toward the small symbiont that swam beside him. *"Fal here was one of the lucky ones."*

Dax felt another electric jolt, this one composed entirely of her own fear for the vulnerable symbionts. Her senses all seemed to become crystalline, hyperacute. "How widespread was this thing?"

"It seemed to affect those nearest the surface the most," the general said, his voice sounding tinny over the helmet speaker.

<<*Neurogenic radiation,*>> the caretaker said, speaking inside Dax's mind. She was momentarily startled, not having seen the elder symbiont since just before passing out. The creature floated above her now, its rust-hued body buoyant and weightless. <<*The Kurlans of old died in the same manner. That secret apparently did not remain concealed with all the others.*>>

"Is it safe to go back to the surface?" Dax asked no one in particular. Her personal fear was escalating alongside the terrible sickness she was beginning to feel because of Cyl's revelations. The fact that she was still alive at all struck her as nearly miraculous. "My suit's environmental module was damaged. I can't stay down here any longer."

"I know. I replaced your module with mine," the general said. *"You have as long as you need to get back to the surface."*

"But how will you—"

"We are becoming unjoined," the Cyl symbiont said, an arc of electricity traveling from the general's abdomen to hers. *"Our travels will take us where you have just been. To the Annuated."*

Dax realized that Cyl must already have conversed for some time with the caretaker symbiont. The general must indeed be near death for the ancient creature to tell him of the final mortal destination of all symbionts, and the accumulated memories carried within them.

She tried to blink away sudden tears. "No! There's got to be some other way. Some way to heal you." She thought of Julian. Surely he could find a way to prevent both Cyl and Taulin from expiring, if only she could get everyone out of this place quickly.

Taulin, the humanoid half of the general's failing symbiosis, spoke again. Being joined herself, she found it easy to distinguish Taulin from Cyl, especially since the melding of the two minds had so obviously come undone. *"There isn't, Ezri. What was done to me on the surface cannot be undone. I have lived a long life, and my symbiont has lived far longer. I think we have served our people well."*

"You're *both* going to die?' Dax asked, her voice choked.

"We do not know," the Cyl symbiont said. *"Taulin Kengro*

will no longer live in this body. The future is unknowable for me. But we must go now. To preserve the past, both Taulin's and Cyl's."

"I hope you found something that can save our people," Taulin said, wincing against a new spasm of pain. *"It has been an honor to know you, Ezri Dax."*

"I hope . . . I hope we'll know one another again someday."

"But not soon," Cyl answered. *"Dax has much living yet to do."*

Tears rolled down Ezri's cheek. For the first time, she noticed how cool the air inside her suit had become, thanks to Cyl's and Taulin's act of sacrifice.

Cyl slipped away from Dax and began to descend, in a slow, lazy free fall. The small symbiont that had accompanied him followed him down.

Dax aimed her wrist light down and watched him sinking away from her.

And then a whisker-thin arc of blue-white energy sparked toward her from out of the depths, connecting briefly to the symbiont in her abdomen.

"Good-bye, Para," Neema said to Audrid, using the childhood nickname. *"I always wanted to see Mak'relle Dur."*

The water below her erupted in a burst of oxygen bubbles. Dax knew that Taulin Kengro had opened his environmental suit to allow the Cyl symbiont egress.

The bubbles floated silently past Dax, and all she saw below her was darkness, utter and complete.

A moment later, she felt a presence behind her. Dax turned, and her wrist lights illuminated the large symbiont who had accompanied her up from the depths.

<<*I regret your loss, youngling,*>> the caretaker said, gently wrapping a pair of its cilia-like tentacles around one of Dax's arms. <<*Shall we continue to the surface now?*>>

16

Stardate 53778.8

After concluding the final surgical procedure he was to perform on this very long night, Bashir carefully made his way across the four wide city blocks that separated Manev Central Hospital from the Senate Tower. Although a few passes of a dermal regenerator had removed the visual evidence of the mugging he had suffered the previous evening, the memory of the assault remained vivid in Bashir's mind. His body, too, reminded him of the incident frequently as he walked; his ribs remained sore because he hadn't yet found the time to treat his minor but annoying deep-tissue injuries.

Sore or not, the attack had left him determined to walk back to the Senate Tower rather than attempt to find public transportation.

As he was ushered past the ubiquitous police barricades by his official escort, Bashir relished the bracing chill of the predawn air. Though he knew that walking was not his safest option, the distance he had to cover was short. And he would be alerted if his most recent patient were to need him while a government hovercar was ferrying her from the sprawling hospital's rooftop to the graceful Senate Tower.

Although the situation on the street remained chaotic, the size of the protesting crowds had diminished considerably throughout the long night, undoubtedly because of the high death toll—among both the joined and the unjoined—in the immediate vicinity of the neurogenic weapons detonations. The police were maintaining a substantial presence, but fortunately no one seemed overly eager to provoke them—at least for the moment. Bashir saw anger and resentment etched across so many faces that the emotions were becoming an almost palpable presence.

Half an hour later, he found himself gazing down at the streets of Leran Manev through the broad, polarized windows that encircled the Senate Tower's top-floor observation deck. The sun was rising across Manev Bay, and its light dappled the government sector's wide reflecting pools with traceries of purple and orange. Standing in silence, Bashir surveyed the chaos below.

Everything looked different from the top of the tower, prompting him to wonder if the unjoined on the streets below would ever see eye to eye with those who dwelled on the lofty parapets of the joined. He counted eight small fires guttering amid the piles of shattered window glass and the hulks of burned hovercars and skimmers. Several hundred people remained visible along the sidewalks, gathered in small, persistent clusters; they seemed to keep a wary distance from a nearby phalanx of equally vigilant armored police officers. He couldn't tell if they were looters, protesters, or members of families seeking their lost loved ones.

To Bashir's weary eyes, the crowd's anger seemed as likely to reignite as it was to dissipate. *Let's just hope nobody down there does anything stupid before the president makes her address.* He tried to see the reinforced presence of the police as a hopeful augury, a sign that the Trill government still functioned, regardless of the previous night's upheavals. But he knew that they could just as easily be seen as symbols of oppressive, arbitrary authority.

How many people died yesterday because of the chaos down there? He wondered how many other Trill cities had experienced similar social convulsions, both from the unjoined rioters and the terrorists who had struck from their midst. Though he hadn't yet taken the time to troll the newsnets for detailed information, he assumed that the worldwide death toll, including the radiation-stricken joined—the victims of more than a dozen separate clusters of neurogenic radiation bombs around the planet—had to be in the multiple thousands. He was grateful, at least, that the neurogenic radiation seemed to have had no lingering effects after its initial explosive release; other than the rioting and related "social fallout," it was once again safe for the joined who hadn't been exposed to the blasts to walk the streets of Trill's cities.

The weird quiet of the distant street tableau was broken by the sound of purposeful footfalls directly behind him. He recognized their cadence immediately.

"Hello, Ezri," he said before turning to face her. He took a step toward the woman he loved, almost surrendering to an impulse to gather her into his arms; once the comm channels had cleared up somewhat, he had learned how close he had come to losing her at Mak'ala. But the brooding shadows of her ice-blue eyes nearly froze him in his tracks, like the stare of a basilisk.

Clearly, her experiences in the deep caverns had had a profound effect on her. He sensed the gulf of centuries that yawned between them as never before, and it chilled him.

"The president is going to make a planetwide address in a few minutes, Julian," she said, her hands clasped behind her back.

He nodded, suddenly unsure of what to do with his own hands. He realized that the past several hours had kept him so busy that he had received only the most cursory of briefings about the potentially incendiary discoveries Ezri had made at Mak'ala. But he knew the gist of it.

It also occurred to him that he knew even less about what she intended to do with the information she had unearthed.

"How much does the president know?" he said quietly.

"Everything," Ezri said. "At least everything *I* know. I gave her a full report before she went into surgery."

"Are you sure that was wise?"

She glowered at him, folding her arms across her chest. "Of course not, Julian. But as you've observed yourself on more than one occasion, our habit of secrecy hasn't been very healthy for us."

He could see from her defensive posture that now wasn't the ideal time to second-guess her decisions. She was, after all, still in command of this mission. "I'm sorry. I didn't mean to criticize. I was just curious about the details."

Ezri seemed mollified by that. "I told Maz all about the ancient Kurlan colony, as well as the disease that arose there. And the genetic engineering project that created the parasites. And . . ." She trailed off, casting a nervous glance at the observation windows.

"And the Kurlan genocide," he said, knowing he was finishing her thought. Ezri answered with a somber but affirmative nod.

Bashir had found the tale of Trill's hidden history almost incredible when Ezri had briefly summarized it for him immediately after her return from Mak'ala. Now the most powerful person on the planet knew the long-buried secret of why the parasites had harbored such an abiding hatred for the symbionts—as well as the fact that their malice was entirely understandable, given what the ancient Trills had done to them. It reminded him of Mary Shelley's *Frankenstein,* whose eponymous scientist had abandoned his monstrous creation and thereby earned its undying enmity.

"How did the president react?" he asked.

Ezri laughed, but without a trace of humor. "Pretty much the way I expected. She didn't want to hear it. At least at first. I really can't say I blamed her for demanding to see some proof."

"I don't suppose anyone could ask for better proof than what came back with you from below the surface," he said. Ezri had told him that once the immediate threat to Mak'ala had ended, Maz had, at Ezri's urging, traveled to the pools to commune with the caretaker symbiont Memh, who had escorted Ezri safely back from the Annuated. By now, the creature was probably already back in the seclusion of Mak'ala's deepest recesses, where it had no doubt returned to its task of caring for its even more ancient charges.

Now that the president had heard Ezri's story—and had experienced compelling evidence of its veracity—she was about to deliver a speech to Trill's entire population. Bashir could only hope that whatever she said would ultimately bring peace to Trill rather than further unrest.

He thought about the operation he had finished just before coming to the Senate Tower. That any joined Trill would voluntarily undertake such a radical procedure was remarkable, to say the least. He hoped that the fact that the patient in question had been President Lirisse Maz boded well for Trill's future.

As he followed Ezri out of the observation deck, he realized with more than a little trepidation that they were about to find out, one way or the other.

Entering the third-level speaker's platform immediately behind Ezri, Bashir saw that the president had already taken a seat behind a wide desk fashioned from dark, dense-looking wood, apparently from Trill's low tropics. Standing on the other side of the desk, a serious-miened Hiziki Gard was speaking with her in low tones even as the president shooed a trio of aides out of the room. Bashir reflected again that for a man so accustomed to operating out of the shadows, Gard didn't seem at all uncomfortable working in the very center of his world's power structure. Maybe he had been forced to step into the breach because so many other government functionaries had been injured or killed during the previous night's chaos. And perhaps Gard's very high-profile assassination of Shakaar Edon, and his subsequent pardon for the deed, had permanently altered the man's formerly covert way of doing business.

Or maybe he'll just maintain his vigil as he always has, just like every Gard before him. Sometimes the best place to hide is in plain sight.

Bashir turned his attention back to the president. Though she looked determined, her face was drawn and haggard, prompting Bashir to reach for the plisagraph he had borrowed from the hospital. Fortunately, the president's vital signs were reading strong and steady; though he was still concerned about her physical well-being, he was relieved to see that the cause of her current distress was more political than medical.

"It's still a powder keg out there, Madam President," Gard was saying, clearly fearful of inciting hysteria among the citizenry. "It might not be prudent to reveal absolutely everything Lieutenant Dax discovered at Mak'ala. Maybe you should consider parceling it out in a series of appearances over the next few weeks."

To Bashir's eye, the president looked almost adrift, as if she were badly in need of advice. It was clear that her world was approaching one of the most critical turning points in its lengthy history. And it was equally clear that the most powerful person on Trill was still making up her mind as to how to approach that fork in the road.

"Facing difficult truths is one thing, Madam President. Simply giving in to the symbionts-for-everyone crowd is quite another," Gard continued after a thoughtful pause. "Now more than ever we have to hold on to our most important traditions."

"Of course," the president said without affect. "Tradition."

Which on Trill always seems to involve tamping down ugly truths until they eventually erupt like volcanoes, Bashir thought. He was sorely tempted to say something out loud.

Fortunately, Ezri beat him to it. "Madam President, the Federation Council is going to expect your government to answer some very pointed questions about the treatment of the unjoined. And to offer redress of their legitimate grievances." Bashir noticed that Ezri's ice-blue eyes blazed with a determination that must have once belonged to Curzon.

Gard shook his head sadly. "I think the terrorists may have already undermined whatever moral legitimacy the unjoined majority may have had."

Bashir found he could no longer hold his tongue. "Rubbish. The people who set off the radiation weapons were only a tiny handful of extremists among the unjoined population." He gestured toward the broad balcony window, through which the milling crowds were visible. "There's no question that the people out there have been wronged, and that the injustice has gone on for centuries. How can you blame them for being angry after they've learned that they've been denied symbiosis based on a lie?"

Gard took a single step toward Bashir, at whom he directed a highly toxic scowl. "They've also been denied symbiosis out of necessity, Doctor. The symbionts aren't *lida* fruits to be picked from the trees. They're rare and precious beings who have to be protected."

Bashir had to concede that Gard was right, at least in part. But he also knew that the fragility and scarcity of the symbionts had long furnished Trill's privileged and powerful with an entirely too convenient excuse for excluding people from symbiosis arbitrarily.

Ignoring Gard, Bashir addressed Trill's chief executive officer directly. "Madam President, I think it's clear that your world's unjoined humanoid majority will no longer meekly accept second-class citizenship, however it's justified by the ruling minority."

Ezri nodded in somber agreement. "And the Federation Council probably won't look kindly on a planet that collapses into civil war over its age-old hidden social problems."

"I agree," said Bashir. "Trill's membership in the Federation might even be in jeopardy. Everything could well depend on your ability to maintain your world's social stability, Madam President."

"Or on how the unjoined react to whatever you decide to tell them," Gard said to the president.

A line from a very old piece of oratory sprang unbidden into Bashir's mind; he decided it needed to be spoken aloud. " 'The world will little note, nor long remember what we say here, but it can never forget what they did here.' Those words belong to a man named Lincoln, who led one of my homeworld's nations through a bloody civil war five centuries ago."

"Those are insightful words, Doctor Bashir," said Gard. "But Trill isn't Earth. Do you really think we can afford to reveal absolutely everything about our past, and still have any hope of getting things back to normal?"

Bashir turned on Gard again. "Mister Gard, the old status quo is clearly no longer a viable option for Trill. Surely you know that even better than I do." To the president, he said, "But I believe Mister Gard is correct in recommending caution. The people outside this building might not be rioting or setting off bombs at the moment, but emotions are still running pretty high out there. I've seen it up close myself."

Ezri frowned at Bashir. Returning her gaze to the president, she said, "But that doesn't mean that you owe the Trill people anything less than the whole truth, Madam President. We're a pretty tough bunch; we can stand airing the whole truth about the Kurlans and the parasites. It's the best way I can think of to properly honor the ancient memories of those times—and to start healing all the damage our civilization is suffering right now as a result of what happened back then."

"Revealing the whole truth right away is just too dangerous," Gard said. "We need time—"

Ezri rolled right over him, though her words were for the president. "It's too dangerous for us to be seen as trying to keep the truth buried." She pointed toward the balcony. "We'll never settle the chaos out there as long as the people think we are continuing to lie about our past, Madam President. Or our present. Maybe we can't give a symbiont to every unjoined person who wants one, but we can stop lying to them about their suitability for joining. We destroyed a whole world once, then lied to cover it up. We can either break that entire pattern of deceit, or risk destroying another world today."

Gard shook his head, his expression a commingling of righteous anger and pitying condescension. "Taking in too much truth too quickly is like trying to drink from a tidal wave, Lieutenant Dax."

Bashir had to restrain himself from murmuring a curse. Both Ezri and Gard were right. And as much as he despised the Symbiosis Commission's mendacity on the issue of symbiotic compatibility, Ezri's position was sounding increasingly reckless to him. Perhaps an intermediate, incremental approach would be better.

He felt thankful that the decision about how much to reveal, and how soon to do it, wasn't his to make.

Leaning back wearily in her padded chair, the president stared in quiet contemplation at the balcony window. In the distance, the crowds milling about in the golden early-morning sunlight seemed to be expanding. Faces were turned up toward the balcony, perhaps in eager anticipation, perhaps in righteous anger.

After a seeming eternity during which no one spoke or moved, the president spoke in a quiet yet determined voice. "Perhaps you're right." Bashir wasn't at all certain to whom she had spoken.

Drawing herself erect in her seat, the president silently motioned for everyone to back away from the visual pickup that was mounted on her desk. It was obvious that she had reached a decision.

Withdrawing with Ezri and Gard to a far corner of the chamber, Bashir watched as a red light activated on the desk, signaling that the president was now addressing the entire Trill humanoid population, including the surviving members of the Senate, via the planet's civilian and military comnets. The lighting around her grew in intensity as the polarization of the balcony windows adjusted to make the president conspicuously visible from the street. For Bashir the moment became elastic, and felt supercharged with uncertainty.

He knew only one thing for sure: it was a damned dangerous time to be the president of Trill.

Dax thought her heart might try to climb out of her throat as the president began speaking to the entire planet. She was surprised, though pleased, when the president began by dealing with the neo-Purists' accusations—not by denying them, but by essentially corroborating most of them. Yes, the president explained unflinchingly, the Trill government had for many centuries concealed the close relationship between the symbionts and the alien parasites. She accepted culpability for continuing the dishonest policies of her twenty-two government predecessors, all of whom had known the truth.

Those earlier Trill governments knew the truth because of what Audrid and Jayvin discovered in that comet, Dax thought, feeling guilt because of Audrid's complicity. *And they were able to keep it hidden for as long as they did because Audrid kept silent.*

Then the president went a step further, explaining that ancient Trill scientists created the parasites millennia in the past—and that they also were forced to try to destroy them, though without complete success. That failure, she said, not only had doomed millions of Trill colonists on Kurl, but had also given rise to the ancestors of the modern parasites.

Dax glanced over at Julian, whose dark eyes seemed riveted on the crowds visible through the balcony windows. She followed his gaze and noticed that the distant clusters of people outside were moving. Arms were flailing in what appeared to be angry gestures.

Switching to a respectful, almost hushed tone, the president said, "This ages-old cover-up has led us all to a precipice. While we do not as yet have accurate figures, we do know that the worldwide humanoid death toll is already in the thousands. The radiation casualties among the symbionts alone have been equally severe; as a result of the neo-Purist bombings, the symbiont population has suffered a terrible 'crash' in terms of its overall numbers, which have been reduced by upwards of ninety percent."

Genuine anger crept into the president's tone. "You may rest assured that the terrorists responsible for this atrocity will be apprehended and punished. Several of the neo-Purist ringleaders—those who weren't killed by their own weaponry—are already in custody."

Dax looked at Gard, whose attention was absorbed by the silent comm unit on his wrist. *A text message,* Dax thought.

Gard's wide eyes and pallid cheeks told her that the news he was receiving couldn't be good. Fear gripped her soul with sharp-bladed fingers. Perhaps Gard and Julian had been right to counsel caution. Had she just succeeded in persuading the president to say entirely too much, and to do it far too soon?

Gard quickly tapped several commands into his comm unit. The president paused momentarily in her speech as she glanced at her desk console; she was evidently now in possession of the same information Gard had just received.

Though Dax couldn't see Gard's text message from where she stood, she had a pretty good idea of its contents. *They're beginning to riot again. The people have heard the truth, but they're just too angry to deal with it appropriately.*

What have I just done?

The president felt shaken to the core by what Gard had just told her. Once again the streets of Trill's most populous cities, from Gheryzan to Tenara, were erupting in spontaneous violence—and the revelations she had just made were the most obvious cause.

The president quietly shook herself; now was the time for leadership, not paralysis. Somehow, in spite of the deep emptiness—the utter aloneness—that she felt, she found the strength to continue with her address.

"Because . . . because of the terrorist attacks, the symbiont population has been greatly reduced. It will no doubt take many years—perhaps many decades—before the symbiont breeding population is once again large enough to allow any symbionts to be spared for symbiosis.

"I must therefore issue the following emergency proclamation: the Symbiosis Commission shall authorize no new joinings, and shall suspend all pending joinings, until further notice and after senatorial and executive review. *All* symbionts currently living in conjoined status with humanoids will be returned to the breeding pools at the end of the lifetimes of their current hosts, and will not be reassigned to new hosts at that time.

"This indefinite moratorium on joining constitutes a wrenching change for our world, to be sure. But this change is dictated by absolute biological necessity. Replacements must be bred for the symbionts who died in the attacks, and those who were injured and left without hosts will require time to recover, as well as to breed. No healthy joined person's symbiont will be taken away. But every available symbiont will be taken to the spawning grounds to help the species increase its numbers as quickly as possible. The symbionts *must* survive. They *must* be protected, if Trill humanoids are ever again to hope to benefit from the long lives, the shared experiences, the accumulated wisdom—and the tandem immortality—gifted to us by our sister species.

"As radical—and perhaps frightening—as this change is, it also affords us a unique opportunity. While we are waiting for the symbiont population to replenish its numbers—and thereby to become ready once again for symbiosis—the distinctions our society has drawn between the joined and the unjoined will shrink and vanish, as will the number of joined Trill citizens who live among us.

"We will put the lie to the charge that only the joined rate positions of power and influence in this society, while recognizing that we have erred badly in this regard in the past. We will remold our civilization into something more all-inclusive than has ever existed on Trill before. No longer will the topmost strata of Trill society be dominated by a tiny minority. In a manner of speaking, we will *all* be unjoined sooner or later."

This is it, she thought, pausing in her oratory. She wished she felt as confident about her next action as she had when she had originally conceived this plan.

Of course, she had still been joined then.

With all the conviction and dignity she could muster, the president rose from her chair. As she stood behind the desk, she imagined she could feel the delicate wings of a nest of *yilga* moths fluttering inside her abdominal pouch. She had yet to get used to its strangely flattened condition.

"I cannot issue such a sweeping proclamation without including myself," the president said, opening her charcoal-colored jacket, along with the lower portion of the formal white tunic she wore beneath it.

She knew that her visibly slack abdominal pouch was now exposed to the entire Trill comnet.

"Because you have entrusted me with the power of this office, I have presumed to lead you. And since I am bringing about changes such as Trill hasn't seen in millennia, I must lead the way there as well. This morning I underwent an experimental medical procedure that successfully interrupted the symbiosis between myself and the symbiont to which I have been bonded for nearly all of my adult life."

She tried to push back a sudden emotional squall, and a haze of tears told her that she hadn't quite succeeded. She bulled onward in spite of it. "I am now no longer Lirisse Maz, but Lirisse Durghan. The Maz symbiont has already been taken back to Mak'ala, where it will participate in the Guardians' efforts to restore the symbiont population to safe levels. I am now, like most of you, unjoined.

"I make no empty promises today. The joined class has little choice other than to implement my ban on new joinings. I trust that the Guardians and the Trill Defense Ministry—not to mention the sheer overwhelming size of Trill's unjoined majority—will tend to make the ban a self-enforcing proposition.

"In the meantime, I stand with you, the unjoined, as one of you. I call upon those of you who have taken your legitimate grievances to the streets to set aside violence now. I ask you to consider carefully all the changes that lie ahead, and how these changes stand to benefit *you*. Consider how we can work together to create a future in which all Trill are treated equally under the law.

"We all stand together at the edge of a precipice. Today we can write a new page of history together. We can record new memories of change for the better. Of progress for all of Trill. Of equality for all of Trill. Again, I implore you to reject violence. Joined and unjoined, let us face our common future as one. Let us build a new Trill together. And let us begin today."

She touched a button on her desk console, and the visual pickup's red light immediately faded to a dull black.

The president sighed and cast quick glances at Lieutenant Dax, Hiziki Gard, Dr. Bashir, and the few staffers who had gathered nearby. Though their expressions all showed varying degrees of apprehension, they were otherwise unreadable.

For better or for worse, the die had been cast.

During the president's speech, Dax began feeling nauseated. It was a sensation she used to experience during her earliest days aboard Deep Space 9; she had been certain then that she could feel the immense Cardassian space station slowly turning beneath her feet. That certainty had been borne out by the same vertiginous queasiness she was experiencing right now.

Only now, she was conscious of an entire civilization turning beneath her feet.

It would be really bad form to throw up on President Maz's carpet, she told herself. *No, that's President* Durghan, *now.*

She considered, as she had many times over the past several hours, that the president's name change might seem more like a complete identity switch in the eyes of some. Would the Trill Senate or the courts try to invalidate the president's symbiosis ban, claiming that only Lirisse Maz, not Lirisse Durghan, had the authority to issue a presidential decree?

It's a good thing Maz signed the order before she went into surgery with Julian. That thought settled Dax's lurching stomach somewhat.

But not entirely. In fact, there seemed to be no end to her misgivings, now that she knew there was no turning back. It was as though she had taken a flying leap off the Senate Tower spire, only to change her mind about the plunge halfway down. Doubts of similar futility nagged relentlessly at the back of her mind. What if the drug Julian had used to end the president's symbiosis were to become common knowledge? She knew that this wasn't beyond the realm of possibility, since Julian had also just used it to safely extract many nonfatally injured symbionts from their otherwise doomed hosts. The president had admitted publicly to undergoing an experimental procedure that had enabled her to survive separation from the Maz symbiont, but she had withheld the details. People would certainly demand them, though, and what then? Wouldn't such a revelation tempt certain unjoined malcontents—people like the late Verad Kalon—to get around the symbiosis ban by simply kidnapping one of the few remaining symbionts still conjoined with a humanoid? Dax already knew from her own symbiont's memories that black market trade in living symbionts wasn't an entirely unknown crime.

Maybe the powers that be will have to see to it that some *secrets remain buried,* Dax told herself unhappily as she struggled to maintain focus on the here and now rather than allowing hypothetical calamities to drive her to distraction.

After the president finished her address, Dax walked to the observation window that faced the speaker's platform. She looked down at the crowd, which had grown steadily throughout the president's speech as people arrived by hovercar, skimmer, antigrav bus, or on foot.

She glanced toward the president, who had slumped limply backward into her chair, her eyes closed in apparent fatigue while Julian hovered nearby, examining her with a small medical scanner. Neither the president nor Julian seemed to be paying any attention to the storm gathering outside.

Beside the president's desk stood Gard, who continued watching his wrist-mounted comm unit intently.

Dax's heart sank when Gard cast a brief glance her way. His appalled expression spoke volumes about what must be going on all across the planet as a result of the president's speech. There were already thousands of confirmed dead; if all the unjoined were rising up now to bring still more blood and fire to the streets, then millions more could follow.

Then, as he continued studying the information scrolling on his wrist, Gard's expression shifted to one of stupefaction. Dax walked quickly toward him.

He grinned at her a moment later, then pressed a button that opened up an audio channel. Dax had expected to hear screams, catcalls, slogans, epithets. Instead she heard an unmistakable rhythmic sound, like the susurration of a waterfall punctuated by sharp, enthusiastic whistles.

The people outside weren't rioting. They were *cheering.* Amid the bursts of applause rose a chorus of voices, repeating the newly unjoined president's birth surname in a rolling, ebullient chant: *"Durghan! Durghan! Durghan!"*

"It might be a little soon to jump to any conclusions," Gard said, still grinning. "But I think your speech could have gone over a whole lot worse, Madam President."

Suddenly overcome by an enormous sensation of relief, Dax

broke with protocol by letting herself sag into a sitting position on the corner of the president's wide desk.

After having endured so much intense upheaval so quickly—and after having been subjected to so many centuries of casual, unacknowledged oppression—Trill's disaffected majority could finally look forward to a new era of hope.

17

Walking between Julian and Gard, Dax wearily picked her way across the Senate Tower's lobby, guiding the trio through the small clusters of arriving office workers. As they headed in the general direction of the landing pad where the runabout *Rio Grande* was parked, Dax found herself avoiding Julian's searching gaze. Instead, her eyes roamed across the wide, vaulted ground-floor chamber.

Almost immediately, she saw a familiar face.

"Ranul!" Ezri shouted as she ran toward him. She hadn't expected to see the massive Guardian again so soon, given the previous day's chaos at Mak'ala. "What brings you to the Senate Tower?"

"I was hoping I'd see you again before you left Trill," Ranul Keru said, giving her a firm but gentle hug.

Dax suddenly realized that Julian and Gard had flanked them. Julian was regarding her silently, with an expression that blended curiosity with impatient anticipation.

"Sorry, Julian," she said, disengaging from the Guardian. "Ranul Keru, meet Doctor Julian Bashir, also from Deep Space 9. And Hiziki Gard, a special officer of the Trill Symbiosis Commission. If not for Ranul's help, I might never have made contact with the elder symbionts."

"You're one of the Guardians," Julian observed after momentarily scrutinizing Keru's utilitarian brown tunic and slacks.

"For now," Keru said with an enigmatic half-smile. "I've only been working with the symbionts for the past couple of years. It's been very restful and therapeutic for me."

"At least up until the last couple of days," Dax said, smiling. She felt some curiosity as to precisely why Keru had felt the need for therapy, but didn't want to pry into his personal affairs; she wasn't his counselor, after all.

The big Guardian returned her smile, though it didn't quite reach his eyes. "I haven't seen so much action since before I left the *Enterprise*. Didn't think I'd ever miss it. Or that I'd start questioning whether I was really cut out to be a Guardian for the rest of my life."

After pausing to smooth a wrinkle on his dark civilian jacket, Gard frowned slightly. "Sounds like you're seriously thinking about going back to Starfleet."

Keru shrugged, smiling. "Maybe, someday. If I found a good reason to make another big life change—and if I thought Starfleet needed me more than Trill does. The symbionts now need the Guardians more than ever. And not just the younger ones, either." He switched to a hushed, confidential tone. "The ancient symbionts you contacted have been taking on a lot of memories from their dying brethren. They're going to need our help as well."

"And you have a chance to learn more about them than ever," Julian said, a familiar knowledge-hungry expression blossoming across his face. "So little is understood about that phase of the symbiont life cycle."

Dax winced, hoping Julian's natural curiosity wouldn't be misunderstood.

"I think maintaining the seclusion of the Annuated will be a far higher priority than studying them," Keru said evenly, a small scowl visible beneath his bushy mustache.

Julian nodded, obviously realizing his gaffe. "Of course. I apologize if I caused offense."

He's so very young, Dax thought, studying Julian's sincere, earnest face. *Such an innocent, in so many ways.* After everything she had seen and experienced over the past day or so, Dax felt as old as the *Mak'relle Dur* legend itself.

Gard cleared his throat, apparently eager to move the conversation elsewhere. "Overcurious scientists will probably be the least of the symbionts' worries for the next few years. I've already spoken to members of the Symbiosis Evaluation Board, and they're telling me that not all of the Trill initiates are taking the president's symbiosis moratorium very well."

Keru nodded, his expression grave and knowing. He obviously either already knew a great deal about Gard's function in Trill society, or had intuited it from the other man's bearing. "You security people will probably be as busy as we Guardians are for however long this thing lasts."

"At least as busy," Gard replied quietly, evidently speaking to Dax as much as to Keru. "If there's another potential radical leader lurking among all the thousands of disappointed prejoined initiates, we'll have to work harder than ever to get out in front of the problem." And with that, Gard bid the group goodbye and turned toward the turbolifts, presumably to apply himself to the arduous tasks that lay ahead. With no new joinings in the offing, Gard would have to seek his monsters and aberrations elsewhere.

Speaking to Dax, Keru said, "I've been told that the Senate has scheduled additional hearings into the symbiont/parasite affair and the bombings. They'll start taking official testimony in a few weeks, after things settle down a bit."

Dax nodded. "The original reason I came to Trill was to testify at those hearings. The Senate will probably want to ask me some follow-up questions. It looks like I'll be coming back to the homeworld a lot sooner than I'd originally planned."

"I've been asked to speak at the next round of hearings as well," Keru said. "Maybe I'll see you then. You can update me on everything that's been happening in Starfleet since I left." Then the big man made his farewells, leaving Dax and Julian standing alone together while office workers continued to arrive, dodging and weaving around them as they headed for the bank of turbolifts along the south wall.

As she watched Keru walk away, Dax's thoughts turned to the thousands of eager young initiates from whom the bright prospect of symbiosis had been summarily withdrawn. Thanks to the memories of most of her symbiont's previous hosts, she was well acquainted with the rigors of a Trill initiate's life. Fair or not, each symbiosis candidate was subjected to a grueling winnowing process that culminated in joining only for a select few. Her symbiont retained the memories of each initiate who ultimately became its host, even though Ezri Tigan had never endured an initiate's trials. Dax felt she understood the bitter taste of disappointment that every not-yet-joined initiate on the planet must be experiencing right now; she could never forget that Jadzia's first application for joining had been torpedoed by no less a personage than Curzon himself. The experience had been absolutely ego-crushing.

How hopeless life must seem now for the initiates, she thought. Though Ezri Tigan had never desired joining herself, Ezri Dax now felt unutterably sad for those whose yearning for the completeness of symbiosis had abruptly come to nothing, as though the Symbiosis Evaluation Board had summarily declared *every* applicant to the program unfit.

Dax's eyes followed Keru's steps as he reached an exit on the far side of the lobby. As the Guardian disappeared from sight, it occurred to her that not everybody expected to benefit materially from an association with the symbionts. Unlike each year's eager young crop of initiates—or unjoined malcontents like Verad Kalon—Keru and the other Guardians were content to give of themselves freely to assist the symbionts. And every member of the Guardian order was unjoined.

Maybe Trill's best hope lies with people who have the strength to stand apart from whatever advantages symbiosis might offer them, she thought. *People like Ranul Keru, or President Lirisse Durghan.*

Or even Ezri Tigan, the person I used to be before Dax came along.

"Excuse me?" Julian said, his eyebrows buoyed by curiosity. Dax suddenly realized that she must have spoken at least part of her reverie aloud.

"I was starting to wonder," she began, slightly flustered at having been caught woolgathering. "Would I have had the courage to give up my symbiont the way the president did?"

"The president probably worked hard for years to prove herself worthy of the Maz symbiont," Julian pointed out. "Remember, you joined with the Dax symbiont initially because that was the only way to save its life."

He just doesn't get it, she thought. Aloud, she said, "Sure, I didn't choose to be joined, but I've *been* joined for almost two years now. Ezri Tigan and Dax are a permanent part of one other now. And my life and career will never be the same again because of that. Ezri and Dax have made memories together that we'll share for the rest of this lifetime. And Dax's next hosts will be able to dip into my experiences the way I benefit from those of Curzon, or Torias, or Emony, or any of the others."

He took her hand gently between both of his; he appeared to notice for the first time that she'd had her phaser burn treated at some point since leaving Mak'ala.

"Isn't that the nature of symbiosis?" he said.

She pulled her hand away, gently but insistently. "Yes. It's a wonderful thing that I didn't even want at first. And now I get to keep it, even though none of the people who really *do* want it get to join the club now."

"I think I understand, Ezri. I believe you're experiencing something called 'survivor's guilt.'"

"Thanks, Julian," she said with an exasperated sigh. "But I *am* a trained counselor."

"Then you should understand that plenty of others are now in the very same position you are," he said, apparently unfazed by her irritation. "Every other joined Trill—"

She interrupted him. "Every other joined Trill is just running out the clock, as of this morning. And if this joining embargo goes on long enough, every last one of the remaining few hundred joined Trill hosts will die. Their symbionts will end up back in the pools, without any prospect of entering a new symbiosis. With no chance of regaining their eyes and ears and arms and legs. Maybe for decades, or centuries. And every humanoid on Trill will be cut off from everything the symbionts know. They might even forget why we bothered to join in the first place. Even people who revere memories can forget what's important, Julian. Trust me, I know."

Julian seemed to be nettled as well, though his words remained persistently sympathetic, perhaps out of habits stemming from his medical training. "You have perhaps another century of life ahead of you, Ezri. Surely the current symbiosis crunch ought to be resolved long before then."

"How can you be so sure of that?"

"Because I intend to help any way I can," he said in a matter-of-fact manner.

Though Julian's words reassured her, at least somewhat, that Trill's symbiosis problems might be resolved sooner rather than later, they did little to assuage her "survivor's guilt," if that was indeed what she was experiencing.

Unbidden, her thoughts drifted again to one of her previous hosts. She recalled an occasion when Julian had all but summoned Jadzia's departed spirit during the throes of lovemaking with Ezri. Though the incident had occurred months ago—and only once—it tended to haunt Dax whenever her relationship with Julian seemed unusually strained.

When he looks at me, who does he really see? Ezri? Or Jadzia?

She tried to brush the thought aside, at least for the moment. It was time to focus on the future—and on the reports that would have to be written during the days-long voyage home that lay ahead. As she resumed moving purposefully toward one of the exits, Julian walked at a brisk pace alongside her.

Neither of them said another word until long after they had reached the runabout.

Stardate 53785.4

The runabout *Rio Grande,* now on course for Deep Space 9, had left Trill more than fifty hours ago.

Fifty extremely quiet *hours ago,* Bashir thought, seated in one of the cockpit chairs—though not in the one closest to Ezri.

He wasn't sure how to go about breaking the seemingly interminable silences that stretched between their shared meals, their uncomfortable, largely separate sleeping intervals, and their brief flurries of report writing, duty-related conversation, and innocuous, superficial personal chitchat. Busy now at the pilot's console, Ezri no longer seemed to want or need to discuss her homeworld's symbiosis moratorium or its aftermath. In fact, she seemed utterly disinterested in talking about *anything*.

He, on the other hand, could scarcely contain himself. There were still aspects of this messy business he had questions about.

For instance, were the parasites really gone for good? Or were there more out there, somewhere beyond Federation space, waiting for the right opportunity to try again?

But now didn't seem an appropriate time to discuss such things. Bashir remained silent, though he thought the quiet tension that had built up in the cabin over the past hour could have repelled a quantum torpedo attack.

Idled by the uncomfortable stillness in the runabout's cockpit, his mind again wandered back to the heavy-handed manner in which Ezri had conducted the mission on Trill. Though subsequent circumstances had largely vindicated her actions, he still felt a lingering resentment about it, as livid and painful as a bone bruise.

Since she seemed unlikely to bring up this subject—or *any* subject—he decided it was up to him to do it.

"Ezri, we have to talk."

She continued staring straight ahead at the ever-shifting star field for several seconds before noticing that he'd spoken. "Hmmm?"

"Ezri, I want to talk to you about the mission."

She turned her pilot's chair so that she faced him. "You're right. I suppose we could append a few more details to the initial reports we sent to Kira." She started to rise from her chair.

He laid a hand on her arm, gently preventing her from getting to her feet. "DS9 is less than half a day away. I wanted to talk to you before we get back and end up getting swept into yet another crisis."

She nodded. "You want to talk about the mission?" As reticent as she still obviously was about rehashing her world's history with him, Bashir thought she was hoping she wouldn't have to discuss anything else.

"Only peripherally. It's really about, ah, the way you handled certain aspects of the mission."

She leaned back in her chair, crossing her arms in front of her in a classic display of defensiveness. Her dazzling blue eyes narrowed. "Trill was attacked by a clandestine global terror network, Julian. Under the circumstances, it seems to me that the mission was as successful as anybody could have hoped."

"I can't argue with that, at least in retrospect." Feeling she was beginning to tie him in knots, he decided he'd better simply come out with his point. "But I think you may have been a bit . . . high-handed when you went off to Mak'ala."

Judging from the puzzled look on her face, he might have just sprouted a second head. " 'High-handed,' " she repeated.

"When I tried to point out that it was a risky thing to do, you simply brushed me off."

"Going diving at Mak'ala *was* risky, Julian. You didn't have to tell me that. But it turned out to be the right thing to do."

He nodded. "Yes, but only in retrospect. At the time, it was as though you had no regard whatsoever for my input."

It was her turn to nod. "Ah. So this isn't really about the mission. It's about your evaluation of my command style."

His frustration finally boiling over, he rose from his chair and stepped to the rear of the cockpit before turning once again to face her. "Dammit, Ezri! Don't trivialize this! I'm not trying to defend my delicate ego. Each of us took wholly opposite approaches to the crisis. Doesn't that bother you?"

"Not especially, Julian. It was my call, and I made it." She paused thoughtfully for a moment before continuing. "And maybe *that's* what's really bothering you—that I've stepped into a role you're not comfortable with."

"That's not true," he said, waving his hands dismissively. "I've always supported your decision to switch over to a command-track career."

"Even though it came as a bit of a shock, at least at first."

He felt a small smile tug at the corners of his mouth. "I prefer to think of it as a surprise, and Daxes are nothing if not surprising. But again, this isn't about your becoming a command officer."

Ezri, however, wasn't smiling. "Then is it about me being *your* commanding officer on this particular mission?"

"Ezri, you were above me in the *Defiant's* chain of command all those weeks we spent exploring the Gamma Quadrant. That wasn't a problem for me then, and it isn't now."

She sighed wearily. "Then what exactly *is* this about, Julian?"

As he paused for a moment to compose his thoughts, he began to realize how difficult a question she had posed. "It's about whether or not my expertise is important to you. My judgment. My advice. My experience, even though I admit I don't

have a backlog of eight other lifetimes of memories to tap into."
He hesitated a beat before plunging on to the real crux of his
complaint. "It's about whether or not *I'm* important to you."

All of the exasperation abruptly drained from her face, and
she looked stricken. "And you think you've become less important to me since I started wearing this red collar."

His response was nearly a whisper. "It seems that way, yes.
At least sometimes."

She rose from her chair, put her arms around him, and buried
her face in his shoulder. He returned the embrace, which seemed
fueled more by regret than by passion.

They stood that way for a long time, in silence, while the runabout's autopilot carried them inexorably homeward.

"Jadzia," Ezri said finally, her head lying against his chest.

He partially disengaged himself from the embrace so that he
could see her face. Unshed tears stood in her wide, cerulean
eyes.

"Sorry?" he said.

She finished dismantling their embrace, then resumed her
place in the pilot's seat. She stared straight ahead at the shifting
star field as she spoke. "You were in love with Jadzia."

"I don't really see what that has to do with anything," Bashir
said, feeling defensive in spite of himself.

"You loved her," she repeated, turning to face him. "You
don't have to be embarrassed to talk to me about it. Worf may
have arranged a place in *Sto-Vo-Kor* for her, but she's still right
here." She placed a hand on her abdomen, where the Dax symbiont stored the memories of all its previous hosts.

And she's in my heart as well, he thought. *And always will
be.* He slumped into the seat next to Ezri's, knowing he was
beaten.

"All right. I *did* love Jadzia. What of it?"

"You were in love with her, but you lost her to Worf before
you could do anything about it. And you lost her again when she
died. Then Ezri Dax blundered into your life. Suddenly, you had
a second chance at Jadzia. And now, here we are."

"I love *you,* Ezri. Not Jadzia's ghost. Don't you believe that?"

She nodded, the tears in her eyes sparkling like distant
quasars. "I do believe you, Julian. But I've always wondered if
the only reason for that is because you loved Jadzia first."

He was feeling adrift; when he'd decided to air his grievances with her, the last thing he'd expected was for her to reciprocate. "What's your point, Ezri?"

"My point is that we came together under some pretty strange circumstances. There was the emotional baggage you had with Jadzia. The Dominion War. The final battle for Cardassia. We became a couple not knowing whether we'd even survive the first day." Tears began painting wide stripes down both her cheeks.

All at once he saw precisely where she was heading. And he was more than a little surprised when he realized that she was making perfect, if painful, sense.

"And none of that bodes well for a stable relationship," he said quietly. He suddenly noticed that his own cheeks were damp as well.

"It isn't that you're not important to me, Julian," she said. "You're a dear, sweet, man. A *good* man. But the part of me that's just plain old Ezri wonders if we'd have been drawn together at all if I didn't see you through Jadzia's eyes . . . or if you didn't see her in mine."

He opened his mouth to protest, then stopped himself. Was it egotistical to acknowledge that he might not have developed feelings for Ezri if not for her symbiosis with the renowned polymath Dax symbiont—and the link to his beloved, dead Jadzia that had come with it?

"I suppose we've both changed quite a bit over the past year," he said finally, knowing that his words communicated little of value even as he said them.

"Me especially," she said, gracefully permitting his obvious dodge as she chuckled through her tears. "And now we're two very different people."

We've matured together, he thought. *I don't think we could have had this conversation just a few months ago. At least not without a good deal more shouting.*

They sat together in silence, watching the stars. Holding hands.

"I suppose we're done now," he said at length. "As a couple, I mean."

They faced each other. He studied her eyes, just as she was clearly studying his. The truth now stood revealed as obvious.

"I hope you don't mind my telling you that I still love you," he said, fixing his eyes back on the interstellar void ahead. "I think I always will."

Her fingers felt cold against his as she squeezed his hand. "And I'll always love you, too, Julian." A brief sidewise glance told him that her gaze now faced front as well.

Very gently, he released her hand. She withdrew it. Whatever cord had connected them romantically seemed to snap with that gesture. They were friends now. Dear friends, and colleagues.

The *Rio Grande* continued hurtling homeward, mere hours away from Deep Space 9. And though Ezri remained seated beside him, the blackness of space seemed not nearly so deep and cold as the gulf that now yawned between them.

BAJOR

Fragments and Omens

J. Noah Kym

ABOUT THE AUTHOR

J. Noah Kym has been characterized by his friends as a tough nut to crack.

For Mom

ACKNOWLEDGMENTS

First and foremost, deepest gratitude to Paula Block for her support, her enthusiasm, and her suggestion of this story's villain.

Muchas gracias also to Heather Jarman and Jeff Lang, scribes extraordinaire, whose help and inspiration were invaluable to the crafting of this tale.

A big shout out to all the folks who make *Star Trek,* on screen and in print, for all the worlds and characters they continue to create.

Finally, a tip of the hat to my editor, Marco Palmieri, for inviting me to explore the world of Bajor.

HISTORIAN'S NOTE

Chapters 1, 2, 11, and all the "Rena" portions of this tale unfold over the three weeks immediately following the *Star Trek: Deep Space Nine* novel *Unity.* The rest of the story transpires during a single day at the end of that period, in late October, 2376 (Old Calendar).

There is no such thing as an omen. Destiny does not send us heralds. She is too wise or too cruel for that.

—OSCAR WILDE

The whole world is an omen and a sign.

—RALPH WALDO EMERSON

SISKO

Eyes closed, Benjamin Sisko listened to his wife's slow, steady breathing. Inhaling deeply, he began a mental list of the smells: lemon-scented laundry soap, Kasidy's face cream, mother's milk, baby powder. *Oh, my,* he thought, *but that takes me back. How many years?* Jake was—twenty-one? Could that be right? *And I thought I'd left baby powder far, far behind me.*

Only a meter from Kasidy's side of the bed he heard a faint stirring no louder than a mouse kicking in its sleep. In response, under his arm, Sisko felt Kasidy's arm spasm and she mumbled something low and unintelligible. "Don't worry," Sisko murmured, eyes still shut. "I'll get her."

He opened his eyes and watched the blades of the ceiling fan churn the early-morning air. Kasidy had installed the fans shortly after she'd moved into the house, one of the many changes she had made to his original design that made their home seem as wonderfully strange as it was familiar. After the years upon years he'd spent in perfectly modulated environments on starships and starbases (and the even less perfectly modulated spaces of Deep Space 9), a ceiling fan seemed a delightfully anachronistic detail. *What a wonderful idea.* He was glad Kasidy had thought of it.

The mouse in the tiny crib stirred again, sighed, and made a wet sound. Lifting his head, Sisko, the Old Campaigner, the Experienced Dad, sniffed, then drew a breath and held it. *Ah, yes, I remember this, too.*

The tiny creature in the crib voiced her displeasure with the recent change in her comfort level. Kasidy's head rose minutely. "Sorry, love," he said, rolling out of bed. "I'm going."

"She's going to be hungry," Kasidy muttered into her pillow.

"Of course she is," Sisko said as he reached into the crib and scooped his daughter up into his arms. *Check for leakage,* the Old Dad instincts told him. *Structural integrity may be compromised.* All appeared to be well, though Rebecca's distress level was sharply rising. Lowering his daughter gently onto the changing table in the corner, Sisko unfastened the diaper, tossed it into the recycler, smiled briefly at the tiny, perfect derriere, then gave it and all other visible parts a thorough but gentle wiping. A spray of powder, then a new diaper, and voilà, all was sealed and in place, and the proud papa stopped only long enough to inspect his daughter's rounded belly. The baby, whose face had been in danger of scrunching up for a howl, suddenly became aware that something significant had changed; she stopped and considered. *Ah,* the face said. *Better. But all is not well.* The lips pursed and Baby Rebecca, Princess of All She Surveys, screwed up her face in a yawp of discontent.

"Well," Sisko said, and carried the unhappy child to her waiting mother. "I can't help you with that." Kasidy slid down the corner of her gown, nestled Rebecca next to her breast, and then covered them both again. The mouth searched, Kasidy guided her head, and then there came a coo of satisfaction. Sisko bent down and pressed his face into his wife's neck, inhaled again: yes, all still there—face cream, milk, powder, love.

Kasidy wriggled away from his rough cheek, smiled, asked sleepily, "What time is it?"

"Early. Go back to sleep."

"*You* go back to sleep. You were up past two last night talking to Jake and here you are up again with the birds."

"I'm not tired."

"You're never tired."

Grinning, Sisko stroked his wife's hair. "The Prophets didn't believe in getting up early. And they're very leisurely about how they spend their mornings. Slippers. Sweatshirts. Two cups of coffee before they even think about what's for breakfast. And then naps all around in the afternoon."

Kasidy stroked the baby's fine curls. "Sounds like it would drive you mad, Mr. I Must Be Up and Doing."

"That's why I had to come back."

"Oh, right," Kasidy said. "That was why."

Sisko straightened and listened to the morning. The *shuff, shuff, shuff* of the fan drowned out a lot of noise, but he was fairly certain no one else was stirring around the house. Birds out in the hedgerow were busily tending their own families, adults making sure their almost-grown chicks were ready to fly. "Coffee," he said aloud, knowing Kasidy didn't hear him; she was already asleep again, Rebecca snuggled close. The baby had stopped nursing, asleep, but her mouth was still firmly attached to her mother's nipple, close, close, so close. Closer to Kasidy than any other human being ever would be. Sisko touched the child's cheek and said, "This is why."

As Sisko stepped from the bedroom, he slipped his arms into the sleeves of his robe. Summer came on slowly in Kendra, evidenced by the cool air from the northern mountains mingling gently with the breezes blowing off the Yolja River. This morning was warmer than the one before and tomorrow would be even warmer, but for an old New Orleans native like himself, anything below thirty Celsius warranted a wrap. Still, Sisko did not wish away these cool mornings. Each graduated environmental change bespoke time passing and he savored the sense of being reconnected to its flow.

Enjoying the way the flesh of his arms prickled slightly in the cool air, Sisko strode into his kitchen only to be greeted by the whiff of overripe garbage. *I thought I'd asked Jake to take that out to the compost pile.* Searching his memory, Sisko had to admit that he could only remember thinking about asking Jake. After all, between the two of them, they had drunk two bottles of the good spring wine last night and he, Sisko, had probably downed more than his share. The nursing Kasidy would only wet her lips with it during dinner. And Jake . . .

Where *was* Jake? On the floor next to the couch were signs of his nest, a loose roll of blankets and a well-scrunched pillow. The shades that had been drawn over the sliding door to the garden had been pulled aside. Sisko padded softly to the door and looked out.

Shoulders hunched, his son was standing in the garden staring into the south, hands thrust deep into his jacket pockets, shadow long behind him, morning dew soaking into his boots and pant legs. Lost in thought, Jake did not hear his father as he pulled the sliding door open. Glad for the opportunity, Sisko stood and regarded his son as dispassionately as he could. *He's grown up to be a fine-looking young man,* the father thought. *Or maybe I need to stop saying "young man." He's a man now. No "young" about it.* Sometime in the past week, Jake had decided to stop shaving, and the unruly stubble of a couple of days past had already become a thick tangle. Everyone had teased Jake about it for a day or two, but Jake had known the change was blessed when his stepmother had run a hand over his chin and commented that all the Sisko men looked better with beards.

But what is he thinking about? Sisko wondered as Jake absentmindedly rubbed his chin. *Never an early riser, this one, not unless he has something on his mind.* Sisko amended the thought. *Or when he's working on a story, but then it's not getting up early; he just doesn't sleep.* But Jake had not been working on a story or, near as his father could tell, much of anything since Rebecca was born. Considering it now, he realized that Jake had been looking restless the past couple of days. Thinking about the past, he concluded. And thinking about the future. Thinking about anywhere but here.

"Hey, Jake-o," Sisko called. "Aren't your feet going to get soaked?"

When he heard his old nickname, Jake's shoulders slowly stirred and he shook off his reverie. Turning toward his father, he smiled the familiar old smile, the happy grin of open, unaffected pleasure, though Sisko felt a peculiar nostalgia creep over him seeing the smile through the beard. It was like when Jake was ten and had just discovered stage makeup. Marveling that he had not thought about it in over ten years, Sisko remembered that summer—the pancake makeup, the spirit gum, the hair appliances, Jennifer chasing a half-denuded werewolf out of their bathroom. How many bathroom towels had the boy ruined?

"Hey, Dad," Jake responded, though not too loud. He looked

down at his drenched boots, then lifted each one off the ground in turn. "Too late."

"Then no reason to hurry in," Sisko said. "Unless you want to help me make breakfast."

Jake's eyebrows lifted. "French toast?"

"Do we have sourdough?"

"I made a loaf yesterday."

Sisko beamed. "I brought you up right, didn't I?"

Jake shrugged, and Sisko saw the smile turn down a little at the corners. Then, in a moment, it was gone and Jake replied, "Yep, you did." Looking again into the south, Jake pointed out across the rolling hills and asked, "Do you know what's in that direction?"

Sisko considered. He knew the names of all the major landmasses on Bajor—the general composition of each continent and their positions relative to each other and the oceans. He imagined he knew as much as any average high-school student, which was to say a lot about a few places and a very little about many others. He answered, "Valley plains and forest spreading out on either side of the Yolja for hundreds of kilometers, and then the sea."

"Anything on the coasts?"

"The usual sort of thing: fishing towns, light industry, ocean farming. No big cities due south of here, though. Why?"

"Just wondering," Jake said as he stared into the rising sun, then added, "Mrs. O'Brien tried to teach us about Bajor's geography, but I don't think too much of it stuck."

"Not everything does, son. It's not like we lived here."

Nodding, Jake said, "But we do now. You do now. I guess I just feel like I'm a guest here. It's not my home. I guess I always thought that we'd end up back on Earth again."

Smiling, finally understanding, Sisko replied, "Well, that's up to you, isn't it?"

"Yeah. Guess it is."

Sisko felt a chill creep up through his feet. It was too cool to be outside without shoes, and his robe whipped around his knees in the morning breeze. "I'm going to go start breakfast. You want coffee or tea?"

Still staring into the purple and gold sky, Jake said, "I'll wipe my feet before I come in, Dad."

Shaking his head, Sisko ducked back inside.

2

KASIDY

Ten minutes later, just as the coffee was beginning to perk and the tea water was coming to a boil, Kasidy came into the kitchen, face scrubbed, hair held back with a headband, and baby Rebecca over her shoulder. After kissing her husband, she spun around and showed baby to daddy, who stopped sawing at the loaf of sour-dough long enough to say, "Hi, sweetie," and wipe baby's spit-up-covered chin with the towel he had over his shoulder.

Kasidy lowered the baby into the crook of her left arm, found herself a teabag, and dropped it in the mug Sisko had left on the counter next to the hot water. "Where's Jake?" Kasidy asked as she poured. He's not out on the couch."

"Outside."

Kasidy pulled aside the curtain over the kitchen window and peered out. "What's he doing?"

Sisko sawed off another slice of bread. "Trying to figure out how he's going to tell us he's leaving."

"Ben?"

Happily engaged with his egg beating, he didn't look up. "Hmm?" he asked.

Kasidy said, "I'm going to go talk to him."

"Then I won't make your toast yet," he said. Looking up at Rebecca in her bouncy chair, sucking her fist contentedly, he grinned and said in the high, excited tones the baby responded to, "I'll talk to Miss Rebecca. Yes, I will. We're going to have a nice chat."

Surprised, she asked. "Aren't you going to tell me to leave him alone? No 'He'll come in when he's ready'?"

Placing the bowl of batter in the refrigerator, Ben shook his head. "Why would I say that? You're his friend. More, you're family. If I were him, I'd want you to come out."

"Oh," she said, not knowing what else to say.

"Not what you were expecting?" he asked as he stooped to lift Rebecca out of her chair.

"Not exactly. Are you sure the Prophets didn't do anything to you while you were gone?"

Sisko made a "Why would I tell you the answer to that?" face, then offered a finger to Rebecca that the baby promptly grasped with raptorlike force and pulled toward her mouth.

"She shouldn't be sucking on your dirty fingers, Ben," Kasidy said.

"Babies," said the Old Hand at Parenting, "do whatever they want to do and nobody can tell them they shouldn't."

The sun was high enough in the sky that the dew was rapidly drying and the *kuja* flies were beginning to spiral up in loose clouds from the grass. Another half-hour and it would be unbearably warm out in the sun. Jake had his head tilted back, eyes shaded, intent on something high up. Stepping out from under the arbor, Kasidy saw what he was looking at: a black shape drifting in slow, lazy circles. Kasidy's pilot instincts kicked in and she judged that the shape might be as high up as a thousand meters and must have a huge wingspan—at least four meters and maybe as much as six.

"Wow" was all she could think of to say.

"Yep," Jake answered.

"Glider?" she asked.

"Nope," Jake said. "It was a lot lower a few minutes ago and I saw its wings pump. Whatever it is, it's alive."

"I repeat," Kasidy said. "Wow. I've never seen anything like that around here. Do you have any idea what it is?"

"None," Jake said. Then he added a bit testily, "I'm not the one who lives here, though."

"Less than a year," she said, trying not to sound too defensive. "And I've been too busy to do much bird watching."

Jake looked down at her, hand still shading his eyes, and said, "Sorry, Kas. I didn't mean it that way."

" 'Sokay, Jake." She took a half-step closer to him, then took his arm loosely in her hands to steady herself.

"They used to have avians like that in South America," Jake said. "On Earth."

"I know where South America is."

"Right." Again, he sounded apologetic, but only barely. "Anyway, one was called *Ornithochirus*. Huge wingspan. It lived most of its life in the air because it could barely move on land. It had to live near cliffs because the only way it could get off the ground was by jumping off something high."

"A pterosaur?"

"Yeah." He looked down at her. "How do you know about them?"

"I had a dinosaur phase when I was a kid."

"Really? Me, too. How old were you?"

Kasidy thought back. "Five. Maybe six. I liked reading about them."

"I memorized all the names," Jake said.

Shaking her head, Kasidy said, "Didn't do that, but I liked looking at holos of them."

"Did they have dinosaurs on Cestus III? Something like them?"

They had talked about Kasidy's homeworld on several occasions, but always in the context of her growing up there and leaving it. "There were prehistoric creatures, sure, but nothing really big before humans starting settling there."

Jake lowered his gaze and stared out again toward the horizon. "How about here on Bajor? Did they have anything like dinosaurs?"

Kasidy had to admit she had no idea. "We should check. I imagine that's exactly the kind of thing Rebecca is going to be asking me in a few years. Or, more likely, telling me about." The idea made her smile. "I guess she'll be just like me—reading about Earth and learning about dinosaurs and wondering what it would be like to find some kind of gigantic bone buried in the sand."

Jake didn't reply for several seconds, and then he said simply, "I feel like I don't know anything about anything."

Ah, Kasidy thought. *Here we are then.* Aloud, she said, "What do you mean? It's always seemed to me that you know a lot of things. A lot more than I did at your age."

Scowling, Jake said, "I know a lot of facts. Sometimes it feels like I don't even know many of those." Pointing out to the south, he asked, "Do you know what's out there in that direction?"

Again Kasidy admitted that she did not. Geography had never been her strong suit, and these days she was not very concerned about anything farther away than the horizon.

"Neither do I," Jake said, the self-disgust making his voice tight. "I have no idea what's out there." He tapped the side of his head and added, "And no idea what's in here, either."

Kasidy sensed how delicate the situation was and did not know whether she should err on the side of sympathy or truth. "You'll figure it out," she said trying to find a compromise. "You're a writer. That's your job."

"Is it?" Jake asked. "And am I? I'm not too sure."

This is worse than I thought. Kasidy decided that sympathy was no longer useful. "Stop it, Jacob Sisko," she said sharply. "I'm not going to listen to you indulge in self-pity. You know you're a writer. If you're having trouble with something right now . . ."

"But that's just it!" he exclaimed. "I'm not doing anything right now!" Looking down at her, eyes wide, he said, "I can't seem to think of anything I want to say right now. Everything seems either too big or too trivial. I can't make sense of it, can't get any perspective!"

"Oh, sweetheart," Kasidy said, trying to soothe her friend, "that will come. A lot has been happening the past year: The end of the war, your father disappearing, your adventures in the Gamma Quadrant, finding Opaka and the Eav-oq, your father coming home, Rebecca being born. That's a lot for anyone, let alone for someone . . ." She bit her tongue, hoping he would let the sentence pass.

He didn't. "Someone?" he asked. "Someone what? Someone who?"

She gritted her teeth. There was no escaping it now. "I was going to say, 'Someone so young.' But that's not what I meant. I just meant . . . you've had an extraordinary life, Jake. All kinds of things have happened to the people around you. . . ." Wincing, she realized her mistake too late.

"Exactly!" He shouted, arms flung wide. "To people around me! But never to me!"

"Now, don't do that, Jake," Kasidy protested. "You had your adventures on the *Even Odds*. Don't make it sound like you're nothing but a bystander. You've seen more in your short span of years than most people see in a lifetime."

"Then why can't I write about any of it?!"

Frustrated, Kasidy decided it was time for direct action. Balling up her fist, she punched Jake in the arm as hard as she could.

"Ow!" he shouted. "What was that for?"

"Did it hurt?"

"Of course it hurt," Jake said, rubbing his shoulder. "You've got bony knuckles. That's going to leave a mark."

"And you know why it hurt?" Kasidy asked, but didn't wait for an answer. She was angry. *These Sisko men,* she thought. *So brilliant and so dense.* "I'll tell you why: Direct stimulus. You get a shot in the arm and you feel it right away. One shot and you feel it very cleanly and clearly. Now, let's talk about everything that's been happening to you lately. Let's say that they're the same as getting one shot after another after another. Understand?"

Jake took a half-step away. "Maybe. You're not going to hit me again, are you?"

"No," Kasidy said, her tone softening. "But if I did, what would that be like? Would you necessarily feel each punch if I got you three or four more times?" She held up her clenched fist. "With my bony knuckles."

Wincing, Jake admitted, "Probably not. My arm would go numb pretty fast."

"You see my point now, don't you?"

Jake continued to rub his arm, but his gaze had drifted off to the horizon again. "I think so," he said. Then, with more conviction, "Yeah, I think I do."

He keeps looking out at the horizon. Grabbing his arm and gently rubbing it, she remarked, "Your father said you were thinking of heading out."

Annoyance flickered across Jake's face. "Did he?" he asked.

"I didn't say anything to him. Well, what if I did? Where would I go? Back to Earth to see Grandpa? He was just here and, frankly, I don't feel like cleaning oysters. Back to the station? I'm not sure I have a life there, either."

"No, silly," Kasidy said cajolingly. "Not anywhere out there. Not on a ship or using the transporter. Use your feet. Pick a direction and start walking." She felt him stand a little taller, as if he would be able to bring the horizon closer. Kasidy felt something in his shoulders relax.

"The house feels too small for all of us," Jake said, his voice cracking a little.

Whatever it was that was coming up out of him was costing him. *Good,* Kasidy thought. *It should.* "You understand," she said aloud, "that it doesn't feel that way to us. Only to you. And it should, too. Young men aren't supposed to like living with their parents."

Jake tore his eyes away from the horizon and looked down at her. The tightness around his mouth disappeared and was replaced by a slow smile. *There it is. The smile. The old Jake.* "How did you ever get to be so smart?" he asked.

Kasidy rolled her eyes and grinned. " 'Always hang around people smarter than you are and you're bound to learn things.' One of the few pieces of good advice my father ever gave me."

He opened his mouth to reply, but before he could say a word, Kasidy saw Jake flinch and hunch his shoulders. Ducking his head, he lifted his arm protectively, as if shielding her from a blow. Looking up and around his arm, she realized that they had both forgotten about the hovering black shape. Somehow, instinctively, Jake had sensed a change in its disposition. The creature, whatever it was, had tipped its wings back along the sides of its body and was now streaking toward them, growing larger by the second. A tiny ground-living mammalian voice from the back of her mind chittered, *Crouch down low and hope it doesn't see you!,* but Kasidy tried to ignore it. The sane, sensible part of her, the part that had accepted the fact that she was married (for better or worse) to the Emissary, was sighing, *Okay, now what?* Abruptly, the creature changed trajectory and winged away from them, slowly losing shape and form until it became a dark blot against the brilliant morning blue, then vanished from sight.

"Why don't you find out where it's going?" Kasidy said thoughtfully after a long moment.

Jake's eyes widened. "You're serious?"

"When Rebecca goes through her dinosaur phase, her big brother can regale her with his how-I-encountered-a-giant-winged-beast story. You'll be her hero."

With an inscrutable expression, he studied Kasidy, then bent and kissed her very formally on the cheek. "Thank you, Kas." Turning, he strode back through the grass toward the house. She followed, noting the muddy footprints across the veranda and into the house; apparently in his excitement Jake had forgotten to wipe his feet. She sighed deeply. *Boys will be boys.* Passing over the threshold into the entry hall, she reached inside the coat closet for a cleanup rag she kept handy for just such an occasion as this.

Ben emerged from the kitchen and frowned when he saw Kasidy on all fours. "I told that boy to watch his shoes. I'll get him back here—"

"No. Let him be." She wiped up the last of the mud and sat back on her haunches to look up at her husband.

"What's going on? He seemed to be in a hurry. Is he going somewhere?"

"Yes," Kasidy said. "For a walk." And, in her own thoughts, she added, *To go see what the rest of his life looks like.*

3

LENARIS

General Lenaris Holem scooped up a handful of ash and allowed the dawn wind to scatter it. He watched it sift between his fingers, leaving his palm stained black, and wondered whose life it represented. Man? Woman? Child? Had they been asleep when the end came? Or had the natural-gas leak already done its work by the time it ignited?

Lenaris surveyed the devastation through the thinning smoke. The tiny hilltop village had been effectively incinerated, reduced to charred ruins and a choking dust cloud that twisted up and across the sky over Hedrikspool Province. Not for the first time, the general wondered how such things fit into the Tapestry. He tried to recall if some obscure reference to this event could be found among the prophecies of Trakor, Shabren, Talnot, Ohalu, or any of the others. Had one of them foreseen it? And if they had, did that mean all this could have been prevented?

Such questions had nagged at him for much of his life. Growing up in the Relliketh camps, under Cardassian rule, Lenaris had always been riddled with doubt. It kept him, he believed, from taking anything for granted. As much as he respected those among his fellow Bajorans more pious than he, he took little comfort in the belief some of them held, that even during the worst times of the Occupation, the universe was unfolding as it was meant to. Looking around him now at what remained of Sidau village, he ached for that kind faith, the certainty that even horrors of this magnitude had some meaning in the greater scheme of things.

"General?"

Knees popping as he stood, Lenaris brushed the ash from his rough hands before responding to the voice. Twenty-five years in the resistance, followed by eight as a senior officer of the Militia, had left their marks on him. His curly gray hair continued to recede, the lines on his face were becoming more pronounced . . . but what troubled him most were the aches in his legs and lower back, which were becoming more distracting as the years passed. "Thank you for coming, Lieutenant," he said. "I apologize for the sudden change of venue for our meeting."

"Under the circumstances, I would never expect an apology, sir. To be honest, I was surprised you didn't decide to postpone our appointment."

Lenaris turned to face his visitor, and found that he still hadn't grown accustomed to seeing Ro Laren back in a Starfleet uniform. Her previous stint with the Federation's exploratory and defensive arm notwithstanding, he'd gotten used to thinking of her as Militia. So much so that sight of her in the black and gray uniform, trimmed in the gold of the organization's security and services division, still surprised him. "How much do you know about what happened here?" he asked.

"I read the initial incident report on my way over from the station," Ro said. "It's tragic. I understand there were nearly three hundred people living here. For all of them to lose their lives in something so easily preventable . . ."

So she hasn't spoken to Kira yet.

Ro stepped carefully around the debris, taking in the view of the fog-shrouded valley beyond the village's crumbled outer wall. "They were an odd bunch," she observed.

Lenaris's eyes narrowed. "Oh?"

Ro hesitated for a second or two before elaborating. "There's little about them in central archives, but from what I gather, they were a pretty insular community. Out here in the middle of nowhere, shunning outside contact for the most part. And, supposedly, they had a strange annual tradition in which they believed they fought off a *Dal'Rok,* of all things." Ro shook her head as if she found the mythical spirit's very name laughable. She turned away from the view and shrugged. "As I said . . . an odd bunch."

"They were Bajorans, Lieutenant," Lenaris said quietly, but with more intensity than he meant to project. "That they were perhaps more eccentric than most, and not as modern as you or I, is irrelevant. Whoever these people may have been—or not been—they deserve better than to be remembered as objects of scorn."

Ro blinked. "I assure you I intended no disrespect, General."

"I'm not sure I give a damn what you intended, Lieutenant," Lenaris said. "What I know is how you came across: arrogant, dismissive, and contemptuous."

Ro's gaze shifted to one side for a moment, the way it often did when she was contemplating a cutting response to someone challenging her. Lenaris had grown quite familiar with the look during those first few weeks after she'd returned to her people following the end of the Dominion War. But then her expression softened, and when she spoke again, her voice lacked its previous edge. "You're right," she said. "That was completely inappropriate. It won't happen again, sir."

Lenaris nodded, letting her know he considered the matter closed. A small part of him, however, was mildly amused that Ro Laren, of all people, was learning restraint. He wondered darkly if he was meant to take that as an omen.

Ro asked, "Has the Militia confirmed how the accident took place?"

"Not exactly," Lenaris said, just as he spied a figure sprinting toward him from the mobile command center at the edge of the village. Wearing a red Militia uniform like Lenaris's own and holding a padd in one hand, the officer kicked up ash and soot with his boots as he ran. Captain Jaza. *Right on time.*

"You asked for a copy of this, sir?"

Lenaris thanked the captain as he accepted the padd. He spoke as he keyed on the display. "Lieutenant, I'd like you to meet Captain Jaza Najem, one of my scientists. Captain, Lieutenant Ro Laren."

Jaza nodded. "A pleasure, Lieutenant. I've been looking forward to meeting you."

"Really?" Ro said. "Why is that?"

Never lifting his eyes from the padd, Lenaris explained, "This is Captain Jaza's last week under my command. He's decided to join Starfleet."

"I submitted my transfer application a few days ago," Jaza elaborated. "I was told to report to the evaluation center in Ashalla next week for an interview. I understand you and Commander Vaughn are overseeing the review process?"

"Initially, yes," Ro confirmed. "The commander and I are primarily evaluating career Militia personnel who qualify for direct transition to active Starfleet duty. I expect Command will be sending instructors for those requiring additional training, and recruitment officers for civilians wishing to enroll in Starfleet Academy. In fact, it was to discuss those very matters that I came to meet with General Lenaris. Are you hoping to remain in-system, Captain?"

"Actually, I indicated a preference for starship duty on my application," Jaza said. "I realize there are no guarantees, but I've grown a bit restless on Bajor."

Ro smiled. "I know the feeling. I'll remember we spoke when your application hits my desk."

Jaza's delight was apparent. "I appreciate that, Lieutenant."

"Thank you, Captain," Lenaris said, finally looking up from the padd. "That'll be all."

"Yessir," Jaza replied. He nodded at Ro. "A pleasure meeting you, Lieutenant. I look forward to speaking with you again," he said, and marched back toward the MCC.

Ro nodded, watching him go. When he was out of earshot, she said to Lenaris, "He seems like he'll make a fine addition to Starfleet."

"Captain Jaza is one of my best officers," Lenaris said. "He'd be an asset wherever he went. I'm sorry to lose him."

Ro turned and looked at him. "I imagine you're experiencing a lot of that these days, aren't you?"

Lenaris shrugged as the two of them started walking toward the MCC. "It isn't exactly unexpected. We've known all along that some Militia personnel would be absorbed by Starfleet once Bajor joined the Federation. But I'm seeing transfer requests from people I never imagined would want to leave Bajor, not after fighting so hard to win our world back from the Cardassians. And I never stopped to consider how many young people would want to attend Starfleet Academy. My sister's children—a girl and two boys—all plan to report to the recruitment office in Ashalla the day it opens next month. It's a lot of change to accept at once."

"They're good changes, though," Ro said.

"Are they?" Lenaris asked. "I thought so too, at first. Then this happened." He gestured expansively at the ruin around them.

Ro frowned. "What does what happened here have to do with—?"

Lenaris held out the padd to her.

"What's this?" Ro asked as she took the device.

"The revised incident report, based on an investigation my people conducted after some anomalies showed up in the initial findings."

Ro frowned as she thumbed through the text. After a few moments, she looked up at him. "Deliberate?"

"That's what the evidence is telling us." Lenaris watched as Ro took another few seconds to absorb the details from the padd, items he'd already committed to memory: residual traces, at the epicenter of the destruction, of triceron, a volatile compound used in some incendiary devices; satellite data showing a single skimmer departing the region shortly after the explosion, headed toward Jalanda, followed shortly thereafter by a Besinian freighter lifting off from the city's spaceport . . . a ship that had arrived on Bajor only hours earlier.

"Son of a—" Ro slapped her combadge. "Ro to *Brahmaputra*. Patch me through to Captain—"

"Kira already knows, Lieutenant," the general cut in.

Ro looked at him. After a few seconds, Lenaris heard the runabout's onboard computer prompt Ro to restate her request. "Cancel," Ro said into her combadge, cutting the connection with another slap. She waited for Lenaris to continue.

"We confirmed the new findings only an hour ago, while you were still en route to Bajor," the general explained. "I notified Deep Space 9 immediately, of course; once the freighter left the system, it was out of my jurisdiction. My understanding is that the *Defiant* set out in pursuit of the Besinian ship immediately, even though the trail was already two hours old at that point."

"What do we know about the ship?"

"Very little. It was a freelance courier. Having found ourselves unable to verify the authenticity of the credentials they presented when they first requested permission to land, we're proceeding on the assumption that they transmitted forgeries in order to cover their real agenda."

Ro shook her head. "But what kind of agenda would anyone have against these people?"

"That, Lieutenant, is why our meeting wasn't canceled," Lenaris told her. "Captain Kira expects you to investigate the matter personally."

4

ASAREM

With the early-morning light of B'hava'el pouring through the enormous bay windows of the first minister's residence, Asarem Wadeen nibbled at a warm slice of *makapa* bread spread with *moba* jam while she read through a padd containing her morning brief, the Bajoran global situation report.

The number-one item in the brief was the incident in Hedrik-spool, though apparently nothing new had come to light since she'd gone back to bed after first being apprised of the matter, four hours ago. It was intolerable that an alien ship could come to Bajor and cause such death and turmoil, and then escape. Kira Nerys, to her credit, had been determined not to allow the perpetrators to get away, but realistically, Asarem knew the odds were against the captain. The ship had come and gone too quickly, before anyone had completely understood what had befallen the isolated hamlet, for even the *Defiant* to have a reasonable hope of catching those responsible. The bottom line was that the security monitoring the traffic to and from Bajor had failed, and would need to be reevaluated if such despicable crimes were to be prevented in the future.

Item two: The new figures from the Ministries of Trade, Agriculture, and Cultural Exchange were encouraging. Bajoran educators and artisans, musicians and writers, designers, builders, and farmers were highly sought after on a number of Federation planets. In addition, exports of every kind were on the rise, including, Asarem noted with amazement, authentic Bajoran cuisine and ingredients, which had apparently earned quite a reputation since the Occupation ended. Less than a decade ago, her people were coping with the threat of famine. Since then, Bajor not only had become completely self-sufficient again in feeding its own people, but was ready to meet offworld demands for native produce and prepared foods. Several planets with interest in Bajoran exports would be reciprocating with resources of their own, not the least of which was Coridan, whose abundance of dilithium would help facilitate a new era of Bajoran colonization.

Item three: On the foreign-policy front, she saw that once the Federation Council convened its new session, hearings were expected to be scheduled on the matter of the Trill government's unilateral handling of the parasite affair, possibly to determine if criminal charges needed to be filed. A footnote on the revised death toll from the recent civil upheaval on the Trill homeworld gave Asarem pause. It was becoming increasingly clear to her that the Trill were already paying dearly for their subterfuge, the very fabric of their society needing to be rewoven. As angry as she still was about the manner in which they had exposed the threat to Bajor, the fact remained that they *had* exposed it, making it possible for her people to take steps against the remaining creatures. Asarem made a note to herself: Although her government would favor holding specific individuals accountable for any crimes committed in the parasite affair, she would also make sure Bajor voted against any punitive action against the Trill people. Bajor had nothing to gain by making the situation on the Trill homeworld any worse.

Item four: A report on the continuing aid to Cardassia Prime concluded that inadequate health care was still the number-one problem there. It made her recall with shame her farcical meetings with Cardassian ambassador Natima Lang months ago, when Shakaar—or rather, the parasitic alien masquerading as Shakaar—had instructed then-Second Minister Asarem to keep the Cardassians at arm's length. Lang had practically begged her for Bajor's compassion, and Asarem had been required to withhold it, despite the way in which it tore at her to do so. Thankfully, Vedek Yevir's maverick act of interfaith diplomacy had rallied popular support for Cardassian rapprochement, which Asarem had been able to officially endorse as first minister once the Shakaar-thing had been exposed. She made a note to pass the report on to Councillor Rava so she could put it before the Federation Council, and to set up a meeting with the Bajoran minister of health to discuss what additional medical support Bajor could offer Cardassia.

Asarem set the padd down for a moment and rubbed her eyes. Her interrupted sleep was going to make the day that much harder to get through. She was supposed to meet Minister Rozahn later in the morning for a springball match, which was to be the setting for the two women to discuss an old proposal of Shakaar's, found among his files, to invite the Federation to establish a Starfleet shipyard within the Bajoran system. She glanced across the room at the ministerial portrait of her predecessor above the fireplace, and wondered how often he felt as smothered by the job as she did right now. She smiled at the painting, thinking that perhaps he'd have been pleased with how Bajor was faring overall. Shakaar looked back at her from the canvas, his expression hopeful. The portrait had once resided in the office of his personal assistant, Syrsy, who had withdrawn from public service after Shakaar's violent death. *I haven't spoken with her since the memorial service,* Asarem realized. *I should get in touch with her, see how she's doing. . . .*

Making another note in the padd, Asarem finished her slice of *makapa* and then reached for the cup her aide had filled before he'd left her to eat her breakfast in private. She took a single sip and winced. "Theno!" she shouted.

A moment later, her aide entered the residence. Theno was older than she by perhaps thirty years, slight of build, somewhat wizened in appearance, but possessing the most pronounced rhinal ridges she'd ever seen. His gray hair was combed back from his forehead, and his soft voice always failed utterly to disguise his complete impertinence. "You screamed, First Minister?"

"If I did, you have only yourself to blame," Asarem said. She held up the cup. "What is this?"

"Cela tea, First Minister," Theno said as he approached. "I asked the kitchen to prepare some for you."

"No, no, no!" she said, setting the cup back down. "How long have you been my aide, Theno?"

"It seems like forever, First Minister," Theno drawled.

"Then you should know by now that I only drink *cela* tea from Rakantha Province. Wherever this came from, it wasn't Rakantha."

Theno picked up the abandoned cup and sampled the tea for himself. "It tastes passable to me."

Asarem pointed at Theno and pounced. "You see, that's the problem. Right there. That attitude. The idea that 'passable' should mean 'acceptable.' Bajorans don't strive for 'passable.' Our culture and our civilization weren't built because our ancestors satisfied themselves with what was 'passable.' The growers in Rakantha are an ancient order of monks who have been cultivating *cela* plants specifically to make tea for centuries. They've elevated it to art, producing a leaf that surpasses the quality of *cela* grown elsewhere."

Theno frowned in distaste. "Isn't this the same group that campaigned a few years ago to have Cardassian voles declared a protected species?"

Asarem folded her arms. "For your information, despite the ecological problems the voles created when they were first introduced to Bajor decades ago, their droppings have been found to have had a remarkable restorative effect on our damaged farmlands since the end of the Occupation. The *cela*-growing monks in Rakantha were the first to recognize this. Because of them, there are now entire farms devoted to the refinement of vole fertilizer, which has greatly reduced our dependence on offworld soil-reclamation technology."

"But . . . they're *voles,*" Theno said.

"You're missing the point. The monks who came to understand their value weren't afraid to get their hands dirty, to look at things from an unpopular perspective, and to speak up in order to make things *better* rather than be satisfied with what was 'passable.' "

"My ignorance shames me, First Minister," Theno said. "Shall I arrange to have myself taken into custody?"

Asarem glared at him before returning to her morning brief. "Just get that swill out of here and bring me some *kava* juice."

"As you wish. Would you like one vole dropping in that, or two?"

Before Asarem could fire off a scathing retort, Theno's right index finger went to the tiny comlink receiver affixed to his left ear. He looked up at her, all trace his customary insolence gone. "It's Second Minister Ledahn. He says it's urgent. He's standing by on comm channel nine."

"Thank you, Theno. That'll be all," Asarem said automatically, moving to her companel as Theno exited the residence and keying the proper channel. The face of Ledahn Muri winked into existence. "What's happened?" she asked without preamble. "More news about Sidau?"

Ledahn shook his head. His strong features, Asarem noted, seemed accentuated since he began shaving his scalp. *"Not yet,"* he said. *"It's something else. Rava Mehwyn is dead."*

Asarem blinked, unwilling to believe at first that she'd heard him correctly. Rava was Bajor's newly appointed first representative to the Federation Council. She'd left Bajor only a week earlier. Thoughts of assassination and new political turmoils, foreign and domestic, raced through Asarem's mind.

"How did it happen?" she asked. "Who's responsible?"

"What? No, no one!" Ledahn said. *"There was no foul play. Rava had a heart attack in her sleep at the Bajoran Embassy, her second night on Earth. She was found dead by one of her aides the next morning, too late to be helped. The embassy physician confirmed it was natural causes. I'm sorry, First Minister, if I led you to think—"*

"No, that's all right, Muri," Asarem said, relief and sadness forming a peculiar mixture in her mind. "I guess I've gotten into a bad habit of automatically assuming the absolute worst."

"That's understandable, especially after all we've been through lately," Ledahn said.

"I can't believe it. I know Rava wasn't young, but . . . I'm sorry, this is quite a shock. I take it her remains will soon be returned to Bajor? We'll need to make sure her life is honored properly. Have her children been notified?"

"Not yet. I thought you'd prefer to contact them yourself. They all live in Dahkur."

"Thank you, yes, I'll do that right away."

"Before you do," Ledahn said, *"there's the matter of selecting Rava's replacement to discuss."*

Asarem was taken aback. "Can't that wait? Prophets, Ledahn, the woman just died—"

"I'm afraid it can't, First Minister."

"Why not? We spent a month wrangling with the Chamber of Ministers over the selection of Rava. The next one will take at least as long."

"No it won't. Or rather, it musn't. The Federation Council has been in recess for over three weeks. The new session convenes in five days. Under its charter, new member planets must have representation at the start of a session. If we don't have a councillor there for Bajor at that time, we'll have to wait for the next session in order to take part in new council business. Six months from now."

"Wait a minute. What are you saying?" Asarem demanded. "Are you telling me that, even though Bajor is now a member of the Federation, we could be excluded for half a year from taking part in the shaping of policy that could impact us? And that issues Bajorans are concerned about may not be raised until the next council session?"

"That's the short of it, yes," Ledahn said. *"Unless we get a new councillor to step in quickly in five days."*

"And just how am I supposed to do that?" Asarem asked angrily. "I couldn't get my first nominee passed because the damned Chamber of Ministers was more worried about sending a 'team player' who would make friends on the council than someone who would take a stand for Bajoran interests. I only agreed to go with Rava because it was clear Sorati Teru didn't stand a chance. Now you're telling me we're back to square one, *and* we're out of time."

"It's not quite the disaster it seems to be," Ledahn said.

Asarem sat back and folded her arms. "Tell me how."

"Under the rules of Chamber, in the event of the death of a Bajoran offworld representative, the First Minister has the right to appoint an interim representative of her choice without Chamber approval. I looked it up. The appointment is only effective for one year. After that it comes up for review by the Chamber, which may choose to allow the appointment to continue for the full term, or it may require you to submit a new nominee. But by that time . . ."

"By that time the interim councillor will be thoroughly immersed in the job," Asarem realized. "And if she does well, the Chamber wouldn't dare revoke the appointment. Magistrate Sorati can be our Federation Council representative after all."

"Yes. And ironically, all it required was the untimely death of Rava Mehwyn."

"Where are you now?"

"With my family in Tamulna."

"Can you be in my office early this afternoon? I'd like you here when I call Sorati with the news."

Ledahn grinned. *"I'm on my way, First Minister."*

Asarem cut the comlink, then keyed her aide. "Theno, please cancel my match with Minister Rozahn and extend to her my apologies. Then send me all the contact information on file for the children of Rava Mehwyn."

"At once, First Minister."

Asarem sat back, shaking her head in amazement at the unexpected turn of events, the twist of fate that brought forth opportunity out of tragedy. *Like springball,* she reflected. *Even during the worst moments of an apparently hopeless match, the ball might suddenly move in just the way it needs to in order to turn the game completely around.*

She had been concerned for some time about Bajor starting its marriage to the Federation from a position of weakness. She'd believed it was imperative to establish from the onset that Bajor was ready and determined to be an active player in the astropolitical arena. To have a strong voice in the shaping of Federation policy, particularly as it pertained to the still-important Bajor sector, which not only encompassed the wormhole, the Alpha Quadrant's gateway to the Gamma Quadrant, but also bordered on Tzenkethi space, the Badlands, and the shattered remains of the Cardassian Union.

Rava Mehwyn, while a competent diplomat, had not been her first choice for the job. Asarem felt she lacked the edge, the strength of character, and the sheer presence necessary for the role of Bajor's first Federation councillor. Rava might have been a likable ambassador and reasonable negotiator, but Asarem had secretly feared she might also be too accommodating, too eager to avoid confrontation, too willing to subordinate the good of Bajor to political expediency. She had been the safe choice, the moderate one, the one that the Chamber of Ministers had been willing to approve.

Now the ball has changed direction, and the move that could decide the game is mine . . . if I'm nimble enough.

5

RENA

The relentless rattle of the rain on the corrugated metal roof smothered the sounds inside the rest-and-sip. Rena observed customers scrape their stool legs along the rock floor, saw an open mouth cheer after a triumphant round of *shafa,* winced as a glass slid off a waiter's tilted tray and shattered on the ground; she heard little of it. Only the storm.

She nestled into the notch at the back of the corner booth, for the moment content to be an observer instead of a participant in the surrounding cacophony. If circumstances required her attention, she would know it. Hadn't Vedek Triu said, only a few days ago, that her path would be revealed as she walked it? Prophets willing, Triu's advice had been inspired and Rena's presence in this place had a purpose. In this moment, Rena wasn't sure what that purpose was; she doubted the answers to Topa's mysteries were hidden in the smoky half-light of a rest-and-sip. But Rena had to believe that if she allowed herself to learn from all possibilities she would find her path.

Her meditations, unfortunately, had been little help in that regard, and that troubled her. Restlessness was an alien state of mind for her and she wasn't sure how to cope. Typically, Rena could linger for long hours over minute details from the subtle gradations of color in the throat of a climbing *lana* flower to the patterns on a beetle's back. She enjoyed being allowed to float atop the surface of her life, propelled by the currents of chance.

But not today. Not yesterday, either, now that she considered it, or rarely since she'd returned from university. Easygoing Rena must have stayed behind in the Dahkur Institute of Art while Compulsively Responsible Rena had returned home. *I have promises to keep,* she thought. *I have kept the first by going to the Kenda Shrine to honor Topa. I need to return to Mylea to keep the others.* Circumstances, however, appeared to be conspiring to prevent her from attending to her duty.

Late that morning, an unexpected cloudburst had unleashed mudslides, forcing a temporary shutdown of the River Way, an ancient road that bisected Kendra Province, starting in the northernmost peninsula, then paralleling the Yolja River to the sea. Rangers had escorted all southern-bound travelers—including Rena—into the neighboring villages to wait until the repair crews had done their work. A rapid rise in the river necessitated that all water traffic stop as well. With Mylea still more than thirty *tessijen*s away, Rena had no choice but to wait out the storm.

Time had slipped by. She'd eaten a hot plate of batter-dipped tetrafin, caught up on the local gossip, and taken a short nap. Now, the sweltering sourness of many bodies being squeezed into a smallish space for long hours combined with deep-fried fish stink saturated the air, while the lethargic orange-gray beams creeping through the windows warned of the aging day. What had been tolerable at midday had grown tiresome. Instead of enjoying the respite from her journeying, Rena struggled to keep frustration in check. Not that she was eager to assume the responsibilities waiting for her at home; more like she had better ways to spend her time than alone, eating bad food in a middle-of-nowhere dive as a veritable hostage of an overeager public servant who worried about a little mud.

She scanned the crowd, searching for Sala's distinctive curly red hair, but couldn't find him. This many customers must be keeping him running, she thought. Draining the dregs from her mug, she signaled Vess, a waiter she remembered from her stop here a week ago, to bring her another. She listened to the rain, seeking a sign of when it might pass, but the storm gave no indication that it had exhausted its pent-up energy. Vess swung by, sending her drink spinning off his tray onto her table, leaving behind a trail of foam until the mug slowed to a stop in front of her. She gulped the ale without fanfare, then picked through a bowl of breadsticks until she found one that seemed less stale than the others. The warm brightness of the alcohol gradually softened her frustration, and she decided she might as well settle in. She might be drunk in another hour, but intoxication might make being stuck more bearable.

Rena swung her feet up onto the bench and leaned back so she was flush against the wall, her bedroll cushioning the small of her back. She reached into her knapsack, searching for her sketchbook. One of her peers at the university had tried converting her to a paddlike sketch unit that could be used with a programmable stylus capable of mimicking brushstrokes, re-creating the texture of charcoal or chalk—even reproducing the drip patterns of ink. The technology was fun, but Rena hadn't been convinced: too much work to learn a new way when the old way sufficed. Besides, she liked the feel of the pebbled parchment beneath her palm, how colored pigment stained her fingernails, reminding her of what colors she's used last.

She unwrapped her sketchbook from the waterproof cloth she stored it in. Skirt draping off her bent knees, she propped it against her thighs and studied the rendering she'd done last night. She gazed at the charcoal smudges for a long moment, examining the curves and figures that had seemed inspired by warm spring moonlight. She frowned. Why she had thought that such a design would be a fitting memorial for Topa's grave marker? She'd have to start over. Again. Maybe. She might be succumbing to the tyranny of perfectionism that inevitably derailed her projects. *For once, you need to finish something, Rena,* she scolded herself. *Time to make good on all that "promise" and "potential" you're supposed to have.*

Or maybe your first instinct was correct and this design is a disaster.

Resignedly, she ripped the sketch out of her notebook, balled it up, and tossed it toward a tray full of glasses perched on an empty table across from her booth. The trajectory of the balled-up drawing drew her gaze toward a table of rivermen who sat nursing mugs of *shodi,* nonchalantly checking out her legs. Following their blurry-eyed gazes, she smoothed her skirt down over her calves toward the tops of her boots. Discontented grumbles and slurred complaints resulted, but Rena ignored them. *Sorry, gentlemen, show's over,* she thought, reasoning that one of these days, Sala ought to hire a band or some dancing girls if his customers were so pressed to find entertainment that they'd resort to attempting to sneak a peek up a girl's skirt. But there was one in the crowd at the table who didn't appear interested in her underclothing; Rena realized he wasn't one of the regulars.

He wore a riverman's requisite soil-smudged jumpsuit, but his brown face lacked the wrinkled, chapped roughness that the wind-whipped rivermen developed over years of pushing barges up and down the Yolja's lower curves. Black stubble covered his chin and cheeks, but it was obvious to Rena's eye that the younger man had only lately decided to sport a beard. The haze made it difficult to determine whether he was Bajoran; he wasn't wearing an earring. He must have felt her gaze, because he looked up from his drink to meet her eyes. He wore a kind, openly friendly expression, and because he hadn't been trying to look up her skirt the way the others had, she smiled; he reciprocated. As they maintained eye contact, she briefly considered signaling for him to come over and sit with her, though she wondered about the propriety of the gesture, considering her—her— *situation. Is that what I'm calling it now?* But she'd been traveling alone for the past four days—ever since she left the Kenda Shrine—and the sound of a friendly voice not her own would be welcome. She wasn't asking to buy him a drink or to share a dance, gestures that might be misconstrued for obvious reasons. Before she could act, a waiter had tapped the young man on the shoulder, diverting his attention. *It's a sign. Decision made,* she thought, wondering what it said about her that she felt a twinge of regret.

She returned her focus to her sketchbook and the empty page in front of her. The same dilemma faced her now as had faced her when she first learned, that before he died, Topa had made three requests of her, his only living grandchild. The first request was that she go to the Kenda Shrine to obtain a *duranja* from the vedeks. Topa had never explained why a *duranja* from Kenda was important save only that a vedek from that shrine had helped him immeasurably during the Occupation. Whatever his reasons, Rena wouldn't deny a dying man his wish.

His second request seemed on the surface to be simpler, especially for an artist: design his grave memorial. For Rena, asking the Emissary himself to preside over Topa's death rites might have been easier than granting *that* request. How to express a remarkable life in a couple dozen centimeters of metal! How to show Topa's bravery, his kindness . . . If they had satisfied her, she could have resorted to the usual labels—resistance fighter, devoted father and husband, advocate for Bajoran independence. The labels failed to explain *Topa*. His nimble mind, always spinning ideas; even in his final days, confined to his bed as his immune system cannibalized his central nervous system, he would order Rena's aunt Marja to keep the Ohalu book on playback. Vedek Usaya would stop by and feign mortification that Topa would pollute his faith with the radical text, and heated debate would ensue. She remembered how, before he was sick, he would stand in the middle of the stone-paved street in front of his bakery—the bakery that had been his father's and his father's father's. Eyes closed, head tipped back, he would turn his flour-powdered face to the sky to be warmed by the sun. Once, as a little girl, Rena had seen him standing in the street swaddled in fog, his face up. Pragmatically, young Rena had pointed out that the sun was in hiding. Topa hadn't budged, saying only, "But I know the light is there. When it finally breaks through the mist, I'll be ready." The metaphor was lost on the child, but not on the adult Rena, who wondered if she was the one now patiently waiting for the light, or whether she'd given up and retreated into the shadows.

"Excuse me?"

Roused from her reverie, Rena realized that the unfamiliar riverman stood at the edge of her booth. His youth surprised her; he had to be close to her age. From his smooth hands, which bore evidence of recent lacerations, she surmised that he couldn't have long been in this line of work. And he was definitely human—a *handsome* human, with an engaging smile. Maybe a recent Federation transplant. She looked at him questioningly.

"I noticed you had some hardcopy," he said, gesturing at her notebook, "and I was wondering if you could spare a sheet."

At university, she'd been subjected to her share of creative pickup lines from men wanting to make her acquaintance, but this was a flimsier attempt than most. "You have a sudden desire to sketch one of your comrades?"

He shrugged sheepishly. "There's a lady over there"—he nodded in the direction of the barkeep—"who's offered to transmit a message to my family for me. I just need to write it down for her."

Ripping a sheet out of the binding and passing it across the table, Rena said, gesturing, "Have a seat. You need a stylus too?" She unfastened a knapsack pocket and removed a writing instrument.

He nodded and scooted into the bench opposite her. Rena watched as the Federation boy—"Fed," as she'd started to think of him—scribbled out several rows of Bajoran characters. As he wrote, he explained, "There's no transmitter on the barge— there's definitely not one here—and I don't expect I'll be to Mylea for a few more days."

"You have business in Mylea?" Rena asked, curious. She'd heard gossip that her friend Halar had met an alien boyfriend who'd been doing dockwork over the winter and wondered if this Fed boy might be him.

"Not so much business as it felt like the right place to go when I took off from home a week ago. I figure I might be able to catch a shuttle or transport out from there. If I like it, maybe there's a fishing outfit that could use a hand."

The stylus flew across the hardcopy with a fluency Rena found highly unusual for an offworlder. Since the end of the Occupation, a number of students from all over the quadrant had dribbled into Bajor's universities, including the one in Dahkur. In her limited experience with them, she'd found that the majority were translator-dependent; few of the aliens spoke Bajoran and none of them could write in it. Odd. She supposed he could be a local. A few Federation citizens came to Bajor when Starfleet stepped in to help the provisional government eight years ago. "So you haven't signed on to work the river for the summer?"

"Nah. Linh was going to let me off at the next stop anyway. Someone back in Tessik told me about a must-see archeological site—Yyn?—that she thought I'd like. I kind of have some experience in archeology so I thought I'd check it out on my way to Mylea."

"You won't have much luck at Yyn for another week—the site's only open to the public during the days leading up to the summer solstice," she said, wondering about the story behind his archeological experience.

Before she could ask, three quick chimes announced a message coming over the comm system. The chatter in the room subsided as the crowd waited expectantly. Rena hoped for good news.

"Due to ground instability and the risk of flash floods, the Provincial Ranger Units have decided to close the River Road and the Yolja barges indefinitely."

A collective groan—of which Rena was a part—pronounced the crowd's opinion on this development. She looked over at the bar, where the uniformed ranger spoke into the communication unit, and determined that he was far too cheerful about ruining their day.

He continued, *"Arrangements have been made for all of you to be hosted in the adjacent village. My deputy will inform you of your housing assignment."*

"You—"

Rena twisted around to see a uniformed deputy pointing at her.

"And you," he said, pointing to Fed. "Will be assigned to the Daveen Vineyards with the rest of the rivermen from your crew."

Rena rose, preparing to protest being lumped together with the motley barge crew, but when she considered the other dour, sneering faces in the place—some of whom appeared to be more intoxicated than Fed's crewmates—she sat back down. With a sigh, she started packing up her art supplies and arranging her pack so it would be easier to carry.

"They aren't bad guys," Fed said, as if reading her mind.

Rena flushed hot, wishing she weren't so obvious. "I'm sure they're fine. I'm feeling a lot of pressure to get home and this delay isn't welcome."

"Emergency?"

"Responsibilities."

"Ah," Fed said. "That I understand." He scooted out of the bench and she marveled at his height—nearly two meters. "I've gotta go get my gear, but I just wanted to offer to, you know, walk with you if it would make you feel more comfortable."

Mildly amused, she looked at him, blinked, and looked longer, uncertain if she should bow in response to his unexpected chivalry or if he would be offended if she laughed—good-naturedly, of course. Manners and rural Bajoran rest-and-sips rarely came together: too many years of eking out survival under Occupation conditions had made these outposts respites for hermits, homesteaders, and other independent types who wanted to be left alone. Seeing genuineness in Fed's face, her impulse to laugh gave way to a smile. "Looks like I have myself a steward."

He arched an eyebrow in question.

"Back in the days of *djarras,* highborn ladies traveled with specially trained protectors called stewards."

Bowing deeply, he looked up at her and with a broad grin said, "Accept my services, m'lady?"

This time Rena couldn't help laughing. "If I must," she said with mock annoyance and slipped her pack onto her shoulders. In truth, however, as she followed behind Fed's crewmates lurching toward the door, Rena knew that any sense of safety she felt came from Fed's presence by her side.

6

RO

Whoever they were, Ro decided from her temporary workstation in the Militia's mobile command center, they knew exactly what they were doing.

To the standard orbital sensor sweeps and the security cameras at the Jalanda spaceport, the Besinian freighter was unremarkable. The medium-powered commercial ship—a nondescript cargo carrier capable of warp five at best—had arrived with an empty hold ostensibly to meet with Bajoran exporters within the city. The export company named in their transmitted request for landing clearance confirmed that the owners of the ship had made an appointment for this very morning three weeks prior, but it was never kept.

Their credentials, as Lenaris suspected, were forgeries. No record of the identities provided by the crew existed anywhere. Nor did the ship's registry. Ro managed to verify that a Besinian freighter fitting the description of the one that landed on Bajor had been purchased anonymously at auction from a Yridian salvage dealer on Argaya just over a month ago. That, along with the appointment made with the Bajoran exporters, made it appear more and more as if this was something long in the planning.

Only two occupants of the craft ever left the ship, and they had carefully avoided the cameras at the spaceport. They did a fine job of making it look inconspicuous, but Ro wasn't fooled. There was intent behind everything these killers had done. They'd even arrived with their own skimmer.

Satellite imaging had shown the heat trails of thousands of similar surface craft knotted in and around Jalanda, hundreds in the countryside beyond, and scores leading into the mountains to the southwest. But only one had cut across the nature preserve to the north, toward the site of the village. It was a three-hour journey in either direction, and the satellites had shown both transits. Those travel times fell precisely between the Besinian freighter's landing, the destruction of the village, and the ship's departure, leaving little doubt about the connection. They were on Bajor less than seven hours, and when they were gone, nearly three hundred people were dead. But while assembling a reliable chronology of events had been a fairly simple matter, the whos and whys of the crime remained elusive.

Ro rubbed her tired eyes while she spoke to her console. "Computer, search telemetry from Deep Space 9 for information on all incoming and outgoing traffic in the Bajoran system for the past twenty-six hours. List any non-Bajoran and non-Starfleet vessels, and pull any scans taken of those craft."

"You're looking at it from the wrong angle," a sharp voice said.

Ro looked up. The only other person present in the command center, a gray-uniformed major, was seated at a workstation some distance away. He wasn't looking at Ro, but his body language was tense.

"Were you speaking to me?" she asked.

"The Besinian freighter," the major said. "You think if you figure out who they are and where they came from, you'll figure out what they wanted."

"That's right."

"It won't work," the major said.

"Is that so?"

"Yes, it is. Short of our actually capturing and questioning them, whoever was on the ship knew it wouldn't matter what we might learn about them. Otherwise they'd have covered their tracks a lot better."

"Maybe they weren't that clever," Ro said. "Maybe they were just careless and lucky."

The major shook his head. "I don't think so. But I do think you're wasting your time investigating the perpetrators."

Ro leaned back and folded her arms. "And I suppose you have a better suggestion, Major . . . ?"

"Cenn Desca. And yes, I do. But I doubt you'd be interested."

Ro's eyes narrowed. What the hell was *his* problem? "Since you're obviously hoping I'll take the bait, let me oblige you: Why do you doubt I'll be interested, Major Cenn?"

"Because it involves looking *at* Bajor, not away from it."

"Excuse me?"

"You think all the answers are out there," Cenn said, nodding his head in the general direction of the ceiling. "I wonder if it's even occurred to you to look for them here, on Bajor?"

"The perpetrators aren't on Bajor."

"But the crime *is*. Why else destroy the village so completely, unless they were trying to hide something?" The major shook his head. "I don't even know why I'm wasting my time. You're Ro Laren. You've made turning your back on Bajor into an art."

Ro stood up sharply, throwing back her chair. It crashed loudly against a console behind her. "I don't know who the hell you think you are, but I am *not* required to put up with this."

"Go on, then, leave. *Again,*" Cenn said as she started to turn away. His accusatory tone stopped her, held her against her will. "That's what you do best, isn't it? I'm sure, now that half the Militia is following your example, you must feel vindicated for giving up on Bajor during the Occupation."

"Major Cenn!"

Cenn snapped to his feet and came to attention. Ro stared at him blankly, scarcely aware that General Lenaris was standing in the open doorway that led outside.

Lenaris's steely voice cut through the sudden silence. "Report to Colonel Heku, Major. Tell him I said you're to assist in sweeping the western slope for additional evidence."

"Yes, sir," Cenn said, and headed immediately toward the exit. Lenaris moved aside to let him pass, then closed the door behind him.

The general turned to Ro, who still hadn't moved. "I'm sorry about that. Do you want to file a complaint?"

"No," Ro said.

Lenaris seemed to relax and started walking toward her. "Any luck yet in your investigation?" he asked.

Ro shook her head, having barely heard Lenaris's question. Anger and embarrassment mixed with confusion as she realized how completely she'd allowed Cenn to get under her skin. *I've endured people judging me before. Why did I let it rattle me this time?*

Lenaris, to his credit, didn't press her on the matter. He seemed content to wait and see if she wanted to talk. Well, he would be waiting a long time, then. She was done talking. Screw this and screw these people. She never needed them before, and she sure as hell didn't need them now. . . .

"Do you—" she said quietly, suddenly unable to keep the words from forcing their way out of her mouth. "Do you think he's right about me?"

Lenaris sighed, then settled into a chair at the workstation next to Ro's. A thick silence settled between them.

"You know," he said at length, "I remember the day you testified publicly before the Chamber of Ministers about your activities after you turned Maquis. Fighting the Cardassians, fighting the Dominion. You gave that testimony right before you received your honorary commission in the Militia."

"I didn't realize you were there," she said, sitting back down and wondering why he was bringing *that* up.

Lenaris shrugged. "No reason you would. I was just one member of the Militia brass among many in the back of the room, and I was only a colonel then. Still, your testimony made an impression on me."

Curious in spite of herself, Ro asked, "Any particular part?"

"Everything you didn't say."

Ro frowned. "I'm not sure I understand."

"Let's just say I've found that sometimes you can form a clearer picture about someone from what they don't say than what they do," Lenaris told her. "That day, the things I didn't hear made me throw my support behind your appointment to the Militia."

Ro found it hard to conceal her surprise. "I . . . I didn't know that. Thank you."

Lenaris waved the matter aside. "No need for that, although

I admit it was an uphill fight. I'm sure it'll come as no surprise to learn that there were a lot of senior officers who didn't want you there. It was difficult to get enough votes in the command council just to keep them from letting Starfleet arrest you, much less give you a job. As far as they were concerned, you were undependable and unpredictable. You were a complication in our relationship with the Federation. Worst of all, in a lot of eyes, you'd turned your back on Bajor when it needed you most."

"Maybe they were right," she said.

"I didn't think so."

She looked at him again. "Why not?"

"Because of everything you didn't say," Lenaris said with a smile. "You never really explained why you came home."

Ro shrugged. "What's to explain?"

"Maybe nothing," Lenaris conceded. "But maybe the lack of an explanation is more telling than anything you could have said out loud. I think deep down in your *pagh* you regret leaving Bajor when it needed every fighter it had, and you've carried that guilt ever since. It's why you kept looking for a new fight. You hoped to find one in Starfleet, but that ended badly, not once, but twice."

Ro kept her expression neutral as the ghosts of Garon II paraded across her vision. She blinked them away. She wondered if she would ever stop seeing them.

"Then the DMZ conflict flared up," Lenaris went on, "and it gave you the first real opportunity to do what you didn't do for your own world. When the Dominion wiped out the Maquis, you just shifted the fight over to them. I'm guessing you didn't even expect to survive. But you did . . . and once you ran out of fights, and thought you had finally atoned for giving up on Bajor, you came home.

"That's what I heard that day in the Chamber of Ministers. That was what you didn't say. And I thought you were right. Whatever sin you feel you committed against Bajor, Laren, you've long since atoned for it."

Ro said nothing.

"For what it's worth," Lenaris said, "Major Cenn isn't usually such an ass. He's actually a good man. That outburst was out of character. It's just that . . . to some people in the Militia, the transfer of so many personnel to Starfleet is a shock to the system, one that they need time to work through."

Ro glared at him. "And I suppose my being here at such a time, with my past, back in a Starfleet uniform, just pushed him too far, is that what you're telling me?"

"You know that isn't what I meant."

"Then what are you saying, General?"

Lenaris leaned forward, and Ro could tell he was making an effort not to lose his temper. "I'm asking you to try to understand what some of us in the Militia are experiencing, now that the reality of the changeover has settled in. We're not stupid, Laren. We know Bajorans need to be in Starfleet, to have a voice in its operations and its policies, and to share responsibility for shaping and implementing them. But there still need to be Bajorans who will put Bajor first, and their voice needs to be heard, too. The more of us who put on a Starfleet uniform, the more the rest of us fear that Bajor's voice will be lost in the multitude."

Lenaris stood up and walked out of the MCC without another word. Ro watched him leave and, alone again, realized that the general had painted a picture she hadn't stopped to consider.

Every Federation planet had its own domestic peacekeeping force. Starfleet dealt with matters of interstellar scope, but every world still needed a home guard to deal with local security issues according to local law. Bajor was no exception, and the Bajoran Militia wasn't dispensable. Contrary to Major Cenn's earlier rant, nowhere near half the Militia was transferring to Starfleet. The real percentage was actually minor for a global military, and would disappear as the Militia stepped up its own recruitment efforts to replenish its lost numbers.

On the other hand, Ro could easily see how a period of doubt and uncertainty would accompany such changes—at least in the beginning, as the new order took hold. She imagined that every world found its own way of dealing with the transition. And again Bajor would be no exception.

Maybe . . . maybe I can even help it along.

Straightening in her chair, Ro tapped her workstation's interface. "Computer, access the Bajoran Central Archives and search *all* databases for *all* references to the Sidau village in Hendrikspool Province. Then establish an uplink with the mainframe on Starbase Deep Space 9 and conduct the same search. Authorization: Ro, phi-delta-seven. Execute."

Having spent her early years in Jo'kala and the camps closest to it, Ro hadn't been to Ashalla in her youth. It wasn't until after the Dominion War that she'd gotten to see other parts of her homeworld for the first time, including the capital. What had struck her on those occasions was how old a city Ashalla really was; its elegantly designed buildings and ornate thoroughfares of red-brown granite and sand-colored fusionstone were built millennia before anyone had ever heard the word "Cardassian." It was sobering to see how much of her people's heritage—how much memory— the city still held, and more sobering still to learn that most of civilized Bajor was just like this, even after everything the Cardassians had wrought. After she'd returned to the planet of her birth, she realized with a profound sense of sadness that she no longer knew this world, had never known it at all.

Was that the real reason I found life here unbearable after the war? she wondered. Had the scope of Bajor's unique cultural identity, restored to fullness in the aftermath of the Occupation, so overwhelmed her that she felt like an alien among her own kind?

Now, as she walked down one of the city's main streets, the weight of Ashalla's vast memory bore down on her again. Except that this time it seemed to lessen as Ro came closer to her destination, until she realized that this district must be one of those that had been completely rebuilt in the years following the Occupation. Where most of the city was defined by structures so ancient it was easy to think of them as eternal, this part of Ashalla showed little of Bajor's past. Mostly it was new buildings, although several had been built in a style clearly designed to evoke what had been lost here. To Ro, it made the losses that much more tragic.

It had been Vaughn's idea that they should meet in this part of town. He had finished early for the day at the evaluation center, and said he had accepted an offer to be given a tour of the Tanin Memorial. The commander hadn't elaborated, but Ro had assumed that it was one of the dozens of monuments across the planet honoring the fallen of the Occupation. As she drew closer to the site, however, she learned by way of the signage leading toward the memorial that it had been created to honor a single man, a vedek who died here some years ago, just after the Occupation ended. There was no statue, no great spire or majestic abstract sculpture. Just a single broken column, apparently salvaged from an older structure, standing in the midst of a meditation garden.

The other thing Vaughn had neglected to mention was who his tour guide was.

She spotted them from across the street, strolling together along one of several flower-lined paths that snaked through the memorial: Vaughn, his hands clasped behind his back, walking alongside Opaka Sulan.

The former kai of Bajor, her short, unadorned gray hair catching the midmorning light, wore none of trappings of her old office. Dressed instead in the simple vestments of a monk, without the traditional hood, Opaka projected a serenity that was striking. She wore a pleasant smile, one that Ro thought was the most genuine she'd ever seen.

Vaughn, for his part, a head taller than the stout woman beside him, seemed to have his attention completely focused on whatever conversation they were having. At one point, he gestured inquiringly at a bed of *esani* flowers along their path. Opaka stopped and stooped to cup one delicate white blossom in her right hand, looking up at Vaughn as she answered whatever question he had asked. Vaughn seemed delighted, and freed one hand from behind his back to help her respectfully to her feet. Then the hand disappeared again, and the two resumed their stroll in comfortable silence. Ro had heard that the commander had come to value Opaka's friendship a great deal since the *Defiant* had returned from the Gamma Quadrant. It appeared that the ex-kai reciprocated the sentiment.

Ro caught up to the pair, but had to clear her throat to get their attention. They looked up. "Lieutenant!" Vaughn said. "There you are."

"Commander, Ranjen," Ro said, remembering that Opaka had eschewed various lofty titles she'd been offered since her return to Bajor, finally accepting a more humble one that spoke to her only current vocation: that of a monk engaged in theological study.

Use of the title seemed to please Opaka. She smiled warmly at Ro. "It is good to see you again, Lieutenant."

"Likewise," Ro said. For all her skepticism of the Bajoran religion, Ro liked Opaka. As kai, she'd given people courage and hope during the Occupation, and her nearly seven years in the Gamma Quadrant seemed to have cultivated that characteristic. Her soft-spoken assurances that Bajorans need not fear to explore their beliefs as individuals had gone a long way to defusing the schism created by the Vedek Assembly's mishandling of the Ohalu prophecies, which had long been suppressed as heretical.

Vaughn looked around at the memorial appreciatively. "It's quite moving, isn't it? When Sulan offered to show me this place, I wasn't prepared for the tranquility it evoked."

Ro looked around. It was all right, she supposed. The garden was certainly lovely, but she always became restless in such places. She'd never been the meditative type, and she suspected that she simply lacked the sensibility to appreciate the memorial properly.

Something on the ruined pillar caught her attention: a partial engraving of a Bajoran glyph in the broken stone, still legible. "Was this originally the site of the Taluno Library?"

Opaka nodded. "It was little more than an empty relic by the end of the Occupation, kept afterward out of a desire to preserve as much of Bajor's past as possible. Not long after the Gates of the Celestial Temple were opened, my friend Tanin Prem, a vedek, lost his life here when a bomb left over from the struggle against the Cardassians detonated, destroying what remained of the building." She gazed wistfully at the column. "This memorial was just being started when the Prophets called for me to leave Bajor. I'm glad to see how beautifully it turned out. Prem would have enjoyed such a place."

After a moment, Vaughn said, "Sulan, I must be going. But I want to thank you for a most enjoyable time. I look forward to speaking with you again."

Opaka inclined her head. "As do I, Elias. Be well. Good day, Lieutenant."

"And to you, Ranjen," Ro said.

Leaving Opaka to contemplate her lost friend, Ro and Vaughn made their way in silence across the plaza that separated the memorial from a large park on the other side. As they started to cross a gently sloping meadow, Ro saw dozens of people, mostly Bajorans but a few offworld visitors as well, enjoying the mild summer day. To Ro's surprise, the commander steered them toward a delicately curved S-shaped bench near a copse of trees overlooking the meadow. Vaughn leaned back and took in the view, watching a group of children working to get an elaborate kite aloft. In the distance, the great copper dome of the Shikina Monastery crowned the hill that rose up from the trees surrounding the park.

"Hope you don't mind," Vaughn said. "But it's such a pleasant day, it seems a shame to waste it in a dreary office, or aboard a runabout."

"No, it's quite all right, sir. This is fine."

"You come from a remarkable world, Lieutenant," the commander went on, his eyes never leaving the scene before him. "The more I experience Bajor, the more I understand Captain Sisko's feelings toward it."

"I'm starting to learn a few things about it myself," Ro admitted.

Vaughn nodded, then got down to business. "You have a report for me?"

"Yes, sir," Ro said. She keyed open a file on her padd while she spoke. "I have the current figures on Starfleet's absorption of Militia personnel."

"Proceed."

"Close to one hundred ninety thousand officers and enlisted personnel in all Militia divisions have submitted transfer applications for Starfleet service. We believe the rush has peaked, and that the numbers will taper off over the next few weeks. Civilian inquiries into enlistment and Academy enrollment have already exceeded the mandatory cap."

"Final estimates?"

"We expect one-quarter million total applications for direct transfer. Two hundred thousand of these will likely sail through, although ninety-five percent of those are expected to require three to six months of retraining and reorientation. Current projections are that ten percent of the remaining direct transfers will be officers. Starfleet enlistment and Academy enrollment are expected to max out with ten thousand new recruits each."

Vaughn stroked his beard, working through the numbers. "It sounds like I'll need to meet with something like a thousand duty-ready officers."

"Right now, the number is still closer to four hundred," Ro corrected, "but it could easily reach a thousand by the time the preliminary evaluations are completed."

Vaughn sighed. "I was hoping I'd be able to speak with them individually before they got their assignments, but obviously that's not going to happen. We'll have to make other arrangements. Perhaps a welcoming ceremony . . ." He looked at Ro. "In any event, Starfleet may need to set up a retraining facility here on Bajor to handle the bulk of the direct transfers."

"That recommendation appears in my report, sir," Ro said, keying the proper page and handing the padd to Vaughn.

"Excellent work, Lieutenant," Vaughn said.

"Thank you, sir."

After a moment of silence, the commander added, "You haven't told me yet how your meeting with Lenaris went."

"It could have gone better," Ro admitted. "He's second-guessing everything now. I did my best to reassure him, but—"

Ro was interrupted by the familiar, quasi-feminine voice of a Starfleet computer. "*U.S.S. Brahmaputra to Commander Vaughn.*"

"Hold that thought," Vaughn told Ro before tapping his combadge. "Go ahead."

"*Incoming communication from Dr. Girani Semna aboard Starbase Deep Space 9.*"

Vaughn winced. "Very well. Put her through."

"*Channel open.*"

"Yes, Doctor, what I can do for you?"

"*You've missed your appointment again, Commander.*"

"And I apologize again, Doctor," Vaughn said. "Perhaps we can reschedule . . . ?"

"*Oh, no you don't. Not this time,*" Girani said. "*the report on the annual crew exams is due to be filed with Starfleet Medical tomorrow. Dr. Bashir asked me to finish them in his absence, and you're the last one, Commander. I may not be Starfleet, but I still have the authority to pull medical rank over any member of the station crew. You're to return to the station immediately and report to the infirmary. That's an order.*"

Vaughn bowed his head in resignation. Ro tried not to smile, but was only partly successful. As his gaze came back up, Vaughn caught her amusement and scowled.

"All right, Doctor, you win. I'm on my way back to DS9. I'll be on your biobed in two hours. Vaughn out." He tapped his combadge again. "Damn doctors. If she wasn't already transferring dirtside—" He stopped, looked at Ro. "That reminds me . . . any progress in finding a new Bajoran MO?"

Ro nodded. "I have several candidates lined up. Their files are available for review at your convenience."

"Good. Kira's expecting a recommendation soon, and I can't blame her. Even more than before, Bajorans will be the primary residents of the station. I don't want to be without a Bajoran Starfleet physician for too long, especially with Bashir taking time off."

Mention of Bashir's absence recalled to Ro the awkward circumstances surrounding the human doctor's return from Trill with Ezri Dax, ten days ago. They had left as lovers and returned estranged. Although, considering what they had been through on Dax's homeworld, a strain on their relationship could hardly have been considered a surprise. Nor Bashir's abrupt decision to finally take some leave time.

"I believe you were about to tell me about your meeting with General Lenaris," Vaughn said.

"It was complicated by the situation in Hedrikspool, which now looks as if it was a deliberate act of mass murder, by aliens, for reasons unknown."

Vaughn nodded. "I spoke with Dax a short while ago. She filled me in on the latest."

"Any word from the *Defiant?*"

"Only that they think they picked up the scent—a warp signature that's a close match for Besinian propulsion systems. It was leading toward the Badlands."

Ro scowled. Any ship in the Bajoran sector intent on evading the authorities inevitably went into the Badlands. Who wouldn't? Sure, you took your chances getting that close to the plasma storms, but once inside, you were home free. That was what made the area so attractive to the Maquis. She made a mental note to look into the possibility of deploying automated sensor drones between B'hava'el and the Badlands; random sweeps of the region might reduce its effectiveness as a bolthole.

"What has your own investigation turned up?" Vaughn asked.

"Nothing useful yet," Ro admitted. "I kept hitting dead ends trying to trace the ownership and previous whereabouts of the freighter. One of Lenaris's men suggested that learning more about the village itself might provide a clue about why this happened. I'm looking into that."

"I imagine Lenaris is feeling pretty frustrated about the whole situation," Vaughn went on.

"Having to turn the matter over to Starfleet galled him," Ro said. "This incident has driven home the downside of the Militia's reduced role as a purely local defense and security force. He thinks they're becoming obsolete."

"He knows that isn't true."

"Intellectually, sure. But it's hard to remember that when you're standing in the ashes of three hundred people you failed to protect."

"It wasn't his failure. And if he believes it was, then it's *our* failure as well. We're in this together."

"But, sir—" How to put this? "We weren't *always* in this together. Bajor liberated *itself* from the Cardassians, without help from Starfleet, or anybody else for that matter. Most of the Militia is made up of former resistance fighters. It's a difficult thing for them to accept a reduced role in protecting Bajor."

"Nearly a quarter million Bajorans in Starfleet isn't a reduced role, Ro. It's an expanded one in which Bajorans will be taking even greater responsibility for protecting their world, and others. Bajor chose this, Lieutenant. It requested Starfleet's help eight years ago, and petitioned for Federation membership. Isn't that the point your people were trying to make by taking a lead in relief efforts to Cardassia? In harboring the Europani refugees when their world was threatened? That Bajor was more than ready to think outside the confines of one people and one planet?"

"I'm not disputing any of that. But if we're in this together, as you say, then those who choose not to join Starfleet—who devote themselves instead to service in Bajor's home guard—still need to have a sense of involvement. They need to know they still count."

"What are you proposing?"

Ro took a deep breath and took the plunge. "I suggest we reestablish the position of Militia liaison officer on Deep Space 9."

"That's the role Kira had before she became station commander, isn't it?"

Ro nodded. "She interfaced with the Militia and with the government in all aspects of station operations. She was a voice specifically for Bajoran interests within the predominantly Starfleet command structure."

Vaughn considered the idea. Then, to her surprise, he said, "All right. What about you?"

"Me?"

"I can't think of anyone better. Kira's role as starbase CO rules her out, and to date you're the only other Bajoran who's worked within both organizations. You're the ideal choice."

"Sir, I appreciate the vote of confidence, but I think what's really needed is for the Militia to be represented by one of their own on DS9, to have a permamant presence there as a member of the senior staff."

"That sounds almost like you're suggesting a token Militia officer."

Ro bristled. "What I'm *suggesting,* sir, is the Militia continuing to have input in matters the station deals with that may affect the security of Bajor."

"Lower your shields, Lieutenant," Vaughn said. "I think it's an excellent idea. I'm behind it one hundred percent and I intend to take it to the captain. I just want you to be prepared for how others may react to the idea, both in the Starfleet crew *and* in the Militia."

"I don't think it'll be a problem, sir," Ro said. "After all, if religious Bajorans can adjust to my agnosticism, and Starfleet hardliners can handle my reinstatement, a new Militia liaison shouldn't be a big deal."

Vaughn laughed. "When you put it that way, I suppose I can't disagree. I take it you already have someone in mind for the job?"

Ro reached out and keyed another file on the padd in Vaughn's hand. The commander started to read, and then noted the time. "Let's continue this discussion on the *Brahmaputra.* I need to head back to the station before Girani sends out search teams. Unless you need to stay on Bajor?"

Ro shook her head. "My business here is done for now. I'll be checking to see if there are any new leads into the Hedrikspool massacre when I get back to DS9."

They stood up together, and then Vaughn looked at her. "You

probably haven't heard this from enough people in Starfleet, Ro, but I want you to know . . . I for one am glad you put the uniform back on."

"Thank you, sir. But . . . why?"

"Because I know what really happened on Garon II." The commander tapped his combadge. "Vaughn to *Brahmaputra*. Two to beam up."

7

RENA

"*. . . raka-ja, ut shala moala . . . ema bo roo-kana-uramak,*"
Rena chanted. In the small confined space—little more than an
empty closet—the smoke from the *duranja* lamp irritated her
eyes, but she forced her attention on the benediction to the
Prophets to protect her grandfather and guide him on his journey
to the Temple gates. "*Ralanon Topa propeh va nara ehsuk
shala-kan vunek—*"

A gentle rap at the door broke her concentration. She shifted
out of her cross-legged meditation posture onto her knees and
blew out the oil lamp before inviting her visitor to enter.

Unsurprisingly, Fed peered around the corner of the door.
"Supper's ready," he said.

Rena followed him through a maze of open-beamed hallways
to a dark-paneled storage room. From the three-meter-high
shelving units pushed back against the rear wall, she surmised
that it had formerly been a wine storage area. Their hosts, an elderly couple they'd met earlier, had cobbled together a makeshift
kitchen with hot plates warming what smelled like *hasperat*. Ceramic jugs fitted with spigots provided water or wine. From the
raucous laughter, Rena assumed the barge crew had resumed
their imbibing from where they'd left off at the rest-and-sip. The
group had staked out a corner of the room, sprawled out on the

floor, and was playing *shafa*. Noticing that their hosts weren't to be found, Rena imagined they had retired for the night. *With this group for company, I can't blame them.*

The *hasperat* was stale. It was served with a sauce that was obviously meant to mask the fact that the flatbread holding it together was about three days past its fitness for consumption. She tried not to let her revulsion show, but Fed hadn't missed the abrupt clenching of her jaw.

"I'm sorry," Fed said quietly, reaching for her plate. "I thought most Bajorans like *hasperat*—"

Rena touched his arm, halting him. "It's the bread," she whispered. "It's way past the point when it should be used this way."

"Wow. I didn't even notice."

"Most people wouldn't. But my family has run a bakery in Mylea for generations. A lot of things, I don't know. Bread, I know." Rena made quick work of finishing her *hasperat,* then washed it down with a large mug of cold, crisp water. Attending to her needs, Fed hovered nearby. She'd told him repeatedly that he could join his friends, but he insisted on staying with her. Though she found his behavior slightly odd, she didn't attempt to dissuade him. During their walk of several *tessijen*s from the rest-and-sip to the winery, she had found him to be an amiable traveling companion.

Conversation had been spare. She had learned that he, too, had been an only child until just recently, when his father's second wife had given birth, and that he'd lived in the Bajoran sector since his early teens. She deduced, based on the timing, that he must have arrived with the first Starfleet contingent that assumed control of the space station, and Fed confirmed it. They had both lost parents in wartime: Both her mother and father had been arrested and tortured by the Cardassian occupiers of Mylea; his mother had died in a space battle far from Bajor. He offered tantalizing glimpses into his past. His archeological "experience" came from working at B'hala. *B'hala!* She'd plied him with questions about the Ohalu texts, but he subtly deflected her inquiries. He had answers—she knew it—but she didn't pry. Long stretches of road had been traversed without words passing between them, and Rena liked that. She'd grown accustomed to the tempo of his steady footfalls, though she had to take a step and a half for each step of his. Having a companion had helped the time pass quickly.

When they'd arrived at the winery, they'd all been assigned rooms in the wine-production facility, not currently in use as the summer fruit crops had not yet ripened. Fed had even obtained a blanket and bedroll for her before the others poached them all. Touched by his kindness, Rena had thanked him profusely, for the first time during the long day feeling relaxed and hopeful that the worst was behind her.

Until the present moment.

Rena was filling her water mug when she became aware of hot breath, sour with wine and *hasperat,* on her neck. "Little missy want to come over and join us for a game or two?"

Squeezing between the buffet table and the riverman, she politely declined. "I'm not much for *shafa.*"

"We don't have to play *shafa,*" he persisted, trudging along behind her, hovering too close for Rena to feel comfortable.

Turning on her heel, she looked him square in the eye. She considered, briefly, whether or not she should play a round of *shafa* in the hope that it would placate her tagalong; he didn't have a malicious air about him. But from appearances, they had more than enough players, including a few women who worked as servers in the rest-and-sip. Rena wouldn't be missed. "No, thank you. Perhaps another time," she said, smiling congenially.

"Look at her!" one of the crewman shouted, pointing. "She smiled at you, Ganty. She likes you." This pronouncement sent the group into gales of cackling laughter.

"Get back to the game, Ganty," Fed said, materializing by Rena's side. Placing a hand on Ganty's shoulder, he leaned over and whispered loud enough for Rena to hear, "I think Volvin is cheating. You'd better check your icons."

"That reptile!" Ganty proclaimed, and tottered off.

She exhaled slowly, releasing tension that she didn't know she had. Whatever remaining appetite Rena had was overtaken by exhaustion. Noticing this, Fed suggested she call it a night. No new word had come from the provincial rangers. There would be no traveling before dawn at the earliest. She received his suggestion gratefully—as she did his companionship when he walked her back to her closet room. At her door, she paused, studying the unusual man who'd been keeping her company. Besides his obvious good looks and genial manner, Fed carried himself with an earnest seriousness she didn't often find in her peers. *Who are you,* she thought, and realized she didn't yet know his name.

"So," he said.

"So." Rena took a deep breath, narrowed her eyes, and said, "We probably should exchange names. I'm Rena."

"I'm Jacob."

"Jay-cub," she said, trying to reproduce the "uh" sound the way he said it instead of as an "oh" sound the way she was inclined to do. "Thanks for . . . for being my steward for the day."

Jacob grinned at her, a mischievous quality in his smile.

Like an idiot, Rena grinned back. A nagging voice in her head reminded her that a bedroll and relative quiet awaited her, but her feet remained fused to the floor. "How does a human barge worker with a background in archeology learn to write fluent Bajoran?" Rena said, thinking aloud. She rested a hand on her cocked hip, tilted her head thoughtfully. "Not who I would have expected to find in this obscure corner of Bajor."

He shrugged. "Yeah, but I consider myself more a writer by profession than a barge worker or an archeologist."

A writer, too? Next thing he'll be telling me that Kai Opaka's his distant cousin. What was it with Jacob that piqued her curiosity so? Peel back one layer, find a fascinating discovery only to find yet another intriguing bit beneath the first. As much as she was inclined to sit and talk with him for a while longer, she knew she ought to be going to bed and she said so.

"I've got some work to do, first," he said, removing a padd from inside his jumpsuit.

"A story?" she said.

He shrugged. "Maybe."

"You'll have to let me read it."

"If I can see your sketches."

"Fair enough." Impulsively, Rena leaned up and gave him a friendly kiss on the cheek, hoping he would know how much she appreciated his kindness, and slipped into her room without a second look. The sight of the *duranja* on the floor triggered a wash of guilt; she immediately regretted her parting gesture. *I have nothing to feel bad about. I've done nothing wrong. I keep my promises, Topa.*

She prepared for bed, stripping down to her chemise, clean-

ing her teeth and brushing her hair. Just as she was ready to dim
the lights, she decided she ought to visit the 'fresher.

As she exited into the hall from her closet, she heard the boisterous shouts echoing from the ongoing "games" Ganty had
been intent on her joining. She discovered evidence from their
most recent visits pooled on the stone floors—wine, possibly
urine—a few doors down from her closet. A chilling scream
stopped her. Soundless, she stood and listened. The laughter resumed and she breathed easier, relieved that whatever had
prompted the scream hadn't been too serious. Nevertheless, she
walked more swiftly, wanting to avoid any more encounters with
Jacob's inebriated crewmates. Turning the corner, she nearly
tripped over Jacob, leaning against the wall, padd on his lap,
mouth gaping open in sleep. *Why would he be out here? He has
a room of his own. This doesn't make—*

In an instant, what seemed to be random pieces clicked into
place, especially his odd behavior at supper: Jacob's reassur-
ances to the contrary, her ongoing safety concerned him. Her initial disappointment at discovering the true motivation for his
attentiveness quickly gave way to anxiety. She shivered, perceiv-
ing Ganty and the others anew. The sooner she could be asleep
behind her own locked door . . .

Her door didn't have a lock.

She slept in a seldom-used storage closet intended to house
nothing more valuable that empty bottles and crates. If anyone
for any reason wanted to get into her room, nothing could stop
them—save maybe a self-appointed steward armed with a padd
and a good heart. If Jacob had reason to worry, *she* ought to be
worrying. Her heart slammed in her throat.

Rena turned back to her room, pulled her clothes on, and
packed up the few possessions she had removed from her knapsack. The noise from the revelers grew louder, increasing her
sense of urgency. Her fingers trembled as she fastened up her
boots, her mind racing through her options. She had no idea
where she would go—back toward the River Road, probably. It
couldn't be as bad as the rangers claimed it was. If she moved
quickly, she could reach the bridge crossing to Mylea before
dawn.

Hefting her knapsack onto her back, she turned on her heel to leave, spinning smack into Jacob. Startled, she jerked back with a shudder. "You scared me."

"I'm going with you," he said, bleary-eyed, obviously still fuzzy from sleep. "Just wait for me to get my gear."

Rena shook her head. "I've lived in this province my whole life. I know the back roads and the dangers better than you do," she said, hoping she sounded more confident than she felt. Without waiting for Jacob's reply, she started off down the hall, going toward where she remembered the entrance as being. Unsurprisingly, Jacob was beside her within moments, carrying his own gear.

"You're going the wrong way," he said.

"How do you know?" Rena snapped, her nerves getting the better of her.

Taking her by the shoulders, he looked her hard in the eye. "I know we barely know each other and there's no reason why you should trust me, but I need you to believe that I'll help you get wherever you're going. You're facing treacherous weather and terrain and you're at least six hours from daylight. You're in as much danger out there as you are in here."

She broke eye contact and slumped forward, the need for sleep aching in her bones. Heavy-limbed with exhaustion, she rested her forehead against his chest for a fraction of a moment. "Fine," she whispered.

Jacob slipped an arm around her waist and propelled her forward. How they wound their way through the halls and stairs of the winemaking facility, Rena couldn't precisely say. Once she heard the drumming rain and smelled the fresh, stirred-up scents of soil and the *esani* she remembered seeing growing beside the main doors, she knew they had found their way. Renewed energy filled her. They stepped out onto the porch.

As Rena's will supplanted her fatigue, she became acutely aware of Jacob's hand splayed against her waist and the warmth of his body beside hers. She disentangled herself and stepped out onto the rickety wood steps, immediately losing her balance on the slippery surface. Jacob caught her by the elbow and helped her upright. As she straightened herself, she glanced up at the dusky sky in time to see beams of moonlight fanning through the mist.

*   *   *

Jacob was a nimble-footed traveling companion, Rena discovered. Swiftly, they moved in tandem toward the River Way, avoiding mud slicks and water-filled divots in the few paved spots. Occasionally, the saturated ground gave beneath their weight, forcing them to scramble to avoid a fall or an injury. Within a kilometer, Rena had settled into her traveling mode, in spite of the problematic terrain. The eerie wine-colored sky prevented darkness from eclipsing their path. Eyes drilled ahead, she glanced infrequently at him, wanting to avoid the intimacy she felt creeping between them earlier. Instead her gaze meandered from the Pah mountain range in the distance on her right, where the dark silhouettes of former volcanoes stood on the edge of the rocky valley floor near Mylea, to the tabletop-flat grasslands spread as far as the eye could see on her left, down to the Sahving Valley, where she'd come from.

The loamy scent of rain-soaked peat and the gingery perfume rising off the reeds and marsh roses saturated the air. She knew they would join the River Way shortly when she heard the rain's steady hiss on the Yolja's glassy surface as the river rambled toward the ocean, but Rena didn't mind the weather. The sweater she'd knit last year proved sufficient insulation from the light rains. Rena imagined that Jacob, having spent time on the river, felt similarly. Up over a slight rise in the landscape, they would find familiar territory. She nearly wept with relief when they took their first steps onto the pathway paved by the ancient Bajora. Relieved of the burden of watching each step, Rena increased her pace to a gentle jog; Jacob followed suit.

As they drew nearer to the coast, sour marsh gases gave way to brine-tinged winds. The road no longer gently rose and fell, but instead sloped steadily downward. Bowed clusters of willow trees gave way to bedraggled shrubs, half-hidden by drifting sands. When white, water-polished boulders began appearing, Rena knew they would shortly arrive at the crossroads and the bridge to Mylea. She almost didn't recognize the junction when she saw it, having never before seen the intersection marked with a placard written in both Federation Standard and Bajoran. *Another sign of change,* she thought wistfully, wondering if this road would feel the same the next time she passed through, or whether it would be the way everything else in her life seemed to be: transitional, shifting like the shore dunes.

Rena mentally calculated how long it would take her to reach Mylea after the bridge, especially without the barges to take them out and around the peninsula, then into Mylea Harbor. She didn't care. She'd walk until she collapsed on the bakery's front step. She raced down the roadway to the bridge, her legs nearly running away with her. The rushing river waters called to her, urged her forward . . .

"Rena!" Jacob shouted.

She almost didn't see the collapsed bank in time to stop her from running off the ledge. Only Jacob, who had approached this last stretch before the Yolja with more caution than she had, had seen how the ground where the bridge joined the land had given way. As she stuttered to a halt, she tripped over a fallen tree branch and fell forward onto her face. The force of her fall split open her knapsack, spilling the contents, including her precious sketchbook, into a muddy puddle.

Her sketchbook. The only part of her university life she'd brought home with her. Her canvases, her paintings—all of them had remained behind in the student studio when she left school to return to Mylea. She left believing she would never see those artworks again, that symbolically, she needed to leave them behind if she were to truly embrace the path she was destined for. The only memory she allowed herself to keep was her sketchbook. Now she watched the dirty water soak the pages through, irrevocably destroying months of charcoal, pastel, and pencil memories. She beat her fists against the ground, teeth clenched. Though she felt that remaining in her prostrate position fit her circumstances, she pushed herself up onto her elbows, pulled her legs up into a kneeling position, finally righting herself by the time Jacob reached her. Tersely, she brushed aside his offers of assistance, ignoring the smarting cuts and bruises on her knees and forearms as she paced.

Cursing, she screamed at the sky, screaming as if she believed that the Prophets themselves could hear her, *demanding* they hear her. "I'm doing what you asked! I walked away from my life to follow the path laid out for me! *Do you hear me?*" She stamped her foot angrily, her hands balled into fists. "If I am submitting to all the demands placed on me—all of them!—why can't you make it easier? Do you hear me, dammit?! Answer me! Send your Emissary or your Tears, but answer me!" Rena continued screaming her diatribe until she was hoarse, her throat sore from exertion. The storm's tempo picked up, and soon she was soaked through.

Throughout her display of temper, Jacob had stood off to the side, leaning against a road marker and respectfully averting his eyes from Rena. Abruptly, he took a few long steps forward, pointing at the river. "There's something out there—I can see the light on the bow."

"They'll never see us through this storm," Rena said, coughing. Heavy with discouragement, miserable from cold, she could see no way out of their predicament; she plopped to the ground, prepared to spend the night in the downpour.

Not to be dissuaded by her negativity, Jacob unfastened a pocket on his gear bag, fished around, and removed a wristband with a small circular object mounted on top where a chrono face would be. He thumbed a switch and a brilliant light beam burst out of the side. Holding the light before him like a signal beacon, he ran down as close as he could to the riverbank, trying to draw the attention of the boat. Minutes passed. Then: "It's changing course! Rena! You can go home!" He let loose a loud whoop of joy.

In spite of all that had gone wrong, Rena couldn't help smiling. *Steward, indeed.*

8

GIRANI

As she marched toward the examination room, Dr. Girani Semna suspected that one thing she wouldn't miss about working in Deep Space 9's infirmary was all the Cardassian instrumentality. Most of the medical staff had grown accustomed to it over the years, herself included. Her patients—the Bajorans, particularly—were another matter. They tended to become uncomfortable in this place, beyond their natural aversion to going to see a doctor at all. Despite the fact that the entire station shared the same design elements and seemed no longer to trouble most of the residents, the infirmary made them particularly uneasy. All things considered, that was no surprise. This was, after all, where they felt the most vulnerable.

Her newest patient, she suspected, was going to be no exception.

"Commander Vaughn," she said as she entered the exam room. "What an unexpected pleasure this is. How nice of you to drop by."

Keeping his arms tightly folded over his exam tunic, Vaughn said, "Spare me the sarcasm, if you please, Doctor, and let's get this over with. I have duties awaiting me."

Girani snorted as she prepped a mobile standing console near the biobed. "Now, Commander, you're not suggesting *your* duties should interfere with the execution of mine, are you?"

Vaughn smiled at her appreciatively, and she knew she'd scored a hit. "Where would you like to begin?"

"The usual way. Just lie back on the biobed and breathe normally while the medical scanners take a read."

Vaughn complied. Girani keyed the exam program to commence, and the ceiling-mounted diagnostic array hummed to life. A narrow stripe of blue light slowly crept back and forth over Vaughn's body. While he lay staring up at the array, he said, "I understand you're leaving us."

"That's right."

"If it isn't too forward of me . . . may I ask why?"

Girani shrugged. "I've been thinking about it for some time. And with the station becoming all-Starfleet, it seemed like a good time to make a clean break."

"Have you considered staying aboard—joining Starfleet?" Vaughn asked. "I know you've been an asset to the station since before I joined the crew. Everyone here thinks very highly of you, especially Dr. Bashir. Your application would likely sail through."

Girani blinked. This was the last thing she expected. "That's kind of you to say, Commander," she told him.

"Is it something you'd be open to?"

Girani hesitated. "I hope you won't take this the wrong way . . . but joining Starfleet simply doesn't interest me. I find my service in the Militia very fulfilling, and I want to continue it. I can still do that on Bajor. Besides, with so many of my people switching over as it is, the Militia needs experienced officers now more than ever."

A frown crossed the commander's features. "Does it concern you? The migration of so many Militia personnel?"

"Concern me?" Girani shook her head. "No, it's the logical evolution of Bajor's relationship to the Federation. It only stands to reason that some Bajorans will welcome the opportunity to serve in Starfleet, while others choose to stay with the home guard. Both are important to Bajor, after all."

Vaughn seemed to appreciate hearing her take on the subject. She wondered if he was encountering some bitterness about the changeover down on the planet.

Girani began to check the current scans against Vaughn's medical file, displayed on a nearby monitor. "Oh, before I forget . . . happy birthday, Commander."

Vaughn closed his eyes, leading Girani to suspect the topic was unwelcome. *Oh, well. . . .*

"Thank you," he said quietly. "But I think it's only fair to tell you that I stopped celebrating my birthday about forty years ago."

"Really?" Girani said, genuinely surprised. "That seems like a waste. Not even your hundredth?"

Vaughn shrugged. "It's just a number. Besides, where I was that day, another birthday was the last thing on my mind."

Girani decided not to pursue the matter. A few minutes later, the medical scanners emitted a low chime signaling that their sweep of Vaughn's body was complete. "Good. Now sit up and strip to the waist, please."

"Is this really necessary? The scanners—"

"Every doctor has her own unique style, Commander. This is mine. I'll study the results of the master scan later. Now kindly shed your tunic and face away from me, please."

After a moment's hesitation, Vaughn did as instructed, shrugging out of the exam tunic and baring his back for Girani. Holding an active medical tricorder in one hand, she used the other to examine Vaughn's upper body directly. Her attention shifted back and forth from the display to her patient: some scarring all across Vaughn's back that had obviously never been subjected to a dermal regenerator; a few areas of increased epidermal pigmentation associated with the elderly—what humans called senile lentigines, or "liver spots." There was also some settling of muscle tone.

She found a large bruise on his left side, over the rib cage. He flinched when she touched it. The tricorder revealed a hairline fracture.

"You're showing another two percent decrease in bone density."

Vaughn's response was immediate: "I've been on a regimen of Ostenex-D for the last twelve years."

Girani sighed. "Ostenex doesn't prevent your bones from becoming brittle, Commander. It only slows the process down. And after a while, it stops working for some people."

Silence. According to her tricorder, Vaughn's heart rate was spiking, but his voice remained even as he asked, "Can you prescribe something else?"

Girani hesitated. "There's a newer version of the drug you might try, but I can't promise you it'll work any better." She reached for her osteo-regenerator, switched it on, and pressed it gently against Vaughn's ribs for several minutes. When at last it beeped, signalling that the bone had been mended, Girani put the device away and resumed her tricorder scan.

Girani then noticed a raised line of flesh that started on the side of the commander's neck and disappeared into the white hair behind his left ear. With his uniform on, she realized, it would hardly be noticeable at all. Upon close examination, however, it was quite obviously the telltale sign of an old and serious injury. "Where'd you get this scar?"

"Back home," Vaughn answered, shrugging. "When I was a kid."

Girani held the tricorder up to the scar. "There are traces of foreign DNA under the skin, but I'm not finding a match in the medical database."

"Expand the search to include class-Q life-forms," Vaughn suggested, "and you'll find it belongs to the species *Draco berengarius.*"

Girani's eyebrows shot up at that. "The original wound was quite deep, though," she said, noting that her tricorder was showing a re-fused skull and indications of slight damage to the left hemisphere of the brain. "It looks to me as if you were lucky to have survived. You've never experienced any side effects?"

"No."

Strange as the wound was, if Vaughn had gone this long without suffering any ill effects from it, it was unlikely to make any difference now. Girani redirected her tricorder at Vaughn's heart. "How often do you exercise?"

"I go swimming for half an hour every morning before my shift. And before you ask, yes, I'm watching my diet."

"According to your medical file, you had a cardiac episode six years ago."

"A mild one. Nothing since."

"What about your energy level?"

Vaughn didn't answer.

"Commander? I said—"

"I get tired more quickly these days," Vaughn snapped. "I'm a little slower getting up in the morning. Are you satisfied, Doctor?"

Unfazed, Girani said, "That depends. Are you experiencing any other symptoms Starfleet should know about?"

That's when he turned and looked at her directly. "I'm *old,* Doctor. And I'm getting older all the time. Starfleet knows that. Putting a microscope on every creaking bone, every aching muscle, won't tell them anything they aren't already aware of."

"And that means what, exactly? I should simply give you a clean bill of health?"

Vaughn's eyes narrowed. "Is there any reason you wouldn't?"

Girani set down the tricorder and came around the biobed to face Vaughn directly. She pulled up a chair and straddled it. "Commander, you're a hundred and two years old. You're more than two-thirds of the way to the end of your natural life, and while you're in good health for a human male of your years, it's still an age when most of your kind has retired."

"If you check, you'll see that many centenarian humans are still on active duty in Starfleet."

"But few of them are in the field," Girani countered, "and with good reason. Medical science and proper self-maintenance may have lengthened the human life span over what it was a few hundred years ago, but as you yourself clearly stated, you haven't *stopped* aging."

"Come to the point, Doctor."

Girani sighed. "Don't misunderstand me, Commander. All things considered, your health is excellent. But at some point, perhaps sooner than you imagine, you'll have to face the end of your ability to continue serving in your current capacity.

"But I'm not telling you anything you don't already know, am I? You've already had this conversation with Dr. Bashir."

Vaughn scowled and looked away for a moment, then turned back to her. "Is it your medical opinion that I'm unfit for duty, or that my current health is a liability to this crew?"

"No, but—"

"Then we're done here." Vaughn pushed off the biobed and reached for his gray tank and red uniform shirt, folded neatly nearby atop his jacket and trousers.

Girani stood up and shook her head. "Julian warned me you were an impossible patient."

"Did he, now?" Vaughn said as he dressed.

"Yes. And I feel no reluctance agreeing with that assessment," Girani said with rising anger. "For someone of your life experience, I expected a little more wisdom."

Vaughn slammed his hand on the biobed. His emotions were palpable, but he succeeded in reining them in quickly. Nevertheless, Girani was sorely tempted to recheck his blood pressure.

Finally he said, "I apologize. Doctor. It's just—" He stopped, struggling for the right words. "I'm simply not ready to give up this life yet."

The forcefulness—or was it desperation?—in Vaughn's voice surprised Girani. She remembered a lot of aging resistance fighters who'd expressed similar sentiments when advised to slow down. During the Occupation, it was difficult to argue that anyone should scale back their efforts to help free Bajor from Cardassian control. The Federation, however, wasn't at war anymore. So what cause was driving Vaughn?

"This issue will not go away simply because you choose to ignore it, Commander," Girani said gently. "You need to face the fact that the time is coming, whether you like it or not, when you will have to stand down. My hope for you is that you'll recognize it yourself when it becomes necessary. Otherwise, someone *will* make that decision for you, and I suspect you're the type who would find such a thing undignified, even humiliating. I doubt that's how you'd want your career to end."

Vaughn stared vacantly into the middle distance. "No. I can't say it is." His gaze refocused, and he looked at her. "Thank you, Doctor. Your candor is sobering. You've given me a great deal to think about. Are you sure you can't be persuaded to join Starfleet?"

Girani laughed. "After the conversation we just had, you still want me to sign on?"

"Yes," Vaughn said simply. "Integrity, directness, and persistence are qualities that shouldn't go unappreciated."

Girani's smile was genuine. "Thank you, Commander. Truly. But getting back dirtside is what I really want. And besides," she went on, seeing the dead face of First Minister Shakaar, "there are things about my time here I want to forget."

Vaughn nodded, accepting her answer. "Just know, then, that you'll be missed. By all of us."

"Thank you," Girani said again.

Vaughn finished dressing while Girani moved to an interface console and uploaded her tricorder's readings to the infirmary mainframe, to cross-check later against the master scan taken by the diagnostic array. She was changing Vaughn's prescription to Ostenex-E when she heard a voice call out, "There you are, Commander! I heard I might find you in here."

Girani turned. Standing in the doorway was Quark, his hands held uncharacteristically behind his back. Girani was about to deliver a scathing reprimand about a patient's right to privacy in coming to see a physician, but Vaughn spoke first.

"Mr. Ambassador," he said, pulling his uniform jacket on. "What a pleasure it is to see you."

Girani suppressed a laugh. Quark's diplomatic appointment as Ferenginar's official representative to Bajor was still hard to take seriously, especially after it became common knowledge that it had come about purely as an act of nepotism on the part of Grand Nagus Rom, Quark's brother.

Quark snorted at the commander's greeting. "Ah, you say that, but you don't mean it."

Vaughn looked at him. "How could you tell?"

"I'm willing to overlook your insincerity, Commander, given your situation and all." From her angle, it appeared to Girani that Quark was holding something behind his back, but she couldn't make out what it was.

"My situation?" Vaughn asked.

"Another birthday," Quark said. Vaughn shot a look at Girani, who shrugged, putting on a face with which she hoped to project, *Don't look at me, I didn't tell him.* "At your age, that's gotta make anybody cranky," Quark went on. "It can't be getting any easier. You're less steady on your feet, less quick with a phaser, less able to remember things, less able to endure the, ah, company of females . . ."

"Less able to endure the company of you," Vaughn added.

"Commander, please," Quark said. "Let's not spoil what should be an occasion to celebrate."

Vaughn stared at him. "You're here to help me celebrate."

"Well, as it happens, I was at the station's florist signing for a shipment of Kaferian lilies, just as Mr. Modo was processing an order—intended for you. Imagine my delight when I learned it was a birthday present from someone on Bajor. As a good citizen, not to mention the senior Ferengi diplomat in residence, I volunteered to bring it to you personally."

"Is that right," Vaughn said, as Quark's other hand emerged, holding a narrow cone of festive paper wrapped around a single, long-stemmed flower. There was a note card attached, and an isolinear rod taped next to it. The flower, Girani saw, was an *esani* blossom.

Vaughn thanked Quark as he took the gift, unsealed the note card, and smiled faintly when he read the contents. Quark's futile attempt to inconspicuously lean over far enough to read the note told Girani that at least he hadn't scanned the message before bringing it to the commander.

Vaughn refolded the note and detached the isolinear rod from the giftwrap. "What's this?"

"Compliments of the Ferengi Embassy," Quark said.

"You mean the bar."

"Just present it to any member of my staff to receive an hour of holosuite time at our special birthday discount. And two free drinks."

Vaughn raised an eyebrow. "Top shelf?"

Quark laughed. "That's a good one. I'll have to remember that. Oh, I almost forgot to mention: For a small fee, you can get an official proclamation from the Ferengi Alliance declaring this Elias Vaughn Day. It comes with a certificate."

"Pass."

"A smaller fee will get you an official birthday greeting from the Grand Nagus."

"You're enjoying your diplomatic appointment far too much, do you realize that?"

"Take joy from profit, and profit from joy. Rule of Acquisition Number Fifty-five."

"My mistake," Vaughn said. "But I'll have to pass on that offer as well, I'm afraid."

Quark made a disgusted noise and shook his head. "No offense, Commander, but your people have no idea how to celebrate a birthday properly."

Vaughn shrugged. "We're only human."

"My point exactly. Would it kill you to spend a little more time in my bar?"

"Don't you mean 'embassy'?"

"Quark's is a full-service establishment," the ambassador said. "I'm just trying to reinforce that fact among the station populace."

"And you think having the station's second-in-command decide to celebrate his birthday there will encourage others to do the same," Vaughn guessed.

Quark spread his hands. "Well, after all, every day is *somebody's* birthday."

"True enough," the commander conceded, raising the *esani* flower to his nose and gently breathing in its fragrance. "As it happens, though, I have a prior commitment this evening. Some other time, perhaps. Thanks for the gift." He gave Quark's shoulder a friendly pat, and nodded to Girani as he strode out of the exam room. "Doctor."

As Vaughn exited, Quark seemed to notice Girani for the first time, a new gleam forming in his eye. "Doctor! When's your birthday?"

HOVATH

Hovath awoke to darkness and the taste of blood. Pain nested behind his eyes, its sharp black beak stabbing his brain. His lower lip was numb and felt twice its usual size. His face was sore, and cold on one side. Through his cheek he felt a low vibration, one he recognized: the deckplate of a spacecraft at warp.

Light assailed him through his eyelids, an instant before his mind registered the sound of a switch being thrown, the echo reverberating off metal walls.

"Up," a harsh voice demanded, just as he felt rough hands grab hold of his vestments and force him into a hard chair. Hovath struggled to open his eyes against the glare, saw that he was sitting at one end of a plain metal table in the midst of an otherwise dark room, a light on the other side shining directly into his face. The stabbing pain behind his eyes grew worse.

Then it all came back to him.

Shards of memory broke through the fog: alien faces, the heat of the explosion, the light of the village burning, screams of agony, the scent of death.

"Iniri!" The wail of grief tore itself from the rawness of his throat, sending him into a fit of dry, painful coughing.

I'm alive. Why am I alive? The crushing knowledge of what had befallen his people was proof that he wasn't dead . . . unless death was not the thing his faith maintained. Though the concept of an afterlife defined by eternal loss and regret was alien to Bajoran thinking, Hovath knew it was powerful idea in human mythology. They had names for it. He knew one of them: *hell.*

"Ke Hovath," another voice said, softer than the first, female. But not his wife's. *Iniri!*

Then a different horror seized him: They knew his name! Prophets help him, they knew his name! They had killed everyone, his friends and neighbors, his family, they had burned the village to the ground—but they had taken him, kept him alive. They wanted *him!*

"Why?" Hovath found the strength to ask before another coughing spasm took hold.

"Let him drink," the woman said. A second later, a sipstick touched his lips. Cool water flowed over his dry, leathery tongue, bringing some relief from the choking taste of ash. He began to drink greedily, becoming aware of two figures on his right and left, standing over him.

"That's enough," the voice said, and the sipstick withdrew.

Hovath looked up, squinting against the light, attempting to see the speaker through the glare. The most he could discern was a dark shape sitting on the opposite end of the table. "What do you want of me?"

"The same thing you want. Answers," his captor said.

"I won't help you."

"I think you will." The dark figure seemed to turn slightly to one of her henchmen. "Show him."

The underling on his right—Hovath thought dully he might be a Nausicaan, though he was uncertain—moved to the nearest wall, where a viewscreen was set up. The alien activated it, and Hovath's heart lifted.

Iniri was alive. She was slumped in the corner of a small room, her red-blond hair in dissaray, her clothing singed. She had her arms wrapped around herself and she appeared to be weeping. She looked as if she'd been beaten, and Hovath's moment of relief turned to rage.

Then he felt the blood drain from his face as he recognized her surroundings. An airlock.

"As you can see, your wife lives. For the moment," the

woman said. "If you wish her to stay that way, I require your full cooperation."

"Please," Hovath moaned. "Let her go."

"No. Not until you give me what I need. Otherwise Iniri dies."

Hovath squeezed his eyes shut and clenched his hands into fists on top of the table, his mind searching for a way out of his nightmare. His teeth bit into his swollen lower lip until he tasted blood again.

"How can I possibly help you? I'm no one."

"Oh, but that is hardly true." the woman said. "Until this very morning you were the *sirah* of Sidau village. But that's not all, is it, Hovath? You've also spent half of each of the last six years as a student in Musilla University, where you pursued what can only be described as an atypical course of study for someone of your upbringing, and published a rather remarkable document."

From the far end of table, something slid toward him across the surface. His fingers caught it. A padd, but not of a design he'd ever seen before. Its little screen displayed the title, *Speculations on the Architecture of the Celestial Temple*.

His name appeared directly below it.

"I've become quite familiar with your work," his captor said.

Tears streamed from Hovath's eyes as he began to understand why all this was happening.

Hovath's spirit had always been restless, distracted; it was for that very reason, he recalled, that the old *sirah* had pushed Hovath so hard before his death, seven years ago. Hovath had stumbled during his first attempt to control the *Dal'Rok*. The old *sirah* had felt Hovath's *pagh,* and found him wanting. Enlisting the aid of two humans from the space station, he crafted a lesson whereby Hovath learned to commit fully to the duty for which he had been trained his whole life.

As the new *sirah*, Hovath served his people well. But the villagers needed his services as storyteller only for a span of five days each year. The rest of that time he was merely a scholar and sometime spiritual guide. Though he had mastered his role, his spirit remained restless, his mind thirsty for knowledge that had no place in the village. A year after he became the storyteller of Sidau, he announced his intent to spend Hedrikspool's autumn and winter months each year in secluded study, away from the village. No one, not even his new bride, Iniri, had known where he went, or the controversial nature of his work: a single line of theological and scientific inquiry that had been circling round and round in his mind since the Emissary had first come to Bajor.

From the day of its discovery, the wormhole had excited him, captured his imagination. For the Celestial Temple to manifest itself in such a manner, it could only mean that the Prophets sought to be understood in ways apart from the wisdom of the prophecies. Or so Hovath believed. *Come,* he felt the Temple beckon. *See what I am.*

After the death of the old *sirah,* Hovath's life walked two paths. On one he was the faithful storyteller of the village, Keeper of the *Paghvaram* and Foe of the *Dal'Rok.* On the other path he'd become a contemplator of Their Manifestation, seeker of secular truth, and student of the architecture of the Temple. He had believed that these two paths, while seeming separate and parallel, would in time converge into a single path of Truth on which he could guide his flock in Sidau, and perhaps others, toward a new enlightenment.

Now a different Truth was upon him, and it stood revealed as his own folly and arrogance.

He shook his head and pushed the padd away. "This is nothing."

"I very much disagree," the woman said. "I find it quite compelling. Your imaginative approach to theoretical physics is not merely unexpected, but inspired. You believe the wormhole is not what it seems to be."

"No," Hovath said tightly. "I believe it is *more* than it seems to be."

"Explain."

Hovath brought his fist down on the table. "If you've read my work, you already know the explanation."

"Indulge me."

Hovath said nothing.

His captor addressed the Nausicaan, who still stood next to the screen showing the image of Iniri. "Space her."

10

RENA

The ranger patrol craft met them a few dozen meters down river from the bridge landing. Rena wasn't surprised to see the fear-mongering officer from the rest-and-sip commanding the boat; she was too tired and irritable to argue with his lecture on the risks involved in recklessly disregarding his organization's dictums. Her reward for enduring the speech was a promise to deliver her to Mylea Harbor before midday. He would transmit any messages she wanted to send in an effort to reassure any concerned relatives.

Afterward, a female lieutenant brewed hot tea for both Jacob and Rena and escorted them belowdecks to small, interior cabin furnished only with a bunk bed. She had left them both with victims' aid packs, each of which included a set of lightweight, one-size undergarments (loose shorts and T-shirt), plus some personal-hygiene supplies. The lieutenant had also laid out a pair of green forest-ranger work-duty jumpsuits, faded from age and use, as well as giving them a few extra blankets. Jacob started stripping off his sopping clothes as soon as the lieutenant left. Indignant at his presumptuous behavior, Rena huffed, turned her back, and waited for him to give the all clear that she was safe to start changing her own clothes. Once she had changed, she scrambled up the ladder and leaped into the upper bunk, snuggling beneath the blankets without a word to Jacob. She waited for sleep to come.

From Jacob's breathing below, she could tell that sleep hadn't come to him either.

"Rena."

She debated answering him for a moment, then, knowing it wasn't fair to punish him for her bad luck, said, "Yes?"

"Your sketchbook . . . I'm so sorry. I know how I'd feel if I lost my work."

"I'm sure it's just the Prophets letting me know they're aware of my rebellious heart, in spite of my outward obedience."

"Why would the Prophets take your art away?"

The finer nuances of Bajoran theology were always difficult to explain to nonbelievers, so Rena pondered carefully how to answer Jacob's question. "The Prophets aren't taking my art. More like, the Prophets have put Bajor on a path. As a result all Bajorans are on a path. When we follow our path, our lives unfold in a way that brings us confidence and peace. When we resist our path, we find chaos and uncertainty. We demonstrate our faith by how we live. As you can see tonight, my faith isn't doing so well or I'd probably be asleep safe in a hostel somewhere instead of on a patrol boat, lucky to be alive."

"Or maybe this is where your path is supposed to take you."

Rena snorted.

"Seriously, Rena. Last year, I thought I lost my father," Jacob said, his voice heavy with emotion. "I believed that if anyone could find him, I could. So, believing I was doing the right thing, I went searching for him."

"You said your father was living farther up in Kendra, so I take it he wasn't dead."

"No. He wasn't. But *I* didn't find him. I ended up on a wild-goose chase, having some crazy adventures, visiting places I never imagined I would, and ended up bringing several someone elses home with me. None of it made sense. Looking back, I know that what seemed like a mistake at the time was just part of a larger pattern that I couldn't see while I was in it. My hopes came true—my father came home—but not the way I planned. Maybe that's where you're at."

Rena, still puzzling over the image conjured by the term "wild-goose chase," understood the spirit of Jacob's words and wished they could be true for her. She allowed his words to hang in the air while she contemplated what she should disclose in return for his confiding in her. "My grandfather died several weeks ago, before Unity Day," she began, slipping back into memories. "He had a degenerative illness that could have been cured if he'd received treatment in his youth, but the Cardassians didn't care about helping Bajorans. So he lived out his last years enduring excruciating pain in a body that betrayed him. He was so miserable and yet so brave that when he asked me to leave university to help my aunt take care of him, of course I left immediately. Before he died, he made me promise some things. So far, I've only been able to honor one of my promises—going to Kenda Shrine. I need to go home to Mylea to finish the others. Right now, it just feels like my life isn't going to start until I honor my promises to Topa, so I just want to get on with it."

"He didn't ask you to give up your art, did he?"

She could sense the disapproving look on his face. "Oh no," Rena said, smiling. "But he asked me to commit to building a life that would honor Bajor, to preserve what is unique about us in the face of all this change. . . ." Her voice trailed off. She didn't want to offend Jacob by expressing uncertainty about the Federation. Like most Bajorans, she supported joining but she had her concerns as she watched the generation younger than hers being plied with holovids from Risa and recreational technology she couldn't have even fathomed. Would their fortune in being born in a time of prosperity—without the demons of Cardassia and the Occupation haunting them—change what being Bajoran meant to future generations? She sighed. "I can best honor Bajor by living in Mylea. After my aunt retires, there is no one in my family to run the bakery. The unique way Myleans have worked, recreated, lived for thousands of years feels like it is on the cusp of slipping away unless some of us try to hold on to our traditions." The lower bunk creaked; Rena assumed that Jacob was making himself more comfortable, but moments later his silhouette appeared at the foot of her bed.

"I hate not being able to see your face when we talk," he said by way of explanation. "If you really mind me being here, I'll go back down."

Sitting up beneath her covers, Rena gestured for Jacob to sit down. He assumed a cross-legged position at the foot of her bed.

"I know what you're saying, Rena, but from the way you've talked about your grandfather, I have a hard time believing he would want you to give up your art studies."

"I won't give up my art exactly. More like, instead of finishing at university, I'll help Marja with the bakery and when I have time, I'll pursue my painting as I always have."

In the half-light, his inscrutable expression made her nervous. She knew, without him saying, that he disagreed with her choice.

Crossing her arms across her chest, she said, "Look, nothing against you Federation people, but you don't have tens of thousands of years of history to protect. I owe it to Bajor."

"You owe it to yourself to paint." Leaning closer to her, he rested a hand on her knee. "I saw you out there, screaming at the Prophets, more angry than almost any person I have ever seen in my lifetime, and considering that I've seen Kira Nerys angry, that's saying something."

Rena's mind caught on something. *Kira Nerys?* The *Kira Nerys?*

He raced ahead before she could answer. "You weren't screaming about preserving Bajor, you were screaming like someone who was having her soul—her *pagh*—torn out of her," he whispered. "Tell me again that you need to give up your art."

Swallowing hard, Rena formed the words, in her mind, but her mouth opened soundlessly, then closed. Her eyes burned with the beginnings of tears. She'd been wrestling with this conflict since returning from school, torn between her past and what she imagined her future to be. *My promises to Topa. He devoted his life to raising me; I promised him I would help save Mylea for his grandchildren.* She clasped a hand against her breastbone, took a deep breath, and said, her voice quavering, "I'll do what I have to . . ." Her shoulders quaked with silent sobs.

Before she could finish speaking, Jacob had folded her into his arms and was rubbing her back as if she were a small child. He spoke gentle, quieting words in her ears. She was too tired and overcome to question whether or not this was right or wrong. Real and true in this moment were his strong arms and the compassion flowing from him. And as she drew comfort from being close to him, barriers that had held back other feelings gradually dissolved, feelings that had hovered around the edges of her emotions since she first saw him in the rest-and-sip.

Beside her, Jacob accidentally pulled her bedcovers away when he shifted, allowing their legs to touch; Rena's heart jarred into a quickened rhythm. A long pause. He moved her leg away. She still felt the ghost of his touch. And she liked it. Unthinkingly, she moved her leg back toward his, heard his sharp intake of breath, felt satisfaction that she evoked in him what he evoked in her.

She couldn't clearly see his face; she didn't have to. Tentatively, he traced the line of her jaw, tangled his fingers in her hair, touched her lips. She inhaled sharply in blissful shock and drew closer.

He kissed her.

Rena knew she should stop this. She had made promises—some of them implied, but promises nonetheless. The late hour, the charged emotionality of the night, never mind the huge risk she took being with an alien stranger this way—all of it warned of foolishness. But Jacob felt neither alien nor stranger: rather familiar and comfortable and home. So she yielded to Jacob's wordless entreaties, parting her lips, allowing the kiss to deepen. He wound his arms around her waist, pulling her closer, and she aided him by draping her leg over his, pulling their bodies flush. The first kiss blurred with another. Kisses gave way to tender caresses and more kisses until Rena joyfully abandoned all reason.

After a time, they collapsed in drowsy oblivion. Drifting off to sleep, they spooned together, Rena noted ironically as she dozed off, with the comfortable familiarity of experienced lovers.

A knock on their door roused Rena from a sound sleep. "Wha-what-what is it?" she said, half-yawning. Beside her, Jacob mumbled something incoherent.

"Mylea Harbor in twenty minutes," came the muffled announcement.

Home.

Disentangling herself from Jacob's arms, Rena sat up in bed and ordered the lights illuminated. She rubbed her eyes and yawned again, realizing that she had no idea what time it was when the gradual recollection of what had happened last night began returning to her. She flushed hot. Swinging her legs over the side, she dropped down to the floor.

I have to get out of here. She found the pile of her damp clothes where she had shed them the night before; they remained too filthy and wet to be practical to wear. Her mud-coated knapsack, its disheveled, dirty contents spilling out the sides, served as a reminder of the miserable night of traveling.

Another groan from the top bunk reminded Rena about the rest. She quickly donned her discarded undergarments, as well as the oversized ranger jumpsuit, gathered up the rest of her victims' pack, and left the quarters in search of a 'fresher. The facility she stumbled on provided a brief refuge and an opportunity to regain some semblance of normalcy, but once she had performed all the cleanup rituals she had the tools for, she knew she had to go back and face Jacob. She had no idea what to say.

Rena had never been one to toy with male emotions. More than a few of her classmates would think nothing of a few stolen kisses and most likely would have few regrets about a drunken night of sex with a stranger if it was pleasurable. Rena didn't behave that way; she didn't kiss men casually, so she had no experience to draw from in determining what to say. She decided on the truth.

With trepidation, she tapped in the door codes and discovered upon entering that Jacob was already awake, dressed, and repacking what few possessions he had gotten out when they'd arrived. The tender expression on his face quickly became wary when he saw her. She cursed her inability to hide her emotions but perhaps, in this case, her readability had served to soften the blow.

"Don't tell me," he began, shaking his head. "It was a mistake, you want to be friends—" He stuffed his dirty clothes into a pocket of his gear bag.

"No. It wasn't a mistake," she said, reaching to touch his arm. "I chose—*we* chose, and it was right because we both needed the comfort."

He jerked away from her. "Comfort? You make me sound like a favorite pillow."

"I can't make this more than that."

"Why not? Because I don't fit into Topa's plan? I'm not from Mylea? What, Rena? Tell me, since I don't have the benefit of having the Prophets lay my path out for me," he said bitterly.

She could hardly blame him. "If I could, I would ask you to

come home with me when we get off this boat. I would invite you to stay in our family's apartments and we'd see what could happen between us. But we can't."

Recognition lit on his face. "There's someone else. Someone that Topa wanted you to be with."

"Yes. And no." She clenched her teeth, exhaling sharply in frustration. "Before I went to university, there was an understanding between me and someone I'd known since I was a child. I was prepared to break it off when I first came home a few months ago, but when I saw how happy Topa was, I felt like I owed it to my grandfather to see if I could make it work."

In one swift, exaggerated gesture, Jacob fastened his bag and hefted it onto his shoulders. "Fine. Far be it from me to stand in the way of your path." He pushed past her without another word.

For a long moment, Rena stood in the middle of the room, too miserable to move. What she was more miserable about—violating her implied commitment or hurting Jacob—she couldn't honestly say. Watching him leave had been crushing. She had consciously pushed down the impulse to chase after him, to beg for his forgiveness and the chance to start fresh without any secrets. His words to her and his understanding about her art—his kindness—the way she felt when he kissed her—all of it had touched a deep place inside. What she would give to have one of those orbs here to help her know what she should do next.

The deep baritone horn announcing the patrol boat's arrival into the inner harbor disrupted her thoughts. *Can't hide anymore, Rena. Time to face your life.* She configured her knapsack the best she could before starting up the stairs to the upper deck.

Rena stood on the opposite side of the railing from Jacob. Unsurprisingly, he wouldn't look at her. Soon, as the boat drew closer to the docks, Rena saw a few familiar faces in the waiting crowds: Halar, her fair-haired childhood friend, clad in her study robes, and rugged, muscular Kail, the person she thought that, once upon a time when she was a girl, she was supposed to marry. Now she wasn't so sure.

When the gangplank descended, Rena waited until Jacob had made his way off the boat before she left. Her feet had barely touched the dock planking when Halar had thrown her arms around her and squeezed her enthusiastically.

"You're safe! Oh Rena! We were so scared when we heard

about the storm." Halar indicated Kail as being part of the "we." "You must have been terrified!"

"I've had easier trips down the valley," Rena confessed. Kail assumed his place beside her, his clothes saturated with the oil smoke from the foundry fires where he worked. She managed not to cringe when he hugged her.

Apprenticed to an artisan, Kail hadn't always worked the fire room, but a recent falling-out with his supervisor had resulted in a demotion. Rena had tried to listen with a sympathetic ear, but she struggled to reconcile Kail's indignation at what he perceived as mistreatment with the belligerence and complaining she'd seen in him since she first returned home. Taking care of Topa during his final days hadn't allowed her to spend much private time with Kail, but from what little time they had shared, he seemed like he'd changed. In that regard, she was grateful that she hadn't accepted any betrothal agreement, hoping that with more time they would get used to each other again; oddly, she hadn't even missed sleeping with him since she'd been back. There had always seemed to be a reason why making love didn't feel right, whether it was the long hours she spent nursing Topa or working in the bakery. With Topa's death, Rena had wanted to be alone to grieve. In light of what happened with Jacob, Rena saw her reticence with Kail and wondered if her reasons for avoiding intimacy were more than circumstantial. She sighed and moved a bit away from Kail, loosening his grip on her waist.

Jacob's height made him easy to spot in the crowds of Bajoran fishermen and aquaculture workers on the docks. He walked confidently, even in this strange place. Remembering the first time she saw him—had it been only a day since the rest-and-sip?—she decided that was what had caught her eye: his being comfortable in his own skin. Rena followed him with her eyes until she felt Halar's gaze on her.

"You're looking at Jake Sisko, aren't you," she said, clasping her hands together gleefully.

Of course Halar would have known who the son of the Emissary was; she'd fanatically followed his "ministry" to Bajor since the kai had announced the reopening of the Celestial Temple eight years ago. And then it occurred to her that Halar wasn't referring to someone unknown to her. Halar was talking about *her* Jacob. Staring, Rena said, "Jacob *Sisko?*"

"Jacob, Jake." Halar shrugged. "No matter—he's a Sisko. Son of the Emissary. I practically squealed when I saw him coming down the gangplank. Did you see him aboard the ship?"

Jacob Sisko. Son of the Emissary. I guess I wasn't the only one keeping secrets.

SISKO

A cool, syncopated rhythm insinuated itself into Ben Sisko's dreams, gently lifted him and tried to carry him back into the waking world. *Not just yet,* he thought. *Let me linger here for just a moment. . . .* And, briefly, for a timeless instant, he thought he remembered how it was done, how to take a second, parse it, and keep it hanging in the air, vibrating. As the piano licks, bass, and drums wove their tale through his mind, he felt the metronome behind his eyes slow down, then stop, and he hung there for an instant, between the tick and the tock. The music still moved, but he, Ben Sisko, did not. *And then the Prophets speak,* he thought. Pausing, he tried to keep his inner eye from wavering, waiting. . . . *Or perhaps They don't . . .*

He opened his eyes, and the moment between moments receded. Pale green light dancing through a leaf canopy. Garden. He touched the patch of grass beside him and felt the chill. Kasidy must have abandoned him once he fell asleep. A sigh-breath against his bare collarbone. Baby. She stirred, hitching up farther on his chest, curling her knees against her body and snuggling into his chest. Sisko smiled, tucking her dislodged blanket back around her legs. But, yes, there was music playing. Coming from the open patio doors. Dave Brubeck, he thought, recognizing the tune. *When did Kas start listening to jazz?* He had done his best over the years to introduce his wife to good music, but she had willfully resisted every entreaty. Kasidy liked what she liked: modern classical, Centauri folk, and the occasional piece of youth-contemporary for mindless humming. Nothing wrong with most of it, Sisko generously concluded.

The bundle on his chest shuddered with a sneeze.

Bless you, he thought, patting the bundle comfortingly.

A shadow passed between him and the dappled sunlight. Kasidy. She plopped down beside him, propping herself against the tree trunk. "I think Rebecca has caught a cold. Which means we'll both have colds in a day or two if we don't take antivirals."

"Can't we immunize her for all these little diseases?" he asked. Careful not to disturb Rebecca, he lifted his head off the ground and pillowed it on Kasidy's lap.

She inhaled deeply, caressed his face. "We can, but Julian recommended we let a couple of these run their course so she can build up immunities. Nothing works better than nature."

"Except when it doesn't."

Kasidy shrugged.

Sisko tried to remember the last time he had lived through a cold. Sneezing, runny nose, headache, congestion. "If she has to be miserable," he asked, "shouldn't we be miserable, too?"

Kasidy laughed. "Sorry, I don't subscribe to that theory."

"Think of it as an anchor to corporeal life."

"I prefer what we did last night," Kasidy teased.

Feeling the residual ache in his stomach muscles, Sisko had to admit he did too.

"When did you start listening to Dave Brubeck?" he asked.

"Is that who this is?" Kasidy asked. "It was on one of Jake's mixes and I liked it."

"Jake's?" He was genuinely surprised. "Something that happened while I was gone?"

"I don't think so," Kasidy said. "The recording was a few years old, from back in that period when he and Nog tried to convince Quark that he should open a dance club." Rebecca, who had been dozing, awoke and immediately began to nuzzle against the cloth of Sisko's flannel shirt. Breathless, frustrated grunts gave way to a puckered-up scowl: the bundle trembled with mewing cries.

Sisko wrapped his arms around her, whispering soothing

words to his daughter, but Kasidy pushed him out of her lap and plucked the baby out of his arms.

"Goodness, little girl. How can you be hungry again so soon?"

"I remember that," Sisko said, "but I don't remember Jake listening to jazz. How could I have missed that?"

"I can't imagine," Kasidy said, loosening her shirt. "I seem to remember something about a war. Ring any bells?"

"Seems vaguely familiar." He sighed, rolling over so he could prop himself on his elbows. Rooting around the grass, he plucked out stems of miniature, blush-faced daisy flowers and started piling them up. "I should make lunch." Deftly, he knotted the flower stems together, making a chain of blossoms.

"Yes you should," Kasidy agreed. "Why not reheat the gumbo you made yesterday?"

"Excellent suggestion. But none for you, little girl," Sisko said, stroking her velvety cheek with his index finger. "Maybe when you're older. None of that replicated lunch food at school. I'll send you jambalaya." He continued the flower chaining, his fingers smudged with powdery orange pollen grains.

Rebecca squirmed and tensed, followed by an unmistakable series of gaseous "phlbets." Relaxing, she pulled away, bloated and happy, offering her mother a tipsy half-smile.

Kasidy draped the blanket over her shoulder, then lifted the baby up and began to gently pat her. Looking at her husband, she asked seriously, "Will you?"

"Will I what?"

"Pack her lunch for her on school days? Do you really see that as part of our future?"

Sisko kept his eyes on Rebecca. "What makes you think I can see the future?"

"Then what do you *want* to happen next?" Kasidy asked earnestly. "You must have some hopes for how you want our lives to unfold, or it doesn't matter whether you can see the future or not."

He rolled off his belly, onto his back, watching the frantic ministrations of a mother bird delivering squirming insects to her nest of young in the branches above. "What I want," he said soberly, "is to be here with you and the baby. But you know the truth: It's never going to be about only what I want. I still have a duty."

"To whom?"

Sisko stared out over his *tessipates* of land, the miasma of variegated greens and browns garnished with straw-colored seed clusters ripening as midsummer approached. He inhaled deeply, drawing in the scents of moldering leaves, the scents of the river, deep into his lungs. In a split second of awareness, he knew the insects gnawing through the tree bark, the schools of fish darting around the water lilies, the plump seed grains burgeoning with life, the katterpod seedlings twining up the garden arbor. The land infiltrated the marrow of his bones, binding him. Just as the sky still did.

"To the Bajorans," Sisko said. "To these people who have placed their trust in me. To the Prophets who allowed me to return here. To Starfleet. And to those others . . ."

"What others?" Kasidy asked, her voice rising with emotion. "Who else is there who's more important to you than your family?"

Scooting back to sit beside her, Sisko threaded his arm behind Kasidy's waist, drawing her head onto his shoulder. The baby heard him coming and, head wobbling, turned toward her father's voice. "My dear love," Sisko said softly, touching her knee, "none of them is more important than my family. But consider this: What do you think we need to do to protect our daughter?"

Kasidy's eyes, which had been growing red-rimmed, suddenly narrowed. "What do you mean, Ben? Do you think someone is going to try to hurt Rebecca?"

"No," Sisko said, trying to keep his voice low and reassuring. "Not specifically for Rebecca, but, yes, something is coming. The Prophets tried to explain it to me." He shook his head. "I wish I could be plainer than that, but it's difficult. The way they communicated—when I was there with them it all made sense, but now, here, meaning fades."

"But it's something that could harm Rebecca?" Sisko saw the fierce gleam in his wife's eyes.

"It's something that could affect us all, every Bajoran, yes."

"Bajoran, Ben? Is that what we are now?"

Sisko held her eye for several seconds, then smiled. "Aren't we?" he asked. He nodded at the world around him. "If Rebecca could answer, what would she say about this place?"

Kasidy looked. Sikso followed her gaze. The tree branches curved to form an archway over the dirt road; wildflowers, a riotous burst of color, carpeted the beds around the house; trails of cloud tufts lazed out over a luminous blue sky. And the house: He had designed it, Kas had built it.

"It's home, Ben. It's our home."

"Yes, it is," Sisko said. "And if we need to defend it . . ."

". . . We'll do what we must."

He kissed her on the forehead, then quickly scrambled up to his feet. "I hear that gumbo calling to me."

Kasidy chuckled, and the sound made the baby jump, then hiccup, a bubble of milk exploding on her lips. Her mother wiped the baby's mouth, then called out to her husband again, suddenly serious. "So what do we do now?"

"First, we should have lunch," Sisko said, pausing where he stood and meeting her eyes. "Then, when we're done, I think we should begin to plan a dinner party."

12

RENA

Rena awoke distressingly early the next morning, a full ten minutes before the house computer was programmed to chime. What could have awakened her? Noise from the street? Unlikely. At this hour, most of the fishermen had been out in their boats for a couple of hours, and few of them lived this far up in the Harbor Ring hills, preferring that their houses be close to the docks. Marja would already be downstairs in the bakery, which was on the other side of the house, and Rena knew from experience that Marja would have to drop one of the biggest mixing bowls or—unthinkable!—slam an oven door for her to hear it up on the third floor. So the question remained: Why was she awake?

Guilt, perhaps. Her stomach knotted as she contemplated the looming confrontation with Marja. When she had arrived, yesterday afternoon, Marja had been at services. By the time her aunt had returned home, Rena had already fallen asleep and was just now waking up for the first time in fourteen hours.

Images from night before last swam up from memory: Jacob. He might be in Mylea now. Would she see him again? Not that he would *want* to see her, or she him, for that matter. To think she'd been with the son of the Emissary all that time and not known it! Thinking back, she couldn't honestly say he'd lied outright about his identity, but he'd certainly withheld it. In retrospect, there had been clues in some of things he let slip, and the fact that she hadn't put the details together before was now a source of embarrassment.

She remembered the single holo the newsfeeds had been permitted to take of the Emissary and his newborn daughter—the Avatar, as some believed. Many, many images had been taken of Sisko over the years, but the press had been cooperative about not taking images of his family, a privacy demand the media had no choice but to comply with. Sisko had made it clear: If one newsfeed ignored his request, all the others would be cut off. Perhaps that's why she hadn't recognized Jacob the way Halar had. Halar had spent most of her middle years digging through the comnet, saving every file and picture she could find, becoming an expert on all things Sisko in the process. If it hadn't been in the headlines, Rena hadn't bothered, being more concerned with her art and Kail. It seemed appropriate now that they were adults that their childhood obsessions still defined them: Halar was studying to become a prylar, Rena was still painting and with Kail—sort of. Or maybe neither.

Rena sagged back against the narrow bed, sighed, hauled herself up into a standing position, and wobbled across the cool wood floor to her tiny 'fresher.

After pulling her wiry black hair back into a loose knot, Rena quickly scrubbed her face, took her allergy medicine, and cleaned her teeth, not thinking about any one thing, but letting a dozen stray thoughts course through her consciousness. After the initial foundation work was completed, she worked up the nerve to look herself squarely in the mirror and was pleased to see that things could be worse. Her complexion, naturally creamy brown, masked the bags (with a little help from a little powder), but the lines around her eyes were difficult to disguise. Scrunching up her eyes, she stared at herself and recalled her grandfather's comment: It's not the years; it's the distance traveled. Only last month, she had plucked the first silver hair from among the black and she could see another growing in its place. Marja had told her that her sister, Rena's mother, had gone completely gray by thirty. Rena hoped that environment had been a factor: her mother's life had been much more difficult than hers had been.

When she was a young girl, Marja and Topa had told her tales of her mother and father, Lariah and Jiram, so many times that they were, to Rena, like characters in a story. Their tale went like this: Her mother, Lariah, and her father, Jiram, had grown up during the Occupation. By day, Jiram had fished, like most of the men, and Lariah had worked with Topa and Marja in the bakery making Cardassian *scorca,* the flat bread the Occupation troops craved. "They were the bravest people in town," Topa had told her over and over. "They could have been like everyone else and just done what they were told, but they wanted life to be better for everyone."

"Especially me!" the young Rena would say (her recurring line).

"Especially you," Topa would say.

No one else in Mylea had been brave enough to give up their soft lives; everyone knew how bad living conditions were in the big cities, the industrial centers, and the mining camps. No one wanted to take a risk.

But bravery was not always enough, or so the story went. One night, someone made a mistake or, possibly, the Cardassians just got lucky. Lariah and Jiram had not returned from their mission to free a group of prisoners, so baby Rena went to live with Marja and Topa. Somewhere along the line, she had learned that Topa, too, worked for the resistance, but had the sense or the luck to not be caught. As she grew older and understood things more clearly, there came a point when he would say, "They were the bravest people in town," and she would mentally append, *Except for you.*

Enough, Rena thought, unknotting her hair and trying to rake the wild locks into submission with her fingers. This was all twenty years ago. *You don't even remember them. The Cardassians are gone now.* Padding back into the bedroom, she took the clothes she would wear today from the hooks on the back of the door: black skirt (or pants), black shoes, black or gray shirt (or sweater, depending on the chill in the air), and a white pullover with purple fluting. Now all she needed was her apron and the transformation would be complete. Seeing herself in the mirror, she said, "Hello, Bakery Shop Girl," and started downstairs to help Marja.

*   *   *

Every late spring, the intercoastal salt marshes north of Mylea were infused with newly warmed seawater from a southerly warm current bringing along the immense schools of tiny fish that, in turn, brought the bigger game fish. At almost the same time, give or take a week, a mass of damp, cool air descended from the mountains and mingled with the warm sea air, creating a dense white fog of such peculiar perspicacity that it was renowned around the planet and treasured by artists, holographers, and, in particular, lovers.

Before leaving Mylea for university, Rena had often enough read the expression "tendrils of fog" in stories and assumed that the author had described a condition that he had seen. Now that she had been away, Rena knew the truth: Most writers didn't know *real* fog. In other towns, fog was wispy and insubstantial. In Mylea, you could practically wrap it around you and wear it like a coat. In other places, fog was merely the ghost of a cloud; in Mylea, fog was like an ambassador of the ocean coming up onto land to remind it who was really in charge.

Lovers walking in Mylean fogs were almost always sure to lose themselves and wander into shadowy gardens and secluded corners. The lonely and the lovelorn claimed to feel soothed by visions of those they had lost too soon or never known. Harsh breezes never disturbed the vapors, but soft breezes would often waft through the streets, making the tendrils curl and dance like ocean waves. Even after the sun rose, the fog would linger and shroud the shops and houses in a translucent silvery veil. In Mylea, in the proper season, at the right hour, those who were open to wonder could find anything there they could possibly wish to see.

As she passed the round window on the stairway down to the bakery, Rena yawned hugely. Outside, the sky was just beginning to turn pinkish gray as the first rays of light began to rend the low morning clouds. She had seen enough early-morning fogs to know it would be a beautiful day, though she might not see much of it if Marja was in a punishing mood. "Here we go," she muttered, and pushed open the heavy wood door that led to the main kitchen.

The heavy door creaked as Rena walked in. Marja, bent over a tray of specialty breads with a glazing brush, glanced up, waved absently, then went back to what she was doing. Except for their pale skin, the same spray of freckles over the nose, and (so Rena was told) the same laugh, the sisters Marja and Lariah could not have been more unalike. Where Lariah had been willowy and tall, Marja was broad-shouldered and buxom, her arms thick with ropy muscle. Where Lariah had been fair, Marja's cheeks and nose were perpetually red, the result of a sensitivity to raw *prusin* seed enzymes, a condition that might have been eradicated if Federation medicine had been available to her in her youth. She walked with a slight limp from a childhood break that never properly healed. Rena's father had been the dark-skinned one, and though she was built more like her mother, only the most observant could see any resemblance between her and her aunt. "Is there any tea?"

"Just put the water on," her aunt said, still fussing with her bread.

"What do you need me to do?" Rena asked, looking directly overhead.

"If you can stay focused, glaze the buns."

It was an old complaint. Rena rolled her eyes. "What do you mean 'focused'?"

Marja shrugged. "No painting the buns with tinted glaze, no decorative flower patterns with the nuts and candies. No concocting experiments with the sweet bread recipes. We're not creating art, we're feeding people. Fofen Genn's replicators broke down. He's a houseful of boarders with no way to feed them. You'll need to take down a few baskets of rolls to hold them over while he waits for the repair person to arrive." Without actually looking up at Rena, she asked, "So did your trip purge that wandering impulse from you once and for all? I hope it did, because Kail came over every day when you were gone and I just know he's ready to make your engagement official."

"We're not even unofficially engaged," Rena said. "And he comes over here because you feed him."

"I hope at least that you finished the design for Topa's memorial. Every time I see him at shrine services, Vlahi from the foundry tells me he's ready to make the mold." Marja's voice was sharp with frustration.

Rena winced, recalling her destroyed sketchbook. "No, Auntie. I'm going to have to start over. But I promise I'll have it done before next week." She looked more closely at Marja, noting the tension in her shoulders. She took a deep breath. "I'm sorry I didn't tell you that I was leaving for Kenda. I contacted you as soon as I could—"

Marja held up a hand to shush her. "After all these years, I should be used to your bouts of wanderlust. But I have to confess this last disappearance surprised even me. Not even a week after Topa's passing. I know he asked you to go on his behalf, but there's work for the living to be done, Rena." She tsked. "And then on the heels of abandoning Kail at the shrine—"

Rena blurted, "I never agreed to go to the vedek with Kail!" Closing her eyes, she gritted her teeth and counted backward until she'd regained emotional control. She was so tired of having this discussion. "I left school for Mylea. Told my professors I wasn't coming back because I was needed at home. Isn't that enough?"

"Enough? Your parents gave their lives so that Mylea could be preserved and Rena asks if she's done enough?"

Rena let Marja's words hang in the air, restraining herself from pursuing an argument. She suspected that her aunt lashed out from her own pain. Marja had buried her grief deep inside her: she missed her father terribly. That Marja was frustrated with her inability to commit to Kail wasn't new. Though it was pretty close to the same conclusion she had recently come to about herself, Rena did not feel like giving her aunt the opportunity to stand with her hands on her wide hips and lecture her further.

"Kail wants me to go to Yyn for the Auster pageant next week."

"Good," Marja said shortly.

A buzzer saved both women from having to pursue the matter. Marja tapped a series of commands into the kitchen controls that unlocked and opened the ovens. Dozens of wire racks loaded with bun-filled trays glided out into the open air, accompanied by clouds of yeasty steam.

Marja lifted a few of the buns to check for readiness. "Give these a minute to cool and we can pack Fofen's order."

Without being told, Rena went to the rear of the kitchen to the pantry and retrieved the handmade rustic reed baskets and long lengths of coarse linen they had always used to pack the bread. Ten years ago, Rena, as a little slip of a girl, would help

Topa and Marja deliver these baskets to market or to the Cardassian barracks. As she and Marja plucked the rolls off the trays, Rena wondered if Marja had similar memories. Once the baskets were filled, they loaded them onto a two-wheeled pull-cart that Rena would tow, a splintery wood handle gripped in each hand, across the hill to the boardinghouse.

As Rena wheeled the cart down the passageway to the court-yard, she passed by Topa's old bedroom, finding his door propped open. She saw through her grandfather's window that the sun was now high enough in the sky to shine down through the mist and make it the same colorless color and density as the spray of flour that pops out the top when the sack is first cut open. He would love a day like today.

Once outside, Rena squatted down by the cart wheels to make sure the axle had been repaired since the last time she'd used it.

"Excuse me?"

Startled, she jumped up. "Yes? What? Sorry . . . what?"

A tall figure stood in front of her, silhouetted against the mist, its hand extended to touch her shoulder, but not touching her. "I'm sorry," the figure said. "I didn't mean to scare you. Fofen sent me down to see if the bread was done—"

At the same time, both of them realized the other's identity and startled, taking long steps in opposite directions.

"Jacob," Rena managed to squeak out. To see him now, emerging from the mist, an otherworldly apparition . . . Rena struggled to shake off the shock.

"Uh. Yeah. Rena," he sputtered. "I should have thought to ask if this was your family—I mean I had no idea that this bakery was yours—I, you know, ummm . . ."

The slap-slap-slap of leather soles on the wet rock pavement sounded; Rena and Jacob's heads pivoted toward the lanky fig-ure emerging out of the fog.

"Hey Jacob! Genn just heard from Marja. The bread is on its way. . . ." Fofen Parsh's voice trailed off as he saw the pair. He looked from Jacob to Rena, then back again. Smiling shyly at her, Parsh dropped his eyes and said, "Rena—nice to see you again. Sorry I missed Topa's funeral. He was a great old guy. If you ever want to talk, I'm always—"

"Thanks, Parsh," Rena said, cutting him off. Avoiding further eye contact with Jacob, she stepped out from between the handles and offered the cart to the two men. "One of you want to take this up? I'm sure my aunt could use my help, since the customers will be arriving soon." She crossed her arms over her chest, thrusting out her chin.

"You'd better believe Marja can use your help," Marja boomed from behind.

Rena jumped visibly.

"Genn's repair people aren't available until after midmeal. In addition to our usual orders and what we need for drop-ins, Genn needs bread for meat and cheese bundles." Marja stood beside Rena, scrutinizing both of the young men from their boots to their hair. "You're looking well, Parsh. Being back in Mylea doesn't agree with Rena, but it agrees with you."

Rena inhaled sharply, flushing with embarrassed fury.

Squinting, Marja jabbed toward Jacob. "And this other fellow?"

Parsh, who had always been a little afraid of Marja, stammered an introduction.

Marja pursed her lips, studying Jacob for a long moment before turning to him with a sniff. "You'll be coming back for the next order, Jacob?"

Jacob stood up straighter. "I expect so, ma'am."

"Bring the cart back with you. It's not like I can transport your food up the street."

Parsh assumed Rena's former position between the cart handles. "Why don't you just stay here a little longer, Jacob, and wait for the next batch? I can handle this myself." Lacing his fingers together, he stretched in an obvious attempt to show his muscles.

Rena rewarded Parsh with a tight-lipped smile.

Rena and Marja watched the young man dissolve into a curtain of fog before Marja pulled Rena toward the bakery. "Nice enough boy," Marja said. "If Kail weren't available, I'd tell you to accept Parsh."

Rena refused to rise to Marja's bait in front of Jacob. No need to give her aunt more ideas.

Marja pressed in the alphanumeric combination that unlocked the bakery's business door, kicked the doorjamb into place, and raised a hinged section of counter, allowing her to step into the staging area. To Rena, she handed over trays of pale green nut puddings in fluted pastries, cookies erupting with candied fruit, and whole cakes frosted in a multitude of colors, the bakery's signature, a series of white, interconnected ovals, etched into the surface. Jacob asked Marja what he could do to help. She tossed an apron over the counter, shoved a bucket with cleaning solution at him, and told him to start wiping fingerprints off the windows and doors. The trio worked in silence until another buzzer from the kitchen announced that the next batch was baked. Marja excused herself, leaving Jacob and Rena alone in the storefont.

"Why hello, Jacob *Sisko*," Rena said under her breath. "Makes sense that the son of the Emissary is moonlighting as a steward to ladies in distress."

"Talked to Kail lately?" Jacob retorted.

"Not today. But if you stay around a little longer, I'll introduce you when he stops by for his morning pastry." Rena unfastened the display cases mounted in the street-facing windows and started arranging the showy dessert pastries.

In his efforts to reach a particularly smudged windowpane, Jacob stood behind Rena and reached over her shoulders to spray the cleaner. Crouched down, Rena stepped back to survey her work and bumped into Jacob's chest. The pastry tray she'd been holding tipped, sending a dozen mousse-filled puffs skidding down the polished surface; her heart plunged to her knees. She shifted the tray's angle, preventing the pastries from splattering on the floor. She steadied her nerves before saying, "I don't know what you're trying to prove."

"I'm just a hungry man who came searching for his morning meal," Jacob said, retiring the cleaning bottle to the bucket.

Marja appeared carrying a smaller bread basket on each of her hips. "You two. Take this to Fofen."

A protest would reveal more about her connection to Jacob than she wanted her aunt to know, so she accepted Marja's basket without complaint and started out the door to Fofen's, Jacob following by her side.

In spite of the strain between them, Rena was surprised how easily she slipped into the cadence of Jacob's walk, just as she had when they hiked for the River Road. She stole a glance at him and wished there were a way they could start again. Starting

over long before yesterday would work, too, back when she left
secondary school and marrying Kail had seemed to fit perfectly
into her life. But she had to remind herself of her commitment to
Topa. *Live for Bajor. Live for Mylea. Don't let our ways pass
into history. Give them to my grandchildren*, he'd said.

Only a nudge from Topa's *pagh* could have served as a
greater reminder of her obligations than hearing Kail's voice
through the fog. Rena gathered that he was discussing solstice at
Yyn with Parsh.

As they came into sight, Kail smiled broadly. "My woman
has brought me food. Excellent." He reached into the basket and
took a roll. Rena slapped his hand; in response, Kail placed a
peck on her cheek. She wished he'd make less of a show of their
relationship. Poor Parsh looked on wistfully; he'd been soft on
Rena since they were schoolchildren, and Kail's displays merely
reinforced what Parsh would never have with Rena. When they
were younger, Rena had found Kail's possessiveness endearing.
Now it seemed a little cruel. Or maybe she was being overly critical because of her frustration. *After Kenda, I should have stayed
gone.*

Throwing a thick, muscled arm around lanky Parsh's bony
shoulders, Kail squeezed him good-naturedly, coaxing a pained
flush in his pale cheeks. "I was just extending an invitation to
Parsh to join our group next week. He's never been to Yyn before."

Rena rolled her eyes. "Parsh isn't the only one."

When Jacob materialized beside Rena, Kail scrutinized him,
probably comparing the newcomer with himself. Rena made her
own comparison, deciding that two men couldn't be more different. Kail, with his ruddy, clean-shaven complexion and
shoulder-length curly blond-brown hair, evinced the strength of
an arena wrestler, while darker Jacob stood taller than Kail but
had a ropy muscularity that suited him for springball.

"Of course you haven't been to Yyn, or we'd have had our
wedding night already." He winked at her.

Jacob looked genuinely puzzled, so Parsh explained the custom that on solstice night a couple need only take one of the
thousands of Auster's candles lighted at the ruins to be granted
the privileges of married couples. The "blessing" lasted only
until morning, in accordance with the legend. Rena felt Jacob's

eyes on her as Parsh explained, in his usual delicate terms, that the tradition typically resulted in a host of births in late fall.

"Why doesn't Jacob join our group?" Parsh asked. "He's not Bajoran. He's a writer. He might find a story at Yyn. Besides, Halar would enjoy his company."

Without moving his eyes from Rena's face, Jacob nodded. "I'd like that. Count me in."

The prospect of spending solstice caught between Kail's expectations of sex and Jacob's mind games pushed Rena too far. She shoved her basket at Parsh and announced that Marja needed her back at the bakery immediately. Kail called after her as she marched back up the hill, but Rena ignored him. If he cared about her feelings, let him prove it. Let Jacob prove it, too. Through the bakery doors and down the hall past Topa's room, she blew past Marja, and stomped up the stairs to her room.

"We'll have customers soon!" Marja called after her.

"I'm working on Topa's memorial," she said, and slammed her bedroom door. Once inside, she threw herself down on the floor and pulled her art supplies—charcoal, pastels—out from beneath her bed. Then she cast them aside and settled on paints. No amount of searching uncovered a canvas or even a large sheet of hardcopy, so she yanked the plain sheet off her bed and tacked two adjoining corners to the wall with hairpins shoved deep into the plaster. Stretching the sheet out the rest of the length of the wall, she affixed the remaining corners similarly. The rising morning temperature started making the attic room uncomfortably warm. Rena didn't care. She peeled down to her chemise and started painting.

She didn't think about strokes or composition or colors as she laid down a thick layer of black-green, the color of Mylea's ocean churned up by a storm. Blue—Topa's eyes—came next, followed by angry reds and gashes of yellow. Flecks of paint stuck to her eyelashes: she brushed them aside with her forearm, leaving a rainbow of smudges on her skin. If Marja had called her, Rena hadn't heard. The shadows lengthened with the changing light. If she felt hunger pangs or thirst, Rena ignored them. She knew only the demands of her brush and the shifting kaleidoscope of emotions pouring out in colors on her wall. At last she came to the browns—the warm, soothing brown of soil, soaked with water, peaty with leaves and dried moss. The color of her father's skin, the color of Jacob's skin, the color of her own. And when the last dab of paint left her palette, in the dimming of the day, she collapsed, weary, on the ground, and scooted back against the opposite wall to see what she had created. She had no idea what had been born of her brush, she only knew that she couldn't go on without it being poured out of her body into something outside of herself. Jacob's words returned to her. She cursed aloud. Why in the name of the Prophets did it keep coming back to Jacob?

. . . You weren't screaming about preserving Bajor, you were screaming like someone who was having her soul—her pagh— torn out of her. Tell me again that you need to give up your art. . . .

She removed the *duranja* lamp from her knapsack and lit the flame. She watched the firelight shadows leap and flicker over her painting. She began the benediction to honor the dead.

"Ralanon Topa propeh va nara eshuks hala-kan vunek."

But I want to honor you, Topa. She buried her face in her hands. *Prophets show me the way that I might do both.*

13

ASAREM

"I'm sorry, First Minister, but the answer is no."

Asarem stared at the monitor in the center of her office's conference table, shocked into silence by Magistrate Sorati's response. "Teru, I . . . I don't understand," she finally succeeded in saying. "You wanted this appointment. You didn't flinch once when you appeared before the Chamber Selection Committee . . ."

"Yes, for all the good that did me," Sorati said wryly.

". . . but as I said, they're no longer part of the equation," Asarem finished. "Under the present circumstances I have unassailable authority to appoint the person of my choice to represent Bajor on the Federation Council. I've chosen you."

"And I must respectfully decline, First Minister. My circumstances have changed."

"May I know in what way?"

Sorati hesitated.

"Teru, please," Asarem said. "At least tell me why. Help me to understand this."

"It's Herek."

"Your husband."

Sorati nodded. *"Our marriage has been troubled these last few years. In truth, had my appointment to the Federation Council gone through last month, it likely would have ended us, and I was prepared to accept that. We had grown apart, and I knew Herek would not have wanted to leave Bajor. Nor would it have been fair to ask him to accept years of separation. But when the nomination failed . . ."* Sorati seemed to grope for the right words. *". . . we rediscovered one another. It felt like we were being given another chance. Our love is renewed, and I find I am unwilling to jeopardize it now for my career. I am truly sorry to disappoint you, First Minister, and I remain honored to have been your first choice for such an important post."*

Asarem mustered a smile. "You need never apologize for loving your husband, Teru," she said finally. "My loss, after all, is Herek's gain, and I'm content to be the one defeated in such a contest. I rejoice for your happiness, and I wish you both well."

Tears formed in Sorati's eyes. *"Thank you, First Minister."*

Asarem closed the connection and sat back. Raising her voice, she called out "Theno!" and then looked across the table to see Ledahn frowning at her. "What?" she asked.

"You didn't try very hard to change her mind," he noted.

Theno appeared at the door leading into the anteroom. "First Minister, there *is* a comm system."

"Just bring me the list of all Bajoran diplomats with at least five years of offworld experience."

"Yes, First Minister."

"In fact," Ledahn went on, "you didn't try at all."

"What should I have done?" Asarem said. "Asked her to put her world ahead of her family?"

"Yes," Ledahn said pragmatically.

Asarem shook her head. "That sounds easy in theory, but I know better. I don't want to argue about this, Muri. Sorati is out of the picture. Let's move on."

"Move on to whom?" Ledahn asked as Theno returned carrying a padd, which he proceeded to hand over to Asarem. "You and I both know all the names on that list. None of them have the qualities Sorati had, the qualities you told me were essential for Bajor's Federation councillor. Let's not deceive ourselves."

Asarem ignored him and began scrolling through the padd.

Into the silence, Theno said, "Second Minister, may I ask you a question?"

Rubbing the ridges of his nose, Ledahn said, "Sure, Theno, what is it?"

"I've recently been informed that Cardassian voles have become an asset to the environment. Why are they not a protected species?"

Ledahn blinked, looked at Asarem, who continued to ignore them as she scrutinized the padd, and then turned back to Theno.

"Well, after all, they're *voles.*"

"My thoughts exactly," Theno said.

"Thank you, Theno, that will be all," Asarem snapped. As her aide inclined his head and withdrew, Asarem tossed the padd aside in disgust. "You're right," she told Ledahn. "None of these are satisfactory. Any one of them is *qualified* for the job, but there isn't one that makes me confident they'll be the kind of voice I think Bajor needs to have."

Ledahn considered the matter. "You found Sorati by deciding to look outside the diplomatic arena," he reminded her. "Isn't there anyone else you know in the legislative or judiciary branches, or even outside the government, with the qualities and qualifications you're looking for?"

"Colonel Enand Adassa," Asarem said without hesitation. "He's the commander of Militia forces on Prophet's Landing. He's sharp and has a good grasp of politics. He's even considered running for governor of the colony. Or he did, before he decided to join Starfleet."

"It isn't too late to persuade him to change his mind," Ledahn pointed out.

Asarem shook her head, reconsidering. "No. As much good as I think he would do for us on the Federation Council, it's just as important that we have some of our best people in Starfleet."

Ledahn nodded. "All right. Anyone else?"

"Opaka Sulan."

He frowned. "I'm not sure that's a good idea."

"Why not? She has the charisma, the intelligence, the integrity, and the strength of character—"

"She's needed here, First Minister," Ledahn said. "The Vedek Assembly has lost a lot of trust among the people over the years. Opaka's return is being seen as a breath of fresh air. I understand there are many who still hope she'll run for kai again. She can do the most good staying close to Bajor."

Asarem sighed. "You're right. Our options are dwindling, though. Prophets, I can't believe I didn't try harder to find more candidates like Sorati the first time around."

"You couldn't have known," said Ledahn. "Once it became clear the Chamber of Ministers wasn't going to see things your way with Sorati, there wasn't much point in looking for others like her. You did what the situation required: You met them halfway."

"And because I didn't anticipate things *ever* going my way," Asarem said bitterly, "I'll have to settle again, won't I?"

Ledahn didn't answer. Instead, she heard the sound of a throat clearing. The ministers turned in the direction of the noise.

"If I may be so bold, Ministers," Theno said from the doorway, "I have a suggestion. . . ."

"Are you still here?" Asarem asked. "Don't you have anything better to do?"

"Sadly, First Minister, that is precisely the reason I accepted this position."

Asarem laughed in spite of herself and slapped the conference table with both hands. "Very well. I'll make a deal with you, Theno: If you have a way to salvage this mess, you can have *my* job."

"I could never hope to run our world as you do, First Minister."

Asarem's eyes narrowed as she considered all the possible interpretations of Theno's reply. "Do you have someone to suggest, or don't you?"

"Your former husband."

Ledahn's mouth dropped open.

Asarem stared at her aide. "I'm going to pretend I didn't hear that," she said quietly.

Ledahn was nearly out his seat. "Uh, you may not have that luxury, First Minister. . . ."

Asarem held up a finger. "Stop right there—"

"I'm just saying—"

"Not another word!"

"If you'll just calm down and think about it for a moment—"

"The answer is no." Asarem pointed at her aide. "Get out, Theno. Get out, or by the Prophets, I'm going to kill you."

Unfazed, her aide walked calmly toward the door leading to the anteroom. "I'll leave you to it, then, Ministers," Theno drawled. "I'm quite confident that between the two of you, you'll find someone *passable*." He closed the door behind him without a backward glance.

Fuming, Asarem turned back to Ledahn. "Now, as for you . . ."

"He has every quality you said you wanted Bajor's Federation councillor to have," Ledahn said, speaking rapidly. "And unless something has changed in the last seven years, he's available. If not him, who?"

Shaking her head, she rose from the conference table and retreated behind the imaginary safety of her desk. "Absolutely not. There's no way I'm going to—"

"First Minister, it's either this, or we hand the decision back to the Chamber of Ministers."

"Then let them have it!" Asarem shouted.

Ledahn stood his ground. "We both know you don't mean that."

Asarem sat down heavily and rubbed her eyes with one hand. "I can't believe you support this idea, you of all people."

"That should tell you how seriously I take it."

"He made it very clear when he left public service that he wanted to be left alone."

"You weren't first minister then," Ledahn said. "Now you are, and your job isn't to give people what they want. It's to provide them with what they *need,* and to let the right people know when *they* are needed. I understand your reasons for not pushing the matter with Sorati, but Aldos was always willing to put Bajor before his personal feelings."

"Yes, and all it cost us was our marriage."

"That's not for me to say. My job is to advise you on the course of action that serves our people best," Ledahn said, refusing to let the conversation be derailed. "And you *know* this would serve Bajor best."

Asarem said nothing.

"At the very least, you have to ask him, First Minister. I'll remain with you while you contact him, if that's what you want."

Asarem closed her eyes, seeing the springball ricocheting wildly. She tried to anticipate where it would fly next, knowing that she was in real danger of losing control of it, even missing it completely.

"No," she said, opening her eyes. "Thank you, Muri, but this is one I'll need to handle alone. And I'll have to do it in person."

14

SOLIS

Mirroring Vedek Solis's mood, the clouds over Ashalla broke, letting the afternoon sun warm the domes and towers and tiled rooftops of the coastal city, so different from his native Ilvia, a sprawling inland community built along the slope of a great mountain. Although this wasn't his first visit to Ashalla, he had never before seen it from his current vantage point, the meditation balcony near the top of the Shikina Monastery. Standing with his right hand pressed flat against one of the four-sided columns that encircled the balcony and supported its roof, Solis looked out at Ashalla and beyond it, to all of Bajor, his *pagh* swelling with hope.

For all the turmoil of the last half-century, Solis Tendren believed that Bajor was once again on the cusp of a great change. As the wars to unite Bajor thirty thousand years ago had changed the course of their civilization. As the discovery of the first Tears had opened up his people's own self-awareness. As their first tentative steps toward new worlds had altered their perception of the universe. As the Cardassians, and the coming of the Emissary, and the Ohalu prophecies had brought changes . . . so now was another transformation coming. He needn't gaze into a Tear to know this. He felt it in his *pagh*, and in the stone against his hand, and in the breeze that came in from the sea.

Bajor is never still, he thought, enjoying the wind in his thinning hair. *Life moves, and Bajor with it.*

It was that understanding that had driven him to come to the Shikina Monastery today. He hoped to insure that, whatever came next, Bajor's path would be lit by the one who had always seemed to see the Prophets most clearly.

Solis heard the shuffle of soft sandals behind him. He turned to welcome she whom he had come to meet with. Opaka Sulan emerged from within the monastery and stepped lightly around the little pool in the center of the balcony. Solis had heard a rumor that the water was merely a hologram disguising a long stair that spiraled deep into the hill on which the monastery was built. Supposedly it had been created secretly during the Occupation to hide the last of the Tears from the Cardassians. If so, visitors to the balcony did well to avoid venturing too close to the pool.

"Vedek Solis, I am sorry to have kept you waiting," Opaka said at once, taking both his hands in hers. "I was delayed in Janir, where the Oralian temple is being constructed."

As always, Solis found Opaka's smile infectious, and he reflected it. "The work goes well, then?" he asked.

Opaka nodded, releasing his hands. "It is far enough along that services may be held within, as of this very day. That's why I was delayed. The Oralian guide, Cleric Ekosha, invited me to join the first gathering of the Cardassian followers of Oralius on Bajor. I could not resist the opportunity. It was a most moving experience. So like, yet unlike, our own devotion to the Prophets."

"Which is closer to the truth, I wonder?" Solis asked.

Opaka's smile widened . . . and was that a hint of mischief in her eyes? "Why, Tendren, they are of course equally true," she said, "and equally false."

"Because if one world's religion is true, all must be?" Solis challenged good-naturedly.

"No, though I believe there is some merit to that argument," Opaka said, lowering herself to the stone bench situated opposite the doorway. She gestured for Solis to join her. "It is because any religion is about attempting to comprehend the universe beyond what we, as merely parts it, can perceive. But though the faithful may scratch the surface of Truth, I believe we each see only a fragment of a much larger and more complex totality. Different religions may see different fragments, none of them wrong, but none of them entirely right either."

"But together . . ." Solis said.

"Together they may begin to form a mosaic," Opaka said. "Or a Tapestry. Just as our lives form the tapestry that is Bajor. Just as our experiences form the tapestry that is each of us."

Solis nodded. Nothing of what she said surprised him, of course. But it was good to listen, to hear her express her thoughts with such enthusiasm, such sincerity and serenity. It made him that much more certain about what he was going to say next. "You know why I asked to see you."

Opaka sighed. "I suspect I do."

"I know I am not the first to ask," Solis went on, "but I feel compelled to add my voice to the others. Will you be kai for us again?"

Her smile grew smaller, but did not quite disappear. "No, Tendren, I will not," Opaka said.

Solis was disappointed, but not entirely surprised. Still, he was not yet ready to give up, either. "The Vedek Assembly never recovered from your loss, Sulan. It fell into discord, politics, corruption. . . . Bareil Antos might have kept us from that decay, but once he was gone too, Winn Adami seemed to feed upon it. We lost our way, and we need desperately to find it again, now more than ever, with so much change in the wind. Ohalu, the Avatar, the Eav-oq . . ." He faltered, overwhelmed. "Can nothing persuade you?" he asked.

"It is not a matter of persuasion," Opaka said gently. "I know of the damage Winn did. My *pagh* ached to learn of it. And yes, recent discoveries are hastening the evolution of our understanding of the Prophets, perhaps with alarming speed. My faith, however, is enduring, and I will continue to walk the path on which They have set my feet, as we all do. But I have come to understand that my path does not lead back to the Apex Chair of the Vedek Assembly."

"Bajor needs you, Sulan," Solis said softly.

"Bajor has me," Opaka assured him. "But perhaps merely not in the way that it imagines it should."

Solis searched for other words that might sway her, but she was no longer looking at him. Her gaze had turned to take in the rest of the balcony, as if noticing it for the first time.

"Did you know," she said at length, "I first met the Emissary in this very place?"

Solis shook his head, but he was intrigued, "What was it like?"

"Troubling," Opaka admitted. "He was in so much pain. *So much.* He was lost, and did not know who he was."

"And you showed him," Solis surmised. "You led him to know his purpose."

Opaka waved his characterization of her aside. "I merely opened a door. He walked through it on his own." She turned back to Solis, looking at him carefully. "That is what a true kai does, Tendren. He does not lead. He does not wield power. He does not decide for others what the will of the Prophets requires of them. He merely helps them to find their own way, and to not fear the journey."

"That is why it should be you," Solis said. When Opaka gave no further reply, he asked, "If you will not become kai again . . . what, then, should we do?"

"What the Prophets teach us to do, when faced with doubt," Opaka said, as if the answer were obvious. "Look for solutions from within."

Solis blinked.

She smiled at him again, and then patted his arm. "Come, join me in my chambers. Let us take tea." She was on her feet and moving before Solis could reply. He rose from the bench and had to rush to catch up to her as she went inside, moving swiftly down the winding steps and through the cool yellow stone halls of the monastery.

"You're saying . . . you're saying I should seek the Apex Chair?" Solis asked.

"I don't believe I said anything of the kind," Opaka protested. "But if you were to ask me if I know of one to assume the mantle of kai, I would have to answer honestly that I can think of no other besides yourself who would care so deeply for the spiritual life of our people. I have heard you gave the matter thought before."

Solis spread his hands as they descended another curve of stairs. "Only to challenge Vedek Yevir. But once you returned, even he abandoned any thought of becoming kai."

"Vedek Yevir turned away from becoming kai because he discovered his true path," Opaka said. "Not because of me. He has a long road ahead of him, and he has at last taken the first true step on it."

"Nevertheless," Solis said as they turned a corner and continued down a another long corridor, "my original motives for seeking the Apex Chair—"

"Are irrelevant," Opaka said firmly. "There is only one motive to becoming kai that matters: the desire to help our people. As a vedek of Ilvia, you have guided and comforted a great flock for years. As an Ohalavar, you have advocated the exploration of faith and welcomed new ideas. And you fought for Kira Nerys before the Vedek Assembly, to have her Attainder lifted."

"I failed in that last endeavor," Solis pointed out. "It was you who helped Yevir to see the injustice he committed in Attainting Kira."

"But you spoke from your *pagh*," Opaka said. "I know, because I read the transcript of your speech. What does your *pagh* tell you now?"

Solis smiled. "That there is much good I can yet do for our people."

"Then do not hesitate to follow that path wherever it leads," Opaka told him, just as they reached the door to her chambers. "Just as I will."

Opaka opened the door and entered first, took three steps inside, and slowly came to a stop, turning to look all around her in amazement. An instant later, Solis saw why.

The modest central room of Opaka's chambers was filled with what must have been thousands of *esani* flowers. They were everywhere. It was like walking into a meadow in full bloom. And though he could tell from Opaka's expression that she was as surprised as he was to see them, her radiant smile seemed to suggest that she knew from whom they'd come.

15

RENA

Rena swirled the ale in the bottom of her glass. Restlessly, she kept checking her chrono, wondering when Parsh would show up so they could finalize their plans for Yyn. Inexorable fatigue had plagued her from the start of the evening. She had been up since sunrise to work in the bakery. She would have left all the planning to Kail and Halar—if she had fully trusted Kail. And why shouldn't she trust him?

Maybe, said a little voice in her head, *because he's been be-having oddly for days now. Today he didn't show up for his breakfast pastry, and tonight he had obviously been drinking for a long time before you arrived at the tavern.* Offering to take over the trip plans for him, she had earlier encouraged him to go home for the night. She had hoped the walk back would give them a rare opportunity to talk without their friends or family around. He had refused and ordered another *shodi.*

Rena sighed. Sitting and drinking all evening, even in this old haunt of her younger days that was built on Mylea's docks, wasn't what she'd had in mind for tonight, but then again any-thing would be better than skulking around the bakery hoping to avoid Jacob.

So far she'd succeeded: she hadn't seen so much as a hair on his chin since that horrible, awkward encounter at Fofen's. He obviously wanted to avoid her as much as she wanted to avoid him. Every time the door chimed, Rena would suddenly find something to clean in the back room. Marja hadn't commented on her flurry of productiveness, though Rena had noticed tenderness bordering on pity in Marja's expressions as the days wore on.

She looked around the table to see how the others were doing, wishing that they'd give up waiting for Parsh and just plan the trip. But Kail, an ugly drunk, had lapsed into bellicose behavior, leaning across the table toward Halar, emphatically making a point about whatever it was that he was on about at the moment. They all tolerated Kail's behavior because they knew the alcohol-infused persona would eventually vanish and the good-natured friend would return. Rena wasn't feeling as patient with him tonight. She knew she was tired, knew that her judgment was suspect, but she suddenly realized that she had been looking at Kail all night and trying to figure out, *Have I changed so much or has he?* Being away at university for a year shouldn't have made so much of a difference. Kail's working full time in the foundry shouldn't have made so much of a difference. Perhaps it was Topa's death. Something in her had changed, and Rena knew herself well enough to know that she had been working very hard all evening to avoid seeing it.

Jacob, a little voice inside her whispered. *Jacob is part of it.*

She told the voice to shut up and go away.

Again, she shifted her focus outward, studying her friends with new objectivity. Halar, the one whom Rena had always thought of as her best friend—what had changed there? She was still as sweet, still as sincere and forthright, as she had ever been. She worked in her mother's shop now and spent a lot of time with her family at shrine services while she began preparations to become a prylar initiate. Outwardly, Halar had generally found a rhythm to her life that Rena recognized that she had not yet attained. *And how do I feel about this?* Rena asked herself. *Am I happy for her? Do I envy her?* She had to confess that she while she didn't begrudge her friend's contentment, she was jealous that Halar had found her peace in Mylea while Rena still struggled to find hers.

Dropping her head to the table, she touched her forehead to the cool, slightly sticky surface and felt her hair tumble down around her ears. *What am I doing here?* she wondered, and knew that the word "here" could apply to Yvrig Tavern, Mylea, Bajor, or the universe itself.

What you're doing here is keeping your promises to Topa, the little voice said. *Or what you think those promises are.*

Rena wished the local band doing bad covers of the latest techno hits from Betazed would play loud enough to drown out her conscience.

She should order another drink—something nonalcoholic and hydrating. But that would mean attracting the waiter's attention, and she was loath to bring him into range considering the current bent of Kail's commentary. Despite her musings, one part of Rena's mind had been keeping track of the trail of Kail's ramblings. He had grown bored with disparaging his friends and enemies (he had fewer of both than he thought), his parents (two lovely people, really), and his shop supervisor, and had moved on to verbally abusing strangers, primarily non-Bajorans. First on the list had been some of the other customers in the bar, but he had quickly grown bored with the students and youthful vagabonds who populated the tavern, so he had moved on to abusing their waiter, a human, who had stopped over in Mylea on his way to Rakantha Province and never left. Rena had served him at the bakery and found him to be fond of all things sugary and always willing to offer a toothy grin in thanks. He didn't deserve Kail's ignorant abuse. He'd never been this way before, had he? True, she was seeing him with the perspective of time and distance between them, but Rena also knew that she wouldn't be attracted to someone who berated others the way Kail was doing now—or in the past.

Looking back, she recalled thinking that no one had seemed to understand how exciting the times were. Bajor had been on the verge of joining the Federation; they would be the first generation who could enjoy all the benefits and responsibilities of becoming true galactic citizens. And what had her peers obsessed about? They wanted to know how long it would be before their parents would get the newest replicator technology. When would the most cutting-edge holonovels become available? The ones who had really driven her crazy were the parasites who tried to figure out the minimum work they would have to do to be given full citizenship rights. Didn't they understand what they were being offered? Not that Bajor was a provincial world, disconnected from the rest of the galaxy, but becoming full Federation citizens meant so much more than finding out what the kids on Earth were wearing. It meant providing hope to those, like Topa, who had been born with degenerative, genetic ailments that could be cured with Federation medicine and the educational offerings on worlds Rena had only dreamed of visiting. It also meant showing the Federation's other worlds the best of Bajor: its art, literature, music, architecture, philosophy, history, and people—all the unique things Bajor had to share that could have a reciprocal influence on the community of which they were now a part.

Her schoolmates who hadn't become obsessed with what benefits they would receive from Federation citizenship were the ones who wanted to stay in Mylea. Instead of pursuing glamour careers in Starfleet, or studying exotic sciences on strange planets, or teaching other worlds about Bajor, these kids would primarily end up working in foundries, in shops, in restaurants, on fishing boats, or in the aquaculture fields. Rena respected these schoolmates, because she saw them as those who would preserve what was unique about their planet—its culture, rhythms, and traditions. In them she placed her greatest hope that Bajor could hold on to its uniqueness and still progress as a Federation world. And where did Rena fit?

Not properly in either category, she reluctantly admitted.

Maybe another ale wouldn't be such a bad idea after all. Which brought her back to the present and the problem with calling the waiter over to take her order: Kail being an idiot.

"Bunch of old people—offworlders!—signed some papers a month ago and suddenly we're all supposed to do our jobs without getting paid," Kail snarled. "Now the flat-noses are everywhere, all of them acting like they own the planet."

"Kail," Rena hissed, appalled. "Hush! Who's been acting like that?"

"You know who," Kail said. Craning his neck, he scanned the dim interior of the bar until he locked his gaze on the waiter, who was standing next to a table across the room taking an order. His customers—a trio of women a year or two older than Rena—were obviously enjoying his attention.

"He isn't doing anything, Kail," Halar said in low tones. "Except waiting tables."

"And why would he?" Kail muttered. "Not like he has to. Not like anyone has to do anything anymore."

Parsh appeared through the tavern's smoky haze and scooted into a chair beside Halar. "Sorry I'm late, but the sonic showers went offline again. Jacob was supposed to meet us here. Have you seen him, Rena?"

She shook her head and amended mentally, *Thank the Prophets.*

"You know the Federation economy doesn't work that way, Kail," Halar said. "No one gets a free ride. Everyone has to do something, but no one gets left behind. No one starves, no one is cold, but not everyone gets their own holoroom."

"No?" Kail asked. "Sounds like you understand all the new rules, Halar. I wish someone would explain them to me. Why should I work down in that hot, noisy foundry seven hours a day when in a little while anyone who wants to can replicate anything I can make by punching a few buttons?"

"You should do it," Rena said, "because you want to. Like we do in our bakery and Halar does in her mother's dress shop. And, besides, you know replicators aren't always the right way to go. Replication takes power and some things you can do cheaper and, yes, better, than a replicator. You know this, Kail. Why are you being such a jerk about it?"

"I've been reading some of the material posted on the comnet," Halar said. "I wasn't so sure about the idea of Bajor joining the Federation for a long time. I thought it would mean that we . . ." She swept her arm over her head to indicate that "we" meant them, Myleans, the "we" she understood. "I was worried we would disappear. But that won't happen."

"Why won't it?" Kail asked, his tone too aggressive. "How different are they really from the Cardassians?" Rena heard the slur in his voice and wondered how much ale Kail had drunk. He had been obnoxious before, but something had tipped him over the edge. "Cardies had guns. The Federation has holonovels. What's the difference?"

Even Parsh must have sensed the difference in his friend's tone. Attempting to distract him, he asked, "Hey, did you see the hoverball finals? I wouldn't want to have to play against Vulcans. Man, those guys have some moves. . . ."

But Kail wouldn't be distracted. "They're not so tough.

There's one thing different between Cardassians and the Feds. Least when the Cardies wanted something, they just came and took it. They were tough. The Feds, they're just cowards." He stared into the bottom of his mug, apparently insulted that it should be so empty. "Every single one of them."

"You think the Emissary is a coward too, Kail?" Halar challenged. Though normally reserved, even cheerful, Halar could be quite forthright when she felt her religion was being insulted.

At the mention of the Emissary, Rena sank deep into her seat, wishing she could disappear. *I wonder how she would feel if she knew about me and Jacob Sisko?*

Rolling his eyes, Kail asked, "The Emissary? Fine, let's talk about the Emissary. Let's start with how convenient it was that he showed up at just the time the Feds wanted to make a favorable impression on the gullible masses. I mean, there couldn't have been any political motivation for that, could there?"

At university, Rena had heard variations on this theme: how convenient it had been that the Emissary had come at the moment the Federation wished to display its good intentions. Not that there hadn't been doubts in every level of society, but how long could doubts stand in the face of a living, breathing example of prophecy come true? And then, not quite a year ago, Kira Nerys had broadcast the Ohalu texts that had predicted the coming of the Avatar. Then, surprise! A few months later, the Emissary had returned and his second child had been born. For her purposes, Rena had accepted what had happened without attempting to assign motive or meaning to it. Knowing Jacob, though, she'd spent the past few days considering the Emissary, attempting to sort the facts from the fictions and gain more clarity on the matter. She'd even cracked open Topa's copy of the Ohalu prophecies to read them for herself. She'd concluded that if the Emissary was anything like Jacob, he couldn't be capable of the political machinations Kail and many others accused him of.

Without consciously deciding to speak, Rena said sharply, "Why don't you just shut up, Kail?"

Shaking his head like a great shaggy *syba* who suddenly realized someone had cut off his antlers, Kail said, "Wha . . . ? What did you say?"

Releasing the emotion she'd repressed felt so, so . . . liberating. "You heard me," Rena said, eyes blazing. "What do you know about about the Emissary? You haven't cared about the prophecies since you were little. You hardly know anything."

Kail's mouth went slack, and his brow dropped down like a hood over his eyes. The muscles in his thick upper arms clenched as he gripped his empty mug. "You're not exactly the portrait of piety, Rena," he said leeringly, glancing from Halar's prim tunic to Rena's bare shoulders and the skirt belted low on her hips, exposing her midriff.

She crossed an arm across her chest, resting it on her collarbone. Kail had always complimented her when she wore this outfit. The tone he'd used just now made her feel cheap. Gritting her teeth, she leaned toward Kail, prepared to lambaste him . . .

But Kail wasn't finished. "Faking sick to get out of shrine services so you could meet me at the docks so we could have—"

"We're done, Kail," Rena said, shoving back her chair. "I thought this could work. I wanted this to work for Topa's sake. But I can't do this—not even for my grandfather."

Halar's mouth fell open. "Rena! Listen to yourself!"

Parsh stared at the floor.

"You going to go find yourself a Federation boy now, Rena? Us Myleans not good enough for you?" Wobbly-legged, Kail stood. In the hand opposite Rena, he held the nearly empty ale mug. A thin stream of liquid dribbled out onto the floor as Kail lifted the mug higher. Rena risked taking her eyes off Kail for a split second to see if Parsh was seeing what she was seeing and, obviously, yes, he was, but was paralyzed by indecision. *This is all happening so quickly. . . .*

Rena scanned the room, searching for an escape route for herself and Halar. *How did I get myself into this stupid situation?*

"I'm leaving now, Kail. Don't bother following me. Don't come to the bakery tomorrow with your apologies."

Kail snarled, and stepped into her path, and his arm began to swing.

16

HOVATH

"Wait!" Hovath screamed.

The Nausicaan's hand was poised over a switch. The underling looked at his master, who said, "Stop. Is there something you wish to say, Hovath?"

Shaking, Hovath stared down at the table, clutching at his hair with both hands. "Please don't kill her. *Please!* I'll tell you whatever you want to know, I'll tell you *anything.* Just don't kill my wife."

"Then we have an understanding?" his captor asked.

Hovath nodded.

"Begin, then. Tell me your thoughts about the wormhole."

Hovath pulled his trembling hands away from his head and placed them atop the table. "The Temple does not behave like an ordinary wormhole," he began slowly, trying to keep his hands from shaking. "Its stability alone is proof of that, but it also has an *interior.* It is a continuum unto itself, outside normal space-time."

"Bajoran and Starfleet scientists have known these things for years," his captor said impatiently.

"They study the wormhole as it appears to them," Hovath said. "Their minds do not venture beyond what their instruments can measure. I began with a simple question: Why does the wormhole open to the Gamma Quadrant? Answering that requires an understanding of the thoughts behind the Temple's makers, the Prophets, who exist within it, outside the linear continuum."

"You attempted to reconcile the theology surrounding the Temple with scientific inquiry into the wormhole."

Hovath shrugged. "I learned early in my life that I have an aptitude for both, and I have tried to keep a balanced perspective." He recalled his private arguments with the old *sirah* on that very aspect of Hovath's personality. Sitting here now, he wished he had listened more, seen the wisdom of focus and selfless obligation that his mentor had tried to impart.

"Bajoran theology is usually consistent with the physical universe," he went on. "The question for me became whether that meant it could offer any new clues about why the Temple behaves as it does, and whether the science of the wormhole could lead to new insights into our faith." Hovath looked up for a moment, once again trying to discern something more about the silhouette facing him. The heat and glare of the light forced his gaze back down to the table. "Bajorans do not question why the Temple opens above our skies. We merely accept it, and see it as validation of our connection to the Prophets. After all, it is upon us that their Tears have fallen, and it is for us that the Emissary was sent."

He paused, remembering the controversy during that first year. "But to learn that the Temple opened in two directions puzzled us," he said. "At that time, there was no discernible reason, from a theological perspective, for why it also opened in the Gamma Quadrant. It left us to wonder if Bajor was as unique as we had believed.

"I considered what was known and observable about the wormhole. We know it is stable, but it is not fixed in space; though its distance to B'hava'el is constant, the wormhole's Alpha terminus moves through the galaxy *with* Bajor's star. The Gamma terminus, we have since learned, is somehow anchored to the star Idran in much the same way.

"I asked new questions. What if the Alpha and Gamma termini of the wormhole were not the only points in this continuum on which the wormhole opened? What if they were merely the *first* two? What if the Prophets' interest in our universe was not confined to Bajor, but extended to other worlds as well? The return of the Eav-oq to this continuum at the wormhole's Gamma terminus is at least consistent with that assumption. But what if it does not end there? What if the Temple has not two endpoints, but many?"

"*How* many?"

Hovath shook his head. "Who can say? Perhaps an infinite number."

"Meaning that the wormhole could, under that assumption, open anywhere in the universe."

Hovath stared down at the table. "Yes."

"How can that be? The termini we know about are triggered at an event horizon. If the wormhole had an infinite number of endpoints—"

Hovath shook his head. "The Alpha and Gamma openings are unlocked. My speculation is that while the Temple may have an infinite number of doors, most of those are locked from the inside."

"Which suggests you would need a key to open them."

"No such key exists," Hovath said, unable to keep the anger out of his voice. "Don't you understand? My ideas were little more than flights of fancy. They have no credibility within the scientific community, nor within the theological one. They are unsupportable. Without a way to test my hypotheses, they are merely philosophy, not theory."

His captor's hand came into the light and set a small golden object down on the table, well out of his reach. Hovath saw a pinpoint glint of green, and knew what it was: the *Paghvaram.*

"What if I were to suggest," she said softly, "that you may have had the key all along?"

Hovath felt as if his chest would explode. He buried his head in his arms and sobbed. "Please . . . let my wife go."

"You disappoint me, Hovath. Your mind is so thirsty, yet you won't drink, even when the well of knowledge is so close."

"It was presumption," he moaned. "Vanity. Arrogance. I thought the wormhole was an invitation to further knowledge, but I see now that it was instead a test of faith. And I failed it. My quest to comprehend the Temple doomed my people, and damned me."

"Hovath, how can you believe such a thing?" the woman

asked, her voice tinged with kindness, with sympathy. "The Prophets haven't punished you. They've rewarded your vision, your willingness to look beyond your little village and peer into the true structure of the universe. You've been unshackled, don't you see? The death of the village is not a condemnation of your choice, but an affirmation, a sign from Them that you are on the verge of something new and wonderful."

"You are twisting my faith to suit your ends," Hovath said. "To justify mass murder."

"Am I?" His captor slid the padd back to him. "Did you not go down this path in pursuit of a truth that you hoped would transcend the one you knew? Did you never even once stop to consider that what you learned would be incompatible with what you believed before? That your discoveries would transform your life? What clearer sign could the Prophets send that you have fulfilled your quest?"

"The death of nearly everyone I love is not a sign from the Prophets. You know nothing of my faith."

"Are you certain of that?"

"Yes!"

Then something altogether unexpected happened. His captor stood up and stepped around the table, moving into the light. Hovath saw her face for the first time, and his world unraveled completely.

"I ask again," she said, "are you certain?"

How? his mind screamed. *How is this possible?*

Aloud he whispered, "Why would you do this?"

She came closer, finally sitting on the edge of the table next to where he sat. "Because, like you, I thirst for understanding. I burn to see what only the Prophets can reveal."

Try as he might, Hovath could not turn his eyes away from her. She stared down at him, as if waiting for an answer. . . .

The room shook. A low boom reverberated through the deck. There was a chime from the console beneath the screen that showed Iniri. The Nausicaan detached an audio receiver from the panel and pressed it to his ear. "Attacked," the underling reported. *"Defiant."*

Hovath's heart surged with hope.

"How timely. Both of you report to the bridge," she told her men. "I'll be there shortly . . . after I secure our new friend."

Iniri vanished from the screen. The two underlings left. His captor gathered up the padd and the *Paghvaram*, secured them in an inner pocket of her jacket, then drew out a hand weapon of some kind and pressed it to the side of his head. The rising hum of its charge pierced his ear. Grabbing his arm with her free hand, she pulled him to his feet as the ship shook again.

Hovath didn't resist. He believed that, one way or another, his nightmare was about to end.

Then he saw the smile on his captor's face, and his hope died. "Now comes the fun part," she said.

17

KIRA

"Stay with them, helm," Kira ordered. "Tactical, I want those shields down!"

"Pulse phasers firing," Bowers said behind her. "Direct hit."

Five hours after departing DS9, moving at warp eight and against all odds, the *Defiant* had located her quarry, the Besinian ship, just a few light-years shy of the Badlands. Kira was determined not to let their good fortune be wasted. Nearly three hundred innocent people were dead because of this ship, and justice was going to be exacted for that crime, one way or another.

Once the freighter had showed up on long-range sensors, Kira ordered battle stations and commenced an attack plan she'd used successfully against Cardassian slave transports more than once during the Occupation—tactics designed to disable, not destroy. Doing it from the *Defiant*'s command chair wasn't all that different from her experiences on the bridge of a Bajoran assault ship, she reflected: she still needed to remind herself to pull her punches when the circumstances required it. This was one of those times.

Or so she thought.

"Their shields are still holding," Bowers reported, the disbelief in his voice echoing Kira's own.

"I believe I know why," Shar said from sciences. "Their shield harmonics are Dominion."

"Dominion?" Bowers said.

Kira shook her head as she stared at the evading ship on the viewscreen. "They salvaged a Dominion shield generator from somewhere. But why didn't anyone detect that when they came to Bajor?"

"They may have a dual generator system in place," Shar postulated. "A more conventional one in order to appear inconspicuous, and another . . ."

"Another to deal with us," Kira finished.

"Sir," Bowers announced, "they're charging weapons—"

"Evasive!"

At the helm, Tenmei's nimble fingers danced across her console. *Defiant* pitched to starboard and climbed, a yellow beam from the alien vessel tracking after her. No sooner did she escape one enemy cone of fire, however, than she moved into another and rocked against the impact of a second beam. The Besinian ship increased speed and pulled away.

"Direct hit to our starboard nacelle casing," Bowers reported. "Torpedo launchers are off line. They're using spiral-wave disruptors."

Dominion shields and Cardassian weapons, Kira noted. *Are they really just opportunists, or are they sending a message?*

"They're making a run for plasma storms," Shar warned.

"I've had enough of this," Kira said. "Close the distance, Tenmei. Shar, triangulate on the probable location of their shield generator and feed the coordinates to tactical." She spoke over her shoulder. "Make this one count, Sam."

"Aye, sir," Bowers said. Minutes ticked by as the *Defiant* reacquired its target and surged after it. "Coordinates received," Sam announced at last. "Pulse phasers locked."

"Fire," Kira said.

On the viewscreen, phaser bolts bridged the void between the *Defiant* and the Besinian ship. An elliptical bubble of force surrounding the freighter became visible against the bombardment—and held.

"Again," Kira ordered. "Fire."

Once more, the *Defiant*'s phasers hit their mark. Their target's shield envelope flared momentarily . . . then gave way as the pulse bolts ripped across the upper hull of the freighter.

"Their shields are down," Shar reported. "Minor damage to their hull. . . . I believe we also took out their second generator."

"Target their port nacelle wing," Kira said. "Go easy this time, Mr. Bowers. I just want to knock them out of warp."

"Aye, sir, phasers firing. . . ." Another flash of orange exploded across one side of the alien ship, and the vessel abruptly vanished from the viewscreen.

"They've dropped out of warp," Tenmei confirmed. "We've overshot them."

Kira let out a long breath and leaned back in her seat. "Bring us about and switch to impulse," she said. "Shar, what's their condition?"

"Dead in space," Shar said, translating the numerical data scrolling up his console display. "They're on emergency power. Their weapons systems appear to be offline."

"Life signs?"

"Twelve. Five of them are concentrated in the bridge, the others are in or around engineering. There seems to be—" Shar stopped, his antennae angling forward. He began tapping his console.

"Ensign?"

"I'm sorry, sir. For a moment I thought there was a slight power spike underneath the ship. It's gone now."

"Sam?"

Bowers shook his head. "I can't confirm it. They've got plasma venting from at least eight different sources all over the ship. The spike could easily have been a ruptured EPS conduit."

"Keep the shields up," she told him, "and Lieutenant, if they so much as twitch . . . be sure to remind them why they shouldn't."

"Understood, sir."

Kira stood up and faced the main viewer, on which the disabled freighter could now be seen again, becoming larger as the *Defiant* approached. "Open a channel."

"Channel open."

"This is Captain Kira Nerys of the *U.S.S. Defiant,* representing the United Federation of Planets. You're ordered to surrender and prepare to be boarded."

She was answered with a burst of static, but there seemed to be a voice behind it. "Can you clean that up?" she asked Bowers.

"No," he answered after a moment. "I'm showing that their comm system is mostly slag."

"I thought we didn't hit them that hard."

"Dominion shield generator or no, it's still a nonmilitary courier, Captain. Overloading the shields and then knocking out the warp drive could have easily had an effect on some of their other systems."

"Are they receiving us?"

"They seem to be."

"All right, send this: By order of the Federation, all occupants of your ship are to be detained for questioning in the matter of more than two hundred and seventy deaths on the planet Bajor. You're to offer no resistance. We have your vessel targeted. Stand by." Kira made a cutting motion across her throat with her thumb, and Bowers closed the channel.

"We'll do this in two teams," she told him. "Have Gordimer take three security people to secure the bridge. DeJesus and Nog will go with me to secure engineering and assess the warp engines. I'll take Doctor Tarses, too, in case there are injuries. Have them all meet me in the transporter bay in two minutes. You have the bridge, Lieutenant." Kira started for the exit.

"Sir," Bowers said. "Request permission to lead the team to engineering."

Kira stopped and looked at him. "You know I can't grant that request, Sam. Not this time." She nodded toward the command chair. "You keep her warm until I get back."

Bowers frowned, clearly unhappy with her decision. "May I respectfully remind the captain that Starfleet regulations call for the ship's commanding officer to remain on board, not to lead away missions."

Kira smiled at him. She knew what he was trying to do, and appreciated it, so she kept her tone light as she strode out of the bridge. "Sorry, Mr. Bowers, I guess I haven't gotten to that part in the manual yet."

As the Besinian ship materialized around her, Kira swept her drawn phaser around the dim corridor into which Transporter Chief Chao had deposited Team One. Kira trusted her people to cover her back, but as team leader, she was their first line of defense against anything in front, and she was determined that none of the killers on this ship would take any more lives.

Fortunately, sensor reads of their beam-in point had proven true: the corridor outside the engine room was quiet. It wasn't until Kira looked at the deck that she saw why.

At her feet lay a dead man.

He was an Arkenite: the distinctive swept-back skull, domed forehead, and large, elegantly shaped ears were unmistakable.

Tarses bent to one knee, held his tricorder over the corpse for a few seconds, and delivered his verdict. "Shot by a phaser during the last thirty minutes," he told Kira, pointing out the dark bloodless burn on the back of the head, which was visible even in the ship's dim purple emergency lighting: the telltale sign of an energy weapon fired at point-blank range.

"Sir, another one," DeJesus said, crouching next to a prone Ktarian male. Both bodies, Kira noted, wore drab paramilitary clothing. Tarses moved to scan the second corpse, and reported the same findings.

What the hell—? Kira thought. She'd seen enough brutality in her life to recognize executions when she saw them. But if Tarses was right, both of these men had been killed while the *Defiant* was chasing down this ship. *Which meant . . . what?*

She tapped her combadge. "Kira to *Defiant*."

"Bowers here, Captain. Is everything all right?"

"We're in, Lieutenant. But we've come across a couple of bodies, very recently killed by weapons fire. Tell Team Two they can beam to their target site, but to proceed with caution."

"Understood, sir."

"Kira out." She gestured with her phaser toward an elliptical door at one end of the corridor. "According to Chao, that should be engineering. Stay alert. I don't want any mistakes."

The door, not unexpectedly, refused to open. Nog unsealed an access panel and went to work on the locking mechanism, DeJesus covering him while he applied the skills developed during his misspent youth together with what he'd learned under the tutelage of of Chief O'Brien over the last few years. Kira and Tarses watched and waited on the other side of the doorframe, backs against the corridor wall, phasers at the ready.

After a few moments, Nog looked up at Kira and nodded

once. Kira nodded back, and her chief engineer touched a final contact on the exposed circuitry before hitting the deck. The thick engine-room door slid open, but there was only silence beyond. No voices, no weapons fire. DeJesus quickly peered inside and then withdrew her head. Finding nothing, she swung her entire body around and entered the room, her phaser pointing the way.

After several seconds, Kira heard DeJesus call out "Clear!" and the rest of Team One crossed the threshold, spreading out as they did so. Kira saw at once why they had encountered no resistance. Four more dead bodies littered the deck: two Tellarite females, a male human, and a male Romulan, all fallen where they'd been shot, as Tarses quickly confirmed, by phaser fire. The last two had been shot in the back; the others bore chest wounds, and still held hand weapons of their own, as if they were preparing to fight back against whoever had felled their shipmates. Like those out in the corridor, they were dressed in paramilitary garb of no discernible affiliation: mercenaries. Judging from the absence of phaser burns anywhere else in the room, Kira concluded they'd never had a chance to return fire. Whoever did this had gotten the drop on all of them.

The warp core stood silent and dark.

"Any life signs?" Kira asked Tarses.

"Just us," the doctor answered, his small eyes and straight, slightly upswept eyebrows enhancing the scowl he wore as he reported his findings. "Wait. I'm picking up something in that direction," he amended, pointing to starboard. "It's Bajoran."

"Maybe it's the one who killed the crew?" Nog said. "A survivor taken from the village, getting their revenge?"

Kira was reluctant to draw any conclusions yet, though she had to admit Nog's guess seemed not an unlikely possibility.

"Dr. Tarses and I will check it out," she decided. "Ensign DeJesus, you'll stay to assist Lieutenant Nog while he assesses the ship's engines. Contact me if there's anything new to report. Which way, Doctor?"

Tarses indicated a short corridor leading out of main engineering and into an adjacent subsection, dimly lit like the rest of the ship in that odd purple lighting. The doctor's tricorder, Kira realized, was leading them toward an airlock. Tarses peered through a small triangular window in the inner hatch.

"Oh, my God," he whispered.

Kira didn't stop to ask him what he saw. She made several attempts to open the inner portal using the keypad in the wall next to it before she finally stepped back and fired her phaser at the mechanism. Applying her full strength on a stubborn manual lever below the keypad allowed her to crank the hatch ajar, enough that Tarses could fit fingers into the edge and pull it open the rest of the way.

The Bajoran was a young woman who could not have been older than twenty-five, huddled in a corner with her knees up, her face buried behind them. It was immediately apparent that she wasn't the killer of the ship's crew. She'd been sealed in the airlock from the corridor, and from the looks of her, she'd been tortured: clothing torn, burns on her exposed skin, hair matted with blood from a head injury. Her earlobe was torn where her earring had been partly ripped free, the bloody ornament hanging by one intact clasp. Her entire body was trembling. She had no other reaction as the door of her prison opened.

"We're here to help you," Tarses said as he approached. She flinched at the sound of his voice, so he lowered it to a whisper as he slowly raised his tricorder to scan her. "I'm a doctor. My name is Simon. Can you tell me your name?"

The woman made a slurring noise and pushed her way to her feet, back against the outer portal. She swung her arms as if to warn Tarses away.

Drugged? Kira wondered. *Or simply traumatized?* Maybe it was both.

"It's okay," Tarses said. "We're going to take you out of here."

Tarses's quiet assurances only spurred the woman to resist even more; she seemed to be trying to push her way through the airlock, making desperate, guttural noises and intermittently clawing at the air in the doctor's direction.

Kira came into the airlock and approached the young woman. "Easy, easy," she said softly. "You're safe. We're not going to let anything else happen to you, I promise. My name's Nerys. Kira Nerys."

The woman's reaction was immediate: she began screaming. She covered her head with her arms and turned away, beating her fists against the outer portal, desperate for escape.

Tarses took advantage of the opportunity she presented in turning her back to them and moved in, hypospray in hand. He pressed it to the side of her neck, and she let out one more piercing scream before dropping into unconsciousness.

Kira caught her before she hit the deck. "What's wrong with her?"

"What isn't?" Tarses said, taking the woman from Kira's arms and lowering her gently to the airlock floor. "Just look at her. She's been the victim of hours of physical and probably psychological abuse. I have to get her to the medical bay."

Kira tapped her combadge. "Kira to *Defiant*."

"Bowers here."

"Two to beam out, Lieutenant. Have Chao lock on to Dr. Tarses and the injured Bajoran next to him. Tell her to beam them straight to the medbay."

"Acknowledged. Stand by." There was a pause as Bowers relayed the orders to the transporter bay, and shortly thereafter, Tarses and his patient were enveloped in a curtain of shimmering light, and then were gone.

Kira exhaled heavily. "Sam, have Shar scan this ship again for life signs. What do his readings show?"

A moment later, she heard Shar's voice over her combadge: *"Nineteen, Captain. The seven remaining members of the boarding party, plus the original twelve . . ."* Shar trailed off, realizing the impossibility of the readings. If they were genuine, then they should be showing one less than the original twelve occupants of the craft, now that one of them had been beamed aboard the *Defiant* with Tarses.

"Let me guess," Kira said. "You're still showing them concentrated in engineering and the bridge."

"Confirmed," Shar said.

"The problem is, with the exception of the doctor's patient," Kira told him, "everyone we've found aboard this ship so far has been recently killed. Something here is sending out false life signs."

Bowers's voice came back. *"Captain, I strongly recommend aborting the mission and returning to the* Defiant."

"Not yet. Stand by," Kira tapped off, then on again. "Kira to Gordimer."

"Gordimer here, Captain."

"Report, Ensign."

"Sir, we've secured the bridge, but the crew was already dead. They were all killed by weapons fire."

"Stay where you are, Ensign. I'm coming up."

Residual energy signatures were consistent: the deaths aboard the Besinian freighter had been caused by the same weapon.

Kira studied the killing field. She noted the single door leading out of the bridge, center aft, saw that all the crew stations faced the forward viewer, considered where and how each of the bodies had fallen, and formed a picture in her mind of how it all happened.

A single killer, making his way through the ship. He or she would have started here, in the bridge. The female Arkenite slumped over the command console was first, shot point-blank like the mercs in the corridor outside engineering. But to get away with that, the killer had to have somehow come in unnoticed . . . or had to have been known to the crew. Someone they hadn't feared. *One of them.*

The sound of the weapon would have caused the rest of the bridge crew to turn. The killer had fired next on the two farthest to port, a female human and a male Bolian; both victims' disruptors were still holstered. Next to go had be the human conn officer, who had perished in the act of taking out his weapon.

The last to die had put up a fight: a Nausicaan who probably took cover behind the tactical station at starboard when the shooting began. By the time the killer's arc of fire had swept to that side of the bridge, the Nausicaan had freed his weapon and started shooting back; the front of the command console was seared. For some reason the Nausicaan stood up—perhaps he thought he had shot his attacker?—and that was all the killer needed to finish him off. The Nausicaan's broad torso was charred black with multiple hits. He'd fallen back against the forward bulkhead, dead before he slid to the deck.

The killer had then proceeded to engineering, met the two in the corridor on the way, dealt with them, and then went on to eliminate the rest of the crew. It made sense for the killer to start in the bridge and work his way aft; the engineers would have been slower to react if they lost contact with the command crew, whereas those on the bridge might have determined more quickly that there was an internal danger to the ship. Taking out the bridge crew first would have given the killer time to cross the distance between the two sections before the engineers were fully aware that anything was wrong, especially if they were occupied with being chased by a Federation starship when it all happened.

Gordimer's people had found an isolinear cube inserted in the command console. The block contained a sophisticated autopilot program, adaptable to fit the conditions defined by external sensor readings. Thus, evasive maneuvers and defensive measures continued even after the crew was dead, and a special signal designed to give outside observers the impression of twelve distinct life signs in two separate areas of the ship convinced the *Defiant* that she was still engaged in a meaningful pursuit. Even the voice Kira thought she'd heard over the static of the comm channel had been fake, designed to mislead.

"DeJesus to Captain Kira."

"Go ahead."

"Sir, I'm still on the engineering deck. I found a shuttlepod bay, just large enough for one craft. The doors were open and the bay is empty, but my tricorder is showing atypical graviton concentrations."

"A cloaking device?"

"That'd be my guess, sir. I think whoever killed these people planned his escape."

That power spike Shar thought he detected, Kira realized. *If it was a thruster burst, a cloaked shuttlepod could have propelled itself clear of the freighter while* Defiant *was still on approach, and then gone to warp without our realizing it.*

Gordimer approached her. "This was all planned," he said, voicing the same conclusions she had. "All of it. But why?"

Kira's thoughts during the chase returned to her: Maybe most of these *were* mercenaries, opportunists. But *someone* among them was sending out a message to whoever would come after them for what happened on Bajor.

Then an earlier notion replayed itself in her mind: the fact that the *Defiant* had beaten the odds against finding the Besinian vessel after so great a head start. Now Kira knew the truth: The *Defiant* hadn't beaten the odds at all. It had been lured out here.

Nog reported in: *"Captain, I've managed to get the warp*

*drive operational, and have already initiated a restart sequence,
which should take no more than fifteen minutes. A minimal crew
should be able to get this thing back to the station for analysis by
0100 tomorrow morning at warp five."*

"Thank you, Lieutenant. Stand by for further instructions."

Kira's mind raced. The killer expected, even wanted, the
freighter to be caught. The crew had probably been misled into
believing there would be a very different outcome to the confrontation, and had been killed to keep them from talking. The
autopilot and the decoy readings were designed to keep the *Defiant*'s crew distracted so the killer could escape.

But why not destroy the ship? Kira wondered. *Why not just—?*

Kira's thoughts froze as she saw it. *The restart sequence.*

"We've got to get out of here. Now," she told Gordimer.
"Contact the ship. Have them lock on to both teams and be ready
to beam us out on my command." Tapping her own combadge,
she cursed herself for not seeing it sooner. "Kira to Nog."

"Nog here, Captain."

"Shut down the restart sequence, Lieutenant."

"Sir?"

"Shut it *down,* Nog," Kira snapped. "That's an order."

"Aye, sir. . . . Initiating core shutdown. . . . Uh-oh."

"What is it?"

*"The antimatter injector isn't responding. It's continuing to
cycle up to release, and the rate is accelerating. Sir, this thing is
going to rupture any second."*

Kira turned back to Gordimer. "Now, Ensign."

"Energize, *Defiant.* Seven to beam out."

The alien bridge dissolved around Kira, replaced by the
cramped confines of *Defiant*'s transporter bay. Chao had successfully snatched all seven members of the boarding party.

Kira tapped her combadge as she bolted off the stage and
started running. "Kira to bridge. Shields up. Get us out of here,
Sam. Best speed."

The ship pitched beneath her, knocking her against a corridor
wall as she ran: the blast front from the exploding warp core.
The artificial gravity winked as the *Defiant* took the hit, throwing her to the deck. Then the ship seemed to right itself; she felt
the vibrating hum of *Defiant*'s acceleration to warp through the
deckplates, and she knew they were clear.

Bowers turned toward her as she entered the bridge. "Are you all right, Captain?"

Kira nodded. "Status?"

"Still in one piece," he assured her. "No serious damage. But it was close. What happened?"

She filled Sam in on the evidence found, the conclusions drawn. His face became a mask of barely contained anger as he understood the extent to which he, along with everyone else, had been fooled by their adversaries.

"We were played," he said.

Kira nodded, suddenly recalling a human expression of Captain Sisko's that seemed to fit their circumstances perfectly. "Someone is throwing down a gauntlet. And we need to figure who, damn fast." She turned to sciences. "Shar, I want you to work on compiling and analyzing the tricorder data collected by the boarding party. Cross-check those scans against the *Defiant*'s sensor logs and prepare a report for our return to the station. If there's anything useful in those readings that will help us figure out what's really going on, I want to know about it."

"I can begin at once, sir," Shar replied. "But the work may best be conducted in science lab one. Permission to leave the bridge?"

"Granted," Kira said, crossing to the command chair and settling into it as Shar exited.

"Sir," Bowers said. "I want to apologize for before. My intent wasn't to challenge your authority to lead as you see fit, only to remind you you had others you could depend on who were ready to walk into danger on your behalf."

Kira shook her head. "No apology necessary, Sam. And I know I can depend on you. That's why I left you in command. But you need to remember that even though this uniform is still new, I've sat in *Defiant*'s center seat before, as well as that of her predecessor." She smiled at him. "Not to mention the fact that I've had the destruct codes for both ships since Day One. I'm no stranger here."

Bowers nodded. "Understood, sir. I suppose some of us, the veteran Starfleet people, I mean, still need a shot of cold reality to remind us of those things. At least, I did. And that surprised me. I thought I understood, intellectually at least, that for a good many Militia officers this transition would be an easy one. But part of me still reacted to you like you were new to the game. I just want you to know it won't happen again, Captain."

She gave him a nod, accepting his honesty without judgment. "Return to station, Lieutenant."

"Aye, sir," Bowers said, withdrawing to his standing console in the aft section of the bridge.

"Captain," Tenmei said from conn. "I'm picking up a temperature fluctuation in the ablative armor, grid sector Z-47."

Kira turned to the engineering station. "Mr. Senkowski?"

"I see it. It's a second-decimal-place differential. I don't believe it's cause for concern, Captain."

Kira noted that Tenmei seemed displeased with Senkowski's response, but had refocused her attention on conn. "Keep an eye on it anyway," Kira told the engineer. "We don't want it turning into a bigger problem."

"Medical bay to bridge," came Tarses's voice over the comm.

"Kira here. How's our guest, Doctor?"

"I regret to report she expired five minutes ago, Captain. She'd suffered multiple internal and external injuries, including cranial trauma. The injuries were inflicted methodically and with great precision. She was definitely tortured, sir."

Kira's left hand curled into a fist. "Have you had any luck identifying her?"

"Nurse Richter transmitted her DNA scan and her earring design to Militia headquarters on Bajor a short while ago. They've verified her identity as Ke Iniri, 24, a resident of Sidau village. More than that, they weren't able to say. I'm sorry, sir. I wish there was more I could have done."

"Don't beat yourself up, Simon," Kira said. "I know you did everything possible. Please see to her remains according to Bajoran custom until we can determine her next of kin. Bridge out." Kira turned to face the forward viewer, trying to keep her voice even, silently vowing to find whoever was responsible for Ke Iniri's death and make sure they were never in a position to harm anyone else. "Helm, set course for Deep Space 9, warp eight."

"Warp eight," Tenmei echoed. "Aye, Captain."

Hours later, moving through the airlock linking the *Defiant* to the station, Kira found Vaughn waiting to greet her on the other side. He was leaning back against the corridor wall, his arms folded.

"Welcome back," he said. "Heard you had some trouble." He fell into step alongside her as she entered the docking ring, and together the two of them moved down the gently curving passageway.

"I assume Dax filled you in?" Kira asked. She'd been in communication with ops during the journey back, and had informed Ezri of all that had transpired.

Vaughn nodded grimly. "I'm getting the sense that this whole thing is much more than an act of terrorism."

"It was a trap," Kira confirmed. "I barely saw it in time. Someone's toying with us, and I don't think they're finished. What makes it worse is that I didn't learn a damn thing about why this is happening."

"Ro thinks she's making some progress on that front," Vaughn told her. "She hopes to have something solid to report soon."

"I hope so," Kira said, sounding weary in her own ears. "I could use some good news."

"Maybe you'll feel better once we're on Bajor."

Kira stopped and stared at him. "That's tonight, isn't it? I completely forgot. What time are we supposed to be there?"

"Twenty-one hundred," said Vaughn. "I already have a runabout standing by."

"Good," Kira said as they resumed walking. "That'll give me some time to shower and clear my head."

"Anything you need me to do in the meantime?"

"Yes," said Kira, handing Vaughn a padd containing Shar's sensor log report. "That's an analysis of every reading we took during the encounter with the Besinian freighter. See if you can reach Gul Macet. Make him aware of what's happened and send him a copy of that report. The fact that the ship was equipped with Cardassian weapons and Dominion shields should be of particular interest to him. Do the same with the Allied commanders of the protectorates. If anyone inside the Cardssian Union has run across that ship, they may be able to tell us something that'll help us to find whoever's behind this."

"I'll get right on it."

Her brow furrowed. "What are you doing here, anyway? I thought you were still on Bajor."

"Had to report for a physical. Dr. Girani got tired of waiting."

Kira smiled. "Now that you mention it, I seem to recall Julian predicting you were going to be a problem when it came to your exam."

Vaughn looked at her as they reached a turbolift. "Does Bashir talk about me behind my back to *everybody* on this station?"

"I don't think he spoke to Morn before he went on leave, but I could be mistaken," Kira said good naturedly as she stepped aboard. "Habitat ring, level one," she told the lift. After it got under way, she asked, "Any word from Julian?"

Vaughn shook his head. "My understanding is that he was in London very briefly, then decided to go to Sudan. I think he still has family there."

"Sounds like he's trying to get as far from his life here as possible."

"That's understandable, I think," Vaughn said. "He hasn't taken a vacation in a while, and between that business on Sindorin earlier this year, the mission to Gamma Quadrant, the parasite affair and the subsequent mess on Trill, not to mention his split with Dax . . . he needed a break."

Kira frowned. "I hope that's all it is."

"Give him time. Once he clears his head, he'll be back."

She looked at him, imagining Vaughn must have gone through similar periods in his own life, perhaps more than once. Come to think of it, so had she. Benjamin too, after his first wife died, and then again when Jadzia was killed.

"Ezri seems to be holding up pretty well," she said.

Vaughn nodded. "All things considered. Joined Trills do tend toward having greater resilience to changes within their lives."

"I suppose that's true," Kira said. "Anything else going on I should know about?"

"I tried talking Girani into joining Starfleet."

"Let me guess: she shot you down."

Vaughn shrugged. "Figured it was worth a try. But her mind's made up; she wants to return to Bajor. Ro made some recommendations for Girani's replacement, and I narrowed those down to three. Their files are in your personal database."

"I'll look them over tomorrow. What else?"

Vaughn told her about Ro's observations regarding the Militia, and her proposal to reinstate the liaison position. He also informed her that Ro's recommendation for the job was supported by General Lenaris.

"Really?" was Kira's reaction.

"She'd like the liaison to start immediately in order to help with her investigation into the Sidau massacre. With your permission, of course."

Kira considered it. Given the nature of the investigation, it made sense to keep the Militia fully involved. Finally she said, "Have Ro report to my quarters, with the officer's file, in thirty minutes. I'll make my decision after I speak with her. But unless there's something in his record I'm not happy about, I think it's a sound idea." The lift came to a stop, and Kira stepped out. She turned and hit the hold button. "Hey, did I hear right? Is today your birthday?"

Vaughn rolled his eyes. "Word gets around, I see."

Kira shrugged. "You know what they say about gossip . . ."

". . . It's the only sound that travels at warp," Vaughn finished.

"So what does someone get a one-hundred-and-two-year-old human for his birthday, anyway?"

"If you asked Girani, she'd probably suggest a few organ replacements," Vaughn said wryly.

Kira grinned. "Much too practical. What about dinner and a belated birthday drink at Quark's tomorrow night?"

"That really isn't necessary—"

"If it was necessary, Elias, I'd make it an order," Kira said. "So I trust I won't have to."

"Tell you what," Vaughn said, patting his uniform jacket until he reached behind his back and produced an isolinear rod. "Quark gave me this as some sort of 'birthday special' he came up with. It's supposed to be good for a couple of free drinks, at least. Why don't we redeem it together?"

Kira arched an eyebrow. "Top shelf?"

"Do yourself a favor and don't ask that when Quark's around," Vaughn said. "Trust me."

18

RENA

"Hey, whoa!" someone shouted. "She hasn't done anything to hurt you!"

Kail's mug halted in midswing. Rena saw a brown hand wrapped around his wrist, holding it back, and a second later she realized that the hand belonged to Jacob. He started to reach for Kail's mug with the other. . . .

Suddenly Jacob was in motion. Kail had a lot of muscle to put into follow-through with his swing. But instead of striking Rena, Kail flipped him off his feet. Jacob cried "Whoop!" and then sailed behind the table and onto the fusionstone floor of the tavern.

Everyone in the room—Halar, Parsh, Rena, the staff and customers—took a breath and held it. Rena saw Jacob holding the back of his head with one hand, the dripping mug with the other, and silently mouthing what Rena suspected were colorful obscenities in his native language.

She blanched, couldn't move. For a long moment, she had to remind her lungs to continue cycling air.

Finally, breaking the silence, Kail slurred, "Wha's wrong with you?"

Mistaking the question for concern, Jacob responded, "I bit my tongue." He set Kail's mug down on the floor and then extended his hand to be helped up, but Kail batted it away.

"Get away from me!"

Rena still couldn't move. Her eyes locked with Jacob's, her nerves thrumming from his close proximity.

"Kail!" Halar shouted. "What's wrong with you?! Help him up!"

Startled by Halar's chastisement and (Rena sincerely hoped) contrite about what he had been thinking about doing a moment before, Kail backed away from the table, then stumbled toward the door. A moment later, Parsh rose, his hands shaking, his eyes wide. He looked at Rena and recognized that she, too, had seen what his friend had been prepared to do. Helping Jacob up, Parsh stammered, "He . . . I'm sorry, Jacob . . . His foreman . . ." Looking at Rena, he said, "Kail got cut today. His foreman . . . They didn't like each other very much and . . . But that doesn't mean . . . He's normally not like this. He used to be . . . different."

Without looking at Rena, Jacob recovered the mug and set it down on the table. "Someone should check on him. You think you know where he went?"

Parsh nodded shakily.

"Then you should go. I'll see you back at the house. We'll plan the Yyn trip tomorrow."

Parsh started for the door, but before he exited, he stopped and said to Rena, "You're really ending it with him?"

She shrugged, nodded, threaded trembling hands behind her back.

Parsh nodded back. "Good." And then he was gone.

Rubbing his head, Jacob muttered something in Standard that had the word *"kwarks"* in it, but Rena couldn't make it out.

She surveyed him quickly, determined that his wounds weren't fatal, and found that the momentary paralysis she'd been experiencing abated upon this realization. Time to get the hell out of here. She had no desire to stay around for the next act of the performance, though she'd been positioned for a starring role.

As the doors swung closed behind her, Rena stalked down the narrow wooden dock toward the mainland, her determined steps coaxing a hollow rattle from each weathered plank. The green-black seawater below slurped around the pylons, shushing and hissing with the lunar pull from the heavens. She'd crossed a quarter of the distance, shivering the whole way, when she realized she'd left her wrap on the chair back at the tavern. Nothing could persuade her to return for it. She would freeze all the way up the hill to the bakery before she willingly chose to face Jacob after the humiliating scene that had just played out. She had rejected Jacob because she felt she had an obligation to Topa and Kail. To have him witness the disastrous end of those promises was more than she could stand. Tomorrow, she would face Marja's disappointment. Tonight, she wanted to deal with only her own.

Behind her, she heard a treble creak coupled with a snippet of synthesized music and laughter from the tavern, followed quickly by the thud-thud-thud of footsteps racing down the walkway after her.

She broke into a run.

Forgetting that she wore her dress boots, Rena threw her feet out in front of her as if she were shod with her flat-soled sandals. Her heel caught in a knothole; she considered slipping her foot out of her boot but decided against it, knowing that the footful of slivers she'd end up with would make it impossible to walk home.

Jacob slowed his gait, though with his long legs, he covered the distance to Rena far more quickly than she was comfortable with. He raised his hands out in front of him as if he suspected she might come at him with one of the ultra-fine-point writing styluses she kept in her bag. "I have your wrap. You left it on the chair," he explained breathlessly. He bent from the waist to rest his hands on his thighs in a stretch. Taking a few deep breaths, he righted himself and took a step closer to Rena, cautiously holding the shawl out where she could reach it.

Rena snatched it away from him, throwing it carelessly around her shoulders. "Thank you for looking out for me. Please leave me alone."

He shook his head. "I want to be your friend, Rena."

Her eyes burned with unshed tears. Damn that he could make her feel so much! Rena knotted the ends of her shawl, scrambled to her feet, and marched down the dock.

"I'm sorry about Kail!" he shouted after her.

She stopped, spun on her heel. "You? Sorry? You saw him in there, his boorish, bigoted behavior. Yes, that was the man I once loved. The person I was prepared to spend my life with. By comparison, you come out looking like the fine gentleman steward. You can bask in your superiority with my blessing."

"I'm sorry because I know how much it meant to you to honor your promise to Topa."

Her shoulders slumped. "I can't seem to finish anything. First I lose the sketchbook with his memorial drawings in it in that blasted storm—I haven't been able to re-create my last design and everything I've come up with since is all wrong. Now I've rejected the man he wanted me to marry. I'm a colossal failure."

"Rena," he said gently. "You aren't a failure." Stepping close to her, he reached for a loose tendril of hair that had wrested free of her headband, twisted it around his finger, then with a tender half-smile, smoothed it back out of her eyes. For a long moment, they stood staring at each other.

This time, she had no excuses to explain away his hypnotic effect on her: she craved it, tilting back her head and lifting her face to receive Jacob's kiss.

Another earsplitting creak announced more exits from the tavern; unidentifiable silhouettes stumbled out of the door, laughing raucously. The trio teetered toward them.

They lurched apart.

"Let's get out of here," Jacob said, reaching for her hand.

She pulled away. If Halar saw her with Jacob. If Parsh returned. Prophets forbid, if Kail came back . . . "I shouldn't be with you. Not like this."

"Why not?"

"I need space to think. I can't—I won't feel how I've felt the last few days again. . . ." Her voice trailed off.

Taking a deep breath, he placed his hands on her shoulders. "I'll walk you home. That's all. Nothing more. Marja wouldn't want you by yourself at this hour."

She shifted her shoulders, dislodging his hands and considered him. "Fine. Let's go."

They kept a swift pace to preserve their privacy. When Rena was certain they were out of earshot from anyone in front or behind them, she blurted out what had been nagging at her since the day on the boat. "Why didn't you tell me you were the son of the Emissary?"

Jacob paused, took a deep breath. "Have you ever been asked to bless a broom?" he said earnestly.

A blurt of laughter escaped that she promptly smothered with her hand. "Can't say that I have." *Not what I expected as an opener.*

"The day I left my dad's homestead, I followed a series of back roads meandering through the nearby farms on my way to the River Way. A farmer on his way to market in Sepawa asked me if I wanted a ride in his hovercart. He gave me his name. I gave him mine. My full name. That's when he asked if I could bless his broom."

"But you don't have any special connection with the Prophets." She paused. "Or do you?"

"In this case, the saying 'like Father, like son' definitely doesn't apply. But tell that to the farmer. Apparently his wife was having difficulty keeping dust out of the house so he thought that a word from me might help her broom work better."

"I see," she said, snickering. "I'm sorry, it's just that—"

"I know it's ridiculous. I'd have laughed too if the guy hadn't been so serious. Then when we reached the Shalun's Hollow Ferry crossing, he told the proprietor about the great honor he would have transporting the Emissary's son across the river, so of course that turned into another big scene." Jacob shook his head, remembering. "My friend Nog would ask what good it is having a name if you're not willing to trade on it. But that's not my style. It took days to put the whole 'son of the Emissary' thing behind me, and that was only by omitting the name 'Sisko' from my introductions, and using the long form of my first name." As they strolled down the pathway, he related various experiences from growing up as the Emissary's son, his narrative continuing even after they'd passed through the Harbor Ring gate. His words evoked sympathy from Rena.

While Rena couldn't relate to having a relative with the Emissary's notoriety, she did know how it felt to live in the shadow of a notable family. In Mylea, hardly a day passed without Rena being identified with or judged in relation to her grandfather or her heroic parents. "She might have Jiram's color, but otherwise, is she not the image of Lariah?" or "Topa was dependable. Always knew you could count on him, but that Rena is always wandering off. . . ."

Rena had considered the possibility that perhaps her lifelong compulsion to wander stemmed from an unconscious need to be known as herself, not "daughter of" or "granddaughter of." And now, as she listened to Jacob, she heard her thoughts and feelings being verbalized by another: the simultaneous pride in family accomplishments and honor, and doubt about whether living up to the standard set by those who had gone before was even possible. She sensed she'd found a kindred soul in Jacob. Before long, they walked shoulder-to-shoulder, the tension between them dissipating into the rising Mylean mists rolling in off the sea.

Inside the gate, they walked beside the weatherbeaten Temple Ring rampart for more than a hundred meters, from pool to pool of puddled, pale lamplight. The occasional skimmer filled with fishermen off to their predawn preparations zinged past. Within hours, the darkened storefront windows would be lively with color and light as the first catches of the day were poured into tanks or cleaned, filleted or chopped into steaks. A little light-headed from the ale, she noticed that the air was lightly scented with the perfume from the late-blooming trees that lined the street. Lovers strolled up and down the street, arms linked or hand in hand. Last year, before she had left for the university, the sight made her feel part of an exclusive club of those who had been lucky enough to find a special someone. Tonight, thinking about love made her feel like a boat cut loose from its moorings.

Turning off before they passed the harbormaster's station, Rena and Jacob walked up brick-paved Moonshell Road, snaking back and forth across the hill past shops and houses.

"What went wrong tonight, with Kail, I mean? You were so determined to make it work."

So now it's my turn to answer the questions, she thought. "Our relationship has been unraveling for a while now. When I came back from school . . ."

"Everything was different," Jacob finished for her. "I know that feeling. Something similar happened to me when I got back from the Gamma Quadrant."

This was new information, and Rena reeled off a fusillade of questions. "You were in the Gamma Quadrant? Really? For how long? What was it like?"

Laughing, Jacob said, "In order, Yes, really. A few months. And, hmm, it was, in no particular order, thrilling, terrifying, informative, exhausting. In brief, just like here, but more so."

"Not just like here," Rena said. "See, all those words you just used seem like the opposite of sleepy, rural Mylea."

"Not to me," Jacob said. "Not to you either, I bet."

"I'm still here," Rena said with a sigh, "because I have to be."

Jacob shook his head. "Promise or no promise, after Topa's services, you could have gone anywhere you wanted—nothing but honor held you to your obligations. But you decided to stay here anyway. Why?"

"I'm not sure that's a question I'm prepared to answer for you, Jacob Sisko."

"I'm sorry," he said. "Didn't mean to pry. Maybe I should have just stayed with the question I really wanted to ask you."

She felt a slow smile bloom on her face. "Which was?"

"What attracted you to Kail in the first place?"

Rena laughed a little heartsick laugh. She hadn't been expecting this. "Because he was handsome. And he liked me. And . . . he wasn't always such a fool. Something happened to him while I was away. He became bitter."

"Or maybe something happened to you," Jacob countered.

The only appropriate response seemed to be a shrug. "Maybe. Who ever knows about those kinds of things?"

Jacob wore an expression of mock hurt. "I do," he said. "I pay attention to those things."

"But you're supposedly a writer," she said. "It's your job."

"And you're supposedly an artist," he countered. "It's your job, too."

Pausing for a long moment outside the door to her family's apartments, they both looked at each other, neither certain as to what they should say.

"I'll talk with Parsh about Yyn—if you still want to go," Jacob said at last.

"As I've already mentioned, I've never been. It would be good to get away for a couple of days."

Silence again.

She didn't want to say "I'll see you tomorrow" because she wasn't certain she would see him nor did she feel a kiss good night was appropriate. She settled on a polite "thank you for walking me home" before letting herself inside.

Surprising herself, Rena stood inside the foyer and watched him disappear into the night. She told herself that she was just enjoying the night air, the sounds of small night birds whirring through the air, the smell of blooming trees, but watching Jacob fade as he walked away, that was part of it, too. An idea for a new painting came to her then, and she looked forward to morning so she could start. She padded up the stairs and dropped onto her bed, falling swiftly into a dreamless sleep.

Morning came too quickly, though Rena felt surprisingly rested for having slept so little. She stumbled out of bed and toward her washbasin when she noticed a large-ish drawing notebook on the floor by her door. At first she thought it was one of her old sketchpads from secondary school; the unwrinkled, clean paper said otherwise. She retrieved the new sketchbook from the floor and a flutter of hardcopy slid out from between the covers. On the top of the page she read, in familiar, spidery strokes of Bajoran characters:

Everything old can be new again, including your art. Jacob.

Last night, He must have returned after they parted and slipped this under her door. She scanned the hardcopy pages and quickly discerned that they were a story. Momentary gratitude that Marja hadn't yet discovered that Rena hadn't locked the exterior door gave way to delight as Rena realized that Jacob had taken a familiar Bajoran magic story and given it a modern twist. On wobbly morning legs, she made her way over to the window seat and, by golden pink tendrils of dawn light, read Jacob Sisko's story. A hopeful smile crept onto her face as she scanned the words.

Everything old can be new again.

19

CENN

Cenn Desca had never been to Terok Nor before. In fact, he'd seldom left Bajor at all, except on three other occasions, all of them Militia business. The first time was when he was still a junior officer, part of the crew on a ship escorting ill-fated colonists to New Bajor in the Gamma Quadrant, almost seven years ago. Although that voyage had involved docking briefly at the station before continuing on through the Temple, Cenn had never needed to leave his ship. For that he was grateful. The view of the hideous structure outside his viewport—an absurd assemblage of rings and arcing towers that the Cardssians seemed to think made a good design for a spacc station—had been enough. There were so many things wrong it, he didn't know where to begin . . . although the arrangement of the docking pylons in such a way that the largest ships were forced to converge on the smallest possible volume of space was certainly high on the list.

The other two times he'd left the planet had been as a sensor-tech on scout ships patrolling the edge of the Bajoran system. Neither of those had required stopovers at the station at all.

Now that he was here, stepping off the turbolift that had carried him from the docking ring to the Promenade, he again felt grateful that his duties hadn't required him to visit before. The place was still far too Cardassian for his comfort. The passage of time, Starfleet's presence, and their changing of the station's name to Deep Space 9 had done little to alter that. He felt uneasy passing through its gearlike airlock portals, walking its dimly-lit decks, stepping over its high-lipped thresholds. The bewildering array of aliens he passed along the way didn't help.

Having to go to the security office was the worst part of all, however. He wondered how many Bajorans had never walked out of this place.

He ascended the short steps, the double doors parting at his approach. Ro Laren looked up from behind the security desk, and Cenn realized too late as he entered that she was in the middle of a conversation with someone on the comm system. He started to back out of the office when she held up a finger, indicating that he should wait exactly where he was.

". . . wish I could be more helpful, Lieutenant," a voice was saying over the comm, *"but as odd as the incident was, it barely seemed of any consequence seven years ago, much less after everything that's happened since."*

"I understand, Doctor," Ro said. "Would you be willing to open your personal logs for that stardate? Any additional details could prove significant. You have my word that I'll keep anything not directly related to my investigation strictly confidential."

"Of course," the voice said without hesitation. *"I'll set up a clearance code for those entries and transmit it immediately. But the person you really want to speak to is Chief O'Brien. I suspect his involvement in the affair may have left him with memories far more vivid than mine."*

"I was planning to do just that," Ro said. "Thank you again. And I apologize for interrupting your leave."

"That's not necessary. The Alexandria *is departing Earth for the Bajor sector this evening. I've arranged to be on it. I should be back on the station in a few days."*

"Vacation lose its charm?"

"Actually, it's been . . . interesting to reconnect with my extended family. So much so that I decided to save my remaining leave time for next year, when more of the Bashir clan is expected to be on Earth."

"Sounds like you had fun. I look forward to hearing about it when you get back. Thanks again, Doctor. Ro out." The lieutenant commed off and turned her full attention on Cenn, her sharp features lacking even a trace of a smile.

Not that I deserve otherwise, he reflected. *I was abominable to her in Sidau. Best get this over with . . .*

"I'm sorry for coming at a bad time, Lieutenant. I was hoping you could spare a few minutes for me to speak with you?"

Ro gestured for him to approach. Cenn stepped to the desk and stood before her, staring straight ahead. "I'd like to apologize for the manner in which I spoke to you this morning. I was out of line. Although I have genuine concerns about the future of the Militia now that Bajor is a Federation member, it was wrong of me to take my frustrations out on you. I hope you can forgive my disrespect, and my lack of professionalism."

The corner of Ro's mouth quirked up. "Apology accepted, Major. Please sit down."

"Thank you. But with all due respect, I feel I should get back to my unit as soon as possible."

"Back to—?" Her smile widened. "You have no idea why you're here, do you?"

Cenn blinked. "General Lenaris told me only to report to you aboard the station immediately. I assumed it was because he expected me to offer you my formal apology in person. I was about to volunteer to do exactly that anyway, and since the general gave me no other specific instructions . . ." He trailed off, suddenly unsure of what was going on.

"I see," Ro said, sounding amused. Cenn began to worry. "I really think you're going to want to sit down for this. Can I offer you a drink?"

"No thank you," he said as he lowered himself slowly into one of the guest chairs. *A drink. This just gets worse by the second.*

Ro leaned back, watching his face. He was beginning to wonder if she was enjoying his uncertainty. Finally she spoke. "You were half right."

Cenn felt his brow furrowing. "About what?"

"About my natural instinct to look anywhere but Bajor for answers," Ro said. "The hell of it is, I didn't even realize it until you threw it in my face. If not for that, my investigation might have continued going nowhere. I'm in your debt, Major."

He hesitated. "Are you telling me you found something?"

"Yes," Ro said. "The beginning of the answer, I think. But I didn't find it on Bajor. I found it here, on DS9."

"I don't understand. You just said—"

"What I meant was, if I hadn't taken a harder look at the information that was available about Sidau, as you suggested, I might not have learned until much later that this station's chief medical officer and its former chief of operations once visited the village. And spoke about it in their logs."

"What did you find out?"

"I'll get into that in a minute. The research isn't complete. We still have a great deal of work ahead of us."

"We?"

"I thought a lot about what you said to me on the surface, Major," Ro said, resting her elbows on her desk. "And some things General Lenaris said as well. I came away from those conversations with a better understanding of what led to your outburst. Don't get me wrong, you *were* out of line, and I'm glad you apologized. But I also came to realize, especially after I continued my investigation, that the Militia and Starfleet still need to work closely together. That's why you're here. With the full backing of General Lenaris and Captain Kira, you've been assigned to DS9 as its new Militia liaison officer, effective immediately."

Cenn stared at her, speechless.

"Nothing to say?" Ro asked.

Cenn remained silent for several seconds more, then decided to go with the uppermost question in his mind. "Is this a joke?"

"The irony isn't lost on me," Ro admitted, "but I'm completely serious. You'll be the Militia's eyes and ears on the station, and coordinate any joint endeavors with Starfleet."

"But . . ."

"What is it?"

Cenn searched for the right way to say what he was thinking. "Lieutenant, I understand what you're trying to do. I applaud it. I'm even honored to be chosen for the position. And I realize that we who serve seldom have the luxury of choosing *where* we serve . . . but I have no desire to live and work aboard Terok Nor."

Ro frowned. "Then stop thinking about it as Terok Nor. This is Federation Starbase Deep Space 9."

"I realize everyone here has accustomed themselves to that," Cenn said. "I'm not sure I can. This station was the Cardassian seat of power during the Occupation. It was a place of slave labor and harsh summary judgment. It was, not long ago, the site of First Minister Shakaar's assassination. That this station has been allowed to continue operating all these years is, quite frankly, offensive. It's an affront to Bajorans everywhere."

Ro leaned back in her chair, studying him from across her desk. Finally she said, "Get over it."

"Excuse me?"

"I said, get over it. You think because you have a few chips on your shoulder, that you're unique? That the people here casually put aside what went on within these bulkheads for decades? Are you really that arrogant?"

"I assure you, Lieutenant, I intended no insult."

"I'm not sure I give a damn what you intended, Major. What I know is—" Ro stopped in midsentence, seeming to turn her attention inward. She let out a short laugh and shook her head.

"What is it?" Cenn asked.

"Just remembering one of my earlier conversations with the general. It's not important," Ro said, refocusing on Cenn. "The point I'm trying to make is that it's easy to be dismissive when you're ignorant. And that's what you are in this case, Major. You're as ignorant of DS9 as I was of Sidau."

"Perhaps I am," Cenn conceded. "But that still doesn't alter the past. This place—"

"This place," Ro interrupted, "is just that, Major—a place. It's defined, at any point in time, by the people in it. You're right: Once this was a place of fear, and oppression, and death. But now it's one of hope, and optimism, and life. It's what we make of it. And it can still be dangerous, no question. Its past is important, and it should never be forgotten. But its present and its future matter more. You can help to define those things." Ro stood up and reached across her desk, offering him her hand. "What do you say?"

Cenn looked at the outstretched hand, then slowly rose to his feet and grabbed it with his own. "I say that I don't think I have the slightest idea what I'm getting into."

Ro grinned. "Then you'll fit in perfectly. Welcome to Deep Space 9."

20

ASAREM

The door was open.

From the air, the house looked tiny and unassuming. Up close Asarem saw nothing about it to make her revise that impression. As secluded mountain retreats went, it was quite easy to overlook and thoroughly forgettable. But then, she supposed that was the point. Following the dirt path that led from the clearing where her executive skycar had landed, to the steep stone steps that ascended to the front door of the humble two-story dwelling, Asarem reflected that "retreat" was indeed an apt description for the place.

She had told her pilot, her aide, and her personal guards to stay with the skycar. The guards had protested, of course. She tried to tell them that Janitza was one of the most remote and sparsely inhabited regions of the planet, and that the likelihood of there being an assassin lying in wait for her unannounced visit was next to nil. It was a weak argument, she knew, and one that nobody responsible for the safety of Bajor's head of state would listen to. These guards were no exception. But then Theno spoke up, reminding them that this trip constituted a familial visit by the first minister, who was therefore entitled to privacy. The security officers would have to content themselves with securing the perimeter of the grounds around the house. The guards capitulated.

Despite the open door awaiting her at the top of the steps, the portal bore no symbol of welcome, no light of hospitality. The encroaching twilight of the Janitza mountain range threw most of the dwelling's interior into darkness, except for a narrow rectangle of light visible on the extreme opposite side of the house. Another open door.

I'm expected, she realized. Feeling her heart thumping inside her chest, she ignored it and went inside.

As her eyes adjusted to the darkness within the house, its modest furnishings and expansive bookshelves registered dimly, including the simple desk where she made out a stylus resting atop a short stack of papers. She almost missed the shrine in a corner of one of the central rooms, but the scent of candle wax, recently melted, was unmistakable. That Aldos remained contemplative and well read didn't surprise her, but she found she had to resist the temptation to stop at the desk and see what he was working on.

At the opposite door, she stopped. The way opened onto a wide wooden deck, painted green. There was a railing all around, adorned with lighted candles, and the view beyond it was breathtaking. The snowcapped Janitza mountain range stretched before her. The sun had already dipped behind the peaks, and the sky above them was awash in astonishing colors. A forested slope descended away from the house and into a lush, wild valley blanketed in the shadow of the mountains. She could only imagine how the scene must look in late morning, when all would be bathed in light.

She saw a powerful-looking telescope aimed skyward in the northwest corner, near the railing. Directly before her in the center of the platform, facing the spectacular view, was a high-backed deck chair. Next to it was a small table on which sat a single empty goblet and an elegant, blown-glass decanter of spring wine.

From the chair, a strong hand reached out and set a second goblet down on the table, half empty. Aldos's profile became visible for a second as he completed the motion. She thought he had changed little in seven years, except perhaps that his hair was grayer. Then his hand withdrew, and his face disappeared within the chair again. Asarem was preparing to make her presence known when he made that unnecessary.

"I've heard it said that you don't realize how much you'll miss people until they're gone," he said. "But what I've come to understand is that you don't realize just how little you miss them until one comes to disturb your peace."

Asarem's eyes narrowed. "It's nice to see you too, Aldos. Your charms are undiminished."

Krim Aldos stood up slowly and turned to face Asarem, the tiny smile he always had for her forming at one corner of his mouth. "I never had much use for charms, Wadeen, as you know better than anyone. Nevertheless, what few I possess worked on you in their day."

"True," she conceded, stepping out onto the deck. "But it was I who convinced you that we should marry. It was you who succumbed to *my* wishes then."

Krim inclined his head, acknowledging the truth of her statement. He reached for the decanter of wine and filled both goblets. "Do you think I'll succumb to your wishes now?"

He knows, she thought, wondering how she should proceed now. Though his body language betrayed nothing, she knew he would be on his guard. Finally she said, "I think you'll do the right thing."

Krim set down the decanter, stoppered it, and picked up both goblets. He extended one of them to her as he closed the distance between them. "And what precisely does the first minister of Bajor think is the right thing?"

Asarem accepted the goblet, watching the candlelight dance on the surface of the wine before she met his eyes. "Must we play these games?"

"That's up to you, Wadeen. You're the one avoiding the reason for your uninvited and unannounced visit." He raised his glass. "To Rava Mehwyn. May her *pagh* know peace."

Asarem touched her goblet to Krim's, but didn't drink. "I didn't want to intrude on you," she said, "but circumstances required that I come. Bajor needs you."

Krim took a sip from his wine. He had enough respect for her not to laugh, at least. "What you mean is that you *believe* Bajor needs me," he said. "I don't happen to agree."

"I didn't think you would," Asarem countered. "Nevertheless, I'm here to ask you to serve your people once again, to become Bajor's representative to the Federation."

Krim turned away, moving to the edge of the deck. He set his goblet down on the railing and watched the last glimmers of color shrink behind the mountains. Overhead, the stars were beginning to emerge.

"I asked one thing of you when we last spoke, seven years ago," she heard him say. "One thing. To be left alone. I saved your political career by unshackling you from my disgrace, and all I asked in return was that you honor my request for solitude. You couldn't even do that."

Asarem's mouth dropped open. "Unshackling me? Is that what you believe . . . ?" Her complete astonishment gave way to outrage. "You selfish, self-pitying, egotistical *pavrak!* How *dare* you? How dare you claim to have done me a favor by ending our marriage?"

Krim turned to face her again, his voice even. "Don't. Don't do this, Wadeen. Don't pretend you didn't agree it was the best course of action for your career. Or that it hasn't been proven out. You're the first minister of Bajor now."

"I didn't become first minister by being voted into office, you idiot. My predecessor was assassinated!"

"But you were Shakaar's second minister. You were *his* choice to succeed him, a choice the electorate supported when he nominated you. That could never have happened to the wife of General Krim, and you'd be naïve to think otherwise. Even your friend Ledahn understood that. Your blossoming political career would have ended very quickly if we had stayed married. Look me in the eye and tell me you didn't believe that seven years ago."

Asarem didn't answer. She wanted to deny it, wanted to tell him she'd merely become his excuse to indulge in his newfound fixation with martyrdom, after already resigning as overgeneral of the Militia for his role in Jaro Essa's coup d'état. Instead she said nothing, because the truth was, she hadn't stopped him seven years ago. Aldos had fallen on his sword, and she . . . she had accepted it and survived, even prospered, while he attempted to vanish from Bajoran memory.

And it was all unnecessary.

"You're right," she told him. "I let you make the choice I was afraid to make for myself, to end the marriage so I could distance myself from scandal." She stepped to the edge of the deck, set down her goblet next to his, and faced him directly. "But now you have to admit something to *me,* Aldos. You have to look *me* in the eye and tell me you still think your resignation was the right choice when, two years after the coup failed, the Circle Commission issued its report and exonerated you."

"The commission's findings with respect to me are a minor footnote in their overall condemnation of the Circle, and irrelevant," Krim said, staring down into the darkening valley. "The fact remains that I picked the wrong side. I made the decision not to stop the Circle's forces from entering Ashalla. I personally led an armed force in a fight for control of Deep Space 9. I was as guilty as Jaro. The only difference is that I'm not rotting in Kran-Tobal Prison."

"You're not like Jaro," Asarem said angrily. "You backed the Circle only because he led you to believe it gave our people the best chance for stability, security, and independence. But all Jaro wanted was power, a lust he disguised with patriotism and misrepresentations of the Federation's real intentions toward Bajor. Jaro *lied* to you. He lied to *everyone.* Add to that the fact that you were also betrayed by your own second-in-command, who murdered Li Nalas . . ."

Asarem trailed off, seeing a flicker of pain cross Krim's face. It was gone in an instant, but she knew she hadn't imagined it. The death of Bajor's most revered hero of the Occupation, on his watch, remained an open wound.

"No one blamed you for those things," Asarem told him. "Nor for refusing to open fire on your own people."

"I allowed myself be misled," Krim maintained. "That cannot be overlooked, or forgiven."

"What you really mean is that you won't forgive yourself. But Bajor forgave you a long time ago, in no small part because you spent a lifetime fighting for our people, and that's something that will *never* be overlooked. That's how you're remembered, Aldos. Not as Jaro's fool."

Asarem paused before continuing. "I know what it feels like to have your faith betrayed, to follow a leader who turns out to be not what he claimed. But I didn't have the luxury of retreating when those deceits were exposed. I had to fight harder than ever because that was what Bajor needed of me, and that's exactly what it needs of you now."

"Have you not even stopped to consider that perhaps I no longer care what Bajor needs?" Krim asked.

"Not for an instant," Asarem answered emphatically. "Service to our people is what your life was always about, whether it was fighting in the resistance, or leading the Militia. Walking away from that life was a mistake. Don't shake your head at me! You knew I was coming here, and you knew the reason for my visit. Why would you continue to stay informed on the most current goings-on within the government if you no longer cared? You can't help yourself. It's who you are. Even when you resigned, you thought you were serving Bajor, that it was better off without you. That *I* was better off without you. You even convinced *me* of that. Well, now I know we were both wrong."

Krim remained silent. She tried to discern what he was thinking, but his face revealed nothing.

"I'm not here to tell you we can get back what we lost," she went on to say. "Our marriage ended for the wrong reasons, and I moved on. Your career ended for the wrong reasons, too, and the Militia moved on. But your value to Bajor isn't ended . . . and you never moved on."

"Wadeen, do you hear yourself? You're spinning a fantasy. Even if everything you've said is true, I was always an opponent of Federation membership. Time may have proven that they are not the 'new Cardassians' the Circle once tried to paint them, and that Bajor has benefited thus far from our association, but I remain skeptical."

"But don't you see, Aldos?" Asarem said. "That's why it has to be you."

"I am not a diplomat. I'm a soldier."

"Then *be* a soldier!" Asarem said. "Walk out onto the battlefield and fight for your people! Defend, advance, strategize, make alliances, attack if you must, fall back when necessary. Do what needs to be done as Krim Aldos would do it. Be the voice of Bajor."

Krim seemed to be studying her eyes as if searching for signs of madness there. Part of her wondered if he'd be entirely wrong to do so.

"This will not endear you to the Chamber of Ministers," he said. "You'll have many more political adversaries if I accept."

"Let me worry about the Chamber of Ministers."

"Be serious, Wadeen. If your popularity slips because of this, it will only make it that much harder for you to govern effectively, and to win reelection."

She let out a sigh of frustration. "I'm not concerned right now with my chances for reelection."

"Then *why* are you doing this?"

Asarem looked at him, surprised that he still didn't understand. "Do you even know why I got into politics? It was because I wanted power. Not the way Jaro wanted it. I wanted power so that, when I amassed enough of it, I would wield it to do the most good. If I don't seize this opportunity to put a strong, effective Bajoran voice on the Federation Council, regardless of the consequences to my popularity, then my power as first minister will have been wasted, and my assumption of this office meaningless." She paused and smiled at him crookedly. "Besides, if you do the job the way I expect you to, my approval ratings will skyrocket. But first you have to give me your answer. I need you to say it out loud. Will you accept this appointment?"

Ten minutes later, night had fallen, and the stars over Janitza shone down from a clear black sky. Asarem's personal guards, keeping their discreet watch on the house, spotted her approaching and signaled her skycar, which promptly hummed to life. Theno emerged from inside and stood alongside the conveyance, holding the hatch open for her.

As she crossed the clearing, she took out her comlink and called Ledahn. *"Yes, First Minister?"*

"He accepted," Asarem said simply. *Game, set, and match.*

There was a moment of silence over the link. Asarem suspected Ledahn was giving a quick mental prayer of thanks to the Prophets. *"That's excellent news, First Minister."*

"I told him a craft would be by tomorrow morning to take him to the capital. I'd like to make the public announcement at midday, from the Chamber gardens."

"I'll alert the communications staff and have them make the necessary arrangements. Will you be returning to Ashalla?"

"Not yet," she said. "I have a commitment in Kendra Province this evening. I'll speak with you in the morning."

"Try to enjoy yourself. You deserve it," Ledahn said. *"And congratulations, First Minister."*

"Good night, Muri." Asarem cut the link as she neared the skycar, halting in front of Theno. She looked into her aide's impassive face, and finally asked the question that had been nagging at her all afternoon. "So what made you think of Krim?"

Theno continued staring straight ahead. "You did, First Minister, when you said you missed him."

Asarem's brow furrowed. "When did I say that?"

"This morning, when you complained about the tea."

Asarem replayed the conversation in her mind. After a moment, she smiled and shook her head. "There are times, Theno, when I don't know whether to thank the Prophets or curse them for your service," she said, and entered the skycar

"I'm often puzzled by the same question, First Minister," Theno answered, and closed the hatch.

21

RENA

"How old is this place?" Jacob asked.

Rena tried to remember details from her last art-history course, one of the few historical classes first-year students were required to attend, but she had studied halfheartedly, distracted by Topa's deteriorating condition, so her memories of the details were scant. "Not really sure," she admitted. "Twelve, fifteen thousand years at least. Not as old as some other cities that have been unearthed. Not like B'hala, but old enough. Do they have ruins like this on Earth?"

Jacob shook his head, then seemed to reconsider the question. "Well, sure, there are ruins. Mostly temples or public buildings like the Parthenon or the Colosseum in Rome. I'm sorry—I know you don't know what these places are—but they're a few thousand years old at most and many of them aren't much better than piles of rubble compared with this place. There have been a lot of wars on Earth and, compared with you, we only recently learned the value of preserving the past." He took a step backward, as if one more step would give him the perspective he needed, then stood transfixed by the edifice before him.

The site—the archeologists called it Yyn—was open to the public only a few days every year, but despite this fact attendance was sparse so early in the morning. Rena assured him that within a few hours the place would be packed with tourists, making it more than worth their time to visit early, though they hadn't been able to convince Parsh and Halar to leave their beds and join them.

Yesterday's ten-kilometer hike to the site had flown by— much sharing of personal stories, discussion about Jacob's new project reworking old Bajoran legends into modern contexts, Halar's religious studies, and Parsh's confession that after university he hoped to open an inn on the coast near Mylea. Kail— or his absence from this trip—hadn't been discussed, thank the Prophets. To placate Halar's curiosity, Jacob had gamely offered insights into Benjamin Sisko and had appeared amused at her gleeful reception of each tidbit. She had been amazed at how little she seemed to know about her friends. Having shared their growing-up years together had presumably created deep connections between them, though Rena wondered, perhaps, if she had assumed much where she had truly only seen the surface. Only Jacob's presence could explain these new insights. He had a steady, kind way about him that allowed people to feel comfortable peeling away their layers to reveal themselves. Take Parsh, for example, who had been the pale, skinny boy who had a crush on her as long as she could remember. Listening to him articulate his future plans to Jacob, she sensed a passion and depth in Parsh she didn't know existed.

Now, though, watching Jacob's face as he studied the cliff face, she wondered what he saw. Did he see rock with faces carved into it or stories coming to life or history? Could he coax them into revealing their secrets the way he had with Parsh? And yes, she had to confess, even her.

Though she had lived within a day's travel of Yyn, had heard about the place her entire life, she had never taken the time to come here. Now, though, seeing it through this foreigner's eyes, she began to wonder why. In and around the low buildings, narrow pillars, and roped-off sections of engraved paving stones walked small groups of tourists, including one or two families, but mostly pairs like her and Jacob, though few were studying the carved wall as intently as her friend. As was usually the case, most of the other tourists were either dividing their attention between reference padds or listening to interactive tour guides through small earplugs as they slowly ambled along.

The cliff they stood before was over fifty meters high, and despite the stone's age and proximity to the sea, the carvings were remarkably unweathered. Perhaps it was some secret of the carver's art that Rena did not know, but the expressions on the faces of the twenty or twenty-five tall, narrow individuals were as distinctive as those on the men and women who wandered through the ruins at the cliff's foot. One—the woman whose feet they stood at—was obviously a pretty but vain young maiden, and another, the slumped figure to her right, was clearly an avaricious merchant who saw none of the wonders around him, not even the pretty maiden. Rena wondered if the artists who had created these works had modeled these characters after individuals, men and women of their acquaintance, or if they were all conjured up out of someone's imagination. There could be no denying that the design of all the figures had been the result of a single guiding individual; though each face was different, they were all the product of one remarkable mind with a compelling vision.

"Do you have anything like this on Earth?"

"I don't think so," Jacob said. "I've heard of large relief sculptures carved into cliff walls, though I can't claim to have seen them with my own eyes, but something like this right in the middle of a town? This was supposed to have been the town center, right?"

"Right."

"Then, no, never anything like this." He inhaled deeply, then let the breath out slowly. When he was finished, his eyes shined brightly. "Does anyone know who did it? Does it have religious significance?"

"Culturally, Yyn is primarily known for the Legend of Astur, the pageant we'll see later. But there's probably some religious meaning too that's been lost over time."

"And Bajor was aware of the Prophets this far back?"

"Sure," Rena said. Recalling her readings from art history, she said, "One theory is that the artists wanted to create something that the Prophets could see from their home in the Celestial Temple."

Jacob smiled, but he didn't take his eyes off the carvings. As they talked, he continued to step backward, to try to take in the whole work. "Well, that's one argument for working on a large scale."

"Yes. The other theory is that these are the Prophets."

This made Jacob look at her. "Really? That's the first time I've ever heard of anyone on Bajor attempting to personalize them. I mean, on Earth most gods and goddesses have some kind of form. Not all of them, mind you. I can think of at least one religion where the believers are prohibited from attempting to visualize the primary god, but for most of the others there's some generally acknowledged avatar. But I can't remember ever seeing a depiction of the Prophets."

"I don't know of any others," Rena said. "It kind of makes you wonder, though. Look at those faces: it's like every one of them was someone the artists were intimately familiar with, like they were people who lived here. Why would someone decide that the Prophets looked like someone who lived down the street?"

Rena looked over at Jacob and saw that though he was still staring at the cliff face, he was no longer really seeing what was before his eyes. "I can't imagine," he said softly. Then he seemed to sense her gaze and looked over at her and smiled. "Maybe the Prophets came down to meet the artist and she said, 'Hey, you look just like my cousin Fila.' "

"You think the artist was a woman?"

"Is there any reason why that couldn't be?"

"None that I know," Rena said. "Which reminds me of something I've been meaning to show you." Slipping her backpack off her shoulders, she unlaced the flap and rooted around inside for her new drawing pad. Flipping open its cover, she held up the sketch, a charcoal and pastel piece.

"Topa's memorial," Jake said. "It's beautiful."

Rena watched as his eyes took in the drawing. "I couldn't sleep last night so I stayed up and worked."

"Is this the final draft?"

"I think so. Putting aside all the baggage of what I thought I should do, I tried to remember how I saw Topa. I mean, I *know* all the facts, and I think creatively, I was stumbling over them."

"I'm impressed." And she could tell from his voice that he was not delivering an idle compliment. Leaning in closer to study the drawing more carefully in the morning light, Jacob reached out, but stopped a millimeter short of touching the page, then traced the outline of the arch, studied the runes and pictographs Rena had incorporated into this latest design. "Will you explain it to me?"

They found a bench across from the stone faces. Jacob kept the notebook on his lap while Rena explained the drawing to him. "I'm working in a few gemstones that are native to Mylea," she began. "Then I chose the style of runes used here at Yyn." Pointing to a row of writing, Rena said, "The text reads, 'I know the light is there. When it finally breaks through the mist, I will be ready.' " And then she explained her memories of Topa from when she was a little girl, of how he would stand in the street and wait for the sun. "It isn't dramatic. No recitations of his exploits in the resistance. But to me, this is Topa. I hope it's enough."

"He asked you because he wanted to be remembered the way *you* saw him—not the way everyone else did," Jacob said pragmatically. "Maybe he didn't want to be known as part of Mylea's history—just as a grandfather."

Rena wasn't sure she agreed with him and said so.

"Sometimes, there are good reasons to let go of the past. If we're constantly looking backward, sometimes we don't move forward." Jacob scooted closer to Rena, leaning down so only she could hear him speak. "Once when my dad tried to explain his first encounter with the Prophets, he told me that in the vision, he was in his ship during the Borg attack when my mother died. The Prophets showed him that even though he had physically moved forward in time, he remained trapped in the past."

"Why would Topa be trapped in the past? He was a hero—one of Mylea's greatest!"

"I probably sound like an old man when I talk like this, but you have to know that what seems heroic from a distance sometimes isn't when you're close up. I lived through a battle in which I saw people at their best and their worst. Many of them were killed or maimed—it was a nightmare. I have friends with similar stories. But to hear the official reports you would have thought we were conquering heroes. Topa's past might be exactly as heroic as you've been told, but it might not. So what you've done here is told the truth—your truth. That's what matters."

"I don't know . . ." Rena said, wrinkling her forehead and contemplating where she might make a few more changes.

Jacob snapped the notebook closed and stuffed it back into her pack. "I do. We're going to finish checking out this ruin, we're going to meet Parsh and Halar for lunch. Then tonight we're going to watch this famous Legend of Astur pageant. An ex-fiancé of a friend of mine informed me that it's quite romantic."

Men. Rolling her eyes, she pulled him off the bench by the hand and dragged him off to see the next cluster of ancient buildings.

Within the last hour, the vestiges of sunset had been wiped away by night. Halar, Parsh, Rena, and Jacob had joined the thousands of visitors spread out over a grassy hillside that formed one of Yyn's boundaries. The audience faced a large semicircle dais at the base of the hill.

A little giddy from the wine at dinner, Halar chatted more than she normally did, but Rena didn't believe the wine could be blamed for Parsh's moony-eyed gazes at her friend. She had never considered them a potential couple, but maybe circumstances had never been right before. The inverse was certainly true: Something that had been right for a long time (her and Kail) could become wrong over time. Thinking of Kail and the ugliness of their breakup, Rena felt grateful that both of her friends had treated Jacob kindly, including them in their plans and conversations; remarkably, Halar had managed to rein in her eagerness at having access to a Sisko. Of course, Rena and Jacob weren't an official *couple,* which might make it easier for Halar and Parsh to accept him without seeing him as a replacement for Kail. Rena hadn't yet defined what she had with Jacob, but the signs were there: occasionally taking her hand, sitting beside her at dinner, the lingering looks when he thought she wasn't paying attention.

A blanket spread out on the grass, Jacob had arranged himself so that Rena could sit between his legs and lean against him. The intimacy of the seating arrangement simultaneously tantalized and terrified her, but the intuitive trust that had existed between them since the start won her over. Once she was situated, he gathered her long, curly hair into his hand and draped it so it hung over one shoulder; he rested his head on the other. Rena propped her arms on his thighs, dangling her hands off his knees. As always, silence felt comfortable between them. Neither felt obliged to speak for the sake of making noise. Instead, matching the rhythm of her breath with Jacob's became a soothing meditation. Fully relaxed, she snuggled back into the warmth of his body. He pulled her tight against him. Glancing over at Parsh and Halar, she was pleased to see that Parsh had overcome his usual shyness and had put and arm around Halar's shoulders. They looked happy.

Soon, the first moon climbed over Yyn's towering cliffs, blanching them cold, white-gray, signaling that the longest day of the year had passed into memory. As if to hold on to the lost light a little longer, a series of massive bonfires erupted on each side of the dais, coaxing a collective "ah!" from the crowd.

Accompanied by sad, soaring flutes, and stringed *belaklavion*s, dancers, clothed in gauzy lavender, sea green, blush pink, and daylight blue twirled onto the stage, their robes flowing out like sea anemones' tentacles floating in a tidal pool. Offstage, the narrator's clear voice introduced the story of Astur, the water spirit who, on solstice morning, had left the ocean in the form of a woman, to search for a young fisherman whose face she had seen when he'd glanced over the side of his boat to retrieve a lost coin. Since the story was conveyed almost entirely through dance, Rena explained the unfolding action to Jacob using the words Topa had told her at a long-ago bedtime.

Astur found her love but couldn't persuade him to leave his life on land to join her in the sea. Because her father, the King of the Reef, had granted her human form only as long as there was daylight, Astur and her lover attempted to hold back the night by a great fire, hoping to deceive the King. But neither a creature of the sea nor a man of the land could withstand the inferno's heat: the lovers were consumed by the flames, conveyed by long lengths of shimmering gold fabric on the stage.

At last, the dancer portraying the King of the Reef came onto the stage and lifted a large milky white glass oval off the ground where the fire had turned the sand to glass. In memory of his lost child, he threw the glass high into the air. The crowd—including Rena—held their breath waiting for the inevitable crash.

Instead, on all sides, small flames appeared as thousands of candles ignited instantaneously, as if by magic, creating the illusion of floating in a candlelight sea. Delighted, Rena clapped. This was far more enchanting than the bedtime version she was familiar with.

"And so it is," the narrator concluded, "that on summer solstice night, sea glass turns to flame as the King of the Reef hopes that his daughter and her lover can live again."

The stage lights dimmed, ending the pageant, but the candles remained, waves of flickering candlelight flowing as far as Rena could see.

As people started getting up around them and leaving, Jacob leaned forward and whispered in her ear, "What happens now?"

"Parsh sort of explained this to you a while ago, but now that you've seen the pageant, it probably makes more sense. The story goes that those couples who capture one of the water spirit's candles have the King of the Reef's blessing for one night of marriage. When the sun returns, the spell is broken."

"Sounds like an excuse for people to make love."

"It is," Rena conceded with a smile, "but it's a romantic one, don't you think?"

Taking their cues from those around them, Jacob and Rena stood; she folded up their blanket, packed up a pair of wineglasses they never used, and slipped on her shoes. Halar grabbed her by the sleeve and dragged her out of earshot of both Jacob and Parsh.

"I want Parsh to bring me a candle," she confided.

Rena blinked her surprise, but quickly gave her approval by enveloping her friend in a big hug. As she broke away from their embrace, she saw Parsh coming toward them, a candle cupped in his palm. She spun Halar around and wished her luck.

When Halar and Parsh had vanished into the crowd, Rena started toward the line of departing audience members, quickly realizing that Jacob wasn't with her. She scanned the throngs of people. She knew that the odds of finding him in the dark were slim, but she hoped his height would give him away. When he didn't immediately appear, she began calling for him, feeling a low level of panic start to rise within her. Logic took over. *If we accidentally separate, we should meet back at the hostel,* she recalled the four of them agreeing yesterday. Since most of the audience appeared content to linger around the candlelit ruins, Rena met little resistance as she raced down the hill and gravel road to the hostel.

The yard surrounding the hostel was nearly empty. The banquet tables held the skeletal remains of their earlier feasting.

Sprays of starlight appeared between the tree branches. Low, throaty laughter came from the dimly lit porch, where groups of festival visitors had gathered around tables to play games or drink wine or talk late into the night. Still no Jacob. Circling around back and through a tree grove, Rena nearly tripped over the legs of a couple who hadn't bothered to find a more private place to begin their celebrating. She was about to start down the path to the beach when a hand touched her sleeve.

"Rena."

Jumping nearly out of her skin, she spun on her heel. "Don't you ever leave like . . ." Her voice trailed off when she saw that Jacob carried a candle between his hands.

She didn't know what to say. In her heart, she had known this would happen—hoped it would—and now he stood before her, his face cast in warm yellow candlelight, and she had to decide.

"I know you've made promises to Topa. I know you feel like you have obligations to Mylea," he said, his voice quaking from nerves. "You have to believe that I'm not asking you to walk away from those commitments—"

"I know," she whispered. She knew from the story he wrote for her, from the inspiration she felt to create when she spent time with him. Through his eyes, she saw Bajor and life more clearly than she ever had. The tightness in her throat released and in its place heat tunneled through her. She threw her arms around his neck and kissed him.

"Whoa—" he sputtered, holding the candle away from his body. "Let's not follow the legend too literally or we'll be glass by morning."

Smiling, she kissed him again; then, wordlessly, she led him inside.

Jacob had time only to place the candle on the dresser and lock the door before Rena had pulled him down to sit on the bedside.

"If this is going too fast for you, we don't have to—"

Placing her finger against his lips, she shushed him. She slipped off her sandals and sweater and she sat beside him on the edge of the bed, resting her head on his shoulder. Because they were comfortable that way, they sat in silence. Jacob traced circles on her bare arm and shoulder with his finger; his feather-light touch became more exploratory, and she shivered.

To halt him, she flattened her palm against his chest. With trembling fingers, she unfastened his shirt, parting it to expose his skin, and pressed her cheek against him. He smelled like musk and candle smoke and the field grasses above Yyn. She began a delicate trail of kisses up his breastbone, murmuring his name, until he captured her face in his hands. The inscrutable expression on his face worried her for a fraction of a second until he claimed her mouth with dizzying intensity. *We're going through with this,* she thought over and over again. *He wants this as much as I do.*

Breaking away from their kiss, Jacob reached over her to de-activate the lights, wrapped an arm around her waist, and pulled her down onto the bed. Lying side by side, they faced each other, at first not touching, having only the candle's sepia glow to see by.

My turn. Sitting up, Rena reached for the tie of her blouse, loosened the neckline and pulled the blouse over her head. She felt his gaze. Before, when they had been together, it had been under the cover of darkness. Now, having him look at her, she imagined the way she studied the subjects she painted, and was filled with nervous excitement.

From behind, his hands went gently around both sides of her waist, fanned against her hips, and he buried his lips in the slope between her shoulder and neck. Arching into his touch, she cradled her neck against his shoulder and closed her eyes, feeling at last that things were as they should be. Complete.

When the midmorning sunlight woke Rena, she rolled onto her side to find Jacob watching her. She must be a sight: her hair in its customary wild and bushy morning style, her lips swollen, and virtually every centimeter of her aching from exertion. She stretched, raising her arms above her head, and then, feeling oddly shy, pulled the sheet back up to cover her fully. "Hey," she said, offering him a drowsy, crooked grin.

"Hey yourself," he said, looking at her expectantly. Resting his head on his elbow, he seemed a little too self-satisfied for Rena to be at ease.

Wrinkling her forehead, she said warily, "You look like you're going to explode if you don't say whatever it is you're thinking—"

"I . . . I think I might be in love with you," he blurted out.

She arched an eyebrow in surprise.

"I know it's sudden and all—"

And then instinctively Rena knew, without being told, that his declaration came from genuine feeling and not from the emotional miasma of sex. Smiling, she leaned over and planted a firm kiss on his lips and pulled him on top of her, relishing his weight. "Besides that other thing, what were you thinking just now?"

"Words . . . ideas . . . the nucleus of something I want to write later. I don't know if it makes any sense, but I feel like I've been seeing life through a broken lens that's suddenly sharply focused."

Rena smiled knowingly against his chest. "That's an artist's job: to see the truth of the world and people and communicate it. Often, we fall back on what we know, not what we see. There's a difference."

"You sound like someone I used to know," Jacob said. "She died. One of Dukat's men killed her. It was . . ." He inhaled deeply, then sighed. "I miss her." Looking down at her and leaning in toward her, he touched his forehead to hers. "You would have liked her. Ziyal was an artist, too. There's a display of her work on the station. Have you heard about it?"

Rena shook her head. "No," she said. "I haven't paid much attention to what was goes on up on the space station. But I'm certainly going to look her up now." As he drifted into memory, she felt a brief flash of jealousy. She asked, "Did you love her?"

He considered her question then said, "In another time and place, I might have, eventually. But no, we were just friends, for the short time we had togteher."

"And you cherish that," Rena said, "just as you cherish every other moment of your life, and everyone in it."

"You understand," he whispered, placing a soft kiss on her forehead. "I feel like you see me."

"I see you because I love you," Rena said without thinking about the words, and knew it was true.

Then he whispered something against her skin that she thought she heard, but couldn't quite bring herself to believe.

She looked into his eyes and smiled. "Ask me that again."

EPILOGUE

SISKO

All in all, it had been a merry evening. His guests started arriving just after sunset: Opaka first, followed by his friends from the station, with the first minister arriving last. Thankfully, they had mostly heeded his edict and dressed in casual civvies: Kira in a dark red dress and boots, Asarem in a long rust tunic and trousers, Vaughn in an evergreen crewneck sweater and jeans. Only Sulan had not shed the trappings of her vocation, but she seemed quite at ease in the humble purple vestments of her order, so Sisko was not disappointed by her choice.

Everyone fussed over Rebecca, of course. Predictably, the baby had quickly become overwhelmed with all the attention and the number of strange faces invading her tranquil world, needing the comfort of Kasidy's embrace to reassure her that all was well. Eventually she grew accustomed to the extra people, and everyone got a turn holding her over the course of the evening before Kasidy finally put her down for the night.

Sisko made crawfish étoufée for dinner. He'd ordered the plump crustaceans direct from Earth two weeks ago, from a company that specialized in exporting seafood offworld; the catch had been packed in stasis straight from the traps and remained thus until ready for use. "Fresh as fresh can get," his father assured him when he first told Sisko of the service. Dad had been right; the meal had turned out exquisitely, if Ben did say so himself. Kas and their guests certainly seemed to enjoy it.

As the night progressed into the small hours of the following day, the group adjourned to the front porch for an after-dinner aperitif. Nerys opened the package she'd brought with her, revealing a strange-looking dark green bottle. Vaughn recognized it at once; his first reaction had been to cover his eyes and shake his head with laughter. Kira explained that it was a Capellan drink called *grosz,* something Admiral Akaar had introduced her to a while ago. "I should warn you, it has something of a kick," she said.

Sisko accepted the half-filled glass of clear, slightly purple liqueur she'd poured him and sniffed it, then sipped appreciatively. He paused to consider how it felt as it went down his throat, deciding as it snuck up on him that "molten latinum" was an apt description. "You weren't kidding," he said, trying to blink the moisture back into his eyes. Kira grinned and refilled his glass, then poured three more; Opaka and Kasidy abstained, taking tea instead.

Sisko had not expected Vaughn to be such a *raconteur,* though he supposed you didn't arrive at that age in Starfleet without accumulating at least a few tales worth telling. When the commander finally wound his way to the conclusion of the story of the tribbles that had found their way onto a freighter full of the *xiqai,* the Orion aphrodisiac spice, Sisko thought that Opaka was going to do an injury to herself from laughing. As it was, she slid out of her low chair and lay helpless on the ground for a few minutes, gasping for breath.

The discussion eventually turned to more serious topics . . . which was, of course, the unstated reason he had gathered this particular group together in the first place, and why they had each accepted his invitation to join him this evening, even after the trials of the day. Had Odo not felt compelled to leave so soon after Unity Day, he too would be here. But Odo was needed elsewhere . . . even more than he himself realized.

Asarem, with whom Sisko had shared several private conversations during the last seven weeks, looped them in on the sudden death of Bajor's Federation councillor, and her surprising choice of a replacement—something the rest of the planet would not learn about until later that day. Sisko remembered Krim Aldos with mixed emotions, of course, but mostly they were favorable. Though the two men had come down on opposite sides of many issues during that uneasy first year, culminating in a battle for control of the station, Krim's convictions about what was good for Bajor had always seemed genuine. The general had both the strength of his beliefs and integrity . . . but it had always seemed to Sisko that Krim also possessed a keen intellect and an open mind. Sisko had no doubt these qualities would make a potent combination on the Federation Council.

Sisko knew less about Vedek Solis Tendren, who, according to Opaka, seemed likely to throw his name into the running for kai. The Vedek Assembly was finally due to convene for statements and deliberations on the matter in the coming weeks, after several false starts over the past year. Though the faithful were beginning to accept that Opaka's return didn't mean she would be resuming her previous role as Bajor's spiritual leader, her living presence was a powerful reminder of what a kai could be, should *strive* to be.

Her eyes met his several times over the course of the evening. More than anyone else in the room, she seemed to perceive the less obvious reasons why this gathering was necessary.

Soon, as it had to, the discussion took on a more grave quality. Kira brought up Sidau, explaining to those not among her crew what had transpired out near the Badlands, and which had unfortunately shed little light on the reasons for the crime that had been committed in Hedrikspool only a day earlier.

The conversation then shifted to the Eav-oq, Bajor's newly discovered sister species (at least in spirit) on the other side of the wormhole. Their existence carried with it strange implications for Bajor, Asarem felt, perhaps even more world-shaking than the rediscovery of the Ohalu prophecies. It was, potentially, a cause for great celebration, to learn that the Prophets had Touched others besides Bajor. But there was still the other half of that revelation, the knowledge Opaka had brought home with that of the Eav-oq, that a third such species was also out there, somewhere in the Gamma Quadrant: the mysterious and violently aggressive religious zealots known as the Ascendants. From her encounter with one of their kind during her years among the Sen Ennis, Opaka believed the Ascendants would eventually return to the region of space near the Temple, and what would follow then was anyone's guess.

Noting the troubled tone with which Opaka expressed her concerns, Asarem volunteered the opinion that they needed to prepare for the worst, with which Kira agreed.

Vaughn suggested moving quickly to reach out to the Eav-oq, begin building a relationship and learning whatever they could about them, their history, and perhaps more about the Ascendants in the process. It was the Ascendants, after all, who millennia ago had driven the Eav-oq into hiding, a retreat that protected the wormhole and those who dwelled within it from being discovered.

"I will go," Opaka said suddenly.

All eyes turned to her. Vaughn, in particular, seemed troubled. "Sulan . . ."

"This is where I see my path leading," she explained to the group. "Toward seizing opportunities to cultivate hope. The Eav-oq are tied to the Prophets, as are the children of Bajor. That is the common ground upon which we may best lay the foundation of a relationship."

"Ranjen," Asarem said, addressing Opaka. "Unless I'm gravely mistaken, this task is indeed meant for you. But whatever kinship you may feel toward them, the Eav-oq are not Bajoran. The gulf between our peoples may prove wider than any of us imagine."

"All the more reason for me to go," Opaka answered, her eyes on Sisko. "We can combat our uncertainty only with understanding. And with faith. I will reach out to the Eav-oq, for the sake of both peoples, so that we may together perhaps see the Tapestry more clearly still."

The discussion went on. Facts were dissected, possibilities imagined, options debated. And through it all, Sisko noted, there was the careful, deliberate skirting of the elephant in their midst: himself.

The world around them was brightening; night giving way to day. Sisko rose and excused himself. He strode out onto the grounds, finally stopping at the great tree under which he'd napped with his daughter only two weeks ago. He laid his hand against the trunk, taking comfort in the solidity of the living wood against his palm, reassured by the simplicity of its stillness. How much longer, he wondered, would he be able to enjoy such moments?

On the rise to the southeast, two dark points had appeared above the fields, slowly resolving into figures walking in his direction. *Odd hour for visitors.* He watched their progress for several minutes, then became aware of the presence that had followed him from the porch.

"You all right?" Kira asked.

He turned and looked at her, smiling faintly. "Just needed a moment."

Kira smiled back. "I didn't mean to intrude. I'll rejoin the others."

"No, stay," Sisko said. "I'm glad you're here."

He resumed watching the approaching figures. Kira followed his gaze. "Who's that?"

Sisko folded his arms and leaned with his left shoulder against the tree. "No idea. But it looks like we'll find out soon enough."

"Rebecca's beautiful, by the way," Kira said. "She looks just like you, too."

"Kasidy says the same thing, but I don't see it."

Kira chuckled. "I think parents seldom do."

"And she's growing so fast, Nerys," Sisko said. "So many of the things that daunted me when Jake was a baby don't even faze me this time around, but I'd completely forgotten how fast they grow as people. I see her changing every day. Every day."

"It's too bad your father and sister couldn't stay longer."

Sisko nodded. "I think they would have liked to, but Judith had a career to get back to, and I think my father was eager to try some new ideas in his restaurant using Bajoran ingredients . . . and to put a his own twist on some Bajoran dishes."

"Let me guess . . . Creole *hasperat?*"

"Don't laugh. He's convinced he's on to something," Sisko told her.

"Have you heard from Jake?"

"Not for a couple of weeks, which is unusual. He was sending messages every day the first week, describing his travels down the Yolja River. Then nothing. But he's a grown man. He'll check in when he has a chance, or when he has something he wants to tell me."

Sisko fell silent for a moment too long, because Kira then said: "You sure you're all right?"

He continued watching the walkers. They were still too far away to see clearly, but he thought they were carrying large backbacks. Hikers, maybe?

"I keep thinking about how close I was to missing it all," he admitted. "Seeing my son again. My wife. Being there as my daughter came into the world, hearing her newborn voice, holding her tiny body in my arms, watching her open her eyes for the first time. And everything that's happened since. But even when I was with the Prophets, outside the universe, outside of time, separated from everything that made me human . . . there was always this thread, this lifeline connecting me to the people I love."

"And now . . . ?"

"Now that thread is running in the other direction, and I can feel the tug. Part of me is still there, Nerys, with Them, in the Temple."

Kira stared at him for a long moment. "You're going back to Them, aren't you?"

"No," Sisko said quietly. "I'm where I belong now. Where I need to be. For my family, for myself, and for Them. This place and time, what's happening out there . . ." He nodded in the general direction of sky. ". . . they're important to the Prophets."

"Benjamin," Kira said, "why are you telling me this?"

"Because you need to be ready for what's coming, Nerys. We all do."

"What exactly is coming?" she asked. "If you know something—"

"It doesn't work like that," Sisko said, turning to meet her eyes. "I don't have any special insight into the Eav-oq, or the Ascendants, or anything else the new day may bring. All I can tell you is that the Prophets' interest in the linear plane has sometimes led them to intercede directly, but always at a cost . . . and to their grief." At Kira's concerned frown, he added, "There's little more I can tell you . . . except maybe to say that whatever comes next, how it unfolds will be up to the people gathered here, at this moment, and those whom we trust the most."

He could tell from the way she searched his face that she had a thousand questions, and he wished he had answers he could offer that were less vague than those he'd just given. But she also seemed to accept that it was all he had, and in the end, Kira's faith in Them, and her trust in him, were all she really needed. He just hoped neither of them were misplaced.

She smiled again. "Whatever comes, we'll be ready," she told him reassuringly.

No. We won't.

"Nerys?"

Sisko and Kira both turned. Kasidy was walking toward them from the house.

"There's a comm for you from the station," she explained. "It's Ro. She says it's urgent."

"Take it in the study," Sisko told Kira. She nodded her thanks and marched back to the house.

Kasidy walked the rest of the way toward him and took his hand. "Everything okay?"

"You tell me," Sisko said good-naturedly. "How was dinner?"

"A meal fit for a kai," Kas declared. "Exquisite in preparation, presentation, and consumption. The Emissary's cooking lights the way."

"Kiss-up," Sisko accused.

"Hey, they get to leave," she said, nodding back toward their guests. "I have to live here."

He took her in his arms. "It's so nice to know I can rely on unbiased feedback."

"Oh, shut up," Kasidy said, and they kissed. Softly at first, the feather-brush tingle of lips meeting, then pressing into something deeper as the world around them seemed to recede.

He held her close, unwilling to let the moment to end, knowing it had to.

Kasidy slowly pulled away, smiling up at him. Her eyes went past him, and then widened. "Jake . . . ?"

Sisko turned. Trudging toward them less than fifty meters away now, were the hikers. And, sure enough, one of them, he saw, was his son.

"Jake-o," Sisko whispered.

Grinning from ear to ear, Jake jogged the rest of the way, embracing his father. His travelling companion, a young woman, Sisko now realized, slowed as she approached.

"Jake, what are you doing here?"

"Sorry I didn't call ahead," Jake said, disengaging from the hug so he could embrace Kasidy. "But I wanted to surprise you." Then he noticed the small group gathered on the front porch. "Wow, uh, I didn't think you guys would have company this early. I hope we're not interrupting anything . . ."

"We were just finishing," Sisko said with a huge smile of his own, unable to contain the joy he felt at having his son with him again.

"So what brings you back?" Kasidy asked, her eyes smiling toward Jake's companion.

"There's someone I wanted you to meet," Jake turned to the young woman, took her hand, and stood with her facing them. She was Bajoran, Sisko saw, and lovely. The way she smiled, there was something familiar about her . . .

"Dad, Kas," Jake began, "I'd like you to meet Azeni Korena." Sisko blinked. *Korena?*

"It's wonderful to meet you," she told Sisko, then turned her smile on Kasidy. "Both of you."

"Did . . . did you say Korena?" Sisko asked.

"Yeah," Jake said, his grin a light-year wide. "My wife. We just got married."

Once the initial shock had worn off, Sisko embraced his daughter-in-law—*My daughter-in-law!*—bearly able to speak past the elation he felt. Kasidy was equally jubilant, and began bombarding the young couple with questions as she led them back to the house, where introductions were made, and congratulations offered. Korena seemed a little shocked to find Bajor's First Minister and former kai among the well-wishers, but recovered quickly. As the sun crept over the horizon, the mood in the Sisko house was merry once again.

Jake followed as Kasidy led Korena inside to look in on Rebecca in the nursery, leaving Sisko to stare after them in amazement. His guests had gone from congratulating the young couple to congratulating *him,* Vaughn pouring another round of *grosz* and offering a toast that Sisko barely heard.

Married, Sisko thought. *To the same woman I once met in an alternate future. A future Jake doesn't even remember.*

And that meant . . . what? That some events were inevitable?

That some things couldn't be avoided? Was this a sign of something deeper?

Enough, Ben, he told himself. *You're a father-in-law. Don't be a killjoy and overanalyze it. Not every event is an omen, and not all events are threaded together. Not everything dovetails back to you. Or Them.*

He raised his glass with the others and sipped, deciding darkly that if *grosz* wasn't illegal, it should be.

Suddenly Kira had rejoined them. "Nerys," Sisko said, beaming at her. "Jake just got back. He's married, can you believe it?"

"Captain," Vaughn said, addressing Kira. "Is something wrong?"

Sisko then noticed that Kira had not come out onto the porch again, but was standing in the threshold of his front door, her expression grim.

"I'm sorry to interrupt the celebration," she said, "but I need you all to join me in the study. Right now."

"What is it?" Sisko asked.

"Ro has new information about what happened in Hedrikspool," Kira said. "And you all need to hear it."

Standing in front of the familiar array of green lights that covered the back wall of Deep Space 9's security office, Ro Laren spoke quickly from the companel screen in Sisko's study, reviewing the chronology of Sidau's destruction before launching into her new findings.

"*. . . As insular Bajoran communities go, Sidau was rather unremarkable in all respects except one,*" she said. "*The villagers had a peculiar annual ritual: They supposedly battled a mythical elemental creature called a Dal'Rok for five consecutive nights every year. I had assumed it was a lot of nonsense. What I learned from the logs of Doctor Bashir and Chief O'Brien, however, is that the Dal'Rok was real. At least, it was real to the inhabitants of Sidau.*"

"Only to them?" asked Asarem.

"*It was evidently a psionic manifestation of their fears,*" Ro explained, "*brought about and repulsed by the villagers' collective will—which was channeled by the community's shaman, the* sirah."

"A storyteller," Opaka said, an instant before Sisko himself recognized the Old Bajoran term. This was starting to sound familiar . . .

"Right," Ro answered. *"Except this one wasn't the kind of scholar we normally associate with the term today. Apparently, at some point in the village's early history, discord among the inhabitants threatened their demise. The details about it are vague, but what Bashir and O'Brien reported was that this led the* sirah *of that time to come up with the* Dal'Rok *ritual as a way of bringing the people together by giving them the appearance of an outside threat to rally against. The fact that they were actually contending with their own fears became a secret passed down from* sirah *to* sirah *for decades, maybe centuries."*

"I remember this now," Sisko said, his expression darkening. He looked at Kira. "Doctor Bashir and the Chief went there while we were mediating the border dispute between the Paqu and Navot."

Kira nodded. "I realized the same thing."

"Lieutenant," said Vaughn, "you said the *Dal'Rok* was a psionic construct. Were these *sirah* telepaths?"

"Sirahna," Ro corrected. *"And good guess, but no. That's where the beginning of the answer to the massacre of the village comes in. According to Bashir and O'Brien, a* Sirah *would employ an artifact to conjure and control the* Dal'Rok."

"What sort of artifact?" Asarem asked.

"It was a bracelet, at the center of which was a small green stone reputed to be a fragment of an Orb."

"An Orb *fragment?"* Vaughn asked, echoing Sisko's own thoughts. All eyes turned briefly to Opaka, but the former kai said nothing, only frowned as she listened to Ro's tale.

"I know it sounds unlikely," Ro said. *"I wasn't even aware myself that that could happen to an Orb. And for what it's worth, I haven't had any luck verifying that it* ever *happened. But it's hard to imagine another explanation for what Bashir and O'Brien experienced. We know the Orbs aren't made of ordinary matter. Starfleet's best guess was always that they were energy vortices that didn't exist entirely within our universe. If the bracelet stone really was an Orb fragment, it might explain why Sidau village was destroyed."*

"Someone learned about the bracelet, and went after it," Vaughn said.

"And maybe got it," Kira chimed in.

"If it *is* an orb fragment," Asarem said, "is there any way to know which Orb it may have come from?"

Ro shook her head. *"I'm afraid not, First Minister. I checked with the Vedek Assembly, and while it's hard to be absolutely certain, given the unusual nature of the Orbs, there's no obvious sign that any of them was ever damaged, assuming such a thing is even possible. The fact that the fragment is supposed to be green isn't a clue; the Orbs have been known to change colors from time to time, though no one knows why. And the use to which the sirahna put the fragment doesn't exactly tie it specifically to any of the abstract concepts for which the Orbs were named."*

Their appellations ran through Sisko's mind: *Prophecy and Change. Wisdom. Contemplation. Time. Memory. Destiny. Truth. Souls. Unity.* Ro was right; it could be any of them.

"Wouldn't it have made more sense to go after one of the actual Orbs," Vaughn asked, "not just this bracelet?"

"The Tears have been hidden," Kira explained. "The close call we had with the parasites led the Vedek Assembly to place them in a secret location for the time being, until new security measures can be implemented to insure their safety in the shrines."

Asarem nodded. "Bajor is determined that they never again be compromised in any way."

"Besides," Ro added, *"a missing Orb would be noticed immediately. The bracelet was all but unknown outside Sidau. I think the perpetrators thought that by incinerating the village and everyone in it, it would prevent or at least delay our learning about the bracelet."*

"How powerful is this artifact?" Vaughn asked.

"That's the question, isn't it?" Ro said. *"The Cardassians captured most of the Orbs during the Occupation as part of the overall plundering of Bajor, but either they were never able to make use of them, or they chose not to risk trying. But if someone with an agenda were to get hold of one, even this supposed 'fragment,' who knows what they could do?"*

It was troubling thought, and Sisko now understood why Kira had elected to share it with the rest of them. *Signs and omens, threads and fragments . . .*

Sisko suddenly realized something else. "Lieutenant," he said. "You said you found out all this only after an exhaustive search of the station's databases."

"*Yes, Captain.*"

"Then how would the destroyers of Sidau have learned about it?"

Ro looked at Kira, whose face was the same grim mask as before.

"The same way," Kira answered. "The only conclusion that fits these assumptions is that the information was obtained from Deep Space 9." Her eyes met Sisko's. "We have a mole."